I0788434

whispers
and
WISHES

Foreword & Dedication

Dear Reader,

Thank you for picking up *Whispers and Wishes*. If you haven't read the first three in the Untouchable series, I caution you to go and grab those right now and read them first.

Book four. Wow. You know, when I started this, I pictured a trilogy with the first book set in the senior year, the second in college and the third after they'd graduated college. That so did not happen. The world they live in and the stuff going on? There's just so much more to it.

Frankie and her boys have been friends forever, but the changing dynamics, the complicated relationships, and the conflicts that arise from the changes in their life just make it so much deeper for me. This truly is a love affair for me to write.

This series wouldn't be complete without the enormous support of Blake Blessing, Rebecca Royce and Sara Vermillion. They've been tremendous as cheerleaders (and in Sara's case, cracking the whip), as sounding boards, and sometimes even telling me to take a break because I was pushing too hard. I flove them to pieces.

Thank you to every single reader who has given this series a shot and to those who left reviews. Thank you to the readers who recommend the series to their friends and to every single person who has reached out to me about it. I see and hear all of you.

Thank you. Thank you. Thank you.

And as always, the housekeeping notes:

For those of you who have never read a reverse harem before, first let me thank you for picking this up and giving it a shot. Second, a reverse harem means the heroine will not make a choice in this book or any other between the guys in her life. It may take her a while to reach that conclusion, but it's the journey that drives it. There are many ways to frame this kind of relationship, currently reverse harem fits it very well.

Also, this is the fourth book in a series. If you haven't read the first three, I encourage you to pause here and go grab them. While there may be no specific happy endings at the end of each of these books, there will be one to the whole series, that I promise you. Some of these books will have cliffhangers, largely due to the size of the story, but the happy ending has to be earned as part of the journey.

Thank you again for reading Frankie's story and I truly hope you enjoy it!

xoxo

Heather

Unopened Letter to the World

We're taught to leave this world better than we found it. Maybe some are taught this by their parents, their pastor, their teachers, or a mentor. I can say with certainty I learned this lesson from my mother and my friends, but not because they tried to teach me. Because through their actions, they showed me that not everyone cares what they leave behind, and sometimes to rise, you have to fall.

I believe that people will always have the ability to rise above their circumstances if they are willing to fight for it. Life, after all, is what we make of it. But we don't always know what our lives are supposed to be or why we are as we are in this world. We can rail against our circumstances and say that they aren't fair, or we can look at them for what they are—experiences.

This is where I am, right now. Maybe I couldn't control how I got here, but I can make the decisions about where to go from here. Buddha said, "Life is suffering." Not the most cheerful of thoughts, but suffering doesn't always mean horrible things. It can mean challenges. It can mean we have to work in order to achieve what we want. It can also mean that what we want is not always what we need.

Life defaults to the difficult setting because without understanding sadness, we cannot comprehend joy. Without grasping loneliness, we can't fathom togetherness. Sometimes, happiness is like a bird. Laughing and calling one moment, then flitting away to somewhere else. It is up to us to pursue that happiness and to rigorously apply ourselves to fulfilling our own needs.

In 2005, Steve Jobs addressed Stanford University in a commencement speech. He said, "Your time is limited, so don't waste it living someone else's life. Don't be trapped by dogma—which is living with the results of other people's thinking."

I have spent a long time living my life according to someone else's thinking—my mother. But the more disinterested in me she becomes, the more I learn about who I am and who I don't want to be.

I made the mistake of assuming where my friends were concerned. In fairness, we all made that mistake. We all thought we knew who the other was and what they wanted. Learning the truth hurt, but it's also freed me. I want to make mistakes and learn from them. I want to follow the rhythm I make, even if no one else can hear it. I want to live without regrets for the things I didn't do.

My mother lives her life on the run, fleeing her responsibilities and her family. She is always looking to someone else to make her happy, to fix what is irrevocably broken in her life, whether it's me or a boyfriend or a married man. She's always looking elsewhere. I have to look to me. I have to live *my* life. Every day, I want to live my life to the best I can.

I want to be excited about the possibilities, and I want to push the boundaries. If my mother showed me what life looks like to run away, then my friends have shown me what it is to face things head on. Maybe I'm idealistic and foolish, but I'd rather risk and lose, then never risk at all.

Every day, I learn more about my friends, about me, and about the potential of who we can be. I know there's a chance that some will fall away. Maybe our relationships won't survive the changes, but we, as individuals, will. We'll grow. We'll change. We'll become the people we can be. That is a life lived in flux and in suffering. We have to live our lives for us. That means celebrating those moments, even if we're growing apart.

Life's hourglass never stops trickling. I want to leave the world around me better than I found it. I want to leave my friends that same way. They have helped me to be better than I thought I could be, sometimes by doing nothing more than being my friends. By doing nothing more than being themselves. To live my best life, I have to be me.

Chapter One
I WANT TO BELIEVE

IAN

"It's been a long couple of days for you," Dr. Diane Miller, the student advocate and counselor stated, or rather, understated. Long didn't begin to describe it. In fact, it felt like we'd been in one continuous day since I got to her place to get ready for the dance. The dance that was supposed to have been our night, our date, before I blew it. Then that crap with Mitch…

"Bubba," Diane said, pulling my attention back to her. Neither Jake nor I had really commented on her statement. The only reason we were even in her office was because we had to do the anger management and work on our communication, per the principal and the coach. That meant two sessions a week, and we'd only gotten started the week before.

Fuck, the only reason we were even at school was to get Frankie's homework and to do this. We were all going to rotate staying with Frankie, or at least the guys were. Hopefully they'd let me pull a shift on Thursday.

"I don't really want to talk about it," I told Diane when she kept staring at me. I shifted in the seat and tried to ignore the throb in my hand.

"Pretty much," Jake agreed with me. Granted, our fight was what landed us up in here, but we were united on this topic. It was no one's business. The kids were all talking about it. I'd heard the gossip everywhere, seen some of the social media posts, and already saved some dumbass sophomore's life when he straight up asked Jake about it.

Moron.

"Okay," Diane said, shifting aside a notepad and staring at both of us. "I'm aware of what happened at the dance. All of the teachers were informed."

Great.

"I also know what happened to your hand Bubba."

"My hand is fine." I'd jammed my finger and dislocated two knuckles. It was worth it. Walking in that room… Red hazed my vision all over again. She'd been so out of it. Her dress had been torn. The knuckles on her hand had been bleeding. She'd punched him.

She'd also scratched the shit out of him.

Frankie was no slouch, but the asshole *drugged* her.

My fists clenched, but Jake sat forward. "Great, then you don't need to ask us about it."

"Actually," Diane said. "I do. Not about the specifics, because clearly neither of you want to discuss that."

She was right about that. No we didn't want to discuss it. "We're not here to discuss that. We're here to work on our anger or some shit, right?"

Jake and she both gave me a look, and I sighed. Yeah, my temper was showing. I didn't want to be at school at all. In fact, I wanted to trade places with Archie and be at her place, looking after her. But it had been really fucking hard to be there the last few days. And I kept messing shit up where she was concerned. The last thing she needed was me being an ass.

So, Archie was there and I was here.

"Sorry," I said, and blew out a breath. "I'm just mad."

"You have a right to be angry," Diane told me.

Jake snorted, but when she looked at him, he shook his head.

"Boys." Diane exhaled the single syllable and leaned back in her chair. "You're in an impossible situation, so let me make a few things clear to you. What you're experiencing right now is tough and traumatic for adults, much less kids—granted you're eighteen," she said with a nod to me. "And you're seventeen, almost eighteen. Someone you care about has been hurt. Badly. Right now, you're both staring at me and thinking 'no shit, and she's the one who is hurt, not me.' And to a point, I absolutely agree with you. However…"

She paused there, studying us for a long moment, and I found myself trying to figure out how she was going to make this about us. It wasn't about us…

"You're blaming yourselves because you didn't prevent it from happening. You're blaming yourselves for not seeing something you feel you should have seen. You think there's something you could have or should have done…"

"I shouldn't have let her go to the bathroom," Jake said. "Not by herself. One of us should have been waiting. So you're right, there's something we could have done. We didn't, and now she's got to deal with it. But we *weren't* going to talk about this."

"I understand not talking about the incident. What I want to talk about is how it makes you both feel."

I laughed, and it came out a hollow, empty sound as I stared up at the ceiling. "What does it matter how we feel? It isn't about us." Or the fact that it was the date *I* asked her out on and ultimately fucked up. If we'd been there as a *date* date, maybe it would have been different. Maybe…

Shit. If I hadn't pushed her away. If I'd not listened to my dad…and now… If I'd seen what the hell Mitch was doing…

How the hell had we missed that?

Why would he target Frankie like that? I wanted to ask him, and I wanted to beat him all over again. Not that he could answer at the moment. The last I heard, his jaw was wired shut.

Good.

I was pretty sure he was under arrest, or at least, I hoped he was. No one was talking to us, and after all the interviews with the cops, Archie got his attorney to take over running interference. They said she'd have to talk to them again and…

"Jake—are you angry?"

"Is water wet?" Jake demanded. "What kind of effed up question is that? Of course, I'm angry. He hurt her. I want to…" He clenched his fists until his knuckles went white.

If Jake's harsh answer bothered her, she didn't let it show. Instead, she focused on me. "What about you, Bubba? Are you angry?"

I just stared at her. What could I say? I was angry. At Mitch. At myself. At the guys. At Cheryl for giving her the damn water in the first place.

"What about this, are you angry with her?"

"No." Jake's answer pounded so closely on the heels of my own, it might as well have been one voice. Then I added, "It wasn't Frankie's fault."

"But you're angry that this happened to her."

"Yes." Was that what she wanted to hear? "I'm pissed off that it happened to her. I'm furious it happened while we were right there, and if we hadn't been looking for her…" I couldn't finish that thought,

When she didn't come back from the bathroom, it had made all of us a little twitchy. Be great if we could have said it had been some kind of sixth sense warning us, but really? I wanted a chance to dance with her, and I kept looking for her to come back and so had they.

"We noticed because we were being selfish," I admitted. Was that what she wanted to hear? If Coach wanted to kick me off the team if I wouldn't go through with this, I'd walk. But I couldn't do that to Jake. I'd already caused enough trouble when he was on uneven ground in the first place. That scholarship of his seemed locked in, and I wasn't going to jeopardize it anymore than I had.

"Why do you say that?" Diane pinned me with a look.

I didn't want to explain it, but Jake said, "Because we wanted to dance with her. We'd been having a great time, and she took off to pee real quick and we kept looking to see if she was back." He verbalized every thought. "One song made sense. But two? When the third song came on, we went looking."

"Sometimes, it can take a girl a while in the bathroom," she suggested.

"Not Frankie," both of us said in one voice again, and Diane almost smiled.

"No," I continued. "Frankie's low maintenance, she really isn't that girl who stands in a bathroom and preens."

"Well, there's always a line, too," Diane pointed out. "It can take girls a while."

"There was no line at the bathroom," Jake interjected. "It doesn't matter why we went looking. Things have been weird for her, she's taken a lot of crap from some of the assholes at this school."

"Ah, so maybe you weren't selfish so much as protective." It wasn't Jake she was looking at, and I sighed.

One glance at my watch, and I wanted to sigh again. We'd barely been in here ten minutes, and we had an hour of this to get through?

"Yeah," Jake said, and I glanced at him. He pinned me with a look that said *pay attention*. "We are protective. All of us are. Sometimes, we're too protective and try to protect her from ourselves. But we weren't too protective on Saturday."

"Okay," Diane said, just like that. "So let's talk about the anger you still have, and what you can do with it…"

"The only thing I want to do is try and make this better for her," I stated bluntly. "How do we do that?"

"Well," Diane mused, spreading her hands. "You start by not denying that you feel something. Those frustrations and that anger, it's not going to just magically disappear. You need a way to work through those feelings, to take ownership of them and give them a positive place to go. Even if that positive place is—tearing down a fence or building something.”

“Physical activity?” Jake guessed.

“Sometimes,” Diane said. “Boys—gentlemen, sorry, you’re not boys. The worst feeling in the world is to be helpless. You’re experiencing some of that right now, and while you’re both really annoyed with me for sticking here on this subject, I want you to consider for a moment that if you feel this helpless and out of control—that other people, who are just as close to the situation if not closer, are also feeling this way. You want to help them, which is great, but to help them, you have to be able to help yourselves.”

To help Frankie she meant. All at once, I straightened in my chair and studied her. I’d avoided discussing all of this with my parents. I’d avoided going home if I could help it. Dad meant well, but this was one more example of where Frankie’s mom let her down, and we kind of felt like we had—you know, screw it, I had let her down.

I didn’t want to anymore.

I wanted to fix this.

Fix us. But I wasn’t putting that on her right now.

I glanced at Jake and raised my brows. This wasn’t just me talking here, but us. He nodded once, and then we both looked at her. “How do we do that?” Jake asked. “Because she’s the important one.”

“Well, you start with acknowledging aloud what you’re feeling, even if you think it’s selfish. We all have a right to our feelings, and if you bury them, you run the risk of letting them become insecurities, and those will bite you in the ass.”

I almost laughed. She just wanted us to say what we were feeling.

“I love her,” Jake said without missing a beat. “And I want to give her back the fun we were having that night, and I can’t. I want to kill Mitch, because while he might not have been a close friend, he was still someone I thought of as a friend and he tried to hurt her. He did hurt her. I hate that I wasn’t the one who broke his damn jaw."

Fuck, Jake made it sound so easy.

"But I'm damn glad you got there," he continued, and I jerked my glance to him and met his gaze. "I'm damn glad you *were* there. I'm glad you're not running away. We need you."

The silence stretched out as he finished, and my breath came out in almost too loud rasps. "I'm…" I clenched my jaw. "I love her, too. And I hate that I'm saying this to you and not her, but I don't want her to have to fix this for me. She already…she always carries so much. This is just one more thing. Homecoming was supposed to be special, and I fucked up before we even got there and then this happened."

I lifted my bruised and battered hand. They'd taped it up at the hospital after they'd set the knuckles. Said there wasn't much more they could do with it. Honestly, I liked the fact that it hurt. It reminded me I had hit the son of a bitch.

"I wanted to kill him when I saw him. Everything just… I get pissed just thinking about it now. I hate everything about it. My part in it. And I don't know how to fix it. How to make it right. It's not fair."

Jake nodded slowly.

"Well, you've taken the first step. The next is asking yourselves, and each other, what can you do right now?"

Right now?

We glanced at each other and then at her. We were stuck at school, stuck going to this session. What could we be doing?

We could be at home *with* her.

The session just seemed to drag after that. I wanted to talk to Jake, but not with Diane moderating it or whatever it was she was doing. As aware of the time as I was, Jake still beat me to the punch when our time was up. He was already standing, backpack in hand and halfway to the door, when she said, "Guys, you made good progress today. Spend some time thinking about what I asked and talking to each other. Friday, we'll meet again, all right?"

I wanted to say no and from the look on Jake's face, he wanted to say no too, but we didn't.

Coop was sound asleep on the couch out in the waiting area. Jake nudged him as we headed out, and he jerked his head up at us blearily. Raking a hand through his hair, he rolled to his feet without complaint and shuffled out with us. We had maybe five minutes before the bell rang. The fact the sessions took our entire lunch period *sucked*. But I didn't have study hall in fifth, so lunch it was.

"Archie texted," Coop said after sweeping a glance around. "She's slept most of the morning. He just ordered food in and coffee. Said we should pick up dinner on our way home."

"Sounds good." We'd ridden in with Jake. Like the guys, I'd crashed at Frankie's the last couple of nights. It might have taken me time to get my ass over there, but once I was there, I didn't want to leave. We'd already told Coach we wouldn't be at practice this week, I was benched because of the hand regardless, and Jake told him family emergency. Right now, we were going to be where we were needed. With that, we split up and headed in different directions. I was almost to my class when my phone buzzed.

Jake

I meant what I said in there. You did something, B. You knocked that asshole out and stopped him. We'll figure this shit out, okay?

Me

I wish it was more.

Jake

Me too.

"Hey Bubba." The absolute last person I wanted to talk to was waiting for me outside of my last class of the day. What little peace I'd put together over the last couple of hours fractured. I didn't look at her, I just walked.

Unsurprisingly, she hurried after me, and I kept my gaze pinned over the heads of the other students. All I had to do was hit the parking lot and head out to Jake's SUV. Then we'd go get food. I'd texted Frankie before seventh, and she'd answered that she'd kill for an ice cream shake.

Her throat really hurt, so I was down for making sure that happened.

"Bubba," Sharon said again as she grabbed my arm, and I made it three more steps half-dragging her before I turned and glared at her. I did not want to talk to her. I didn't give a damn what she had to say. She'd been a total fucking bitch to Frankie, and I was sorry I'd ever given her the time of day.

"What?"

Paling, she pulled her hand back like I'd bitten her. "I wanted to ask about Frankie."

I stared at her a beat. Was she for real right now? Shaking my head once, I turned and walked away.

"C'mon," Sharon said, jogging after me. "We all know what happened. I just want to know…"

I kept moving.

"She was my friend, too, you know." Her voice took on a shrill note, and it carried. I wasn't the only one who stopped. Because really, she was Frankie's *friend*?

"Is that a joke?" I rounded on her. "Really? You're making jokes?"

"It's not a joke…it's—" She broke off whatever she was going to say and paled further as she took a step back. "I'm not the one who did it, Bubba. Why are you so pissed at me?"

"I don't give a damn about you." Harsh but true. "I thought about apologizing to you once. You don't deserve it. The only thing I'm sorry about is I ever asked you out. Forget my name. Forget hers. Go away. I don't care what you do, but leave us alone. You're like a bad rash, and they make antibiotics for those these days."

"Nice." Coop slung an arm around my shoulders. I had no idea where he came from, but he looked right at Sharon and then through her before he glanced at me. "Just wave off the plague flies and keep walking. They eventually run themselves into doors."

Yeah. Fine. That fit.

I nodded and turned away.

"Really? You treat me like I'm some kind disease? What does it matter what he did or didn't do? She's already putting out for all of you. What's one more?"

Silence seemed to rock across the quad, and for the first time in my life, I wanted to punch a woman. Her yelp, however, had me spinning.

"Holy shit," Coop said with a snort, and there was Sharon on the ground, nose bleeding and Rachel stepping over her. "Problem, Rach?"

"Just tripped. Nothing to see here," she said with a smirk. "Rodent problems. This school is really going downhill."

We were far from alone though, and a lot of people were staring, so I stared back. One perk of being on the football team, most of them didn't know what to do when I glared at them, so they hurried away.

"C'mon," Coop said. "Jake's waiting."

I didn't bother to see if Sharon was all right, and honestly, I found it hard to care. Why had I ever dated her?

"What the hell is wrong with me?" I muttered as we reached the first row of cars.

"You want the list alphabetically or in order of highest to lowest?" Rachel. Shit, I forgot she was there.

"Not helpful, Rach." Coop's easygoing demeanor was enviable, even if I knew he was as worried as I was, if not more.

"I don't know, I think if it saves shit for brains a trip to the proctologist, I can be very helpful. How is my girl?"

"She's fine," Jake said from behind as he swept past. "I'll tell her you asked about her."

Undeterred, Rachel stuck with us all the way to Jake's car. "I've texted her but she hasn't answered, and I'm not pressing because I know she's got a lot on her mind."

"Thanks for that," Coop said as he dragged open the back door and tossed his stuff inside.

"I know she's not *fine*." The last she spat out with a glare at Jake. "So do me a favor, tell her I'm here if she needs someone else to talk to."

I could argue she had us, but… "She'll probably text you when she's ready," I offered her instead, and Rachel swung her dark-eyed gaze in my direction and stared at me. "It's been a long week, and her wrist hurts." Not to mention her other bruises. Bruises that made all of us livid, and she knew it. So I was trying not to react to them, but that just seemed to backfire, too.

Rachel compressed her mouth into a thin line and nodded. "Thanks. Just…tell her I'm here. I don't want to bug her, but I also don't want her to think she's alone."

I felt every word of that statement. "I will."

"Let's go, Bubba," Jake said. He already had the SUV started, and Coop leaned between the seats from the back.

"Hey, Rach…"

She spared him a look.

"Nice trip."

For a split-second, the corners of her lips curled, then she pivoted on her heel and walked away. As Jake headed for take-out, we didn't talk. Not really. At the same time, the air in the car was thick with all the things we weren't saying.

"Don't forget to get her—"

"A double chocolate chip chocolate shake," Jake finished. "I know."

When my phone rang, I sighed.

Mom.

Holding up a finger, I hit answer and said, "Hey, Mom, what's up?"

"I thought I would call and ask you that." There was no admonition in her voice, which was a bad sign. She was almost too calm. "I talked to Alicia today."

Shit.

"She told me about what happened at Homecoming." There was the reproach. "Why didn't you tell me what happened to Frankie? Sweetheart, I could be over there helping."

I blew out a breath, Jake and Coop were dead silent, no way they hadn't heard my mom so, I manned the fuck up. "Because I didn't want Dad to know. He's already talked about going to CPS about things, and while I appreciate that he cares and wants the best for Frankie, trying to send her away with strangers isn't what she needs. We're taking care of her."

Mom was quiet for a moment. "Tell me the truth, Ian. Is she all right?"

"Not really," I said. "She's Frankie. She's strong. But I don't know if we know what we're doing." I ignored the dark look Jake sent me. "But I know we're the right ones to do it." Jake's expression shifted. "I know we're the people she needs. We're kind of figuring this out as we go."

She sighed. "All right, where is Maddy?"

"Europe, I think." Yeah, I wasn't lying to Mom. Not telling her stuff was one thing, but directly lying? Not happening. "Can you not bring this up with Dad?"

"I'll deal with your father. That girl doesn't need more trouble, but at least I know why he pushed to get us certified as foster parents so much the last few weeks."

What?

Even Coop jerked.

"Tell me if she needs anything. Some things you boys can't do. I know Alicia's probably told Jake the same things." I shot him a look, and he shrugged, then nodded. "And I'll call Carly." That was Coop's mom. "We'll figure this out. In the meanwhile, do you want me to bring you clean clothes? I'm assuming you're staying over at the apartment."

I had been. "I'm good, Mom. I can come and get stuff." Honestly, I wasn't sure we'd be able to get her to leave Frankie alone if she came over. I wasn't sure what the right move was. "Sorry, I cut you out of the loop."

"You were protecting her," Mom said. She sounded almost proud. "Just remember we're not the enemy and don't worry about Dad, okay?"

"Thanks, Mom."

"Love you, baby."

I grimaced but said it anyway, "Love you, too." After she hung up, I stared at my phone.

"I love your mom, too," Coop said without an ounce of sarcasm.

"Me, three," Jake told me with a grin, and then it was our turn at the pick-up window and he paid for the food. I had no idea they'd applied to be foster parents. I suppose that helped if they really pushed it where Frankie was concerned, but she didn't need any more major changes.

While I might not know what she needed, I definitely knew what she didn't.

"Hey," I said as we pulled out of the drive-thru. "Stop by the grocery store real quick."

"What do you need?"

"Not for me," I told him. "I want to pick up some roses."

She needed something pretty, and roses had made her smile before.

"Well, well," Coop said with an almost satisfied sigh. "It's about time."

"Shut up," I told him over my shoulder, but Jake chuckled.

"Not gonna happen. You gonna write her a poem, too?"

"Nope," I answered as he pulled up to the front of the store. "Don't have to. I wrote her a song." Then I was out of the SUV before they could say anything else.

Let them give me shit.

If roses could make her smile, then I'd get her roses, and if those didn't work…well, I'd come up with a plan B.

Then a plan C.

And I'd go all the way down the damn alphabet until I found one that did.

Chapter Two
DON'T READ THE COMMENTS

ARCHIE

The phone vibrating nudged me out of my doze, and I eased my arm out from under Frankie then flipped the phone over to see Jeremy's name on the screen. After pressing a kiss to her forehead, I slid out of the bed and pressed answer before I murmured, "Hang on."

Two of the three cats were curled up with her, and after the nightmares from the night before, when she'd wanted to go back to sleep, I hadn't argued. Hoping Tory was hiding out under the bed, I pulled the door mostly closed before hustling down the hallway.

"Sorry, Jere, I didn't want to wake Frankie up. What's up?"

"I understand, Mr. Archie," Jeremy said, his calm and patient voice settling me before he'd said more than four words. He just had a way of responding to even the worst situations with such confidence that I knew it would be all right, even if I didn't know how. I tried to emulate that sometimes, even if I didn't know how to fix something, I always wanted Frankie to think we would figure it out.

Because we would.

"I have located Mr. Edward and Ms. Curtis."

Yay? "Not sure I actually care anymore, but where are they exactly?"

"It would appear they've traveled from Paris to Berlin, and are currently en route to Prague."

Didn't Frankie's mom still have a job?

Or maybe Edward was her job. I shuddered at the thought. This was so not going to end well. His affairs never did.

"Great, do you know where they're staying? Maybe we can get a message ahead of them, since Edward's secretary is useless." The woman was nice enough, but she'd filtered his messages for so long, I seriously doubted if she even passed on anything that came from Muriel or myself. Jeremy had a slightly better than average chance of getting one through.

"I've taken the liberty of leaving a message for them to contact me," Jeremy said as though reading my mind. "I've also packed a bag for you, and I'll bring it along with lunch to the apartment shortly, unless you've been able to persuade Miss Frankie to come back here to recuperate?"

To be honest, I hadn't made the offer. She wanted to be safe, and this apartment, small and cramped as it might be, was hers. So here we stayed. We'd all taken shifts sleeping with her, and someone inevitably ended up on the sofa or on the floor in her room. It didn't matter as long as she wasn't alone.

Hell, I doubt anyone would have gone to school today if we didn't have to start rotating absences. Jeremy had me covered today, but I would have to put on an appearance the next day. Frankie had a doctor's note keeping her out all week. Her wrist hurt, and so did her face.

She didn't even have to tell me how much it hurt because she was taking the painkillers we'd had filled for her. That told me more than anything she was in pain.

"No, she needs her place and the cats," I told him. "So it's better we're here, and thanks. You don't have to bring the bag over. I can run and get it when the guys get home."

"I don't mind delivering it, Mr. Archie, then I can say I have actually seen you and you are fine when asked."

I laughed, "Fair enough."

"Do you think Miss Frankie would enjoy the beef roast, or would she prefer something more comforting? Like the chicken and dumplings?"

Frankie liked food. "She'll love anything you make, you know that. But, the roast and the potatoes are one of her favorites."

"Then I'll get that in the oven. It should be ready in ninety minutes or so. The potatoes are just about there. I'll have a pot of chicken and dumplings ready for the weekend. I've also fixed up the room attached to yours if she changes her mind. If you'll make me a list of supplies the cats would need, I can get those set up as well."

"You're the best, Jeremy."

"I try, Mr. Archie."

"Any word from Muriel?" She'd gone off on a shopping weekend or something right before Homecoming. Honestly, I didn't remember where she'd been going, only that she'd been leaving and I was glad to have her out of my hair.

"I have heard from her, yes. She is taking time at a spa retreat in Arizona. I believe her itinerary will have her there for at least a week. I have the number should you require contacting her, but…" He didn't need to finish that sentence.

I hadn't needed to contact Muriel in a long time. "Great. What about Wittaker? Has he called?"

"No, I have a call to him scheduled for three this afternoon. Would you like me to move it up?"

"Three's great, Jeremy." I scrubbed a hand over my face and grimaced at the stubble. I hadn't shaved in two days, and it was going to start stinging her face if I wasn't careful. Not that we were making out. She'd been too bruised and battered for that. Cuddling, however, had been high on the list.

"Very good. I'll be over with lunch and your bag at twelve-thirty. If you could gather your things for washing and anything of Miss Frankie's as well, I'll get it laundered and returned."

"You really are the best."

"Just doing my part to make it easier for her. If you require anything else, let me know."

"Will do."

Then we were off the phone, and I checked my messages. Some from Coop, mostly just check-ins. Thankfully, email meant we could get most of our assignments directly from the teachers, not that I'd even looked at mine since we got her home from the hospital.

Opening it now, I headed into the kitchen. There was still coffee in the bottom of the pot, so I just poured it into a mug and stuck it in the microwave.

Coop had done dishes before school, and Jake took the trash out. I had dish duty for after dinner tonight. Funnily enough, it didn't look hard, but I could count on the fingers of one hand the number of times I'd had to do "chores." Spoiled?

Yeah, probably.

I scrolled through my school mail. Most of this stuff was just reading and a couple of assignments. I'd have to make up a pair of tests, too. No biggie.

The government test Frankie and I could study for together, but not like it was hard. Coffee ready, I pulled it out and sipped. Reheated it wasn't too bad. There were notifications in my email for Instagram tags. Tabbing out, I switched apps and opened Instagram.

Homecoming pics were everywhere. Lots of them had us tagged. Anger swarmed through me, stinging like I'd kicked over an angry hornet's nest, or maybe the pictures had. There were a few where we were all out there dancing together, Frankie had this great smile on her face.

The first three were only a few minutes before she left to use the restroom. A few minutes before the rest of the night went sideways. I still couldn't wrap my mind around it. One minute, we were dancing and having fun, the next, she was just gone.

Those had been the longest five minutes of my life.

I didn't want to even think about how long it had been for her, or how long he'd had her *before* we realized she was gone. Moving to the sofa in the living room, I sat down and just scrolled through the pics.

Frankie and Rachel.

Frankie and Rachel's girl with Rachel. I had no idea what that chick's name was, and at the moment, I didn't care.

Frankie dancing with Coop. Another where it was the two of us. I wanted that pic. I screenshot it and saved it to my album with her. For a moment, I flipped through those pics. The most recent ones were from when we were getting ready and then mugging it up at the beginning. Fuck, I'd been having a good time. I was sorry Bubba screwed shit up, but I was damn glad it was all of us getting to be there and hang out, and we weren't stepping on anyone's date.

Sighing, I went back to Instagram. After…after we found her, and after Bubba knocked Mitch out. It had all gone a little crazy. I was still blurry on some of it. My head hurt, and my stomach had been rebelling. It wasn't until we hit the hospital and Frankie was so out of it, I even thought about the water she'd come back to the table with.

Water she'd nearly drained and I'd had some, though it had been warm, and I figured that was where the funny taste had come from. At least they'd been able to test me to figure out what had been done to her. That helped.

Not much.

In between the blurrier moments though, one thing that stood out was the fact that Homecoming was still happening. The music still played. People still danced. Kids were having fun.

And we were putting Frankie in an ambulance, and Coop hopped in to go with her.

Fuck me, there were pics of her on the gurney and others of Mitch being put in one with the cops there. The comments on Mitch's made my stomach roll.

Feel better soon!
OMG What happened?
We're with you Mitch!
Was there a fight?

Was there a fight? We're with you? There were so many more of the same. Fuck all of them. Did they not know what he did? They were *with* him? I hated every one of these jackasses. I hovered my thumb over the one of Frankie on the gurney, it had comments, too. A lot of them.

Five bucks said they'd tagged her. Currently, her phone was off, and we'd kept it that way unless she wanted it for something. The well-meaning text messages got out of hand at the hospital, and after we got her home, we just shut it off.

Fuck it, I downed a mouthful of the coffee and clicked the picture.

What happened?
Is that Frankie?
Was there an accident?
Is she drunk?
Heard she attacked Mitch.

Pain pulsed behind my right eye, then I caught the reply to that last one.

Then get your hearing checked or your sources. Jockstrap attacked her. Now shut the fuck up.

Rachel.

I hearted that comment.

She was all over the comments, too. Where they were nice or asking questions, she left them alone. But the stupid ones? Damn.

Her blistering tone left my skin chapped.

I was glad she was on our side. Well, Frankie's anyway…

Leaving that picture, I scrolled some more, then switched apps again. The more I looked, the more tired I became. The squeak of the door and Tiddles bounding out of the hallway had me standing. The bathroom door closed, and I blew out a breath. Sweeping the living room with a glance, I made sure there weren't any messes. We'd been trying to pick up after ourselves, especially after coming home to the mess of mum building.

Jake had offered to get rid of her mum from her room if she didn't want it to bother her. But the reproachful look she gave us had us all raising our hands. Do not touch her mum.

Got it.

A part of me was oddly grateful she still wanted it. The door to the bathroom opened, and I picked up my coffee cup so I didn't look like a dork just standing there waiting for her to come out. She might go back to bed or she…

She shuffled around the corner and gave me a faint, but genuine smile. Apparently, she'd taken the time to comb her hair while in the bathroom. The bruise on her face looked better, and I used that term judiciously. The swelling had gone down, and it was more a mottled green and blue rather than angry black and purple.

The bruise on her back actually pissed me off more, but don't think about it.

"Hey," she said, and I grinned at her.

"Hey, Sleeping Beauty, get tired of napping the day away?"

She snorted and shuffle stepped over to me, and I put the coffee cup down to wrap her up in a hug. This I could totally do. Face tucked against my shoulder, she let out a little sigh. With care, I rubbed her shoulders gently. The tank top and sleep shorts were thin enough, if I glanced down, I could make out the dark bruise still on her back. Better to not set it off.

"I can't believe I slept this late," she murmured.

Rubbing my cheek against her hair, I smiled. "If it makes you feel any better, I only got up about fifteen—no, twenty minutes ago."

"You got up earlier, too, when the guys were getting ready for school." So had she, but I didn't call her on it. She'd been disappointed they got to go and she didn't. Frankie loved learning and hated being behind more than anything. I didn't think we'd have much luck getting her to take it easy after this week.

"True," I admitted. "Then I promptly snuggled up to the prettiest girl in the world and went back to sleep."

Her laugh lifted me a little higher, and I leaned away to glance down at her.

"Hey, why don't you throw on a hat and a hoodie, and I'll run us out to get expensive coffee? Jeremy is bringing us lunch in a little bit."

She bit her lip, then winced. There was still a small, if healing cut that she'd been worrying at. Another nail I'd like to drive into Mitch's coffin. "Sure you want to be seen out with me? People might get the wrong idea."

Yeah, I didn't give a fuck about what other people thought. "Babe, I'd be your arm candy any day of the week. We all know I'm the good looking one in this relationship."

"Oh my god," she groaned, and rolled her eyes, but I counted a win when she laughed and smacked my shoulder. "Ass."

"Sometimes," I agreed. She ran her fingers through her hair and then studied me.

"You sure it will be all right?"

"We can do whatever you want," I promised. "If you don't want to go, I can ask Jere to stop on his way. He'd love to do it."

"He's already bringing us lunch," she argued, just like I knew she would.

"He's gone out of his way the last couple of days to bring stuff over here." She wasn't wrong. He'd sent food, as had Alicia and Carly – Jake's and Coop's moms respectively.

"He *likes* doing it," I reminded her. "If Jeremy could spoil you every day, he would. Just like me. Good thing you're not into older guys, or I might have to worry."

That got me another hit and second set of rolled eyes. Oh, I was scoring big today. "Just for that," she told me, "I'll give you my freebie list after we get coffee."

Oh, someone was getting feisty. Wait… "You have a freebie list?"

"I do now," she told me, then tapped my chest. "I'll go grab a hoodie. Should I put on real clothes?"

I glanced down at her long, lean bare legs. "You look great. We're not getting out of the car unless you want to go someplace else."

Fuck, I'd take her anywhere she wanted to go. I'd take her to mini-golf if she wanted it.

"Okay." She made it three steps away, then turned around and came back. "Problem?"

"No, I just…" She rose on her tiptoes and pressed her lips to mine. It was a quick, blink and you'll miss it kiss, but I savored every nanosecond of it. "Forgot to say good morning."

"Morning, babe," I answered, and she gave me another little smile before she padded back toward her room.

Ten minutes later, she leaned back in the passenger seat next to me as I pulled out of the apartments. Not only did she have on a hoodie over her tank top and a baseball cap that I was pretty sure had to have belonged to Coop at some point, but she'd also put on sunglasses. It was a decent enough day out, not too hot and not too chilly, so when I offered to roll down the windows, she'd given me a thumbs up.

As soon as we had our coffees, I studied her profile. "You want to head back, or you want to take this nice day out for a spin?"

Frankie cut a look toward me. "Isn't Jeremy coming over?"

"Yep," I said, but then tapped the time on the dash. "We have an hour, maybe a little longer. Time for at least taking a loop around the lake. Music, coffee, my girl, and me?"

The corner of her mouth kicked up. "That sounds really nice."

"Then tell you what, just this once, you get to pick the music." I unlocked my phone and passed it over. Frankie put her coffee into one of the cup holders before cradling my phone like I'd handed her the holy grail.

"You mean it? I really, really get to pick the music?"

Yeah, give me shit. That was what I wanted to hear. "You better pick it fast before I change my mind."

She snorted, and I hid a grin as I took the next turn and angled for the lake. At the next light, I'd text Jeremy, until then—the first song that blared out of the speakers had me groaning.

"Seriously?" Her laughter was worth every ounce of my pain at that damn hamster song. No, LMFAO didn't record a hamster song, but since it was used in all of those commercials, she'd played them to death on YouTube.

"You said I could pick the music." She held up my phone, but I didn't have to look to know she'd hit the Frankie's playlist on my music app. "Also, this is beyond adorable that you've got all my favorites on here."

"Adorable, yep. Totally scoring the boyfriend points."

Another laugh, and she handed me the phone back. With her right arm still in a splint and wrapped to stabilize her wrist, she was doing almost everything one-handed.

When she started singing along though, I relaxed a little more. I was sorry the other guys weren't here for this, but daily drives where she could just relax and sing were now officially added to my to do list.

We made it back to the apartment about five minutes ahead of Jeremy. The coffee was done, and Frankie was tired and aching, but she seemed a little more settled.

"I think I want to try and take a shower." But she eyed her wrist.

"If you can wait a few, I'll help." Jake had helped her with the first, she couldn't get the splint wet, so we wrapped it in a plastic bag, but Frankie had a lot of hair.

"I hate that I have to ask for help."

No kidding. "You're not asking," I reminded her. "I'm offering."

At her sigh, I backed off a little.

"We could run a bath." It wasn't much of a concession, but she didn't need me if she wanted to just sit in the tub.

"Hard to wash my hair there."

"I know. Look, I get that it's not something you want to ask me to do," I told her. "But getting to look at you naked is definitely something I like doing. So, win win?"

It was a gamble. I didn't want to push anything. In fact, I wanted to maintain a healthy distance from anything that made her uncomfortable. The fact that she still wanted our hugs and didn't retreat, even when she grew a little distant at times, was a godsend.

I wasn't trading that away for some cheap laugh.

"True," she said slowly, and I let out a breath. "I'd get to see you naked, too."

"No, I'm sorry, that will cost you extra."

She made a little sound of outrage, but before she could say anything, there was a knock at the backdoor.

"Hold that thought," I said with a grin. "Jeremy's here."

The little growl she released tickled me, but I kept that to myself as I opened the door. Jeremy stood there with a duffle bag in one hand and a large dinner box in the other.

"More in the car?" I asked him as I grabbed the duffle.

"I can go get it, Mr. Archie," he informed me primly before handing me the first dinner box.

I'd argue with him, but I was pretty sure that in almost eighteen years, I'd never won an argument with him.

"Yes, sir, I'll get my laundry." I set the first dinner box on the table and then carried the duffle deeper into the apartment. Frankie eyed the bag, then me. "Clean clothes. And he asked for our laundry, so I'm throwing all your stuff in with mine."

Her eyes widened. "I can't ask Jeremy to wash my clothes."

The back door opened again. Damn, Jeremy was quick. "It's really no trouble, Miss Frankie," he informed her. "Truly, I would love to take care of more for you. I have a room ready for you at the house, and I asked Mr. Archie for a list of pet supplies, so if you wanted to come stay, you could bring the cats with you."

He was setting the table, and I divided my attention between him and Frankie. Wearing a shell-shocked expression, she surprised me when she said, "Jeremy, I think that's the sweetest offer you've ever made me, and I remember the first time you went to the store to get stuff for French toast because I asked."

The older man smiled. "It was my pleasure, I like cooking for people who enjoy food. In fact, I've made the roast and potatoes. I also included a salad and some cheesecake. I know you prefer ice cream, but I thought the cheesecake would make a nice difference. There should be plenty for all the boys as well."

She blinked really hard and turned, but not before I caught the sight of tears. Oh shit. "Hey," I said softly, rubbing her biceps before I hugged her gently from behind. "If you want something else, you have to tell him, or he's going to blow up my phone."

It was a joke, and she gave a watery laugh that promised she got the humor.

"It's okay," I said in a lower voice. "If you don't want me to send your laundry, I won't, but he wants to help. We all do."

And her trying to do laundry with a broken wrist was right at the top of my nope list.

"Course, if you want, I'll do your laundry. You can even show me how the machines work. It can't be that hard."

"There's no way that could possibly go wrong," Jeremy decried in his dry tone. "I implore you, Miss Frankie, that if you do teach him how to do his own laundry, you explain it in full, or I'm afraid you'll find all your colors bleeding into your whites if he doesn't blow up the washing machines themselves trying to *improve* them."

"That was once," I argued, gleefully taking the bone he threw me. "And I was ten. I didn't know that soap dispenser wouldn't know to only dispense the correct amount of soap."

Jeremy gave me a patient look, and a small wink.

Frankie laughed again, the watery sound far more amused this time. "That's a story I'd like to hear."

"Well then I shall gladly tell you while I set up your food and Mr. Archie gets the laundry."

Glancing up at me, then at Jeremy, Frankie pulled off her hat and said. "Okay…do you mind if I send the bed sheets, too?"

"Not at all. In fact, do you mind if I take pictures of Mr. Archie trying to make the bed?"

She giggled. Honest-to-god giggled.

"I don't know, that might be mean." Then she glanced at me. "Do you *know* how to make a bed?"

"I know how to wreck one," I said, keeping my tone dry. "How hard could it be to do it the other way?"

Jeremy's snort spoke volumes, but it made Frankie laugh again. "Tell you what, I'll show you how after we eat and I have my shower."

"Works for me." I dropped a kiss on her lips, just lightly brushing them. I did not want to upset that cut there. "Go sit and let Jeremy spoil you while I do the grunt work." Then I whispered next to her ear. "He really needs someone to look after since I'm staying here."

"Uh huh. Don't peek at my panties while you're stacking the clothes."

"What panties?" I asked as I backed away. "If you don't have any, you don't need to wear them…"

"Mr. Archie," Jeremy's prim verbal smack stopped me in my tracks. "You will include all of Miss Frankie's things without comment or teasing. Are we clear?"

"Crystal," I said with a salute, and when Frankie looked away from me laughing, I met Jeremy's gaze and mouthed 'thank you.' He nodded serenely.

"Come along, Miss Frankie. As I recall, you were quite fond of the horseradish with your roast beef, and I brought some just for you."

"Oh, you really are going to spoil me."

That was the idea.

In the bedroom, I fired off a text to the guys to let them know she was doing all right. I know I'd want to know, and I better get updates from them when I had to go in.

That done, I whistled as I stripped the bed. See, that wasn't so hard…

The laundry though, there was a lot of it. All the guys had their stuff in here.

Ah, hell with it. I bagged it all. Her stuff and theirs.

Jeremy wouldn't mind.

Chapter Three
IT GETS WORSE AT NIGHT

JAKE

They started out the same way every night—she'd go from sleeping peacefully to beginning to twitch. After the third night in a row, the first tremble of her hand would rouse me. Most of the time, I'd open my eyes, and she'd just be shifting. It was harder when I slept on the floor. So far, only Bubba hadn't taken a turn sleeping with her, even if we'd all made it clear that it was all right— even Frankie.

That first night, he'd crashed on the sofa, but after that, he made a pallet on the floor in her room. Coop, Archie, and I rotated who slept with her. The bed could fit two of us with her comfortably, and three if we wanted to squeeze.

Since her wrist was still in the splint and she had bruises on her back, face, and arms—fucking asshole—none of us wanted to squeeze. So for one night out of every three, I slept on the floor. The night before, I had, and it had been hard to sleep because I couldn't tell if she twitched, so I found myself waiting for shifts in her breathing.

I wasn't the only one. More than once, when I opened my eyes to check on her, I'd find Coop shifting either on the other side or on the floor, we'd both look at her, and if she was still sleeping, we'd go back to sleep.

Tonight, when the twitching started, I rolled onto my side and stared at her. Archie had the other side, but there was a light on in the corner, and when I glanced over, I found Bubba frowning at the bed. He had a notebook open and had been writing something in it. The roses he bought her filled the room with their scent, and she'd smiled so wide at them, the cut on her lip had started to split.

Worth it, even if we had to ice it a little.

Still...I didn't care that he was awake so much. The light he had on let me make out Frankie's face. The smallest of frowns tightened between her brows, and her eyes shifted swiftly under the closed lids.

A dream.

But a dream or a nightmare?

The nightmares had been bad. She had them when she was younger, usually after a horror movie—hence why we *never* made her watch horror flicks. Frankie's imagination didn't need the help. While she hadn't really talked about what happened with Mitch, I didn't doubt that it was worse than a horror movie because it happened to her.

Fucking asshole. If I ever saw him again, a broken jaw would be the least of his problems.

Still, at the first whimper, I pressed my forehead to hers and whispered, "Shhh..." I gripped her left hand carefully, wrapping my fingers around hers so she could squeeze. "It's okay," I murmured close to her ear. "You're safe."

I felt more than saw Archie wake up, and he wrapped his arm around her, hugging her. That was the other thing we'd discovered. If we caged her in and hugged her close, it seemed to settle her, and the last couple of nights, we'd gotten her out of the nightmare and back to sleep before she woke all the way up.

I hated that panicked look when she'd jerk awake and the fact that she'd be shaking. Worse still, she wouldn't tell us what was in her nightmares, and I wanted to push her, to make her tell me, because I couldn't fight what I didn't know was there. Any other time, that would be exactly how I tackled it.

But I couldn't do that to her right now. I didn't want to be the asshole.

No, that title was reserved for that fucking asshole who…

Her eyes flickered open, and Bubba rolled forward to his knees, ready to move. She let out a little sigh, and they drifted closed again as she burrowed.

"Sleep, Baby Girl," I whispered. "We got you."

The corner of her mouth tipped, and she squeezed my hand, then her breathing deepened and evened out. I sighed, and Archie lifted his head long enough to press a kiss to the back of hers. We shared a look, and then he dropped back down with a yawn.

Bubba scrubbed a hand over his face and went back to leaning against the pillow he had propped against the wall and glanced down at his notebook. I raised an eyebrow. "You should be sleeping," I whispered. "You still have school in a few hours."

It was my turn to stay with Frankie, we'd drawn numbers for it to keep it fair. Coop would stay with her the next day, and then we were at the weekend. We'd make the call for Monday once we made it through the weekend.

"Not tired," Bubba said. "Want to finish this. Get some sleep. I'll keep an eye on her."

I frowned. I got it, I did. But man… "Bubba," I said, pitching my voice lower when Archie lifted his head to glare at me. "You need sleep. Leave it for tomorrow."

He just shot me a dry look. "Good night, Jake." When he turned his attention back to his notebook, I just sighed and settled back down on the pillow. I still had Frankie's hand in mine, so I hugged it to my chest, and when she snuggled closer, I let my eyes close.

The next time I opened them, she was poking me. "I gotta pee," she said by way of explanation, and the faintest of snores rose from behind her. Archie was probably dead to the world.

"Yep," I said, rolling off the bed and to my feet so she could scoot out. I wasn't making her climb or do anything awkward. She winced as she unfolded, though she wasn't moving as stiffly as she had the last few mornings. Smothering a yawn, I debated falling back on the bed, but if she was up…

Tiddles yowled at me.

Then Tabby and Tory threaded around my legs. I swore that Tory only came out when food was involved, otherwise, the little hermit played hide and seek.

"Got it, you want to eat."

Bubba was asleep on his pallet in the corner, the notebook closed next to him. Hopefully, he'd gotten some actual sleep. Leaving the room, I headed for the kitchen with the cats following and yowling all the way. Coop sprawled on his stomach on the sofa, also dead to the world. What the fuck time was it?

The clock in the kitchen said it was five minutes before the alarms would go off.

Heh.

Fine.

I fed the cats and got the coffee started. Frankie surprised me when she padded into the kitchen.

"Not going back to bed?"

She shook her head. "I'm still tired, but I'm kind of tired of sleeping."

"K." I kind of got that. "Want to work on homework after we kick the bums out and send them off to school like good little boys?"

She snickered, and I grinned. Then her smile faltered. "I kind of thought I might try to go, but my face still hurts and so does my throat."

"The doc gave you a pass for the whole week," I reminded her. "You might be better off just sticking to the plan. It's not just going back to school."

It was all the assholes there.

"But if you want to," I continued, even though I would prefer she didn't. "We could give it a shot. You'll have one of us with you all day." There were only two classes we didn't have with her, and Rachel was in one of them. That just left finding a way to cover her TA period. Maybe they'd let her sit that out.

"I want to, but I won't," she said, scooting over to lean against me when I lifted an arm. I wrapped it around her and pressed a kiss to the top of her head. "I start off being all 'I can do this,' and then I get tired thinking about it."

That was because my Frankie was an overachiever from hell. She did not like sitting anything out. Even when she got sick for real, she kept trying to do stuff. It could be maddening. Course, it didn't help that she seemed to embrace the concept of guilt when it came to blowing off shit and just taking a day.

Especially when she worried about things—like her job and money. Fuck. Her. Mom. I worked and helped my mom out, and she'd never in a million years put this kind of responsibility on me. Even if I could stand it. Even my dick of a dad wouldn't pull this crap.

Ugh, I hated that woman.

"Then we do homework here, watch YouTube videos, eat ice cream."

"Cheesecake," she corrected me, and I grinned.

The coffee filling the pot hissed to its conclusion as Coop's alarm went off, and then the others began to sound through the apartment. Not mine, I'd turned that shit off, but hey, look where we were.

The next hour drifted by with coffee and cinnamon rolls—Frankie and I made them and got those going in the oven. She hadn't had a fritter in a few days. I'd get up extra early the next day and do a donut run.

The guys drifted through, morning kisses deposited with care and no pushing whatsoever. Except Bubba, he just gave her a side hug. Again, not pushing.

"What do you want for dinner?" Coop asked.

"Oh, and Jeremy will probably be by with the laundry later," Archie said as he looked at his phone. There was something up, because he frowned but swiped out of whatever message before he focused on the rest of us. Yeah, I'd ask him about that later. If Frankie noticed it, she didn't say anything.

"We have so many leftovers in there," she protested. "I say potluck so we can clean out the fridge."

"Potluck works," I agreed. Coop and I had taken turns working on this schedule, too. Archie and Bubba could both be there in the evenings, but if I could slip in a few hours of shift that was extra dollars in the pocket. At the same time, I didn't want to be away from her.

I'd work this evening since Coop worked the night before—and likely why he'd slept on the sofa.

After the guys left, Frankie let out a long sigh.

"Okay, Baby Girl," I said while rinsing the breakfast plates. "Talk to me. What's going on in that beautiful brain?"

"Nothing," she said, but then made a face. "Just…tired of everyone tiptoeing around me."

"We're not tiptoeing."

"Yes you are." Then she shrugged and faced me, leaning against the back of the chair. "And I get it. Things are kind of screwy, and I look like this and I have this." She motioned to her face then waved her splinted wrist at me. "Hard to forget. Unless you're me, and then you have this blank wall."

One she wasn't happy about, so no, I wasn't taking that bait. "You're recovering. So we're taking it easy. That's not tiptoeing. Nor is taking care of you."

"You guys have practically moved in, everyone is making sure I'm not alone, at any point. I can barely go to the bathroom by myself."

"Sick of us already?" I teased, keeping it light.

"No, shockingly enough. You'd think I would be, but I almost don't mind it—though I feel guilty that Ian keeps sleeping on the floor."

"Hey, the sofa's there, and you offered to let him crash on the bed a couple of nights ago." It had been a strained offer on her part, and we all knew it.

He'd turned her down gently, and he'd even teased her, so…that was something. "Besides, I think he's doing it to show you how devoted he is."

That got me rolled eyes.

"He brought you roses," I reminded her, and the corner of her mouth kicked up. "Not that I'm going to plead his case." On this portion of it, Archie, Coop, and I were in agreement. We'd be supportive, but Bubba dug this hole and Bubba had to be the one to fix it. That didn't mean we couldn't root for him, but Frankie came first.

"I know he did, and I like them," she said, and then chuckled. "It's kind of funny, I wanted you guys to be the ones sending the roses, and then it turned out to be Rachel, and now he brought me roses, and I'm wondering if he's bringing me flowers because he wants to give me flowers or because he thinks I want them."

"I followed that—mostly."

"Good, because when I think about it, it gets all tangled up in knots, and then I don't want to think about it anymore."

"I get that, too."

She pushed her left hand through her hair and then made a face. "Do you think you'd mind helping me put this in a ponytail?"

It cost her to ask me that, so no way in hell was I teasing her.

"How about I braid it?" Then it would be out of her face and off her neck. At her blink of surprise, I spread my hands before shutting off the sink. "Three sisters. Trust me, I can braid hair."

"That's true. I've even seen you braid it, but I was sworn to secrecy."

"That was when Blake was into drill team." I made a face. "I cannot tell you how happy I was when she gave up that crap."

"Louisa still does cheer though. All three of them dance."

True. "But drill team is where…" Then I winced. "Okay, I'm shutting up about that."

"Drill team is where the football team starts trolling for girls," she pointed out, and I sighed. "Jake, you don't have to edit for me. I get it. I tried out for drill team, remember?"

And she'd been on the spirit squad too, yeah. I remembered. "You were hella cute making us those spirit boxes, too."

Her snort made me grin. Drying off my hands, I motioned her to the living room.

"Come on, let me braid your hair for you. It'll be fun."

"Will you put ribbons and trinkets in it?"

"Yeah, let's not go too far." I'd only done that for Blake once. "But if you really want a ribbon, I can thread one in there."

"I really don't want a ribbon," she said, a hint of laughter in her voice. "Though maybe some other time."

"Good deal."

I turned on the TV while she hit the bathroom and came back with her brush and some hair ties. When she sat on the floor, between my legs, I took the brush and handed her the remote. "You are in charge of entertainment."

"I thought we were going to do homework. Do you know how far behind I am?"

"Nowhere near far enough to be that stressed about it. But feel free to find us something educational to watch."

"Meh." The moue of disgust was the right answer. Still, I took my time running the brush through her hair. It was easy to forget just how much she had. I loved her hair. I loved it when she tumbled over me with it or when it was spread out on a pillow below me.

I loved it even more when I could fist her hair and guide…

And new subject, Jake. I gave myself a good solid mental shake. The last thing I needed was a boner while I was brushing her hair. I'd barely gotten rid of the morning wood. Not getting a boner around Frankie took effort.

I thought about Mitch for a split second, and that helped to deflate it but aggravated my temper.

She scrolled through the channels as I smoothed out her curls. They were not quite a riot today, though the extra waves would make separating it a challenge.

"Jake?"

"Yeah, Baby Girl?"

"Do you think I could have done something differently?"

I froze then forced myself to keep moving. A French braid would take a lot of concentration, and I needed to not yank on her hair. "Saturday night?" I clarified after clearing my throat.

"Yeah." She had the TV on, but it was muted as she scrolled the channel guide. We'd end up switching to Netflix or YouTube, but we always started out on the guide. Like we had to verify there was nothing on.

"You didn't do anything wrong," I said as evenly as I could manage. Even when we'd talked to the cops and that advocate at the hospital, that fact had been stressed. Frankie hadn't done anything wrong. She went to the fucking bathroom.

The fault?

That was Mitch's.

And a little bit Cheryl's. Though I'd been stewing on that one on my own. Cheryl gave her the water. Even if Mitch gave it to her, why the fuck would he need to roofie his own girlfriend? There was just something off about that. She'd been a complete wreck the one time I saw her at the hospital and we kicked all of them out. Frankie didn't need to be the one to look after her or make it better for her. Rachel had been with her.

I didn't like Rachel, but I trusted her a little.

Cheryl?

Not so much.

"Jake?"

Fuck, I'd gone quiet. "Sorry, Baby Girl, I was just thinking about that night." I blew a breath out between my teeth.

"You don't want to talk about it." It wasn't a question.

"I didn't say that."

"You don't have to."

"Okay, one." I managed to push that word out without gritting my teeth. "Don't put words in my mouth. Two, I don't want *you* to have to talk about it. There's a difference. It pisses me off, Baby Girl. It pisses me off every time I think about it, but that doesn't mean you shouldn't talk to me. It just means I have to resist the urge to punch holes in the wall or go find that lousy fucking asshole and beating him bloody."

"Oh."

Just that. Oh.

Then. "I almost don't have a problem with that last part."

A laugh worked up through me, and I nearly lost the thread of the braid I was weaving into her hair. "Almost?"

"Almost," she said. "I am confused about what I should feel. I'm upset. That's a given. I hurt—my wrist really aches right now, and so does my cheek."

"How's your back?"

"Sore, but it's not as bad."

"You want one of your pain pills?"

"I hate taking them."

"I know, but I hate you being in pain."

"If I take them, then all I'm going to do is be a little sleepy and silly all day."

"Then you can snooze on me," I said. "You're recovering. You're allowed to rest."

She was quiet for a long time, and I let her work it out while I finished the braid. When I was done, she tilted her head back to look up at me. "You're really good at that."

"Shh, I'm a big bad ass football player with anger management issues, don't let anyone know I can do hair."

"Your secret is safe with me."

"I know it is." I dropped a kiss on her forehead. "Take your pain meds? For me?" There was no mistaking the wince around her eyes or the fact that she'd gotten pale beneath her tan. The bad dreams didn't help her rest either.

"You really think I did nothing wrong?" Those deep green eyes held all of my attention.

"I *know* you didn't do anything wrong, Baby Girl. You scratched the shit out of his face for one." Then I reached down to touch her splinted arm gently and lifted it. "And under these bandages, I know for a fact your knuckles are bruised, which tells me you pegged him with your right. You did everything right, Frankie. That fucker is the one who screwed up. He's the asshole. He made mistakes. Not you."

She blew out a breath. "And if you guys…"

"No," I said firmly. "We're not playing the what if game." We couldn't. We really couldn't. I already wanted to kill the guy. Straight up. When I'd said as much to one of the cops, he'd been really clear with me. I couldn't make threats like that. So fine, I'd keep them to myself. I still wanted to kill him. "He fucked up. He's the bad guy. You didn't do *anything* wrong. Clear?"

I hadn't meant to growl those last words, because dammit, I was supposed to be keeping things easier for her, but they came out that way regardless.

She let out this little relieved breath and then nodded. "Clear."

Frowning, I traced a finger over her forehead. "Have you really been worried you did something wrong?"

"A little."

Fuck.

"I just don't remember so much of it, and Denitra said that was normal. That it had to do with the drug in my system. But there's this blank wall. I remember dancing. I remember having fun and laughing. Then I kind of remember needing to pee. But I was still…happy." Her eyes took on this lost look, and I didn't think I could hate that asshole more than I did at the moment. "Then nothing. So I don't know what I did. I don't know if I went with him or if I lead him on or…I don't know."

Okay.

"C'mere," I said, helping her up and then tugging her into my lap. When she melted right into me and wrapped her arms around my neck, I balanced her and then touched her chin so I could look her right in her eyes. "You fought him. No matter what he did or said, or what you worry you did or said, you fought him. You scratched his face. You punched him. You were so out of it when we got there, but you fought him before. That tells me in bright, bold, neon fucking letters that you did not want to be there and you did not want anything to do with him."

She studied me, and I knew she searched for something in my eyes. Maybe she wanted to know if I really believed it—I did. Maybe she wanted to know if she could believe it—she should, but I couldn't force her to. I just needed her to hear me.

I could go on, but I bit my tongue. I just needed her to focus on that one point right now.

"Okay," she said after a long moment, and I let out a breath. "I believe you."

"Yeah?"

"Well, I believe you believe that. And I really do have a mean right hook." Then she glanced down at her wrist almost mournfully.

"Yeah you do, but how about you let me punch people for you for a while, at least until that's healed." And like forever. I had no problems knocking people's teeth in.

"You're not supposed to fight. I don't want you getting kicked out of school."

"Fine," I said with a sigh, playing it up a little. "I'll teach Archie and Coop how to throw a hit. They can take some heat." Bubba damn well knew how, much to my delight.

She grinned a little, but then winced again.

"Please take a pain med? Then we can watch whatever you want. I'll even watch one of those romantic comedies you like."

"You like them too, Jake Benton, don't play that game with me."

I pressed a finger to her lips. "That's a secret. Remember?"

Dammit, why was I mentioning memory? What the fuck was wrong with me?

"We're alone, remember?" She countered, then nipped my finger, and my heart did a little squeeze.

"True. Fine, tease away—but take your pain med first."

"Ugh, you're going to be such a pain in the ass until I do it, aren't you?"

"Yes, yes I am."

And I would take great pride in it. I wanted to take care of her, and sometimes that meant being a pain in the ass.

"Fine, I'll take it. Find me a movie, very sappy and maybe something that will make me cry."

I made a face. "Does it have to be that bad?"

"Yes," she insisted, then kissed my cheek. "And thank you for my hair and for listening."

"Anytime," I promised. I helped her balance as she stood and then watched as she headed into the kitchen to get her meds. My phone buzzed, and I checked it while she filled a glass with water. We'd learned not to rush in to do everything for her, even if we wanted to.

Mom

I hate to ask, but Louisa has tutoring until six. Blake and Becca have dance until seven. Can you pick up Louisa for me and feed her? I'll get the girls and then meet you all at home?

Me

No problem. Need anything from the store while I'm out?I planned to work tonight and then back to Frankie's, but I can grab stuff if you need it.

Mom

Bread, milk, cereal, and Pop-Tarts. Strawberry and Chocolate.

Yeah, I had to get both or the girls would fight.

Me

Will do. I'm not at school today. Just a reminder in case they call.

Mom

I remembered, but thanks for the reminder. How is she?

I glanced in the kitchen where she stared in the pantry. Someone was hungry.

"Want me to make some popcorn?"

"It's eight-fifty in the morning!"

"That's not a no," I said.

"Hmm… I could go for cheesecake."

"It's eight-fifty in the morning!" I mimicked her tone, and she stuck her tongue at me.

"Cheesecake is at least *dairy*, so it's breakfast adjacent."

I snorted. "I'll come get it. Let me just text Mom back."

"Tell her I said 'hi.'"

"Will do."

Clicking the phone off, I stood. "Why are you still in the kitchen… Frankie, I said I'd get it." She had the cheesecake balanced as she tugged it out of the fridge.

"I'm good," she said. "Pain meds need time to kick in. So not loopy yet."

Shaking my head, I went to help. "You are so impatient sometimes."

"It's cheesecake, and there's actual leftovers."

Like all of two pieces. We both stared at what was on the platter, then at each other. "Split them?"

"Deal."

Not even an hour later, I sprawled with Frankie tucked into my side on the sofa, her cheek against my chest as she released the most adorable little snore. I was also stuck watching *Ghost*, which wasn't a terrible movie. But I couldn't reach the remote without moving her, so I'd watch it while she slept.

Though the idea that your best friend was the reason you got killed *sucked*.

Chapter Four
I'M WIDE AWAKE IT'S MORNING

COOP

"You sure you want to do this?" I asked for like the third time, and the sour look she shot me said the question irked her to hear as much as it irked me to ask.

"You guys have both been working on and off all week. Yes, I want to do this. I need to get out of the apartment, but I don't want to go in places while my face looks like this." The bruise on her face was definitely better, though it remained angry. "And I have an appointment with the doctor this afternoon, so why not let you work and I can ride around in the car with you?"

I sighed. As plans went, it wasn't a bad one. "If you're sure," I hedged, then studied her for a moment. I had the keys in the ignition, but I hadn't turned the car on. "Frankie, you want me to go work for a couple of hours and let you have the apartment to yourself?"

Everything in me *loathed* the idea. I didn't have those kind of reactions often, but just the thought of leaving her by herself made my skin crawl.

Fifteen minutes.

She had been out of our sight for fifteen minutes, and it cost her. The thought of another fifteen minutes, much less a couple of hours, made me sick. At the same time, we couldn't smother her. It wasn't healthy for her or us. Not that the guys wanted to hear that. The only one listening on that particular front had been Bubba, and even he'd been reticent to entertain it this soon.

"No," she said, and the relief swamping me was pathetic. "I like hanging out with you guys, I just want to get out of the house. Archie took me for a drive on Wednesday, and it was nice. But I was a little out of it yesterday, so I didn't bug Jake to go out."

"Bug him next time," I advised. He'd kick himself if he figured out she hadn't wanted to ask him for any reason. "Trust me. And I don't mind going to do some work, or we could, you know, just go for a drive." The freedom of having a car was still new for me. I loved being able to take her wherever, whenever, or just getting in the car and going.

Sis had gotten used to asking me for the weirdest crap just to get me to say I'd run to the store with the car and get it. Though, she'd been pretty good this week and only asked a couple of times. She wanted to come over to see Frankie, but I wanted her to stay home. I didn't want Frankie worrying about putting on a show for Sis or for anyone. It was bad enough she'd been doing it for us. Not all the time, but enough it was noticeable.

"But you like working, and if you get some hours in today, you won't have to work as much this weekend."

Suspicion itched through me. "Frankie?"

She shot me a sideways glance. "Hmm?"

"Are you feeling guilty because you're not working this week?" Marsha had been clear that she needed to take as much time as necessary. I'd gone in and spoken to her myself. I hadn't wanted to tell her over the phone, and I didn't want Frankie to have to deal with it. When Frankie called her on Tuesday, Marsha hadn't told her I'd clued her in. She'd just told Frankie to take a couple of weeks and to call her when she was ready to go back to work.

"I'm feeling guilty for a lot of stuff." She sucked at her bottom lip, then winced. The cut there was better, but it kept getting irritated because she'd gnaw at it. The stitches in her cheek were dissolvable, or so they'd said, and they seemed better, even if the bruise still managed to look bad.

"You know you don't have anything to feel guilty for, right?" That was important.

"Doesn't mean I don't," she said. "I'm pretty sure Archie paid my rent. I know he paid to have the locks changed. Jeremy is doing my laundry. You guys are taking care of the cats and the apartment. All of you have shopped, and your moms sent food."

Okay. I got it. "You feel like you're taking advantage?"

"I kind of am."

"No," I informed her, opening up the app on my phone and checking to see how busy it was. It was a little before lunchtime, which could be good. I hadn't worked during the day during the week, so this would be different. "You're not."

"Coop…"

I backed the car out and shook my head. "Frankie, you can make up all the lists you want. No one feels an ounce of pressure to do what we're doing. First, you're the last one to demand this. You tend to try and do everything yourself. Second, we *want* to do this. You look after us, we look after you." Then thinking about it, I added, "We look after each other, too."

"Like when Archie was in the hospital." She grimaced and the guilt thickened in her voice.

"Yeah," I said, reaching over to cover her left hand with mine. "Like then. Like when Jake and Bubba were trying out for football. Or when we got drunk for the first time."

That pulled a laugh out of her. "Oh my god, I don't want to think about that."

"Yeah, it wasn't pretty," I admitted in a sad, sad tone.

"No," she agreed. "It was not. I don't think I've ever seen so much puke in my life."

"And yet, you still kiss us." Her groan was worth the disgusting tease. "But that's my point, we help each other. We take care of each other. So don't feel guilty, okay?"

She sighed, then squeezed my hand. A bell sounded on the phone, and I hit accept on whatever order I got and then the phone gave me directions to the restaurant.

"That's it?" Curiosity filtered through the guilt and lightened her tone.

"Yep, not sexy, right?"

"I didn't say that."

I snorted. "Yeah, I just log on and when orders are available, it offers them, I take it and then follow the directions. It's pretty simple. Mostly driving and waiting."

"Huh."

"Feeling envious about my way cooler job?"

Her snort lifted my spirits. "You don't have to wear a uniform."

"That is definitely a plus," I admitted.

"And you don't have customers running you everywhere. Well, I guess you do but…"

"But mostly one at a time." As though to make me a liar, the app offered me a second delivery from the same place. It also gave a bonus for that, so hell yes, I clicked on it. "Except I'll get two from this place then we deliver them both, and I'll pick up whatever comes next."

"Huh."

The grunt made me curious, but she didn't add to it. Instead, she curled her legs up to sit cross-legged in the seat. There were flipflops in the well, but she was in shorts—my old boxers, and yes, I definitely appreciated that she wore those for sleep shorts—a t-shirt and an unzipped hoodie. I cranked the A/C up in the car because the sun shining in made it hotter in there.

Her hair was still braided from the day before. The sunglasses hid her eyes though, and I kept glancing over at her.

"I'm okay, Coop," she promised. "I'm just thinking."

"Okay." I let it go, since sometimes being quiet was the best we could do. "Let me know if that changes or you need anything, okay?"

"Deal."

For the next couple of hours, we listened to music as I drove from restaurant to house or business, picking up and dropping off. Once I had the first two orders, they kept flowing in, and fortunately, it turned out to be a day that when I showed up, the food was ready rather than having to wait around.

Frankie watched with interest now and then, once she seemed like she'd gone to sleep, so I left her alone. But when one of my last stops turned out to be a barbecue place, her stomach growled so loud it echoed in the car.

"And I think on that note," I informed her. "This will be my last delivery, and we'll grab lunch on the way back."

"I can go a little longer," she insisted. But really? This was Frankie. She could redefine hangry if she went too long when she was hungry. She'd also not had any pain meds today, and the lines around her mouth were tight. "You've been really busy and getting good tips."

"And I'm happy with the fifty I've made so far," I told her. "I can afford to grab us some lunch."

Her sigh tugged at me.

"You want to go somewhere and eat? We don't have to go back to the apartment." Maybe she was just sick of being inside?

"Could we? Archie drove me around the lake, but maybe we could go find a picnic table or something?" She glanced down at herself. She didn't have on real pants, but the old boxers covered everything.

"I'll find us somewhere. Pick what you wanna eat."

The surge of excitement in her expression gave me wings. She was sick of being trapped inside. Frankie was an active person. Okay. We could fix this. It took me fifteen minutes to get the last order delivered, and she'd picked Korean barbecue—not a shock considering by the time I got to that place *I* was ready to eat their food. I logged off and then turned us back around.

She looked a little pale by the time we had the food in the car, and I flipped open one of the boxes and offered her the edamame. "Munch while I find us a place to eat."

The lake would be the obvious choice, but I had a better idea. Somewhere that also wouldn't be heavily populated this time of day. She didn't want to see people, she just wanted to be outside. So I cut across town and past flag pole hill toward the Pennywhistle Park. It had been a little amusement place for kids back in the day, but since it closed, they'd cleared a lot of the area and tried to fix up the outdoor park. Still, no one hung out there—at least, not that I'd ever seen.

But there were picnic tables and trees and quiet and sunshine. So I navigated around the old dilapidated building and parked under an oak tree. In the spring, that thing shed pollen like mad, but the leaves hadn't even begun to turn colors yet. Our autumn wouldn't really hit until sometime in November. While they counted snowflakes up north, we might get some rain and eventually colorful trees.

I could count on the fingers of one hand how often we got snow *here*. Anyway, Frankie let out a little laugh as she glanced around. "Okay, this place is creepy when deserted."

"Yeah, but it's daytime, so not scary creepy, right?" 'Cause if it was scary, fuck that, we'd go somewhere else.

"No, not scary. Kind of weird though." She opened her door after I shut off the car, and slid her feet into her shoes before climbing out. I snagged my drink and the bag of food while she grabbed hers. It wasn't hot, if anything, it was actually a nice day. Warm, breezy, and sunny. The humidity didn't suck.

Mouth widened into a yawn, she broke off with a laugh, then cast me an apologetic look. "Sorry."

"Nope, you can be sleepy. We just drove around for hours. Mom used to do that with Sis when she was little, remember?"

"Vaguely," Frankie said. "I remember you complaining mostly that you had to ride around in the car and be quiet, and you'd get bored."

Yeah. That sounded like me.

I shrugged and nodded toward the picnic table. There was playground equipment not that far away. It had been there since we were kids. Though they'd definitely upgraded some of it. "It was boring, but it made her go to sleep, which was the point."

Spreading out our feast, I let her pick where she wanted to sit and then nodded to the spot next to her.

She grinned and patted the bench. Good, better to be invited than to hover more. We'd gotten a little bit of everything, but Frankie's favorite was the beef bulgogi, so I got that out for her first and passed her a plastic fork before I dug into my barbecue chicken. When she offered me a bite of hers, I traded with a bite of mine.

"You remember when we used to come here?" She motioned toward the old building with its mini-amusement park inside, or what had been a mini-amusement park. At five and six, that place had been *awesome*. We had to be good to come, too. My mom brought us a lot.

"Yeah, I remember," I told her. "I was kind of sad when they closed it."

"We were twelve," she reminded me. "We'd already outgrown it."

"Sure, but you don't miss it? It was fun."

"A little, but I kind of like going to the bigger amusement parks with you now."

I grinned. "Well, lucky for you, we still have that option."

"I'm glad your birthday was before," she admitted, and I paused mid-bite.

"Selfishly, me too. But I'd have been okay if this was how I spent my birthday with you." I'd had a damn good time on my birthday, before, during, and after the trip to Six Flags.

She nudged her sunglasses up and then pushed them higher so they rested on her hair and she could meet my gaze. I loved her eyes. They were the perfect shade of green. I'd never found anything that matched them, not a shirt, not a blade of grass, nothing. They were her eyes. Hell, I'd even looked at emeralds in a catalog once.

Nope. Not her shade at all.

"I somehow think truth or dare wouldn't have been on the table."

My cock swelled at the reminder. Fuck. "Then we would have played it later," I told her. "You forget, I'm really patient."

"You've also not given me a real good morning kiss since before."

Frowning, I said, "Your lip was split, and you're hurting. I'm not going to grind into you like I can't control myself until you're feeling better."

"That's fair," she admitted, then grimaced. When she turned her attention to her food, I bumped her knee with mine.

"Talk to me."

"I talked to Jake a little about it yesterday."

He'd mentioned it. No details, just that she'd worried she'd done something wrong. "Okay, is there something you want to talk to me about?"

"No, I think my pity party is firmly full with the table for one I have set."

"Pfft, you won't be at a table for one if I can ever help it. At least two, better if it's three, and to be on the safe side, we should always get one for five."

Sooner or later, Bubba would fix this thing with him and Frankie. The flowers were a great start. So was being there for her every damn day. I'd told him not being a boyfriend might actually be a blessing right now. It was hard to walk that line between what I'd do as her best friend and what I wanted to do because she was Frankie.

I wanted to protect her.

She needed me to kick her in the ass.

These things weren't mutually exclusive, but I'd much rather do the former than the latter. At least until I was sure she was okay.

So, maybe it was time for Bubba to be pushy.

The corner of her mouth kicked up. "I don't know if I want to talk about it or not. But Denitra gave me numbers for some counselors."

"Okay." I offered her another bite of chicken and kept it low-key while she chewed the bite. Denitra had given her quite a bit of literature. And had called to talk to her a couple of times.

The nurse was awesome.

"And I know Ian's dad does counseling, but I don't…"

"Yeah, no." I jumped right in there at her hesitation. "Whatever counselor or psychologist you end up seeing, they have to be someone you don't have a personal connection with. It's important that they are as unbiased and apart from the rest of your life as you can make them."

She studied me for a moment. "I figured. The idea of talking to Ian's dad would just be weird."

"Agreed."

"So is the idea of talking to Diane at school."

"Fair." The guys were talking to her for their anger management, not that either of them had filled in me or Archie. I didn't think they'd talked to Frankie about it either.

"Besides, she's also working with Ian and Jake, so that would just add to the weird factor."

"Yeah, I can see that, too."

She stared at her food. "I looked up some of the names on my laptop last night." She'd been working on 'homework' after we'd had dinner. And apparently doing research.

"Most of the counselors require you to get a parent's permission to talk to them."

Fuck.

"Do you think your mom would sign a permission slip for me? She's on the list of people authorized for me at school."

"Frankie, she'd sign it in a heartbeat." I didn't even have to ask. "For that matter, *I* could sign it."

At her raised eyebrows, I shrugged.

"Unless they physically need to see your mom, how do they know who signs it?"

She blinked slowly. "That's…dishonest."

So was her mother.

"Not if it gets you the help you want." If she was bringing this up, then she wanted it. So dammit, we were going to make it happen. "I can call my mom right now and ask her if you want me to."

"No," she said, stopping me with a hand on mine. "I just—I haven't figured it out totally. I've never seen a psychologist before. Curtises don't do counseling."

"That sounds like a terrible catchphrase."

It was Frankie's turn to shrug. "I don't know how to do it. How do you trust someone you don't know with stuff that's really personal?"

"You build trust. You start slow, you take your time. You talked to Denitra, right?" This bordered dangerously close to pushing. We'd let Frankie bring up that night. Archie wanted to erase it all and try and make it go away. Jake still seethed, a simmering volcano of pissed off. Shockingly, Bubba seemed to teeter between furious and depressed about it. The former was not him. He wasn't usually an angry guy.

But I got why this made him angry.

Me?

It pissed me off, too. But I was more worried about her and whether she'd bury it like she had everything else shitty that happened. You could only pretend everything was all right for so long before you popped.

"Well, it was kind of hard to not talk to her." Frankie stabbed at some of the meat still in her container. "But she seemed to know everything before I said it. Nothing surprised her."

"That's the job," I told her. "That's what psychologists and other specialists train for. You're not their entertainment or there to shock them. They're there to *help* you."

"Feels weird to think I need help."

Oh sweetheart. There was so much I wanted to say, and I bit my tongue. Instead, I focused on what she might need to hear. "Maybe. Then again, look at Jake and Bubba. Jake's always had an issue with his temper."

"Yeah, but he's only going because he has no other choice."

"True. Same can be said for Bubba, but they're still going, and I haven't heard either one complain about it, have you?"

She shook her head slowly. "No, now that you mention it. They haven't brought it up at all."

"Exactly, they aren't complaining or fighting for that matter. Again, this isn't about what other people do, but it's something to think about. If you have questions, ask them. I doubt they'd mind talking to you about it."

They might, but I knew Jake. He'd put himself out there. He'd open a vein if she needed it. Bubba wanted to rebuild that bridge, so it might be a good place to start.

"Have you ever thought about therapy?" She pinned me with a look, and I shrugged.

"Only every single day for the last few years."

Surprise flickered in her eyes.

"Mom and Dad tried the marriage counseling thing, remember?"

She nodded.

"Well, during all that, Sis was also acting out." I had her full attention. "One of the fights Mom and Dad had was over Sis's behavior, and they wanted to put her in therapy. I volunteered 'cause why not, I figured it'd be fun. An hour every week to just talk about me? The best subject on the planet next to the subject of you? What could be better?"

Frankie laughed. Genuinely laughed, even her eyes lit up. "An hour a week to talk about you, huh?”

“Hey, don’t knock it until you’ve tried it. I’m a fantastic subject.”

I meant it on some levels. Mostly it was playing, and yeah, I had thought about therapy. For my parents. For Sis. For Frankie.

For the most part, I did okay. But everything I’d read and learned taught me that we needed more opportunities to open up, not less.

“I wish I could just talk to you about it.”

There it was. I wished she could just talk to me about it, too. “I’d love to be your sounding board, and you can talk to me about anything,” I promised her. “I mean it. You can talk to me about everything from hair and nails to Rachel’s choice in chicks to how much better in bed I am than the other guys…”

Her cheeks flushed pink, but her smile was so wide, my grin stretched to meet it.

“You can Frankie. I’ll listen to everything. But I am horribly biased where you are concerned. I’d do my damnedest to give you advice and to just listen, but there’s a big part of me that just wants to fix it, and as sad as I am to admit it, I’m not an expert.”

Stretching out her left hand, she cupped my face, and I covered her hand with mine before turning to press a kiss to her palm.

“I adore you,” I reminded her. “I’ve known you forever, and I plan to know you forever. So what you need and when you need it, I’m here. And if you want to make appointments or consultations with those different psychologists, do it. Most offer a free consultation, and you can meet them and see if you click or not.”

Her expression softened. “You know I adore you, too, right?”

My heart might have done a backflip at that admission. Scooting forward, I rested my forehead against hers while still holding her hand. The breeze stirred around us, and her bare leg was soft against mine.

“It’s because I’m perfect, I know,” I teased, and her laughter was a heady thing.

"Sometimes," she admitted, and I raised my brows. "Sometimes you're a little shit."

"Okay, I can live with that assessment." What else could I say? She wasn't wrong.

"Coop?"

"Hmm?"

"Can I ask you a hard question?"

"You can ask me any question you want." I pressed a kiss to the tip of her nose before threading my fingers with hers.

"Do you guys talk about me?"

That wasn't a tough question. The easiest answer was yes, we did. Except… "We do," I said. "We talk about how you're doing. They text me when they're home with you so I know you're doing okay or if you need something." Catching a tendril of her hair that had pulled from her braid with my free hand, I tucked it behind her ear. "If you're having bad dreams, we talk about that. We try to coordinate so we know our schedules and what you need. But what we do or talk about when it's just us?" I shook my head.

"At all?"

"Nope." The surprise on her face we all deserved. "Frankie, what you do with Archie or Jake—that's your business and theirs. What you and I share? That's ours. No, I'm not telling them how it feels to kiss you or feel you wrap around me. When you talk just to me? Then that's between us, too. Unless…" I held up a finger, and she tracked it with her gaze for a moment before focusing on me. "Unless you're really hurting. Then we talk because we all want to take care of you, and as far as I'm concerned, we're all boyfriends, even Bubba— okay, maybe not Bubba, but he's kind of boyfriend level."

Her nose wrinkled.

"Fine, he's a good friend. I'm not making his case for him."

That pulled a smile from her.

"That said, if you're worried I'm going to tell them about this conversation?

Then rest easy because the answer is no, I'm not. I'll only bring it up if I think you're really hurting and need all of us to talk to about it. Otherwise, what you tell me stays with me. I'm a vault."

And had been for all of them. Frankie did that for us, too. It was how we'd always balanced this friendship.

When she leaned in and pressed her lips to mine, I held still. Just the barest of brushes, and I wanted to deepen it. But I cupped her face and forced myself to take it easy. Then she teased her tongue against my lips, and I groaned.

Okay. Good intentions crumbled as I opened up and met her tongue with mine. It was just a long, slow kiss. I held her hand and cupped her face as we tested and tasted each other. The hints of Korean barbecue just added to the spice of the kiss. She pressed her bandaged wrist against my other leg, and the raspiness of it kept me grounded.

When she finally pulled back, I wasn't the only one breathing hard. Fuck, that had been nice. I studied her expression and smiled. "Thank you."

"You're welcome," she whispered. "I wanted to know if that was still okay?"

Was kissing me still okay?

"Hell yes, it's still okay." I closed the distance and kissed her this time, a little more forcefully, but she gave a little moan and scooted forward. Then I wrapped my arms around her and buried my face against her throat. She gave a little shudder, and I sighed. "It's always okay. We go as fast or slow as you need."

Relief swam off her, and I pulled back a little.

"Frankie, did you think we wouldn't want you?"

"You're all being so careful, and... I know I've been confused."

I pressed a finger to her lips. "We're all respecting your space, but don't for a second think I don't want you. I can't tell you how many times I've jacked off in the shower just to make sure I wasn't pressuring you in anyway."

"Well, the next time you do that, do you mind if I watch?"

Heat flushed right through me, and my erection told me my dick was one hundred and ten percent on board with this idea.

"Whatever you want," I told her. "But don't push anything you don't want to. Trust me. You are *worth* waiting for."

The press of her lips against mine threatened my sanity. I didn't want to hurt anything on her, but I could definitely go for making out.

"Maybe we go slow," she whispered against my lips. "But I would love to see you get yourself off. I bet it's pretty."

I groaned. "You're killing me."

She chuckled, then pulled her hand from mine and slid it down my front. I caught it before she reached her destination.

"And that would kill me," I chastised her. "If you really want to play, we go home and we play. But I don't want to hurt you."

None of us did.

She met my gaze, and I held my breath.

"Maybe we experiment a little?"

I glanced at the time on my phone.

We had about ninety minutes before the guys were out of school.

"Whatever you want," I told her, and pressed another kiss to her lips. "Let me clean this up, and we're going home."

And hopefully my dick didn't die from strangulation before then. The heat in her eyes wasn't manufactured, but then neither was her earlier confusion.

Take it slow would be my mantra. But I wanted her to know I wanted her. That hadn't changed at all.

If that meant a little torture for me, I could handle it.

I could handle pretty much anything for her.

Chapter Five
LIFETIME PILE-UP

FRANKIE

The experiment with Coop didn't go anywhere, because when we got back to my apartment, Mr. Wittaker was waiting for us. I hadn't known the attorney was coming over, and he gave me an apologetic look as he exited his car to greet us.

"Miss Curtis, I tried to call, but I never got past your voicemail."

Oh.

"I haven't really had my phone on much." The guys were here, and even when they were at school, one of them was with me. Otherwise, I'd have felt disconnected. I just didn't want to answer messages yet. I still needed to straighten out how I felt about a lot of this in my head.

"I understand," he said. "I spoke to Mr. Standish—the younger—this morning. He let me know, but this is important, so I came to you. Do you have time to talk to me?"

I glanced at Coop, and he gave me a nod. "Sure," I said, blowing out a breath. "Would you like to come in?"

It had taken a lot to work up to propositioning Coop. The guys had been amazing. Really, really amazing. But I missed more, and I wanted…well, it didn't matter what I wanted right now. Mr. Wittaker said this was important, and I wanted my official independence from my mother. So, one thing at a time.

My wrist ached and so did my back. Every day, I felt a bit better and could put off the pain meds longer and longer. But the aching twinges in my hand and wrist grew more pronounced with each passing hour. If it wasn't better by the time Mr. Wittaker left, I'd take something.

I didn't like taking any of the pain meds. They either made me loopy or knocked me out. Most of the time, it was both.

We sat at the table in the kitchen. Coop flipped on the light, and I opened the blinds that I almost never opened to let the sunshine in. In his suit, Mr. Wittaker seemed horribly out of place here, but he made no comment on the apartment size or state. At least it was clean.

The guys had been pretty fastidious.

Even in the bathroom, I'd only had to complain once about the toilet seat being left up, and they didn't do it again. Kind of unfair I supposed, one of me and four of them, but they were being sweet.

Flipping open his black briefcase, Mr. Wittaker pulled out two folders. Then he glanced at Coop before he looked to me.

"It's fine, you can talk to me in front of Coop." He had talked to me in front of Archie, but Archie and Jeremy had paid the bill, so I supposed that might be different.

"Actually," Mr. Wittaker stated. "It's not fine. Mr. Benton is eighteen, correct?"

Coop nodded slowly as I frowned.

"That's what I thought." Mr. Wittaker focused his whole attention on me. "As your attorney, we share attorney-client privilege. Anything you say to me is protected. However, if Mr. Benton stays, he can, since he is eighteen, be compelled to testify should it come down to that to anything you said here."

Scowling, Coop said, "I'd never tell her secrets, compelled or not."

"Mr. Benton, that's a truly noble thought. However, if you lie on the stand, then you would be committing perjury. That is also a crime."

My stomach flip-flopped. The last thing I wanted was for Coop to get into trouble.

"I'm telling you this, Miss Curtis, because as your attorney, when we discuss matters of the case, it should only be us. Then anything you say is protected. I can't prevent you from telling him after the fact, but just understand— anything you share may be up for grabs if they are compelled."

Oh this sucked.

"What are the chances of them being called?" I didn't want this to spill over onto the guys. I just wanted to get out of this mess with my mom.

"What are the chances your mother will fight this?"

She'd have to want me to fight it, right?

"I can go back to the bedroom," Coop said, though he clearly didn't like it. "You can call me when you're done." But he wasn't talking to the lawyer. Instead, he focused on me. "If you're okay with being alone with him. Otherwise, I'll just go get my headphones and sit in the living room and turn them up real loud."

I wasn't worried about Mr. Wittaker at all, but Coop's offer warmed me.

"I'll be okay."

He nodded, then pressed a kiss to my forehead. "I'll just get you guys some water real quick."

Mr. Wittaker waited a beat as Coop filled a pair of glasses then set them on the table.

"Give me a yell when you're done," he said, then headed out of the kitchen. A part of me wished he didn't have to go, and at the same time, I couldn't risk him getting sucked into this. I doubted Mom would fight. I missed him as soon as he was gone.

She didn't care about what I was doing now, right?

"Excellent. I have two briefs here for you to see. I'll leave copies for you to read, but I want to go over them with you now so you understand what I'm doing, and if you want any changes made, we can tackle those right up front."

A chill raced over my skin, apprehension and something else. This was something I needed to do, and at the same time, it felt incredibly disloyal to my mother. She wasn't an evil person. She wasn't even truly bad, she was just…

"Okay."

"We'll start with this one." Mr. Wittaker flipped the folder open and turned it around to face me. "I will be filing this, with your approval, and at the same time, we will be serving your mother, Ms. Curtis, with the notification."

I sucked against my lower lip, then stopped immediately. The cut there had mostly healed, but it still pulled and stung.

"Legal age of majority in Texas is eighteen, pretty standard. You can become automatically emancipated if you marry or if you join the military. However, in Texas, you still need a parent's permission to marry before eighteen, so this won't help you."

My heart did a little skip jump at the marriage comment.

Mr. Wittaker gave me a sympathetic smile.

"Since that's not an option or your expressed desire, we go for a declaration of emancipation in court. Once this is filed and your mother is notified, we'll petition the court for a swift date for a hearing. In order to address the specific considerations that a judge will want to know, I've listed many of the things we discussed in my office here." He flipped the page to an itemized list.

My mouth went dry at the first line indicating neglect. I disliked that word intensely. Taking a sip of the water, I tried to keep my hand from shaking. Not that I was having much luck. My gut churned, too.

"First, we indicate a pattern of neglect on the part of your mother and the number of hours, days, and weeks you've been self-managing. This helps us on two levels, it establishes that you would not be hampered, but in fact, you would be better off without her presence, and also that you are capable of managing yourself." He ticked down to the next on the list. "You have stable living arrangements now, but it's my understanding the lease here is in your mother's name?"

"Yeah."

"But she has moved out?"

I nodded. He tapped a line on the paper.

"This is her new legal address?"

"As far as I know. I haven't been there, and she's in Europe, somewhere at the moment."

Mr. Wittaker frowned briefly, then picked up his phone and made a couple of notes.

"All right, I'll make sure to note that, because notification has to be served. But her absence can be factored into neglect. When were you notified of her trip?"

"Technically, I haven't been notified. Found out when the guys tried to track her down when I was in the hospital."

While I couldn't pinpoint it, his expression shifted subtly from professional to disapproving. "I hate to ask this, but can you get me a copy of your hospital records? I'll need your authorization to get them."

"I'm a minor still, right?"

"True, but you can request them and then give them to me. Legally, they do have to give them to you."

I sighed. "Okay. I'll call today."

"Good, if you want to have them fax it to my office or email it…" He slid the card over to me. "You can always have them sent to you, and then you can forward them on."

At my nod, he continued, "The rest of this lists if you're financially self-sufficient. With your rent paid up through the end of May, you just need to be able to cover your utilities. The income statements you gave me show that you can.

There's also your work history, these both play in your favor. The scholarship you won and the internship option you've been given are both positives toward post-high school. Largely, we just need to show you can handle all of this ahead of your eighteenth birthday, which is in April, correct?"

I nodded again. It seemed a really long way away.

"I know this seems a little boring to go over everything again, but I don't want a single mistake to slow this process for you."

"I appreciate that."

Next he went over the other items and evidence listed that included whether I was mature enough to make adult decisions and my school records, including my attendance and GPA.

"Is the fact that I've been home this week going to play against me?"

My leg bounced steadily as I tried to keep the rest of me still.

"I don't believe so, you are under doctor's orders, and you have been responsible. The police reports you filed and the questions you answered will cover any lingering concerns there. If and when you need to speak to a district attorney regarding this case, I do want you to let me know. I'll be there to help look after your interests."

My gut bottomed out. I was going to make a lousy witness. I didn't remember. I had the injuries, I had what Denitra told me, as well as what I'd gleaned from the guys, but there was this blank wall. I couldn't tell them what really happened.

"So that's all of this. The next few paragraphs are standard legal information and then we have one last concern. Were you able to track down your birth certificate?"

Shit. "I forgot I was supposed to be looking for it. I'm sorry…"

"No worries, it's been busy. I've already requested a copy of your birth certificate. It took me some time to track it down, since you were born in California."

I was?

"It lists the father as unknown."

Not a shock. "Okay."

"Do you have a name for him?"

"Nope. And he's been kind of a no show for seventeen years." So I probably wouldn't know him if I met him walking across the street.

I'd been born in California?

"And that plays to our advantage, but like I said earlier, I want to eliminate any surprises or delays."

"Thank you." Honestly, I'd had no idea what it would say. Mom *never* talked about him. I'd been six or seven before I even realized I didn't have one and that I was supposed to. There were no photos of him either.

"Do you know anything about your father?"

I shook my head. "She never talks about him. I asked her once when I was six, and she told me he'd died. That was it. Then when I was thirteen or fourteen, we had a fight 'cause I was mad that I didn't even have pictures of him, and she wouldn't tell me his name. She said I should be grateful she wanted me when he didn't. So really, your guess is as good as mine." Those words had hurt.

They still kind of stung.

"I see." No judgment echoed in his voice, though admittedly, his stern expression said otherwise. "We'll cite abandonment for now. We can amend it later if necessary. We'll move for an expedited hearing, and in the meanwhile, I'll be filing this as well..." He flipped to the second folder. "This is an emergency order to emancipate you until the time of the hearing where the final decision can be made, citing the incident at Homecoming, the inability to reach your mother, and the fact that she has moved out as key factors, with the original filing providing the necessary support. If I can get this in front of a judge today, we could possibly have the order in place by next week."

"That fast?"

"Yes, Mr. Standish the younger requested we move with due diligence and to try and expedite this, particularly after the issues with getting authorization for your care."

I hadn't really thought about it or how frustrating that had to have been. Once I was awake, I answered a lot of questions and consented to some things—like the sexual assault kit—but I couldn't authorize everything. Not even if it had to do with me.

"Then I'd very much like you to get that done." Even if it made me heartsick to cut ties with her. She was my mom. I didn't have anyone else. Just me and the guys.

Not that I seemed to have her anyway.

"I think that covers all the stickier issues," Mr. Wittaker said. "If you'd call Mr. Brennen back out, we can have him witness you signing these."

"It doesn't really matter if they ask him whether I signed the documents."

"No it doesn't," he told me with a kind smile.

I called his name, and Coop rejoined us in seconds. I could almost picture him leaning against the door in my room just waiting for me to yell. It was sweet.

After we explained to him what we needed, Mr. Wittaker motioned to the blank lines at the end—these pages were mostly blank except for where the signatures went. I guess that covered Coop too.

"Miss Curtis, I just need you to sign here and here."

I hesitated and looked at my splinted wrist and hand.

"You can sign it with your left, we know it will be awkward, that's why we'll both witness you signing it."

Signing with my left hand proved unwieldy. No way the scrawl I made resembled my natural handwriting. Still, I got it done, and Coop added his signature to the witness line and put in proof of ID before the attorney also signed it.

Flipping everything closed, Mr. Wittaker rose. "I'm going to let you get back to resting. I'll have copies of this messengered to you. And I'll update you as soon as we get a response."

"Thank you. Do I need to try and track down my mom…?"

"No, I'll take care of that. If she is unavailable to be served, I need to have a paper trail established for how we attempted it that I can show the judge."

Coop stood, but when I went to, Mr. Wittaker waved me back to the chair.

"You rest, and I hope you feel better. Remember what I said about any potential questioning. Really, if you need anything at all, call me."

Then he was gone, and it was just me and Coop again. I couldn't say the playful, experimental mood survived the last hour and ten minutes.

"C'mon," Coop said, nudging me out of the chair. "Go make yourself comfortable on the sofa. I'll get your pain meds."

Honestly, I didn't argue about it this time. As soon as I curled up on the sofa, I had Tiddles in my lap and Tabby up on the back of the couch. Coop took up the other end and propped my feet in his lap after I swallowed down my pills.

"That was a lot," he commented quietly.

"I think I'm getting pretty good at the big-time drama," I admitted, and it pulled a real, if reluctant smile to his lips. "The weird part is I have an attorney who is helping me sue my mom because she's not around, and it's like I'm divorcing her. In some…weird way."

He gave a little shrug. "I can tell you from experience, the divorce part sucks while it's happening, but it gets better on the other side."

I canted my head so I could study him. When his parents got divorced, it hadn't been a picnic. His parents fought about everything. Coop and his dad still had issues with each other. Not that he talked about it that much. "I know you don't like her," I said slowly. "But she's my mom, and I have this…sick feeling in my stomach that this is going to ambush her. Then at the same time, I'm all like, good. It's not like she hasn't ambushed me."

"You know there's no right or wrong way to feel," he said, running his fingers along my ankle to my calf and back. It was just a light petting motion, almost mirroring the way I stroked Tiddles where the black cat sprawled against my chest. His purring was almost as soothing as Coop's fingers working over my leg to the top of my foot.

"Just…she's my mom." I didn't know how to express it beyond that. I didn't like talking about her with anyone, I actively avoided it.

"Frankie," Coop said, clasping my ankle. "I mean it. How we feel about her should not in any way affect how you feel. I get it—she's your mom. You care about her."

"She's the only family I have, Coop." Saying it aloud made it a scary kind of real. "I don't know my dad, if I even have one. I mean, I know I have to have one, but he's never been around."

He nodded slowly, but didn't say anything. Maybe the lack of comment more than anything else let me talk about this.

"I think she did her best, and when her mom came to visit a few years ago…she didn't stay that long. She didn't even stay here."

I licked my lips.

That had been so strange. I had a grandmother, and I'd been excited. Coop's grandmother was awesome. I liked his grandpa, too. So when Mom said we were going to see my grandmother or, more precisely, she was coming to see us, I'd been excited. Coop's grandmother smelled like peppermints and made cookies. Mine?

I shook my head. "We went to her hotel to see her. She barely spoke to me the whole time I was there. Just nodded at me and told me to sit up straight. The rest of it was her and Mom having a fight without being a fight." After… Well, after, we'd left and gone home, and that was the first and last time I ever saw my grandmother.

Honestly, I didn't even know if she was still alive.

"You know mine still love you, right?" Coop said, giving me a comforting squeeze. "I'll totally share them with you."

Heart heavy, I tried to smile. I did appreciate it. But I was so tired just thinking about it. "I'm glad. Your grandmother gives great hugs." Mine didn't. She hadn't touched me once. "I'm sorry we didn't get to play."

"Hey, we have all the time in the world," Coop promised me as he put his feet up and grabbed the remote. "You look tired."

"I feel tired." I felt worse than tired. It had been a good day, but I still had so much to figure out. "I have to call those therapists and the hospital and…"

"They can wait," he told me firmly. "None of them are going anywhere, and if you're tired, you can nap. The guys will be home soon, and even if you only get thirty minutes, you're going to feel better."

I didn't want to miss the guys. "Wake me up if I don't when they get here?"

"Nope," he told me with a grin. "'Cause then they'll get mad at me. Trust me, everyone is more than willing to hang out and wait. I bet you can even convince them to order pizza tonight."

We kept ordering out food or Jeremy brought over food or one of their moms sent food. There was so much food in the fridge. "Potluck," I said around a yawn. "We can't let that stuff go to waste."

"Right," Coop murmured, rubbing slow circles against my leg. My last glimpse of him was his smile as he glanced at me. I didn't even see what he turned on the television.

The pounding on the door jerked me awake, and I winced even as I blinked around the room. The television was on but quiet, and Ian sat at the coffee table working on his notebook. He jerked too at the pounding on the door.

Jake was halfway across the room heading for the kitchen as I started to sit up. Tiddles leapt off me at the first movement, and I put my right hand down and then winced. A little sound must have escaped, because Ian slid an arm around my back and helped me up.

"Easy," he said, sitting behind me so he half-propped me up as I cradled my splinted wrist. "You okay?"

The pounding on the door came again just as Jake wrenched it open. "What?" That growl was all kinds of hostile, and I strained to see who it was, but between the door, the angle, and Jake, I couldn't see who it was.

"Good evening, dickhead. I've come to see my BFF, so if you wouldn't mind…"

Rachel's voice carried, and the combination of insolence and annoyance made me smile, even if my wrist ached.

"You could have called," Jake said, unmoved from his position. "Why the hell were you pounding on the door like that?"

"One, I have called and you guys keep telling me she's asleep, and she hasn't answered my texts. Two, I knocked like that because I'd rather you didn't pretend you didn't hear me."

Guilt stabbed at me, and I glanced up at Ian who wore a frown. "I'm okay," I said quietly, then held up wrist. "I think I forgot while I was asleep." The pain meds always muddled me anyway.

"Yeah, good." But he didn't move away, if anything, he just sat there and let me lean into him. And you know, it was nice, so I let myself lean into him, too.

"Rach…" Jake began.

"Save it, dickhead. I brought her coffee and chocolate, and I'm not budging until I see her. You guys have played guardian at the gate for a week. It's cute, I appreciate it. Now get the hell out of my way."

"I need to go and deal with that," I told Ian. The last thing I wanted was Jake slamming the door in her face or for it to escalate.

"She's asleep," Jake replied, the testiness in his voice hitting epic proportions.

"I got this," Ian promised. "Not anymore." He pitched his voice a little louder, and Jake yanked around to glare at him, though the moment his gaze connected with mine, it softened a bit. It also gave Rachel an opening, and she squeezed right past him with a pair of coffees in hand and a bag dangling off her wrist.

She looked good. Dark hair pulled back into a ponytail and dressed in jeans and t-shirt with some band logo on it that I didn't know. "You look like crap," she said by way of greeting, and I almost laughed. Expression thunderous, Jake closed the door and stalked after her.

"This is your idea of checking on her?"

"Well, it is when she's sitting here all pale and leaning on shit for brains like a good stiff wind will knock her over. On the other hand…" Rachel set the coffees down and cocked her head to the side as I met her dry gaze. "You also look a little bit like a badass."

"Only a little bit?" I said, sitting up more as Ian pressed his hand against my spine to support me until I swung my feet around. He kept his touch below the remnants of the bruise on my back. I didn't think about it much unless someone put pressure on it, and then it reminded me that it hurt. The blanket tangled around me, I had to tug it off before I stood.

"Well, maybe a lot," Rachel conceded, and then she took another step toward me and put the coffee on the table. "Can I give you a hug?"

"Sure," I said, and it wasn't as awkward as I feared as she wrapped her arms around me.

"Be careful of her back," Jake ordered, and I met his gaze over Rachel's shoulder. Worry filtered through his eyes, and I mouthed 'I'm okay.' He frowned but nodded.

"I'm not going to hurt her," Rachel snapped back. "Go be a dickhead somewhere else. You too, shit for brains." She flicked off Ian and Jake like they were bugs. "I want to talk to Frankie without an audience."

"Rach…"

But before I could continue, she rolled her eyes as she released me and then said, "Please, would you give us a few minutes to catch up? Take a break. Take a shower. Take a walk. Just—go away."

"Frankie?" Ian asked, not missing a beat. "You want a minute with your friend?" The hesitation he put on the word friend spoke volumes, but Jake just rolled his eyes.

"I'll be in the bedroom, don't be a bitch and don't wear her out." With that, he leaned over and pressed a kiss to my cheek before murmuring, "Coop and Archie went out to grab dinner, and before you say potluck, Bubba and I killed half the leftovers when we got home. I was starving." Then he gave me a wink before he retreated toward my room. Which, you know, as weird as it was, I'd gotten kind of used to having them there.

"Thanks," I called after him and then glanced at Ian. "And yes, I'd like to talk to Rachel. I've not been a very good friend the last week. Do you mind?"

"Nope," he said, then pressed a kiss to my forehead, and my heart did a little squeeze. It was the first one he'd given me since everything happened. "I'll go let Jake rant while I work on this." He scooped up his notebook and glanced at Rachel. "Just—dial it down a notch?"

"For you, stud, anything."

"Sorry, all taken here. Better luck next time."

My snicker at Rachel's smirking tone dried up at Ian's retort, but he was already vanishing down the hallway. A light touch against my chin jerked my gaze back to Rachel.

"Don't drool, girl, it's not really attractive."

I wasn't drooling. "If you came all the way over here and stormed the gates just to tell me that, I'll be disappointed." It was the best I could come up with. Ian knew Rachel wasn't really interested, so the response didn't have to be that. But why had he said that?

"Hey," Rachel countered. "I also brought coffee." She handed me a peppermint mocha with a grin. "And best of all, I brought you me."

That really was best of all. Smiling a little, I sat back down and nodded to the sofa. She dropped onto the other end and picked up her own coffee cup.

"I'm sorry—" But she didn't let me finish.

"Nothing to be sorry for. You needed time and space, and I gave you as much as I can. They told me how you were doing, and as much shit as I give them, I like that they've closed ranks and been protective. But it's been a week, and I needed to see you for myself. So, you can throw me out whenever. Until then, I figured we could hang out for a few?"

"It feels a lot longer than a week, and I'd love it if you hung out for a while. At least until Coop and Archie get back." I had no idea when they left, I was still a little muddled from the pain meds.

"Cool," Rachel said, then crossed one leg over the other. "So what do you want first? The good gossip? Or the really good gossip?"

Um…

That felt like a trick question.

Chapter Six
PLAYING RUBBER CHICKEN

Running.

I was running.

Only my feet weren't moving.

Everywhere I turned, the walls were blank. It was like I was in an endless hallway of dead ends. Frustrated, I turned in a circle. Something was after me.

No. Some *one* was after me.

I couldn't see them either.

Just the drag of their footsteps. I struck out blindly. Boxing with shadows. My wrist popped and hurt. My shoulders burned. I struck out again, and my face burned. I fell.

Then I was running again, only this time, I ran right into a wall.

It was a dream. I knew it was a dream. Why the fuck couldn't I wake up?

"Shh…" The soft hush of sound whispered against my ear. An arm tightened around me, and Coop's familiar voice penetrated the endless walls.

Then Jake's voice joined him. "Shh, we've got you. You're safe."

Relief swam up as I cracked an eyelid open. The light was on in the hall, enough for me to see Jake sitting on the bed in front of me. He was mostly dressed. With care, he brushed the hair away from my face.

"You got her?" It took me a minute to register he wasn't talking to me.

"Yeah," Coop said around a half-yawn. "I got her. Go do your sickeningly healthy thing."

A soft chuckle drifted over me as my eyelids fought to lower, but I didn't want to go back to sleep yet. Coop's arm was warm around me with his chest pressed firmly against my back. I was lying on my left side, and there was a pillow propping up my right arm. It had been on Jake, I thought.

Maybe.

"Hey, Baby Girl," Jake tipped his head to the side as he found my gaze with his. "Go back to sleep. It's still early."

"Where are you going?" It was the weekend. Why were they up early?

With a long sigh, he said, "Arch, Bubba, and I are going running."

"Why?" The disgust must have reflected in my tone, because there were more soft huffs of laughter.

"Because they're getting lazy," Archie murmured. "And I haven't gone running all week. Coop's here, and we'll be back in a couple of hours."

"With donuts," Ian tacked on.

Two hours?

I made a face. No way in hell was I leaving my warm, comfortable bed to go running, much less for two hours.

"Want to go?" Jake asked, amusement curling his lips.

"No." I wiggled back against Coop, and he groaned into my neck. Oh. The thick erection nudging my ass had me curling my toes. Yeah, I'd stop wiggling.

"Go back to sleep, Baby Girl." Jake chuckled, then pressed a kiss to my forehead. He rose, and then Archie was there. He had his Bluetooth earphones around his neck and his phone tucked into a Velcro armband.

Oh, he was wearing shorts and a tank just like Jake. They were gonna get hot and sweaty when they ran. I might need to get up before they got back.

He brushed his lips against my forehead, and I caught a whiff of peppermint toothpaste. "See you in a little while, babe."

I smothered another yawn, then blinked because Ian had taken Archie's place, and he brushed the hair back from my face. "Sleep well, Angel." He shouldn't be calling me that.

His kiss was far briefer as he grazed his lips against my cheek, but there and gone as he straightened. And all chance of going back to sleep vanished as he left the room with the guys. I could hear the cats following them, meowing. They'd gotten used to the guys being there, too.

The crinkling of a can being opened drifted back up the hall, and Coop chuckled against my hair as he flattened his hand over my stomach. "They are so pussy whipped."

The minute the words registered, laughter swelled through me and I cracked up. He shook with laughter.

"I heard that," Jake yelled, and the laughter bubbled up through me faster.

"Don't hear you denying it," Coop answered in the same tone.

"You can't see me, but I'm flipping you off."

Coop's laughter deepened, and my chest ached from the out of control giggles.

"Be good," Archie added. "Frankie's pussy is all taken care of."

I sucked in a breath, then lost it laughing all over again. Masculine laughter chased Archie's words, even as Coop clutched me to him still chuckling. The back door closed, but it did nothing to quiet our humor. Wiggling, I rolled onto my back and met Coop's gaze. The guys had shut off the light in the hall, but it wasn't really dark. We must be close to dawn. Coop touched my nose with a finger. The laughter surged up again, and he caught my splinted arm carefully as he hugged me.

Practically panting to catch my breath, I lay there. My stomach hurt, we'd giggled so much. Next to me, Coop didn't seem to be doing much better. One arm against his forehead, he snorted as he released another chuckle.

"We're not going back to sleep, are we?" Since he sounded almost as awake as I was, I turned my head to look at him.

"Probably not," I admitted. "I can try." But I was *really* wired up.

"I blame them," Coop declared in an attempt to be grumpy.

I couldn't help it. "The pussy-whipped?"

His guffaw made me grin until my cheeks ached. I had to stop 'cause it pulled on my bruise cheek too much, but I wanted to keep smiling. He rolled up to sitting, still laughing.

"I'll be right back."

He was only wearing boxers and some of my laughter dried up as he walked away. Coop was wiry, and it was hard to see in his clothes, but without them?

Whew. Hot.

Sitting up, I checked my breath against my hand and then tested my back by stretching. There was still a pull. Coop took longer than a minute, more like ten. But when he came back in, he made a face when I slid off the bed.

"I gotta pee," I told him, and rose on my tiptoes to kiss his smooth cheek. A second grin stole through me. He took long enough to shave?

"K."

It took me a couple of minutes, but I peed, brushed my teeth, and washed my face—one-handed. I was already sick of the splint. But I had to wear it for at least another week, and then they'd see whether I could take it off or if I needed something else.

Blegh.

My hair was kind of a mess. It had begun to pull out of the really nice braid Jake had put it in, so I freed it and used my fingers to comb it. It was all kinky waves and kind of huge. But I had to wash it at some point today. I kind of wished I could shower and do all the things on my own, but that was still tricky.

Gathering my courage before it could flee, I padded back to the bedroom. "Coop," I said before swinging in the door. "Do you think you could—oh."

I paused.

Coop sprawled on the bed, completely naked. Not that he had that far to go, he'd just had boxer shorts on earlier. But he had one arm hooked behind his head while he palmed his very stiff cock with the other.

"Hi." All the breath kind of went out of me. Not that I hadn't seen the guys in various states of naked for the last week. But it was really hard to appreciate in the shower when they were actually helping me wash and I had to keep my right arm out of the way.

And I couldn't lie, I riveted on the way his hand slid slowly up the length to the tip then back down again. There were already drops of moisture gathering, and each glimpse I got of the vein running along the underside showed it throbbing.

"Frankie?" At the husky, yet questioning notes in my name, I dragged my gaze up to meet his. There was just a hint of laughter in his gray-green eyes. "Truth or dare?"

The soft question sent a thrill through my system, and I moved closer to the bed. "Truth."

He stilled his hand and studied me. "Do you still want to experiment?"

Oh, that shiver in my system seesawed between nervous and excited. "Yes."

Sitting up, he shot me an expectant look, and I rubbed at my lower lip carefully. "Truth or dare?"

He grinned. "Dare."

I laughed.

"You're already naked."

"I know." He leaned forward and crooked a finger unto the waistband of the boxers—Jake's this time—I wore then tugged me toward him. "But you're not."

"But this is my dare." And my heart jumped again when he slid his hand under the tank top and began to nudge it upward.

"True, but I want to be helpful while you're thinking about it."

Helpful. He slid his hand just under my breast and then captured the nipple with his teeth through the shirt. The combination of sensations threatened to short-circuit my brain. It was so simple and at the same time, they'd been so careful in *how* they touched me. I'd half-worried it wasn't going to be the same.

No.

Couldn't say that worry lingered at the moment. He slid his free hand under my shirt and covered the other breast. My legs trembled, and I slid onto my knees onto the bed. When he lifted his head to look at me, I traced my fingers against his cheek. The damp tank clung to the nipple he'd just sucked, and it ached even as he tweaked it.

"Kiss me?" I whispered. "Like, really kiss me?"

When one of his hands slipped away from my breasts, I almost complained. Almost. But he pushed up onto his knees and cupped my chin before gently running his finger over my lower lip. "Still hurt?"

"A little." I could lie and say no. "But it doesn't sting anymore."

He pressed his lips to where the cut had been. A butterfly kiss, there and gone again. "Hurt?"

"No."

Another kiss, this time to the corner of my mouth. "Here?"

"No," I said with a smile.

He brushed his lips to the other corner. "What about here?"

"No," I whispered, and put my left hand on his chest to steady myself. He caught my right and lifted it gently until the splinted hand was on his shoulder. Then he pressed his lips to mine, a whisper of a touch. "No," I said quickly before he could say anything.

"You don't know what I was going to ask," he teased. Another gentle touch. "What if I was going to ask if I could slip you tongue?" He traced his tongue over my lower lip as if to make a point. "Or if I was going to ask can I take off your shirt before I kiss you?" He squeezed my breast, and my nipples tightened more.

"Coop…" It came out more a whimper than a complaint, but he nuzzled a path of little kisses to my ear.

"Can I take off your shirt, Frankie?"

I shuddered. "Yes."

It would be easier with his help anyway, or I'd have dragged it off by now. He caught the hem of the tank top and lifted. Even if everything in me screamed to rush, he took care to free my left arm first and then moved it gently down my right and over the split and off without jostling anything.

All of my complaints fled at the fierce and focused expression on his face. The cool air against my breasts had me moving close to him until I was chest to breast. When I slid my hand down his chest toward his very erect dick, he paused and watched me with a small smirk.

"Not going to wait for me to say truth or dare?"

I snorted. Indignant. "You haven't even *done* your dare yet, you don't get to com—" His mouth closed over mine as he clasped my nape, and I groaned. This was what I'd been missing. He darted his tongue in to duel with mine, chasing it as he deepened the kiss. These wet, long, tongue-twisting morning kisses. I closed my left hand on his cock, and his moan vibrated right through me.

If not for his hand on my hip and his other on my nape, I might have fallen because I only had my right for balance, but I didn't want to stop kissing him, even as I began to stroke him. I'd really missed this. Missed touching him—any of them. The hugs, the cuddling, and the holding were great, but I drowned in the feel of Coop devouring my mouth.

His dick was hot in my palm, and with every squeezing stroke I made, he pushed forward against my hand.

"Fuck," he muttered, releasing my mouth long enough for me to gasp in a breath.

"I think that's the idea."

He paused with his lips touching mine, and I swore his eyes widened a fraction, then laughter flowed out of him and I grinned. The corners of his eyes crinkled as his mouth stretched into a smile. "You really are feeling better?"

There was hope and hesitation in that question. I licked my lips. "I know a way I could be feeling a lot better."

He sucked in a breath before covering my hand on him. "You keep that up, and I'm going to be over before we get to the fun part."

This was kind of the fun part, but I appreciated the warning.

Then, focusing on me, he said, "Truth or dare?"

I groaned, but I couldn't deny his playful smile. "Whichever you want."

"That is not how this works, Francesca."

"Call me that again while I have my hand on your dick, Cooper." I glared at him. "I *dare* you."

"No, I'm good," he replied, all sweet smiles. Then he pressed a quick kiss to my lips. "Truth then…top or bottom?"

I hesitated, because I almost wanted to say top, but I didn't want to whack him with the splint. It was heavy, and without something to rest it on, it would start making my wrist ache.

"Bottom," I decided, and goosebumps raced over my skin as he traced his hands to my hips. "I'd say wherever with you too, but I have a feeling you might swat me." I loosened my grip on his dick, albeit reluctantly, and he gave a little sigh as I reached for my shorts.

"Uh uh." He nudged my hands away and then lifted and twisted until I could lie with my head on the pillows. Then he took the time to fluff up one and placed it under my right arm.

I really missed having it right now.

He stared down at me for a moment, and my face heated. The flush spread down my chest as though warmed by his gaze as he stroked it over me.

"You're so pretty, Frankie," he whispered. "I don't think I ever tell you that. But you are. You're gorgeous."

Now my cheeks flamed for real, and he grinned.

"But one second."

I swallowed as he slid off the bed. Where was he going? Admittedly, I had a really nice view of his ass as he bent, but I wanted him here not there. The sound of a zipper sliding on his backpack answered the question. He turned around with a pair of foil wrapped squares.

"Ambitious," I teased, and he chuckled.

"I've been hard for a week. I'm pretty sure I'm going to go off like a shot and then need to recharge, but I'm all about giving it the effort." I just wanted him to touch me. He set the packs on the bed and then reached up to catch the waistband of my shorts. With one light tug, he pulled them down and then stared at me.

No barriers at all.

"Really. Really. Pretty." After pressing a kiss to my ankle, he brushed another to my knee as he worked his way up to my thighs. My heart hammered triple time as he pressed a kiss to the crease where my leg joined my hip. "It's your turn."

Fuck.

My turn?

"Truth or dare?" Right. I knew that.

He grinned as if reading my mind.

"Truth or dare, idiot."

He chuckled the bite down lightly on the same place he'd kissed. His hands were so hot on my thighs where he began to stroke them up and down. The seesaw of nerves to excitement from earlier ratcheted higher as the tension in my belly drew ever tighter.

I ached to touch him and have him touch me. And at the same time, I grinned down at him. It was hard to not smile at Coop when he grinned up at me.

"Truth," he decided before licking me from entrance to clit, and my hips arched as my brain cells scrambled. I couldn't form words because of the way he slid his tongue in hard circles around my clit before sucking on it, and I twisted in his grasp, but he kept my legs open with his hands on my thighs. Everything in me clenched as I squeezed my eyes shut. He didn't let up for an instant, the pressure intense and demanding, and then relief burst through me as I tipped over the edge.

I was still trembling when he chuckled and kissed a path up to my breasts. When I got my eyes open, his lips were shiny as he licked them slowly. "I'm sorry, I didn't hear that."

Laughing, I fisted his hair and dragged him up toward me. He kissed me without hesitation, and I sighed against his lips. He had most of his weight on his hands, but he still draped me, and it was damn nice. I rocked my hips up against his, the first brush of his cock against my pussy had us both hissing. The angle was just there, and he pressed forward, the first nudge of his tip demanding, then we were both straining.

I stretched, oh, I'd forgotten the intensity of the stretch as he rocked into me, pressing deeper each time. The drag was so much more, and I bit down on his shoulder by the time he sank all the way in.

"Fuck," he exhaled against my ear, and I shuddered.

It was too much and not enough. Oh, I wanted to move. Why was it so much more intense? Everything in me seemed wholly focused on him. My inner muscles fluttered, and then I clenched, and he let out a hiss.

"Fuck. Fuck. Fuck."

The punctuated cursing dragged my eyes open, and I met his stare. "What?" We were both panting, and I swore my heart raced at woodpecker speeds to escape my chest.

"I hate to do this, sweetheart," he moaned, and I swore I pulsed around him as he started to pull out.

"Wait," I groaned as he eased out of me.

"Have to Frankie," he said, his jaw tense and the muscles there clenched. "Need the condom on."

Shit.

I banged my head back against the pillow as I stopped locking my legs and freed him so he could pull all the way out. It had felt so good. Not that it didn't feel good with the condom, but that had been so different.

"One sec," he said in between pants, and there was something gratifying about the fact that his hands shook as he got the condom opened and rolled on. I licked my lips as I watched him.

"Thank you." The whispered words pulled his glazed eyes up, and he stared at me. "I didn't notice and it was…it was really nice to just feel you."

"You have no fucking idea," he replied in a ragged tone. "You feel beyond fucking amazing. But…not risking you."

No.

Better safe than sorry.

"Maybe someday…"

"Oh yeah," he said slowly. "We'll figure it out." With shaking hands, he shifted me a little and then moved forward. The first brush of him wetting the tip against me sent little shocks through my system.

I ached for him all over again. "I'd like that," I told him, and he grinned as he nudged forward again. Inching in with that gentle rocking motion like he hadn't just been in me, and we were both straining by the time he sank inside.

"I'd like a lot of things with you," he admitted before he kissed me, and I managed to get my legs wrapped around him. Coop was doing most of the work and having a great deal of care with my right arm, not that I minded if he jostled it. Instead, I ran my left hand over him everywhere I could reach and sucked on his tongue as he thrust it against mine in time to the rhythm he set.

Somewhere in between kisses, he huffed a laugh.

"Still your turn."

I giggled, torn between want and hilarity. I adored him so much. This was why we'd been friends forever. "I forgot what you picked."

He kissed a path to my throat as he hooked one arm under to brace my shoulder, and then he lifted my thigh with his free hand. It shifted the angle, and I swore I was seeing stars with every stroke.

"Truth," he reminded me, then sucked down against the top of my breast.

Right.

Truth.

"Um…" Oh fuck. It was hard to think while he was doing that. I dragged my hand to his hair to pull his head up. He came at my call, but his thrusts grew fiercer and faster.

"Yes?" he managed to tease me, but the veins in his neck stood out. This was just as much a strain for him as it was for me.

The tension coiled tighter and tighter, liquid heat sprawling out through my system.

"What things—" Dammit. "What things do you want—" Oh, he was going to kill me like this. "—want to do with me?" Triumph surged through me for getting it out.

His groan echoed my own, and he kissed me, his tempo increasing. I was burning up, and my skin slid against his. The friction sent shivers racing everywhere. Lips pressed against my ear, he whispered, "Watch you with the guys." Holy shit. "Maybe join in." The images that conjured. "Definitely sandwich you with Jake."

I came. The image alone sent my whole system into overdrive, and it spilled over me as I shattered. I might have screamed. Pretty sure I cried out, but I was shaking and clenching against him as he went rigid and then shuddered. Clinging to Coop, I floated as he buried his face against my throat. It might have been my imagination, but I swore I could feel him pulsing.

Oh.

Coherent thought just wasn't there. His skin was sticky and tacky against mine. The rush of his breath as it puffed against my neck. The hammer of his heart, or maybe it was mine. Those came into focus and then, bit-by-bit, my body made its protests known. I ached from head to toe.

So. Did. Not. Care.

This ache was so good.

Coop…

He lifted his head and grinned down at me. "We have…ten minutes, I think, before the guys get back."

Oh. Yay.

Guys.

I might be able to move by then.

"You want a shower, sweetheart?"

I looked up at him, blinking slowly. Handsome. Sweet. Fun. Coop was kind of the whole package. I flexed around him, and he gave another shudder.

"Did you mean it?"

"About the shower?" He quirked an eyebrow.

"About me with the other guys?"

A slow grin spread across his face. "Oh yeah. That'd be hot."

He was still in me and I was still shaking from that orgasm, and I still blushed. "And a sandwich with Jake?" 'Cause now that he'd brought it up, all I could do was see it.

"Figure he's gonna be more willing. You know, Archie doesn't always like to share. Might have to work him up to it."

Oh. Shit. Now I was trying to picture that.

"And Bubba's still working on getting his head out of his ass."

I bit my lower lip.

"So Jake it is." Then his grin turned teasing. "Does that turn you on?"

"I didn't say truth."

His mouth formed a little 'o'.

"And I think we're putting a pin in the game for now."

"Bad Frankie," he teased, then nipped my lower lip with absolute care. "I wanna know."

"Ask me again…" I encouraged him. "When I'm not still riding this pleasure high."

"I will," he whispered, and then he kissed me slowly. "I'll ask you as many times as you like."

By the time we pulled apart, I was all spaghetti legs and arms. Coop chuckled as he helped me stand, and then we leaned on each other on the way to the shower.

"And, Frankie," he promised. "You don't have to do anything you don't want." His stare held me in place. "You just asked what things I wanted."

I had.

"I really enjoyed experimenting," I told him, and he laughed again. After turning on the water, he got the plastic over my arm while I sat all loose limbed on the closed toilet.

"Definitely. Great start to the day."

You know, he really wasn't wrong.

And now that he put those images in my head?

Yeah. I was definitely turned on.

Chapter Seven
LIES, LISTS, PLANS

The rest of the day passed in a rush that dragged unbearably in places. It rushed when the guys first got back, and Jake got a knowing look in his eyes. It took Archie a beat longer, and then I was blushing when he slapped Coop on the back and gave me a very firm and warm kiss. Still, it was kind of nice. It dragged when I had to try and work with my splinted wrist. The guys were all about helping me, but a little part of me really hated the fact they had to help.

Okay, a big part of me. I just despised being 'helpless.'

Still, we spent the day getting me caught up on homework with the guys playing the part of my hands since writing was right out. It was weird to try and work out math problems with Ian when he started to solve it for me, and I had to pinch him to make him stop.

Papers for lit with Coop typing was hysterical, 'cause he kept adding his own asides. Archie had government all laid out, and it was a lot of reading, and he typed up my paper for me as I pulled the facts together.

I was exhausted by late afternoon, and the guys decided to cook dinner with me supervising. In retrospect, that wasn't the best idea. They didn't burn down the kitchen, but they did set off all the smoke detectors, freaked out the cats, and had to toss the charred chicken they'd broiled for thirty-five minutes rather than three to five.

I don't think I'd laughed that long or that hard in a while. The tears rolling down my face were as much from the laughter as the pain the laughter left me in when my side cramped.

After the evidence had been disposed off and the smoke aired out, Archie and Coop left to grab dinner for everyone, and it was down to me, Jake, and Ian. The fact that a storm had rolled in during the day and lightning kept flashing outside promised Coop and Archie might be a hot minute.

"I'm going to grab a shower," Jake said, giving me a studying look before flicking his gaze to Ian then back to me. "You okay with that?"

"I'll be fine. I think Ian and I can manage unsupervised for a few minutes."

"But only a few," Ian countered, his tone dry. "Because we know Frankie gets mean when she's hungry."

My stomach chose that minute to gurgle, even as I glared. "Hey!"

Really, the gurgling just undermined my outrage. Jake snickered, and I stuck my tongue out at him.

"Real mature," he said with a grin and a wink. "Behave." Then he strolled up the hallway, leaving me flopped back on the sofa with my feet on the coffee table. Ian had packed up my books for me and slid everything into my backpack. I still had some more homework to do, but we were leaving it for tomorrow. Calculus assignments were mostly done, there was one more and Ian said we had two quizzes. Government was done, that was probably the easiest.

There was a test in there I had to take, too. I had to do some reading for lit, fortunately I didn't need my wrist to read a book. I was worried about European history, but Jake wouldn't even discuss it until the next day. The TA work wouldn't need to be made up, and that just left French.

I'd been tempted to message Mathieu, but the look of reproach I got from all four of them had me discarding that idea. Fine, I'd sent an email to Madam instead. Geez. Mathieu could probably catch me up faster, but it wasn't worth the argument.

"You'll get caught up," he said lightly, and I slid my gaze to meet his. His blue eyes warmed as he smiled at me. "Don't look at me like that, I know you. You're making lists in your head."

"A week is a lot of school," I admitted.

"Pfft, for someone else, maybe. But not for you." He pushed up from the floor. "You want something to drink? Or one of your pain pills?"

I grimaced. I had managed to not take one all day, even though I had been sore after Coop and I played. The shower had helped, but I'd gotten a little stiff from sitting around so much.

"You don't have to take it, but you keep wincing," he told me. "If you're hurting and I can help, I want to."

"I haven't eaten in a while, it might be better to wait until after food, or I'll end up face planting."

He nodded and rubbed his right hand. The bruises were still livid marks across his knuckles. They'd turned a beautiful shade of green and yellow. There wasn't much they could do about his knuckles after they'd relocated them.

"I'll get you a soda, then, yeah?" He didn't wait for me to answer as he headed for the kitchen.

"Ian," I said, and he paused, swinging his glance back to me. "Did I ever actually say thank you or just imagine it?"

He frowned. "For what?"

"For hitting him." For stopping him.

His jaw tightened. "You don't have to thank me for that."

"Yes, I do. I don't remember it, but I saw your hand, you know. After you got over here, and the cops told me some of it and so did Denitra and the guys."

Dropping his chin, he let out a sigh. "Frankie, it shouldn't have ever happened. He should never have been anywhere near you, much less drugged you. I barely remember punching him." Anger clicked under the words. "I just wish I'd done more."

Then he headed for the kitchen. It took him more than a minute to get a Coke out of the fridge. I wished I could remember the part where he got there, if nothing else. Something so I could say definitively one way or the other.

That blank wall just sucked.

"I'm sorry," he murmured as he came back with two cans. He sat on the coffee table next to my feet and popped open can before he passed it to me.

It was my turn to ask, "For what?" The can was cold against my palm, and his fingers were warm where they lingered until he was sure of my grip.

"For being pissy. You don't need to deal with my baggage from last weekend."

"Well, at least you remember your baggage," I said, giving him a small smile. But his expression didn't change. "Okay, so not my best work."

"Why are you trying to make me feel better?"

"Because you're my friend," I said. If nothing else, we'd been friends for a long time. I'd been trying to salvage that, even if I'd been hurt. The hurt wasn't gone, but the last week had definitely muted it some. "You're not happy."

"Of course, I'm not happy. *You're* hurting." He stared at me, his brows drawing together tightly. "Frankie, tell me you understand that I do still care and what hurts you—fuck."

"No," I said quietly, pulling my feet off the table and sitting forward. "Finish it."

He exhaled a breath, tongue against his teeth as he shook his head. "The last thing you need is me unloading on you."

"The last thing I need is you telling me what I need." The words came out sharper than I intended, but he gave a little jerk, then blew out another breath.

I took a sip of the soda before I set it down on the table, then focused on him. There were shadows beneath his eyes. There were shadows beneath all of our eyes. No one had slept well the last week, even if I'd gotten more sleep than all of them.

"You're right," he said slowly, and those words came out a little rough. "Will you tell me what you need?"

"Well, talking to me would be a good start," I said. "I don't really have a lot of experience with…" I held up my wrist then motioned to the two of us. "The only guy I ever 'broke' up with wasn't really one I dated for long, and last weekend was full of new experiences."

The humor didn't land, but damn it, I was trying. A muscle ticked in his jaw, and the knuckles on his left hand went white before he relaxed his clenched fist.

"I suck at this, Ian… Just tell me what you were going to say. Unload on me. Maybe it will help, and then I won't feel like…"

"Like?" he prompted.

"Like I'm useless," I admitted. The words tasted like ash on my tongue, and some of the day's good mood just drained away. "You guys have had to do everything. I don't know where I would have been this week without all of you." Or how I'd get through the next week or the week after that. I couldn't go back to work until the wrist was better. There was stuff I could do at Mason's, but so much of my job required both hands. Maybe if it were my left wrist…

"Hey." He exhaled the word as he leaned forward and caught my left hand. The warmth of his fingers wrapping around mine betrayed just how cold I was. "You are *not* useless. But you are freezing. What the hell?" He didn't wait for me to answer, just stood and snagged the blanket off the back of the sofa before he pulled it over me and slid onto the sofa next to me. "Snuggle?"

I raised my brows.

"I'm not freezing," he said. "You are."

I hadn't realized I was until he'd held my hand, and I eased toward him as he wrapped an arm around me. My splinted wrist ended up resting against his leg, but his arm around my shoulders was like an electric blanket, and I let out a little shudder as the warmth chased away the chill.

"Thanks," I said. "I didn't even realize I was that cold." The A/C was on, but that was normal. I'd been in shorts and a tank top all day. The thunder outside rolled like a bowling ball racing down to strike the pins. The rush of rain striking told us the storm had finally hit.

"No problem," Ian murmured, then pressed a kiss to the side of my head. "Sorry," he said almost as soon as he did it. Then sighed. "Dammit, I used to think I was good at this."

"Which this? 'Cause we have a lot of thises going on."

He chuckled. The soft vibration of it shook me, and the corners of my mouth began to twitch. "We do have a whole lot of thises going on."

I snickered, then his laughter deepened and he squeezed my shoulder. "In *this* case," he said as he tried to get his laughter under control. "I meant talking to you."

"Oh, so you used to be good at talking to me?"

"Yeah." He hesitated a beat. "Why? Do you think I wasn't that good at it?"

I leaned my head back against his shoulder so I could look up at him, eyebrows raised.

"Okay, Angel, that's just mean." Then he winced, but neither of us commented on the slip. "I was good at talking to you."

"You still are," I said in the effort to make some peace. "When you aren't deciding what I need to hear." That sobered us. "Speaking of which, you said what hurts me…?"

Not looking away from me, he nodded. "I care about you. That hasn't changed. What hurts you, hurts me. I don't want you hurting. You've been hurting for days, and I can't make it just go away. You're not sleeping well. You're putting on a brave face. But…"

"But?"

His mouth twisted, and he glanced from me to the hall. The rain outside was coming down loud against the windows, and the rumbles of thunder came more frequently. He shot a glance toward the window, then back at me.

"But you're not okay." He clenched his jaw like he needed to brace for my response.

"No," I agreed with him. "I'm not."

Silence greeted my statement, and he frowned.

"Surprised I'm agreeing with you?"

"A little," he admitted. "Yeah. You…"

I shrugged, then shifted a little so I was leaning a little more comfortably against him with my head pillowed on his shoulder. I wasn't so much looking at him as the wall over the television. It was still muted, though there was some game on. I didn't even know who was playing.

To be honest, I didn't care.

"I don't usually talk about stuff that goes wrong."

"No," Ian said. "You don't. You generally tell us everything is fine, and we have to pull teeth to find out what's happening."

"Kind of hard to pretend when you guys know more about it than I do."

"Frankie…" He sighed.

"You do. You remember it. I don't. A part of me is glad. But most of me hates that blank spot. I hate not knowing what happened. I got the wrist and the face and the bruises on my back—I know what he *tried* to do, and I know I hurt him back. But there's still a blank spot."

He didn't respond to that, not at first. Not that there was much he could say, not really. "I'm sorry," he said finally. "I can't imagine what that has to be like for you. A part of me is glad you can't remember it."

I frowned.

"Hear me out?"

Still not caring for the idea he might be glad about it, I nodded. Thunder cracked overhead so loud, I jumped and Tiddles fled from the back of the sofa to race down the hallway toward my bedroom. He and the others were probably under my bed.

Ian squeezed me gently. "It's just thunder."

"No shit. It was just really loud thunder, Captain Obvious."

He paused.

Then snickered.

Despite my best efforts, I was laughing again.

"Anyway," he managed to push out. "The part of me that's glad is just—I don't know if you were afraid or if you were angry or…what you were feeling. I just know I don't want you to have to relive it."

I guess that made sense.

"Then, not knowing means you just kind of fill in the blanks."

"I hate horror movies."

"Yeah," he said slowly. "We know."

"This is like being in my own. There's a door you shouldn't open, but they're going to open it. The suspense of waiting to see what's on the other side chokes you, but you do it anyway. What's worse? Opening the door to see what's there?"

"Or imagining all the horrible things that could be there." The fact that he got it helped. "Shit, Frankie, I wish I could tell you."

"You could tell me what you saw when you got there."

He went very still.

"If you can." Maybe that was asking too much?

The door to the bathroom opened with a squeal of hinges, thunder rumbled, getting louder and louder, then the back door opened with a bang. I jumped, and the fact that Ian did too made it a little better.

Coop and Archie made it inside, dripping wet, and Ian grimaced. "I'm going to help them," he murmured, and I nodded. "Stay there, guys, I'll grab you some towels."

They looked positively drowned.

"Are you all right?" I asked, leaning forward to stare at them, even as I tried to get my racing heart under control.

"We're fine," Coop laughed. "Just Ferraris and big ass puddles don't mix."

"Bite me," Archie said with a grin. "We got the food. I hope you're hungry, babe. We got a little bit of all your favorites."

Ian was back with Jake right behind him. Hair damp and wearing a clean t-shirt over boxers, he winked at me on his way past. "You good on a drink, Baby Girl? Or you need something to go with your enchiladas?"

My stomach growled. "I'm good, Ian got me a soda."

Coop and Archie stripped out of their soaking wet shoes and clothes in the kitchen, then toweled off while Jake and Ian got the food set up on plates. Then they all piled into the living room. "Okay, someone turn up the A/C before everyone freezes." Jake slid onto the sofa next to me and pulled the blanket over his legs too.

"Hey," Coop complained. "You're not cold."

"Nope," Jake said with a smirk. "I'm not. You can go find clothes." Then he balanced my plate on a pillow in front of me. "You good? Or should we shift to the floor so you can sit at the coffee table?"

"I think I can do this." If I used my splinted wrist to brace it, I could mostly eat with my left hand. I'd been getting pretty good at it. I couldn't cut food at all, but the great thing about sour cream chicken enchiladas, refried beans, and rice, was that I didn't need to cut up much. It all broke apart easily.

Archie shot me a grin from the floor where he sat on the other side of the coffee table, and Coop took the spot by my feet while Ian settled on the other end of the table.

He met my gaze and mouthed 'later?' and I nodded. Yeah, I would like to finish our conversation later. The corners of his mouth tipped up.

"Okay, movie time," Archie said. "It's Coop's turn to choose."

Jake and Ian both groaned, and I laughed.

"You know he's going to pick *Die Hard*." It was his default movie if he couldn't figure out anything else to watch.

"Nope," Coop said. "I'm not picking *Die Hard*."

I snorted, and he grinned up at me.

"Don't believe me?"

"I'm just saying it's the movie you usually pick."

"Well, not tonight. Tonight, I think we'll watch this." He had the remote, and he navigated over to the latest streaming service Archie had added to my box. I swore I had them all now, but over the course of the week, he'd just logged me into all of his accounts. It was kind of nice.

"Seriously?" Ian said, and even Archie canted his head back to stare at Coop.

"Yep." Coop grinned wider, and Jake snickered.

"It's in French, Coop," I reminded him, and he winked at me.

"*I know*," he murmured, giving me a playful leer. "I love it when you speak French, remember?"

Face hot, I bit back another laugh. Yes, I did remember. It was something he'd admitted to while we'd been making out on this sofa. "All right, Amelie is not me."

"It's all good," Coop assured me as he rubbed my foot under the blanket. "You can repeat any lines we miss."

Jake snorted, but the protests died off as the movie began. The film was an older one, but it was also delightful. I felt so bad for the main character, but her quirkiness won over the guys, and it wasn't long before they were laughing along with me as she set out to fix things for people she'd never met.

It was a sweet film.

By the time it was over, we were all yawning and I hurt more than I wanted to admit.

"Pain meds," Ian said as he and the others were cleaning up. "You've eaten and you're going to bed, right?"

I sighed.

He wasn't wrong.

"Yeah," Jake said after studying me for a beat. "Pain meds." I didn't argue.

Fifteen minutes later, with my teeth brushed and my face washed and changed into boxers—Archie's—and a tank top, I crawled into bed. Archie waited until I was settled before he slid in, and then Jake settled on my other side. Coop stretched out on the floor on a pallet he'd made, and Ian was over in his corner with his pillows and stuff.

Jake tucked a pillow under my right wrist and curled sideways before Archie shut off the last light.

It was weird how normal this had gotten. Despite the fact that I was so tired, I almost didn't want to close my eyes.

"Guys…"

Archie shifted so he could catch my left hand and then interlaced his fingers with mine.

"Thanks."

Jake pressed a kiss to my temple, and Archie squeezed my hand.

"You're welcome," Coop said into the quiet. "We know we're awesome."

There was a downbeat, then an upbeat before laughter eddied through the room. A pillow must have been thrown, because the soft thud of it hitting served as the first salvo, then another went flying. The scrabble of the cats racing out made me laugh harder. Then a pillow whacked me in the face in the dark.

"Hey," Jake growled as he snatched the pillow off of me. The bed depressed and then bounced as he launched off of it. Archie must have caught the next one. I couldn't hardly see any of them, but their laughter and the whacks carried just fine.

It took another ten minutes before one of the pillows totally gave out. The rip of sound ended the horseplay.

"Watch your eyes," Coop warned, then the light snapped back on. I squinted mine open and then winced at the pillow stuffing spread around the room.

"Okay, so…who sleeps without a pillow tonight?" Jake asked.

"That would be me," Ian said with a grin. "I started it."

He looked damned pleased with himself, too. When he glanced at me, I grinned. To be honest, they were all laughing and smiling. It had been a while. A week really, since I'd seen any of them this relaxed.

Well, okay, Coop had been pretty damn relaxed earlier in the day, but this was different.

"Fair enough." It took them another couple of minutes to clean up. Finally, Jake crawled back into bed, and Archie smirked before the lights went out. He hadn't left his spot, but that was more to shield me than anything.

Some of the tension bled out of my muscles, and I wasn't sure if that was more the pillow fight or the pain meds. Either way, I relaxed. Surrounded by their scent and the soft sound of their breathing, I said, "As I was saying…"

Archie groaned. "You're gonna incite a riot, babe."

"Shut up, Archie," came from the other three, and we all laughed.

"See what I put up with?" he complained, but squeezed my hand gently.

"You put up with a lot, and we're really happy you do."

"See, you get me. We're connected."

Jake snorted. "Shut up and let her finish so she'll go to sleep."

"Yeah, yeah."

I grinned hard enough to make my cheeks hurt. "You know what—it doesn't matter. We can figure it out tomorrow."

"It matters if it's important to you, Baby Girl."

"No, right now, it just matters that all of you are here." Even Ian. Or maybe especially Ian. He didn't have to be. But he was.

"No place else I'd rather be," Jake promised.

"Ditto," Archie said.

"Well, I'd rather be in the bed," Coop offered. "But I'm close, so I'll live."

"Glad we're here, Angel," Ian said quietly, and that wasn't a slip. I could call him on it. I should call him on it.

But I didn't want to spoil the mood. Not right now.

We could figure out next week the next day. As much as I liked having them here, they had parents and homes, and I was pretty sure those people wanted them to come home sooner or later.

Tiddles made his way up the bed and curled up between Archie and me. Tabby settled half on Jake and half on me. I bet if I turned on the light, Tory would be making herself comfortable on Coop.

For a minute, my thoughts flitted to Ian. He was sleeping in the corner of my bedroom. He didn't take the sofa and he hadn't taken a turn in the bed, even though I had offered. So had the guys. It would be a little awkward, but we weren't making out, we were just sleeping.

"FYI," Archie mumbled. "Change the sheets in the morning."

Heat whipped over my face again.

"Jeremy wants me to bring the laundry 'round again before the week starts."

"So why are you bringing it up now?" Ian asked, a yawn punctuating the words.

"'Cause he doesn't want to have to make the bed," Jake suggested, and it was my turn to yawn.

"Does Archie even know *how* to make a bed?" Coop mused.

"Yes," Archie stated with a little vehemence. "I do. I'm pretty good at it, too."

"Yeah well, you can prove it tomorrow."

I didn't say a word. Archie had figured it out just fine with me giving him a few pointers. When he lifted my hand to press a kiss to it softly in thanks, I smiled into the dark. I rubbed a circle against the side of his hand with my thumb.

Another yawn stretched my jaw, and the meds swarmed up. We had to make some plans…

Chapter Eight
DUCK. DUCK. MOM

Monday morning rolled around, and I wasn't the only one groaning at the sound of the alarm. Though we were two fewer than we'd been Saturday. Archie stayed over along with Coop. Jake and Ian went home because they had football practice early.

It was weird to crash the night before without them there, but I was glad Coop and Archie stayed, even if I'd half-expected to be on my own.

"Okay, we need to hit a grocery store today," Coop said as he studied the contents of the fridge. Honestly, there wasn't much beyond a Styrofoam container of some leftover fries that no one was going to eat, a splash of milk that wouldn't do anything for cereal, and some condiments.

The guys ate *a lot*.

"It's okay…" I began, but Archie nudged me over so he could get to the coffee maker.

"I'll send Jeremy a list, and he can pick it up. If I leave the extra key for him at the office, he can swing by and stock everything while we're at school."

I glanced at Coop, and I had a feeling his expression mirrored mine. His eyebrows were high, and his mouth shaped in a little 'o.' Closing the fridge, he said, "Arch, maybe we just hit the grocery store after school."

We were out of cat food, so I had to go regardless. I'd opened the last cans this morning, and I was pretty proud of myself for getting the can lid open while bracing it with my splint.

"It's not a problem," Archie said, taking a sip of his coffee, then cutting a look toward me. "Unless I can persuade you to bring the cats and come stay at the house for the week. Jeremy would love to spoil you some more."

We'd talked about that. "I don't know if that's a great idea, especially right now with my mom about to get served with the emancipation papers."

"Fair," Archie admitted and blew out a breath. "Then let's just make a list for Jeremy. He's coming by later with the laundry anyway."

"Archie, he has a job. He works for your family, and he takes care of everything there…"

"And he's offered to help out here," he pointed out. "You know he adores you, right?"

"The feeling is mutual." Still. I shifted and then glanced at my coffee. "I just don't want to impose." Or take advantage of everything Archie kept doing. He was covering a lot.

"Tell you what…" Coop suggested. "Let's decide at lunch. This is your first day back, it's probably going to be exhausting. If you're really tired, we could ask Jere, or you can give me the list and I'll do it after school. How does that sound?"

Meeting Coop's gaze, I read understanding.

"That sounds good," I said, then glanced at Archie. "I know you want to just fix everything."

"I can handle it, babe. You've been doing a great job of letting us take care of you. But seriously, if you're tired, let me text Jeremy. He *wants* to help, and so do I." The last three words twisted around my heart. I hated telling Archie no when he got like this.

"I will, I promise." It was an easy enough promise to make.

"So let's go ahead and make a list?" Coop suggested.

"Good plan, then we'll hustle 'cause we need food in case Frankie needs to take her pain meds."

Yeah, I really had no interest in taking them at school, but I was bringing them with me. Normally, I'd check them in with the nurse, but that required a parent note as well as the prescription so… "Archie, do you mind if I leave those in your car?"

"Nope," he said. "I'll run out and grab them if you need them."

Fifteen minutes later, with a shopping list longer than my arm, we walked out of the apartment. I did not need that much stuff, though Coop and Archie both pointed out they were all likely to be around a lot the next couple of weeks while I needed help. That was going to be a dent in my bank account.

Yes, Archie would absolutely offer to pay, but that wasn't fair to him. Not that I started that argument now, he was unlikely to ever stop offering. It was just who he was.

It was still raining when we headed out. Coop took his own car, while I rode with Archie. I'd be riding with Coop on the way home. Likely Jake the next day. Apparently, we were going to rotate who drove me where the same way we rotated who slept in the bed.

The closer we got to the school, the more my stomach tightened. With the exceptions of Coop's sister and mom once, Jeremy a few times, and Rachel's drop by visit, I hadn't really spoken to anyone but the guys since leaving the hospital.

Chills raced up my spine as we pulled into the lot. Archie slanted a look at me. I'd been fine until we stopped for coffee. Unlike the last couple of times, when Archie just took me out for a drive or when Coop took me to the park, we were going to walk into the high school.

I had to turn my phone back on, and I hadn't done that yet. Honestly, I wasn't sure I was ready for any more messages. But I couldn't turn the other students off if I was standing in front of them.

It wasn't until he parked and put a hand on mine that I even realized I was shaking.

"We can blow this shit off right now," Archie said without an ounce of hesitation. "I'll text the guys, and we're gone. Just say the word."

"I can't." Not even if I wanted to, which right now, I really kind of did. "I have to be up front about everything. I gotta prove I can take care of myself and handle my responsibilities."

"You don't have to prove *shit*."

I cut a look at him and smiled. The fierceness in his dark brown eyes offered me a lifeline. "I do though, a little bit to me, but also because of the emancipation."

Archie sighed and drummed his fingers against the steering wheel. "Fuck."

"It's okay, I can do this."

"You don't have to make yourself." But even he didn't press that argument. There were other cars in the lot and kids on the way. It was still raining, chances were football practice had been moved inside, or maybe Coach made them play anyway. They usually could if there was no lightning.

"Yeah I do," I told him and squeezed his hand. "You getting my backpack?"

"Yep, stay there till I get around with the umbrella."

I didn't roll my eyes, even if I really didn't want them fussing. I could take the backpack, but that was another fight I just wanted to avoid right now.

Coop opened my door before Archie made it all the way around. "I got the coffee."

I passed him the drink carrier, but kept possession of my own. Then Archie was there with his umbrella. He slipped into his own backpack before he snagged mine.

One perk of their hands being full? I got out of the car on my own. The walk across the lot turned chilly, and I suppressed a shiver. The ripped jeans I wore seemed like an even better idea than they were my favorites.

Inside, I waited while they shook out their umbrellas before we headed to the cafeteria. We ran into a few kids in the hall, but most of them barely glanced at me. It was going better than I hoped.

Unfortunately, that relief proved very short-lived. One step into the cafeteria, and the weight of a dozen gazes landed on me. Archie took point heading for our table, but that meant crossing a good chunk of the open floor space to get there. Despite the spirit stuff emblazoned on the walls and the purple flags here and there, it was almost painfully white and bright in here. Had it always been this way? The railings along the edge were the only other spots of gray.

The bruising on my cheek had gone down, but it was still visible. The stitches there had at least dissolved, so they didn't stand out. I could have tried to do cosmetics or called Rachel to help, but I hadn't really thought about it until right this moment.

The rolling hush gave way to a sweep of whispers across the room, and Archie dropped our bags before he nudged out a chair for me. One that put my back to the majority of the room, and in this case, I took the escape. Archie settled in the chair next to me while Coop shifted to move opposite us.

My hand was shaking a little as I set my coffee down.

"You good?" Coop asked, and I gave him a little smile. I wasn't, but I would be. I couldn't even put my finger on the source of my unease. It would hardly be the first time I was the butt of gossip. The last few weeks had been a crash course in public humiliation.

I could totally do this, even if the ice on my skin and the rapid race of my heart tried to make a liar out of me. "I'm good. I have my coffee, and I'm back on routine. That's pretty cool."

I didn't even have to drop the doctor's note off at the attendance office, the guys had made sure to deliver it last week. So really, we were just back to normal.

Coop slid a breakfast burrito over to me. "Fair, but say something if that changes, okay?"

Sure. I'd get right on that. Faking it until I could make it.

"Right on time," Coop said, but even as he skipped his gaze past me, Archie's remained fixed on me.

Glancing at him sideways, I raised my brows, and the corners of his lips tipped upwards. Not a real smile. The worry on his face pulled at me, and I bumped his knee with mine.

The other drawback of being at school meant we needed to keep our distance again. His smile deepened, and he mouthed, 'It's going to be okay,' more than said it aloud.

Warmth fisted in my chest. Yeah, it was going to be okay.

Jake all but fell into the chair on my other side, breaking the spell, and I glanced at him to find his hair damp and his expression a little wild-eyed. "I think it's official."

"Agreed," Ian said as he slumped next to Coop. They both reached for their coffee, and they both looked exhausted.

"What's official?" Archie asked as he bumped my knee and then nodded to my burrito. Yeah, yeah. I needed to eat. I stuck my tongue out at him, and he grinned.

I took a bite of my burrito while Archie watched before I looked back at Jake. He groaned. "Coach hates us."

Ian chuckled. "He hates you more."

"Oh yeah," Jake said as he stretched. "I'm going to hurt tomorrow."

I frowned. "What did he do?"

"Just made us run several different patterns in the rain after we ran two miles and did fifty pushups, crunches, and burpees."

They were the only reason I even knew what a burpee was.

"Someone's getting flabby," Coop said with a slow grin.

I hid a snicker as Jake and Ian both glared at Coop.

"Well, one perk I see," Archie said. "At least you're both on the same side in wanting to beat up Coop."

"Yep," Ian and Jake said in the exact same tone. There was a beat, then all four of them cracked up and some of the unease drifted away. This was normal.

"Oh my god, Frankie!"

Dammit, I shouldn't have thought I was out of the woods so soon. The tension in my gut ratcheted up to a hundred, and I shifted in the chair.

"Crap," Jake muttered as he twisted until he faced the direction Cheryl came from, one arm against me so he was more or less between me and her.

I hadn't spoken to or seen Cheryl since Homecoming.

Since she gave me her bottle of water and wandered off.

Since her boyfriend attacked me.

Wide eyes wet with tears, Cheryl flew right across the cafeteria like a laser-guided missile. A flash of chestnut hair behind her promised Rachel was in hot pursuit, but there was no way to avoid Cheryl, and the whole cafeteria was watching,

Coop rose, and so did Archie, but Jake blocked her even as Archie shifted closer.

"I can't believe you're here," Cheryl said, her voice equal parts ragged upset and thrilled. "I've tried to call you like three hundred times."

"Cheryl," Rachel said before I could. "Ease up."

"You didn't tell me she was coming back today," Cheryl continued whirling to Rachel. "We could have done something, we should do something…" She swung back to me. "We're definitely doing something. Lunch? No that's a time limit…"

"Cheryl, timeout," Ian said, his tone firm, and Cheryl snapped a look at him. "Back off. It's Frankie's first day, and we're taking it easy."

"Well, no duh," Cheryl said with an exasperated look. "But we're like best friends, and I've been worried, and you guys haven't let me see her or given her my messages, have you?"

I caught Rachel's eye, and she rolled hers. "Cher, come on, let's go finish breakfast. We'll catch up with Frankie after she's had some time to be back."

"You got to see her," Cheryl answered, whirling on Rachel. "I haven't, and *my* boyfriend is the one who ended up arrested."

All the air seemed to back up into my chest.

"Hey, Cheryl," Coop said as he caught her arm. "Let's chat. Rach, you busy?"

"Nope," she said, then tossed me another look. Any other time, it would have been funny. She wore the same look the guys had all week—worry for me, and at the same time, looking for reassurance that I was okay.

I gave her a tight smile, even as Cheryl complained—*loudly*—all the way back across the cafeteria. She was upset that I didn't want to talk to her, and at the same time, the words had all died before I could even utter one.

Aware of scrutiny from the nearby tables, I turned back to my breakfast burrito and coffee. The fact that I had zero appetite, however, made the prospect of eating unpleasant.

"Hey," Jake said, as he shifted again, but his arm stayed along the back of my chair. The heat of it was a physical presence, even though he wasn't quite touching me. "Cheryl's a little high strung about all of this."

"That's a bit of an understatement. I don't think she's a total idiot but…"

"But what?"

Ian sighed. "It was a long week for her last week. She got hit with a lot of questions, and I'm pretty sure it was overwhelming." But he didn't sound sympathetic, if anything, he sounded more irritated.

"And she's milking it," Jake muttered. "But that's *not* your problem."

Honestly, I had no idea what to say to Cheryl at the moment.

Nothing.

"Actually, I think I just want to head to class before the bell."

"You sure?" Archie asked, and at my nod, he started cleaning up. "Okay. Let's go. I've got your bag, and we're all going to take care of making sure you get from class to class, okay?"

Yeah, we'd had this discussion. I didn't need to have it again. Maybe I was imagining it, but there were so many people looking at me right now, I was ready to take Archie up on his offer to ditch.

I might not even make it through our first class.

"We'll see you soon, Baby Girl," Jake said, pitching his voice lower. "Your phone is on, right?"

I nodded and patted my back pocket. "I've got it set to vibrate."

The corner of his mouth twitched, and I could almost read the dirty thoughts dancing across his mind.

"Hush," I murmured before he could vocalize even one, and he grinned.

"You're no fun."

"I'm lots of fun," I countered.

"Yeah," he said grinning wider. "You are." That smile didn't quite make it all the way to his eyes. The worry kept darkening his pale blue eyes. "Like I said, see you soon."

Coop was already on his way back as Archie grabbed my bag, and I lifted my chin toward him.

"We'll tell him," Ian promised. "And I'll see you in an hour."

Not even leaving the cafeteria behind could help me shake the itchy feeling between my shoulder blades. Archie stopped about a dozen feet from our classroom door. The hall was mostly quiet, and there was one kid all the way down at the opposite end.

"Tell me right now," Archie said when I glanced at him. "You sure you're good?"

"Nope," I admitted. "I think I started to freak out a little."

"You want to go?" He shot a glance to the watch on his wrist. "We have time to get out before the bell rings."

"I can do this, just stay close?"

"So close, you're going to wonder if we're attached."

I snorted, but the promise helped.

It helped through government when the kids seemed to spend more time staring at me than the teacher. It helped when the bell rang, and he had to keep people from stopping me. More kids than I knew said hi to me or called my name.

Being that noticed had never been on my bucket list. In calculus, the teacher made a big point of welcoming me back, which just drew more attention to me. Ian had already arranged to help me with notes, and he snagged my desk right up against his, only he put himself between me and the class.

In French, I had to see Mathieu, and the depth of concern on his face just kind of hammered it home. Madame hugged me and pulled me out of the class after getting them started to make sure I was all right. And seriously, I should have seen it coming. Not fifteen minutes into French, and Diane showed up.

When she pulled me out into the hallway, I met her steady stare and said, "I really don't want to talk right now."

"I can understand that, and I'm sure this has been an overwhelming day already."

I neither agreed nor denied, instead, I just said, "I'm just trying to get caught up. I missed a lot."

"I'm sure, but I want you to come see me. For any reason. Even if it's just that you want to get away from the noise and need some place quiet to be. Okay?"

"Sure," I said. It seemed the fastest way to get rid of her. I told Coop I needed to call one of those therapists, and I did. I got that. It was not going to be Diane. It was not going to be the student advocate, no matter what her degree was.

It just couldn't be.

"Okay, go on back into class. I'm not going to keep you out here."

"Thanks."

"And Frankie?"

Dammit.

"It's good to see you."

I nodded.

The rest of class was kind of a blur. There weren't notes per se, and it was mostly vocalization, but Madame didn't call on me. Or maybe she did, and I didn't notice. Coop was at the door when the bell rang, and he came in and grabbed my bag.

I didn't even ask him how he got there before the bell. Knowing the guys, they arranged all of this ahead of time. Exhaustion nibbled at me, but I sucked it up. Lit was moderately better. The kids must be getting over the novelty of staring at me, because other than a few side-eyes, they didn't say anything.

Lunch was off-campus, thankfully. Jake and Ian were stuck with their anger management session, so Coop and Archie took me to get sushi, which was hands down one of the easiest things to eat with only one hand.

Back at school, study hall with Jake was probably the most peace I'd gotten all day.

"You look like hell."

"You just know how to sweet talk a girl." We weren't even pretending to study. Jake took over a couple of the bigger chairs in the corner by the windows and dragged them closer so I could lean back in one and put my feet in his lap.

"My girl, anyway."

I smiled.

"Take a nap?"

Fuck, that was tempting. But I didn't know if it would help. My arm ached, my back ached, my head hurt, and honestly, I was so tired I thought if I went to sleep, I'd have a hard time getting back up.

"Thirty minutes," Jake pushed. "I'll be right here, and I'll make sure to wake you up."

He'd be right there and nothing would happen. This was also why I hadn't taken my pain meds at lunch. I didn't want them to make me too loopy. As it was, I had a feeling I'd pass out as soon as school was over.

"Thirty minutes," I agreed. While I didn't think it'd be easy, I dropped right off.

It seemed like I blinked and Jake nudged me awake. He offered me water, and then it was time to head to my TA period. He walked me all the way there and told me to hang out, he'd get me after.

The teacher I assisted just told me to grab a seat in the back of the room and work on homework if I wanted. She wanted me to take it easy. I checked in with the guys. They'd been texting on and off. It was kind of weird, in a way.

I hadn't texted them most of the week. Even when some had been at school and I'd been at home. I just hadn't been on my phone.

There were a handful of messages from Cheryl—not hundreds. I hadn't read the latest ones. Rachel sent a couple asking if I wanted to get together on Tuesday, or if she could just swing by and see me. One from Archie with the promise that Jeremy would have delivered the groceries before school was over and he was also dropping off dinner for us.

Yeah, by lunch, there was no way I could go do the shopping, no matter how much I wanted to. Archie wouldn't let me pay for the groceries either. I'd find a way to pay him back.

Somehow.

Ian mentioned he'd be over after he ran by his house. He just had to pick up a couple of things.

Mondays were planning days.

That was another bit of normal.

The office runner arriving with a message to get me out of class wasn't. The kid's name was Robert, or maybe Robbie? I didn't know him well. He was a senior, but we just never hung out. He carried my bag for me, and when I asked why I was going to the office, he shrugged.

"They just said I needed to come give you a hand with your bag."

I fired off a message to the guys chat.

Me

Got called to the office.

I needed Jake to know I wouldn't be in my TA class.

Jake

Everything ok?

Coop

What's up?

Archie

Why?

Ian

I can cut out of here and meet you if you need me.

Hopefully, it was just the principal or something wanting to talk to me. Though I'd really rather have skipped that.

The last thing I expected when Robbie pushed open the door to the office was Mr. Standish standing there speaking to the principal in serious, hushed tones and my mother, eyes blazing as she whirled toward the door.

Oh.

Shit.

I still had my phone in my hand and the message open. I just typed in one word with my thumb and hit send before I clicked it off.

Bad News

Frankie

Mom

Jake

What?

Coop

Where?

Archie

Ian

She's not answering.

One minute later…

Jake

Getting out of class.

Ian

Already left class. Heading to the office.

Coop

Right behind you.

Archie

Tell me she's there.

Frankie

They want to check me out.

Archie

Do not leave.

Frankie

Wasn't planning to.

Ian

OMW

Archie

Fuck it, I'm coming.

Jake

Ditto.

Chapter Nine
DON'T TAKE ME FOR GRANTED

"**S**he's all signed out, Ms. Curtis," Mrs. Dearborn, the office administrator, stated with a quick smile in my direction. "Have a great rest of your day, Frankie."

Mom swept a furious look over me, then nodded. "Let's go, Frankie. Now."

That tone sent ice down my spine. "I have stuff I have to do today." Arguing wouldn't go well, but with the audience, it might buy me some time.

"We'll take care of it," Mr. Standish stated as he claimed my backpack where Robbie had set it down, then opened the door. "Let's go." His expression was far more neutral, but his eyes were practically frosty.

Gut churning, I glanced at the office staff. Robbie had gone back to his homework and barely seemed to even notice the rest of the room. So the crackling tension was just us.

Got it.

I lifted my phone and scanned the messages, then typed one-handed as fast as I could.

"Frankie," Mom snapped.

"Just letting Coop know I'm going."

Not that I planned on going far.

She gave me the curtest of nods, and even dragging my feet, the guys weren't in the office before we stepped out to between the public doors and finally out the front.

A dark car idled near the curb with a driver.

Ugh.

"Why are you here?" I asked as soon as the main doors slammed shut.

Mr. Standish took another couple of steps, but Mom wheeled on me. "Get in the car, Frankie. We'll discuss that and *everything* else."

"I don't want to go with you." It took every ounce of courage I had to push those words out. Inside, I shook like a leaf shredded by a windstorm, but even when Mom glared at me, I didn't back down.

"I am *still* your mother."

"Really?" I raised my brows. "How was Europe?"

"Busy," she snapped. "And we're jet-lagged, we flew straight back. Now stop being such a stubborn brat."

"Ladies," Mr. Standish stated smoothly. "Shall we adjourn this discussion to the car?" There was another parent heading in our direction. Mom glanced at Mr. Standish, then me.

"He's right. We have a lot to discuss, Frankie. Get in the car and stop being stubborn."

"No."

She made it three steps before my answer sank in.

"Excuse me?"

"I said no. I'd also appreciate it, Mr. Standish, if you'd put my backpack down." I wasn't going to close the distance and take it if I could help it. Then again, if I had no other choice, I'd tackle that problem, too.

Mom stared at me, her jaw tightening. The mom passing me nodded to all of us. Mr. Standish gave her a smile that didn't touch his eyes. Mom shifted her weight.

They were both dressed pretty casually. Well, casually for Mom anyway. Mr. Standish wore a button-down shirt sans tie or jacket. Though the slacks looked expensive. Mom, on the other hand, wore far too expensive tan slacks with a paler, almost eggshell-colored halter-top. Her hair was loose and tousled.

Honestly, he looked more put together than her, but she sported more expensive jewelry than just her ring. As soon as the door closed on the other parent, Mom charged me.

"I'm not kidding, Frankie. Get in the damn car. We need to talk. We need to do it somewhere privately. I refuse to air your tantrum for the rest of the world."

My tantrum?

I almost laughed. "My tantrum?" I don't know whether it was my tone or the hollow sound of my laughter, but she frowned. "Tantrum." I lifted my splinted wrist. No way she could miss the bruise on my face. "You drop into the end of my school day to check me out of school without so much as a phone call in almost two weeks, and you want to talk about my *tantrum*?"

Who was this woman, and what had she done with my mother? Granted, Mom had always had her issues, but once upon a time, I held onto the absolute certainty she cared about me. This stranger in front of me offered me no such illusions.

"Oh don't be so dramatic. You were the one who made the choice to stay, if you'd simply stopped pouting and moved with us, that wouldn't have been an issue."

Stopped pouting.

Her failure to communicate wouldn't have been an issue.

"You are so full of shit," I said, staring at her. "Do you actually believe the crap you say, or are you just putting on a show for Mr. Standish?"

Her hand flew and this time, I caught it before she connected. I had to drop my phone to do it, but I ignored it bouncing against the ground as I held her right wrist.

Mom's eyes widened, and Mr. Standish let out a whoosh of breath as he said, "Madeline."

She yanked her hand out of mine, and I backed up one step.

The door behind me slammed open, and Ian slid up next to me. "Everything all right?"

"No," I said, and Mom's eyes blazed. "It's not. Could you get my backpack from Mr. Standish?"

"Sure," he said as the door slammed open before it had closed all the way. Coop fell in on my right. "You got her?"

"Yep," Coop said as Ian nodded then headed toward Mr. Standish.

"Mr. Standish, I'll take that," Ian said, his tone absolutely polite. "We've been handling taking care of Frankie, and we've got it."

Mom swung her gaze from Ian to me and Coop. "You boys should be in class. This is none of your business."

"Sorry, Ms. Curtis," Coop stated, edging slightly ahead of me. "We'll just have to agree to disagree. Frankie is very much our business."

The doors popped open again, and I didn't even have to look to know who had just arrived.

"Wow, Edward. You figured out where the school was, you should get a cookie."

Archie strolled past me, pausing only long enough to recover my phone and pass it to Jake. After a studying look toward me, Archie focused on his father. Jake closed in on my left.

With an impatient glare, Mom focused on me. "We need to talk."

"So talk," I challenged her. "I'm standing right here."

I kept my attention on her. I didn't doubt Jake or Coop would stop her from hitting me again, but I didn't want to invite a mistake.

"I'm not having this discussion with you in front of your school. Credit me with some class."

Jake snorted but said nothing. Ian had my backpack, and Archie was right in his father's face. "First time for everything, right, Edward?"

"Archie, stop being melodramatic. This is an issue between Madeline and Frankie, and doesn't concern you." Mr. Standish glared at Archie. "In fact, allow me to propose a compromise. There's a park directly across the street, it's not busy at the moment. We can adjourn the conversation there."

A muscle twitched in my eyelid. At least Ian had my backpack.

"I'll give the ladies a lift over there, and you boys can meet us there when classes are done."

"Frankie's not getting in that car with either of you," Archie stated. "You've pretty much burned any trust you might have had with her. She doesn't have to do a damn thing if she doesn't want to."

"C'mon, Baby Girl, we can go if you want." Jake put his hand on the small of my back, but made no other move to get me in motion.

"You are all acting like we're going to attack her," Mom sounded disgusted. Really, I didn't care.

I shouldn't care.

Dammit. I really shouldn't care.

My heart pounded so loud, they had to hear it, but no one seemed distracted by it.

"Let's make this simpler," Coop said, then cut a look at me. "Do you want to talk to your mom?"

The answer was both a hesitant yes and a very firm no. Mom glared at me. "Fifteen minutes." It split the difference. "And I'm not going anywhere with you."

Anger simmered in her eyes, and an ugly look passed over her face. "Fine. But I do not intend to have this conversation with an audience. We can go across the street to the park and meet there. Then your watchdogs will give us some air."

Watchdogs. "Stop being a bitch, Mom. You don't get to set the terms because you're suddenly in the mood to parent. Give it five minutes, you usually get past it really quick."

I felt more than caught Jake's sharp look, but Coop nodded once. Mom? She just looked stunned.

Good.

"I'll give you fifteen minutes after I get across the street, and the guys can stay for it if they want or they don't have to, but you aren't dictating the terms."

Not that I had a single doubt where they stood on it.

"Fine." She practically ground the word out between her teeth. "Then let's go."

"I'll go with you," Coop said as Jake slid my phone into my back pocket.

"Bubba, give me her backpack." Jake caught it, then glanced at me. "I'm going to get my car, and then I'll meet you over there."

I nodded. Archie smirked as he turned away from his father. "I'll grab mine, too. Be five minutes, babe."

"Thanks, Archie."

"Always," he murmured. The look in his eyes told me he wanted to give me a hug, or at the very least, catch my hand, but he did neither.

"I'll tag along and keep Coop company," Ian volunteered. "As long as you don't mind." His gaze locked on mine, and I blew out a breath.

"Thank you."

"Oh, for the love of Christ." My mother spit out the words and wheeled on one heeled foot and stalked toward the waiting car.

Well, score one for me.

Maybe.

I exhaled as Archie's dad disappeared into his car and then it pulled away.

"You all right?" Coop asked.

"Not really," I said flexing my left hand and trying to stop it from shaking. "Thanks for coming."

"No problem," Ian said, and then held out his hand to me. "Come on, we'll walk you over, or we can just ditch them and head out."

The offer made me smile. "I would love to. I really don't even know if I should be talking to her."

Coop frowned. "Good point. Call Mr. Wittaker?"

"Yeah," I said tugging my phone out and eyeing Ian's extended hand. "Sorry."

"Not a problem," he replied, dropping it. It was still dark and overcast. "We're ready when you are."

I nodded and hit Mr. Wittaker's contact. When I got his voicemail, I left him a quick message about my mother arriving at the school and wanting to talk to me.

After I put the phone back in my pocket, I walked with Coop and Ian toward the park. Mr. Standish's car was already there, so was Jake.

Archie pulled in as we crossed the street. I hadn't meant to take so long, but I also didn't care. I needed the time. The icy hot feeling under my skin hadn't gone away.

"The minute you want to be done, you say it," Coop told me. "I don't know what her plan was, but we're not going to put up with any shady crap."

I smiled a little. "Shady crap?"

"Showing up out of nowhere to check you out of school after being virtually unreachable for more than ten days?"

"Right," Ian agreed, catching my hand as we crossed the street, and I gripped his fingers probably tighter than he expected. The trembling inside seemed to be vibrating its way out. "You don't owe her anything, okay?"

"I know." For once, that part I did know, even if I struggled with reconciling what I wanted—what I should do—and what I'd always done. Mom was Mom. I'd made excuses for her all my life. She was complicated and high-strung. But I didn't deserve this, not right now, and especially not after the last week.

She stood outside the car by the time we arrived. Jake and Archie leaned against their own cars but hadn't gone anywhere near her, and thankfully, Mr.

Standish stayed in his car.

"You want us close or to give you some privacy?" Coop asked as we crossed the last bit of ground between us and where the benches were. I didn't head toward my mom so much as those places to sit. Maybe I should stand, but tired kept hitting me in waves, and even with the adrenaline hit from seeing Mom in the office, it wasn't helping.

"Stay close, but maybe give us a little space?"

It seemed like a concession, and I didn't want to give her any. At the same time, I wanted to get this over and done with. The less posturing the better.

"You got it." Coop ran his hand down my spine lightly. "And as soon as this is done, you take something, okay?"

I didn't plan to argue. I hurt too much, so I just nodded. Ian squeezed my fingers once before he let me go, and I continued to the benches. Mom had to cross the damp grass to where I was standing, and her heels kept trying to sink.

Nope. Not a shred of guilt did I feel.

"Fifteen minutes starts now," Archie called, and I threw him a smile. He held up his phone with a timer on it, and my mother scowled, though with her back to all of them it was unlikely they saw it.

"That boy's arrogance knows no limits, does it?"

I wanted to fold my arms, but the splint made that hard, so I settled for leaning against the back of the bench and setting my hands on it. It was damp and moisture seeped into the denim, but it was better than falling, and I didn't want to sit and let her loom over me.

"I'm here," I said.

Though I'd really rather be anywhere else. I don't know when Mom and I became this bitter camp of antagonists rather than family, but I'd never felt further apart from her than I did right now. What did it say about me that when I looked at her, I saw the enemy? I also saw all the things I'd wished she'd been and hated because she wasn't. If I spent too long on it, I wondered what had I done wrong. It sucked.

But here was where we were. "What do you want?"

"Is that really any way to talk to me?" Mom demanded.

I shrugged, because it hurt and I was tired. "It's the best I can do at the moment. Would you rather I ask you how Europe was again? Oh wait, you never mentioned a trip, so I don't see why I should."

"I don't understand what has gotten into you," Mom said, almost exasperated. "Why are you doing this?"

What? I frowned. "Doing what?"

"This," she said, flicking her hands at me. "Why are you doing *this*? Why are you fighting me on every little thing?"

"I'm not," I said. "Fighting you on every little thing would require you be around. You're not. You moved out, remember? You have your new boyfriend. You know, the married dude back there who happens to be the father of the arrogant boy?"

Honestly, I wasn't trying to be quiet, and I had no idea how much carried back to the guys, but the flicker of a smile on Archie's face told me he got that much.

Embarrassment flooded me as I caught Coop's eye and the tautness in his jaw. If Archie could hear, then the others could, too. Archie understood crappy parents. The other guys had good ones.

Caring ones.

Jerking my attention back to Mom, I stared at her. She frowned. "What happened to you?"

"Life." Because I wasn't discussing Homecoming with her. Not a chance in hell.

My phone vibrated in my pocket, and I pulled it out. There was a message from Mr. Wittaker on the screen.

Mr. Wittaker

Any questions regarding the emancipation from her direct her to speak to her lawyer and to have her lawyer contact me. Do not answer her questions directly.

Fine by me. I cleared the message then shoved it back in my pocket.

"Frankie," Mom exhaled as she took a step toward me. "What *happened* to you?" She nodded toward my arm. "How did you get hurt?"

"I fell down."

"You are not that clumsy," Mom snapped. "There were messages… I had calls from the hospital about you being admitted. It was why we came home."

A week later.

"Must not have gotten those messages really quick."

"We weren't in Europe on a vacation." From concerned to annoyed. "We came to get you to check on you, to take you to our place. I think you should still come. You don't need to be on your own."

"But I'm very good at it. I've had *years* of practice. You might almost say I'm an expert." The longer we stood here, the angrier I got. I resented her. I resented that she was casting me in the role of bad guy because she'd *rushed* home a week after I'd been let out of the hospital and I seemed ungrateful. I resented that her life revolved only around her—her wants, her needs, and her interests.

More, I resented that she dragged me out of school to do this. Going back had been harder in some ways than I'd imagined and now *this*?

"What do you want, Maddy?" I almost said Mom. Almost.

But I suddenly understood why Archie did it.

'Mom' implied a relationship that just didn't exist anymore. If it ever had.

She recoiled as though I'd slapped her. For the first time in my life, she retreated a step and disappointment flooded her eyes. Or maybe fear. I had no idea.

"Seriously, what do you want? You have your boyfriend and your perfect new place and you haven't looked behind you for a while. So what do you want?"

The fist around my heart turned to lead. I didn't want to care about her. I didn't want to care what she thought about me. And I *really* didn't want to have this conversation right here and now.

"I wanted to make sure you were all right," she admitted slowly, hesitantly. Maybe she wasn't terribly certain. "I wanted to take you back to our place. I wanted to give you a chance to see how nice it could be. It's a real upgrade from that apartment, and you won't be able to afford it shortly. Not if you still plan on college."

And there it was.

How did she still have the power to disappoint me?

"I'm fine," I said, aware of Coop straightening and taking a step in my direction. I shook my head. I didn't want them to intervene. "I have no interest in your new place or this new life you've been transitioning to for the last year or so. I didn't have a place in it before, I don't see wanting one now."

"That's not true," Mom—no, Maddy said, her voice torn between sounding like she could barely hold back tears and at the same time her eyes were so angry. "You're my daughter."

"Could have fooled me." I was so tired. "And if that's all, I'm going to go now. You pulled me out before I got to finish my last class. And I have homework to do."

Was that a flash of guilt?

Did I care?

I pushed away from the bench and headed for where the guys waited. Archie's car or Jake's, right now I didn't care. Ian had ridden in with Jake for practice, and Coop had his car back at the school. We needed to get that…

"You can't just walk away from me."

"Why not?" I asked, not slowing down, and Coop was moving now.

Archie had pushed away from his car, and Jake planted himself between Archie's dad's car, Archie and me.

I could have kissed him for having Archie's back like that.

"Just putting into practice what you taught me, Maddy. Don't like something, walk away from it. I'm sure you two are very busy doing…whatever." I made it two more steps then paused and glanced at her. "I'm not a doll you get to decide you want to play with and discard when you're bored. You've done that to me my whole life. When you feel like being a mom, you can be great. Most of the time, you're not. I'm not letting you do that to me anymore."

Turning away, I continued my trek to toward the guys.

"Francesca Elizabeth Curtis." Her voice grated. "Don't you dare take that tone with me."

Yeah, the guilt died a swift death. I didn't look back. "Sure, Maddy. I can say it politely if you want. Have a nice day." Coop was there, and he slid an arm around my waist and headed me straight for Jake's SUV.

The car door on Mr. Standish's car swung open, and Archie passed us. "Keep going, get her out of here."

Ian moved with Archie, but Jake opened up his passenger door, and Coop gave me a hand getting in. I dragged the seatbelt on and kept my gaze firmly away from Maddy. Edward. Any of it.

What happened to me?

She had her nose pushed in because she couldn't even let me know she was leaving the country or dating or even truly moving until after she'd done it? Eyes closed, I leaned my head back against the seat.

"Hang on, Baby Girl. We're going to drop Coop at his car, and then we're going home."

"Okay," I murmured. Coop slid into the back seat, and the doors slammed. Raised voices carried from outside, but I only checked to make sure Archie and Ian were okay.

As Jake pulled out of the lot, it sunk in to me that Ian glared at my mother.

And was yelling at her.

Oh.

"They're going to be okay, right?"

"They're going to be fine. Archie is making sure we can go without having them up our ass. And I want you home before they decide to head back to the apartment and find out they can't get in." Jake put a hand on my knee.

"Do you have your pain meds?" Coop asked. "Your backpack is here."

"No, Archie had them."

"Got it, texting him now."

That whole interaction hadn't taken thirty minutes. School wasn't even out yet. At the same time, it seemed to have taken years. Jake drove us right up to Coop's car.

"Come straight in," Jake advised. "We might go in the front if we have to."

"She won't follow," I said.

"Frankie, you don't know that."

"Yeah I do. To follow would imply she cared. Right now, she cares about being right. I made her look bad, so she's going to try and make up for that with Mr. Standish." I shuddered, but just shook my head. "She won't come."

Of that much, I was certain.

She also didn't know about the emancipation.

Chances were she hadn't been served. Jake opened my window, and Coop leaned in when I glanced to him and pressed a kiss to my lips. It was soft and swift.

"It's going to be okay."

I nodded.

Maybe.

"See you at home?"

"Wild horses couldn't keep me away."

Then we were pulling away, and Jake closed the window. When he covered my left hand with his right, I held on tight.

"He's right, Baby Girl. It's going to be okay."

"You guys are going to get busted for skipping class."

"That is really not important right now," he assured me.

But it kind of was. They'd all been getting into trouble lately because of me.

"I worry."

"I know you do," he answered. "We worry about you. No way we were letting you have to take on that fight alone, but you know what?"

He waited so long at the end of that question, I dragged my tired eyes open to meet his gaze. "What?"

"You were fucking awesome, and you didn't need us."

I smiled a little. "That's not true."

"Yeah it is," he said, stroking my hand. "You really do look after yourself. You've had to do it on your own a lot, but we've got your back."

They did.

"I know," I whispered. "And I'm really glad you were there."

"Nowhere else I'd rather be…" He gave it a beat. "Well…I can think of a few places to be, not that I don't like having your back, but your front is pretty damn sweet."

That did it.

I laughed.

"Idiot."

"Hmm-hmm," he said, lifting my hand and kissing it. "I like your ass. Your back. Your tits. But I gotta say, I think your mouth is my favorite."

I flushed and shook my head. "You cannot seduce me into a better mood." Even if I wanted him to.

"Oh, Frankie," Jake drawled slowly. "I like a challenge."

"You know, I knew that about you."

He grinned and some of the bricks on my chest eased up. The more distance he put between me and Maddy, the better.

Chapter Ten
WELL HE'S A ROLLING STONE

ARCHIE

Edward's behavior shouldn't shock me. It really shouldn't. In nearly eighteen years, I'd never seen him at a single school function or darken the door of any school I attended until today.

The hell of it was, he wasn't there for me.

Go figure.

Frankie's pallor worried the fuck out of me, but she didn't back down from her mother once. I never got that phrase 'so proud I could spit' until I'd seen her shut her mother down not once, not just twice, but three times.

That last comment though, about not being a doll she just got to pick up and play with when she felt like it, deflated all of my pride and left a hollow place for rage. What the hell was wrong with her mother? No one deserved to be treated that way.

Especially not Frankie.

For a spare second, our gazes had locked as Coop hustled her to Jake's car. Edward's car door swung open, and I cut behind them so I could block any approach. Jake was ready to run interference, but I needed him to move.

"Keep going, get her out of here."

I half-expected Bubba to go with them, but he didn't. Instead, he faced Frankie's mom as if he had every intention of bodily blocking her from following. Worked for me.

Expression cool, Edward flicked a look from me, to Frankie's mom, to Jake's SUV as he backed out of the slip he'd parked in and then accelerated to leave the park. "Are you proud of yourself, Archie?"

I shrugged. "Most days. Not that you care. Must suck that not everything is going the way you want it to."

"Do you really want to wage this war with me?" The question almost made me smile.

"Pretty sure my actions speak for myself, Edward. I want you to leave Frankie alone. Period. End of story."

In an ideal world, he'd leave her mother alone, but that bridge had already been breached, it had been burned, and there was no putting it back up. At least not easily, and after everything we'd learned in the last few weeks, I didn't want to reconstruct it. I wanted both of them as far from Frankie as I could possibly get them.

That woman didn't deserve a daughter like Frankie.

"Did you forget who controls your accounts?"

"Nope. Grandpa has a very firm grip on my trust fund. You might control the family accounts, so knock yourself out." It wouldn't be the first time he threatened to cut me off.

Probably wouldn't be the last.

Bringing up Grandpa, however, penetrated his veneer of control. "You are treading on thin ice, son."

I snorted. What was Edward going to do? Take on his father? He hadn't managed it in all the years we'd been here. I doubted very much he'd take the fight now. It had taken me a while to figure it out, but I had it now.

He'd moved here to wait for Grandpa to die. In an ideal world, for Edward anyway, that death would occur before I turned eighteen. Then Edward would be the one in charge of everything.

That advantage vanished in about ten more days.

"Cut me off," I said, sliding my hands into my pockets. "I dare you."

Because bring it on. I was done playing nice or political. Muriel was off at her retreat or spa or whatever the hell it was she'd checked herself into, in order to cater to her mental and emotional breakdown, or pills and alcohol addiction, I'd lost track. At this point, I'd also lost the effort to care.

Muriel Standish remained in miserable marriage because she could. Maybe it was to punish Edward. Maybe it was because she refused to lose. Or maybe, just maybe, she couldn't be bothered to separate herself from the Standish fortune. Not that she didn't have her own money.

I no longer had it in me to give a damn.

The pair was a sperm and egg donor only. Beyond that, I needed to have nothing else to do with them.

"Hell, kick me out. That could be fun." I half-lived at Frankie's right now, anyway. I somehow didn't think Jeremy would go along with his plans, regardless of the circumstances. "Oh wait, you really can't. The house belongs to Muriel."

His jaw tightened, and his eyes went flat. "That's enough, Archie."

"Oh, I'm just getting started, *Eddie*." I hated that nickname and all it implied. I locked gazes with my *father* and raised my brows. "Stay away from Frankie. She doesn't want anything to do with this farce you and your mistress are putting on, and neither do I."

He actually took a threatening step toward me, but I didn't flinch. Unlike Frankie's piece of work for a mother, Edward had never raised a fist to me. He threatened. He bullied. He yanked credits cards and privileges. But a guy who was never around didn't have a lot to work with. For the most part, he got ugly, then he left.

Like that was a burden.

If it weren't for the way he'd looked at Frankie or that damn dress he bought her, I'd ignore him in this game. Now he'd shown up at the fucking high school to get her. I didn't care that her mother was with him. Edward edged too close to the line, and it wasn't ever happening.

"Don't push me," Edward warned. "You're putting ideas in her head and making this far more difficult than it needs to be."

"You know what, you're a bitch." Bubba's voice cut into our conversation. "And I say that without any due respect. You can't even be bothered to *care* why a hospital called you here. Not to mention, you never bothered to call anyone back about why she ended up in a hospital to begin with. Frankie's right. Leave her alone. You don't deserve her."

Edward jerked around at the rising accusation in Bubba's voice. I braced to move. I'd never seen him actually start a fight, but he wasn't going to get the chance to blindside Bubba either.

"How dare you," Ms. Curtis said, her voice a little warbly. It bugged me that she looked like Frankie. Different eyes. Older, sure. As much as I hated to admit it, she was a good-looking woman. Frankie took after her in a lot of ways.

That made it worse, in my opinion, because the surface similarities was where it ended.

If Frankie possessed a selfish bone in her body, I'd yet to encounter it. In fact, I wish she had more.

"I dare because, unlike you, I care about her." Bubba's uncompromising tone had my eyebrows rising.

"You have no idea what you're talking about."

"Right, and I've only known her for close to seven years. How would I know that you abandon her regularly, you can't be bothered to show up, or that you have left her to fend for herself so often, she doesn't even see it as unusual?

I have real parents. I know what a parent is *supposed* to be like."

Damn, Bubba. My admiration climbed a notch. From the corner of my eye, I caught Jake's SUV leaving the high school lot again. Not a minute later, Coop exited driving the Lexus.

Instead of responding, Ms. Curtis stared at Bubba, her mouth agape and her face flushed red. She looked almost ill.

"Yeah, I didn't really think you'd have anything to say. Bullies usually don't. Frankie was right. You don't get to just decide you want to be a parent because you're in a mood."

"Bubba." Edward said his name almost distastefully. "This is really none of your business, and you should have more care in your tone for how you address my fiancée."

I couldn't help it, I snorted. "You're still married, Edward. Makes it hard to have respect for what is potentially leading to an illegal relationship."

Instead of glaring at me or even responding, Edward simply said, "Maddy, come. You tried."

For a moment, just a split second, Ms. Curtis hesitated. If I hadn't been watching her, I doubt I would have seen it. But her expression, far from hostile, turned worried. "I still don't know what happened. The hospital wouldn't release her information to me."

Good.

Technically, the woman was still her mother. But there were laws, and the advocate had stressed that she was there for Frankie and no one else. Maybe they'd blocked it somehow? Course, I wasn't sure how the cops hadn't reached out to them, but then again, Frankie wasn't the perpetrator.

"Not our problem," I said before Bubba could respond. "C'mon, Bubba. We have things to do."

The wavering look on Ms. Curtis' face erased as her lips compressed. The look she sent me could have boiled oil. Not that I gave a damn about her opinion. In fact, I welcomed her ire. Bring it on. I wasn't afraid of her. I'd rather she pointed it all at me, anyway.

"Archie," Edward stated in a cool tone. "You're going to regret this."

"I've been regretting you my whole life." I told him with a crisp nod. "This…" I motioned between him and Frankie's mom, "hasn't really been a factor, other than to prove once again what a selfish narcissistic ass you are." I paused, more for dramatic effect than anything else, then smirked. Bubba had crossed the lot and stood a foot away from me. "Then again, maybe that's why you two deserve each other."

I let that grenade drop and walked away, and I didn't glance back even once as I slid into the car. The passenger door opened, and Bubba gave it a beat before he slid into the seat. He hadn't even gotten his seatbelt on before I pulled out and turned onto the street.

"Holy shit, Arch."

I shrugged. Didn't occur to me until right then that Bubba hadn't really seen me and Edward go at it. They weren't really that exposed to my parents, and I preferred it that way. Jeremy was a successful surrogate and far more desirable an authority figure.

"Text them and see if they need anything before we head that way." I didn't mean to snap it out like an order, but the fact Edward showed up with Frankie's mom to pick up Frankie when he'd not once shown up at a single one of my schools irked me.

I got it, I preferred Frankie to me, too. But what the fuck was he up to? And why were they so intent on getting her to their new place?

The rain suddenly began sheeting down. I kicked on the windshield wipers and the headlights. At least it waited until we were out of it.

"Jake says she's half-asleep in Coop's lap. Maybe coffee. Otherwise, just come in quiet."

I nodded and took the next turn. Coffee sounded like a good idea. One drawback to staying at Frankie's was the lack of alcohol. Her mother didn't even keep wine there, and I debated asking Jeremy to stock it, but I figured he bent the rules enough for me at home.

When I pulled into the drive-thru line, I glanced over at Bubba, who stared at his phone like it held the secrets of the universe.

"Problem?"

"Just worried about her."

I nodded. "She'll be fine." Not that I wasn't worried, but Frankie had been surviving her mom for years without us being aware of how bad it could be. Now she had us in her corner. We would make damn sure she was fine.

"You say it like it's easy."

I shrugged. "I say it like we don't really have a choice. There are worst things in life than crappy parents who do a crappy job of being parents."

Like assholes who drug my girlfriend.

The silence next to me was heavy.

"Just spit it out, Bubba. You're not going to offend me."

"Your dad's a real dick."

"Yep," I agreed. "He really is. Edward's not a father though. He's a sperm donor."

"Do you think he'll actually cut you off?"

"Not the first time he's threatened it. Won't be the last. Doesn't matter anyway." It was our turn, and I cracked the window to give the order. I knew everyone's drinks now. It was damp outside, and she was hurting, so I got her a hot one with the peppermint and extra whip cream. Rain spattered inside, but I ignored it. The temperature outside seemed to be rapidly descending, too.

He waited until after I'd paid for the drinks and we were pulling back out into the suddenly heavy traffic that marked the end of the school day before he said, "I'm sorry."

"For what?" Sure, there were a lot of things he could be sorry about, and I wasn't in the mood to guess.

"'Cause your dad is an ass. Your mom...well, I don't really know your mom."

"Don't overthink it. I don't really know Muriel, either. It's not a big deal."

"That's not the way parents are supposed to be."

I chuckled. "Bubba, did it ever occur to you that you got lucky? Jake and Coop's parents are divorced. Jake barely mentions his dad without latent hostility boiling over. Coop avoids his like the plague. They're both good with their moms, but their dads? Not so much. Frankie doesn't even know her dad's name much less who he was, and her mother has had one foot out the door for years. My parents? Pfft. Before we moved here, I hadn't lived with them in years. I saw them at holidays, and I lived primarily at boarding school."

It was just how it was.

"You got lucky. Your parents are together and apparently like each other and you." I shook my head. "It's almost cute." I might have resented it a little in the beginning, but I actually liked his parents, too. They meant well. Even his dad.

Wasn't that the damnedest thing? His dad's interference created a fuck up of epic proportions, but the man *meant* well.

"Thanks," he said, making a face. "I never thought of myself as naïve before."

"You're not naïve," I corrected. "You're optimistic. In a different way from Coop. I see all the bad shit that could happen. I have to. Helps me anticipate how to fix it if it goes wrong. You see all the positives."

"Then why was I the one obsessed with whether this could possibly work if she had to choose eventually?"

"I said you were optimistic, not smart."

There was a beat of silence, but he chuckled. "Ass."

"Yep." I sighed. "Look, Bubba, seriously man, don't overthink it. Some people just shouldn't be parents. I look at Edward, and I wonder what the fuck happened to him. My grandparents were awesome. Nana, Grandpa—they were the best. But the distance between Edward and Grandpa? It's epic. Kind of like the distance between me and Edward. So, who knows? I don't worry about it.

I can't fix the relationship, and I don't want to. You feel bad because you think I'm missing out…"

I pulled into the apartments and headed down the hill to park. I'd always thought of this place as being a little on the lower end side. It was definitely shabby, but the upkeep was neat and the neighbors fairly reputable and kind.

It was also home to two of my favorite people.

The rain was a steady downpour. After I parked, I glanced over at him. "Don't feel bad. You can't miss what you never had."

"Tell that to Frankie," he countered.

"Frankie misses what she thought she had. What she convinced herself she had." I'd seen that today. "She's hurting for a lot more than the crap her mother is pulling. But we're not letting her go through it alone."

"No," he said slowly. "We're not."

"The roses were a nice touch. You got something for her today?" I had another set of charms, but I'd put them away. Her bracelet was still in fucking evidence, and while I'd been half-tempted to just order her another one, I'd wait. I'd already asked Wittaker to try and get it back.

"Don't laugh?" Bubba asked, and I nodded once.

I could do that. "Hit me."

He tapped his pocket. "I recorded a song for her last night after I went home."

"Nice man," I patted his shoulder. "Really nice. You got those?" I reached behind us to snag my backpack. His must have ended up in Jake's SUV.

"Yep." Before I could open the door, he said, "Arch?"

I waited.

"If they push back? On Frankie's emancipation? And if your dad cuts you off? What then?" He winced. "You're paying for stuff, but if he takes it away…"

Not an unfair question. Really. Except… "I'm not worried about it." One, I'd made sure to cover all of Wittaker's retainer. While he was also one of Edward's attorneys, he had committed to the case. The fee wouldn't be the issue. Second, Frankie's rent was also covered. "Even if he cuts me off, which he won't. But if he did, Muriel would open the floodgates just to get even with him. But let's say she didn't notice, entirely possible. I turn eighteen in nine days."

Bubba frowned. "Your trust?"

I nodded. "I don't get the bulk of it until I'm twenty-five, but trust me, what I get at eighteen and twenty-one? We'll be fine."

Nana had seen to that and so had Grandpa.

"Edward's going to do what he does. So is Muriel. I know the potential fallout. I can handle it." Plan for the worst. A motto to live by. "Now, let's get inside and see our girl."

I snagged her pain meds out of the cup holder before we got out of the car. We were both wet when we reached the back door. Jake had to have been watching for us, or maybe Bubba texted him when I wasn't looking. He opened the door when we got there.

I actually shuddered before we got inside though, because the rain had definitely turned cold. The interior of the kitchen was warm though.

"She's asleep," Jake said in a low voice.

"I'm not," Frankie countered from the living room. A yawn followed her words, and I toed off my wet shoes before setting my backpack down and stripping out of the damp shirt and socks before following Jake and a similarly stripped Bubba into the living room.

Jeremy had dropped off more clothes for me, so I had stuff to change into. As Jake had said earlier, Frankie was curled up against Coop, but they were both sitting, even if it looked like they'd been lying down.

The traces of tear tracks on her face renewed my earlier aggravation. The first thing her idiot mother should have done was ask her how she was and maybe spent more than thirty seconds on what happened rather than immediately escalate into demands.

"Got you coffee," I told her, and she gave me a wan smile.

"'Cause you're the best."

"I am the best," I agreed, and the corner of her mouth tipped up. "Have your coffee. I'm gonna change, and then we can figure out what's next, yeah?"

"I'd like that," she said, and Bubba carried her coffee over to her and handed out the others.

"I'll be back."

In her bedroom, I glanced around and shook my head. Jeremy really couldn't help himself. It had all been straightened, the bed stripped and remade with fresh sheets and a brand new comforter. Frankie was gonna be irked.

But I got it, Jeremy cared.

My bag sat at the foot of the bed, new clothes laid out at the top, all the laundry from the basket in the corner was gone, and there were other stacks for Jake, Coop, and Bubba.

"Yeah," Jake said as he slid into the room. "I noticed this when we got home and I came in here to get her a blanket. Jeremy?"

"Yeah," I said, pulling on a clean t-shirt. "I'm guessing the kitchen is spotless and the fridge is fully stocked?"

"So is the pantry, there's also a baked ham in the oven and hot veggies in trays on the stove along with some stuffing."

I'd smelled that when we came in, but I'd been more interested in Frankie than the food.

"I'll thank him." I should have known he'd go overboard with the offer.

"Dude, there's chocolate pudding in the fridge."

I stripped out of the damp jeans and pulled on sweatpants. "Of course there is." Frankie loved chocolate pudding.

Honestly, she loved food. It was one of the great things about her.

"How are you doing?"

Okay, I'd already gotten it from Bubba, so I met Jake's concerned gaze. "I'm fine. More concerned we might have to deal with her mother again this week. She's not giving up, but how she's going about this doesn't make sense to me."

It made even less sense when I considered Edward's choices.

Folding his arms, Jake said, "Maybe she feels guilty about abandoning her."

I met his gaze and raised my brows. "Did you see real guilt on her face?" I had, there at the very end, a brief flicker of it along with indecision. But Jake and Frankie had been long gone by then.

"No," Jake said with an aggrieved rake of his hand through his hair. "I didn't. Frankie was pretty sure they wouldn't follow. Said it would mean her mother cared if she did, and she highly doubted that was the case." Anger rolled off him waves, like heat shimmering off of pavement. "Why the fuck did they just show up today? It's been a *week*."

"I don't know," I said with a shrug. "But we dealt with it, and she's safe and sound here, so I say we don't worry about them and we focus on her. Did you notice anyone giving her shit today?"

"Outside of the crap with Cheryl? No," Jake said with a short shake of his head. "They're keeping their distance. But they're talking."

"Yeah, we can't stop that. But we stick close. The hardest periods are third and sixth." It hadn't escaped my notice that her mother showed up during the one class we weren't with her.

Then again, that might have just been dumb luck on their part.

"You two having a party in here without me?" Frankie asked from the doorway, and I pivoted to face her.

"Babe, it's never a real party until you get here."

She snorted and flicked her fingers at me. Some of the shadows shifted out of her eyes as she smiled. When she crossed the room and wrapped her arms around me, I held her tight. I would never not want these hugs. "Thank you for having my back," she whispered.

"Always," I promised. "We always have your back. And your front. Your sides are pretty sweet, too."

It was Jake who snorted, then smirked as Frankie laughed. "Too late, Jake already complimented my ass and breasts.”

“Well, then we’re just making it official that we agree,” I said, pulling back enough to press a kiss to her forehead. “You good?”

“I am now,” she said, meeting my gaze and not shying away from it. “I just wish I understood what she wants.”

“I don’t care what she wants. The only people whose wants I care about are in this apartment.”

“And Jeremy,” she added on with a glance toward her bed, and I grinned.

“Well, Jere’s pretty good about taking care of himself.”

“And us.”

“I told you, we want to spoil you. Now, let’s go drink your coffee and do our homework breakdown. I’m sure you’re due at least one academic meltdown.”

At Frankie’s groan, even Jake grinned. Because that was our girl. Our overachiever would not care for being even an ounce behind.

“We got this,” I reminded her, and then Jake caught her hand and between us, we got her back out to the living room, to the coffee, and then the food.

We got around to homework eventually, but Frankie was asleep before eight, because she lost the battle to exhaustion. Even after Jake and Bubba headed home because they had practice early, Coop and I were both awake and neither of us seemed to want to rest.

Something was going on. I just didn’t know what.

That part bugged me.

When Coop finally said he was going to try and sleep, I stayed in the living room arguing with myself. There was one person I could ask about all of this.

One person who might be able to help, but it kicked over a whole other anthill.

But I wasn’t willing to wait nine more days or for the other shoe to drop. I sent an email rather than a text. It would probably be a day or two before I got an answer, but at least I could get one ball rolling.

Surprising no one, by the time I turned in and slid into the bed on Frankie’s side, neither Edward nor Frankie's mom had shown up at the apartment.

I'd take the reprieve, but I'd get ready for the war.

Chapter Eleven
PARENTAL DISCRETION ADVISED

COOP

I pulled up to the curb and sent a message to Sis. Two minutes later, the front door to the house I waited in front of opened and she jogged out. Her friend waved to her, and then she was sliding into the front seat next to me.

The smell hit first. "Since when do Mandy's parents smoke?"

"They don't," Sis said sliding me a look. "And don't start."

Seriously? I raised my eyebrows. "Since when do *you* smoke?"

"I just said don't start, Coop." She dragged her seatbelt on. "We had a couple of cigarettes. It's not a big deal."

Not a big deal? Mom would kill her. Then kill me. If not the other way.

"You and the guys did way worse than me, so I don't want to hear it."

"It doesn't matter what I did or didn't do," I countered. "Smoking is a filthy habit."

"So is sleeping with a bunch of girls, but that didn't stop you."

I glared at her for all of a moment, then blew out a breath. "You need to not believe everything you hear."

"But that part is true," Sis stated. "And I didn't judge you, so maybe you could cut me a break."

Gripping the steering wheel, I shook my head. She was fourteen going on forty. Putting the car in gear, I pulled out. It was still raining on and off. The temperatures had fallen off. It had only gotten up to the mid seventies during the day, and right now it was sixty and still dropping.

"You stink, and if you smoke that shit again, I'm not picking you up. That crap is gonna make the car smell."

"You just got this car, and I'm hardly going to make it smell that bad." She had no idea.

"Yeah, you tell Mom that when we get home."

"Hmmph. She's working late."

Actually, no she wasn't. Mom *thought* she had to work late, but she texted while I'd been out making deliveries that she was home. I'd told her I would still pick Trina up.

Unfortunately for Trina, Mom had a nose like a bloodhound. We'd barely walked inside when she sat up in her chair and glared. "Which of you two has been smoking?"

While she hadn't focused on me, I raised my hands. "Not it. In fact, I'm gonna shower 'cause it's all I can smell at the moment."

"Thanks, Coop," Sis said with a scowl.

"Trina!" Mom's voice climbed into the red alert range, and I headed out of the line of fire. Trina needed to avoid that crap. But she and Mom were forever banging heads on some subjects. This was going to be another one.

I paused just inside the hallway heading toward my room and shower. Trina and I had to share a bathroom. Our apartment was laid out a lot like Frankie's, only we had three bedrooms instead of just two.

"Trina," Mom said with a sigh. "We've discussed this…"

Yeah, that was going to be an argument in three, two…

"Dammit, Mom. Why is everything I do put under a microscope? But Coop gets to do whatever he wants whenever he wants?"

"We are not talking about your brother," Mom said. "We're discussing you. This is not a matter of comparison or false equivalency."

I swallowed a smile and continued to the bathroom. Trina always wanted to argue about what I got to do versus what she was allowed to, and she was forever pushing the envelope. If she kept this up, we'd end up having a visit from Dad.

Which was the point, I supposed. I barely saw him, and after he and Mom divorced, I was fine with it. Twisting the water on and letting it heat up, I stripped and checked my phone.

Two messages.

One from Jake. He was staying at Frankie's tonight. It was Tuesday evening, and he didn't have practice in the morning. He wanted to know if I was coming back.

The second was from Frankie.

Frankie

Just checking on you. My turn to ask, are you okay?

Tuesday had been a much better day at school than Monday. For one, her mother hadn't put on an appearance and we'd managed to avoid the Cheryl intercept again. I got it, Cheryl was a nice girl for the most part. A ditz, but a nice girl. Then again, she'd also been the one to give Frankie the water. While I didn't want to think she had anything to do with it, I couldn't escape the idea that she had been involved.

That made me want to punch her.

Not a healthy mental space to be in.

Me

> All good here. Picked up Sis. Grabbing a shower. Want me over?

I wanted to go, no argument. But if she and Jake needed some time, I could be generous. Saturday morning had rocked my world. And I'd meant every word about watching her with the other guys. I'd seen enough of their asses over the summer, that part never fazed me, but the idea of watching them go down on a girl never turned me on before I thought about it being Frankie I watched getting off.

Fuck. I was getting hard just thinking about it.

Everyone had their own kink. Apparently, a little bit of voyeurism was mine. Not that I just wanted to watch. No, I had all kinds of ideas.

Her message popped up just as I headed for the shower.

Frankie

> Jake said he doesn't mind, and I would like you here.

Snagging the phone, I fired off a fast response.

Me

> Then you'll have me. Be there after I shower and check in with Mom.

In the shower, I sped through washing my hair and shaving. I'd gotten pretty good at cleaning up the scruff without needing a mirror. I preferred not to leave rasp burns on her skin if I could avoid it. My cock ached as thoughts of her spread out in front of me kept dancing behind my eyelids.

One hand braced against the tile, I gripped my cock and got myself off in a few swift strokes. It wasn't anywhere near as satisfying as getting myself off inside of her, but it would do. I'd had a lot of practice jerking off to thoughts of

162

her.

But now that I'd had the real thing?

Yeah this was just a stopgap to get me through the rest of the evening without pouncing on her. Right now, Frankie called all the shots. The fact that she'd been more than willing to play with me on Saturday had delighted me to no end. But no pushing.

Period.

I'd walk around with blue balls before I let her feel pressured.

Shower done, I toweled off, then wrapped a towel around my waist before straightening up the bathroom and snagging my dirty clothes. The yelling from the living room had stopped, so either Mom and Trina had solved it or…

Trina's door yanked open, and she stared at me with a sigh. "Sorry." As apologies went, it sucked, but since I hadn't asked for one, I just shrugged.

"Just worried about you, Sis."

"I know," she mumbled. "Mom's mad. She called Dad. We're having a 'family meeting' this weekend."

Good to know. I'd be elsewhere. Instead of retreating to her room, Sis followed me to mine.

When I circled my finger for her to turn around, she rolled her eyes. "Like I want to see your hairy butt."

I snorted.

"Anyway," she continued, facing the door. "Sorry I was rude about it. I really don't think it's a big deal, and it's not like I'm buying the cigarettes."

"Well that's good, since it would be illegal for you to buy them."

Her scoff made me smile as I dragged on clean clothes. I also grabbed a change of clothes for the next day.

"You going over to Frankie's tonight?" The quiet question tugged at me, and I glanced over at her.

"That was the plan. What's up?"

"Nothing," she said, but even when she turned around, she avoided meeting my gaze. "You're just always over there now. You sleep there more than here."

"That's true. You need something, Sis?"

She lifted her shoulders again.

Dropping to sit on the edge of my bed, I patted the spot next to me. "Come on. Tell me what's going on."

"You don't want to listen to me, you just want to go over and see Frankie."

"Yes, I do want to see Frankie. But I also want to listen if something's bothering you." I studied her. The only times she got like this was when she really wanted my advice but didn't know how to ask for it. Four years didn't seem like a big age difference some times, but at others? It seemed forever.

Pushing away from the door, Trina crossed to sit down next to me. The waft of ash and smoke still clung to her hair, even if she'd changed out of her clothes. It would probably be there until she showered.

"You sure you have time?" The skepticism in her tone nearly mocked the hope in her expression.

Retrieving my phone, I opened it to message Frankie where Trina could watch me typing.

Me

Sis needs me for a bit. Gonna be a few.

Frankie

We'll be here. Tell her I said hi.

Me

Done.

"Frankie says 'hi,'" I said, tone dry. Sis laughed and bumped my arm. She'd gotten taller over the last year, but she was only an inch taller than Frankie. That still made her shorter than me, and I was fine with that. "So, spill. What's going on?"

Twisting, she sat sideways and stared at me. "Do you remember Noah Auburn?"

The name wasn't familiar. "Nope." But he was a boy so… "Should I?"

"Well, maybe. He's kind of a sophomore."

"Why are you hanging out with sophomores?" Trina was in eighth grade. She and Jake's sister Becca had a couple of classes together. Weirdly, they weren't that close.

"I'm not—well, just Noah. Really. His sister, Jenny, she's in my class, and I've gotten to know him a little when I go over to Jenny's."

I knew most of her friends. This was the first I was hearing about a Jenny. "Sis, when do you go to Jenny's?"

Trina bit her lower lip and worry swam across her expression. Oh, I was not going to like this answer. Tipping my head back, I considered her.

"Just tell me. I'm already irritated about the smoking, and whatever this is, it's bugging you enough you want my advice." Which in and of itself said it could be bad news.

"Actually, I wanted to talk to Frankie about it, but I don't want to bother her right now."

Some of my irritation evaporated. "Frankie would talk to you about anything," I told her. Even if I wanted to shield Frankie from the rest of the world dumping on her, if Sis needed to talk to Frankie and I blocked that, Frankie would kick my ass.

Justifiably so.

"I know she would," Sis said with a faint smile. "But I don't want to bother her. I just want her to get better, and maybe I can talk to her about this later if you're not any help."

"Thanks?" I said, teasing just a little. "I think."

A flash of a smile warmed Trina's face. "You're welcome. *Anyway*… Jenny lives across the street from Mandy. So a lot of the time when I'm at Mandy's, we head over to Jenny's or Jenny comes over to Mandy's place."

"Got it."

"Noah is Jenny's brother."

"Got that part, too."

"He… Well, he's really cute."

Kill me. "Okay."

"That's it?" She stared at me, doubt written all over her face. "Just okay?"

"He's a guy, he's cute. I don't have much more to say to that than okay." I was too busy keeping the rest of my responses in check if she was about to tell me what I thought she was about to tell me.

Sis stuck her tongue out at me. "He's a sophomore."

"You said that already."

"Fine," she said with a frustrated shake. "He asked me to go to the movies this weekend. Like—him and me—on a date."

On a date.

Sophomore.

I had a name…

"You talk to Mom about this?"

Her eyes were darker than mine, far more gray than green, and she rolled them at the moment, then looked at me like I was stupid. "After she just busted me for smoking…"

"He smokes." It all clicked into place, and Trina winced. "That's why you've been playing around with cigarettes."

She gave a little shrug. "It's not a big deal."

I stared at her.

"Okay, yes, he smokes. But Mandy thinks he's cute, too. When he offered her one, she took it and he gave her this great smile, and I wanted him to smile at me. So I took one, and they aren't great but he is."

Uh huh.

I rubbed the back of my neck.

"If we have to do that family meeting this weekend, I'm never going to get

Mom to say yes to the movies."

Oh, I had no doubt about that.

"Noah doesn't have a car yet."

"And you need a ride?"

She nodded slowly. "If I tell him no that I can't go, he'll probably ask Mandy, and I know she will go and then he won't ask me again."

Cause he was a douche if her saying no once would mean that was it. On the other hand... fuck.

"So you want me to what?"

"Maybe take us to the movies? I want to tell him yes and I need a ride for us to go, and you could take Frankie and we could double date if you took Frankie to a different movie."

Yeah. That sounded like a plan—a double date with my sister, the eighth grader, and Noah, the sophomore who shouldn't be looking at her sideways.

"Will you think about it? Please?" Sis continued. "And maybe don't tell Mom?"

"I'll think about it, but you have to tell Mom. You are way too young to date."

"You took Frankie on dates when you were in eighth grade."

"No, I didn't. I hung out with Frankie in eighth grade. She's also my age, and I'm not two years older." When the older guys at school had noticed her when we got to high school, I hadn't liked that, nor had Jake. It hadn't taken long before Jake picked his first fight to keep that attention off of her.

It helped we met Archie day one. Archie proved very useful in keeping wandering eyes and hands away from her, too.

"Coop, you know what I mean. I really, really like him."

I sighed. "Fine, you tell Mom and she signs off on it, then I'll take you."

"And you'll ask Frankie?"

And probably Jake. He would help me deal with wandering hands no problem. I gave her a smile. "I'll see if Frankie's up to it."

Trina gave a squeal and then hugged me. I chuckled then tugged her hair.

"Yeah yeah, go shower. You smell, and Sis…"

"I know, you don't want me smoking."

"If the guy only likes you cause you'll smoke with him, he isn't the guy for you." Period.

"Maybe." Not that she seemed to be agreeing with me. Then she bounced off the bed. "But I really like him."

Ugh. "I can see that."

"Does Frankie know that your cool and relaxed attitude is all an act?" Sis dared me with raised eyebrows, and I smirked.

"Ask her. Now get lost. I'm going to go see my girlfriend."

At the door, Sis paused. "You know I'm happy for you, right?"

"Yeah?"

"Yeah. Like Mom said, it was time for you to get your head out of your ass where Frankie was concerned."

Yeah. I'd known how I felt about Frankie a lot longer than the rest of them. "See, miracles do happen."

She snorted a laugh, then let herself out. I grabbed my bag and headed for the living room, pausing in the kitchen to find Mom. She was making herself a cup of tea and had just shaken a pair of ibuprofens out of the bottle.

"Sis is making you crazy, huh?"

"Oh, don't start," Mom said with a laugh. "I swear, you were the easy child, so she's making up for it and determined to drive me mad."

I laughed. "Eh, I was just better at hiding what I was up to."

"Hardly," she countered, then patted my cheek. "But I always knew who you were with, and you had good friends, baby. Even if you all had your own kind of crazy. You tried to make up for that this summer though…"

I ducked my head. Mom had caught me coming home drunk a couple of times, and she hadn't been thrilled. "You don't have to worry about me."

"Ha, I always worry about my kids." She poured the boiling water over her tea bag and studied me. "It's my prerogative. You spending the night at Frankie's again?"

"That's the plan."

"You two are being safe?"

"Yes, Mom." Almost slipped on Saturday. Almost. I wanted to do that again, but I wanted to be sure it would be safe for her. For us. That had felt amazing. "Not risking her."

She nodded. Arms folded, she studied me with the same look Sis had given me earlier.

"Go ahead and ask," I told her, leaning against the doorjamb.

"How is she?"

"She's good. Has good days and bad. School was a little rocky. Didn't help when Ms. Curtis showed up at the end of the day yesterday."

Mom frowned. "I thought she'd moved out."

Mom was aware of a lot of it. I'd kept her in the loop. She also wouldn't use that information against Frankie. At one point, I thought Mom and Frankie's mother had been friends. I had no idea what happened in the intervening years, but they'd grown apart.

"She did. Apparently, she got the call about Frankie being in the hospital and came to see her."

A snort of derision escaped her then she shook her head. "Well, Maddy's timing has never been stellar. Just…take care of you and Frankie, baby, and be safe. I know you said that nothing happened, but that's still a shock for the system. The assault. The aftermath. She might be more fragile than she's letting on."

Oh, I was aware of that. "I know, Mom. She's my priority. We're all making sure she isn't alone."

"You're a good boy. So are they—even when you're little hellions." She finished her tea as I gave it a beat. "Your turn, spit it out."

"Sis likes a sophomore brother of one of her friends. He asked her out."

I swore my mother aged in front of me as she dropped her chin. "I am not ready for her to date."

"Ditto. But he asked her to a movie. She asked if I'd take them since he doesn't drive and obviously neither does she."

Nose wrinkled, she glanced at me. "And you said?"

"I told her I would *if* she talked to you and got you to okay it. She figured I could take Frankie and we could double date."

We both grimaced.

"Fine, I'll warn your father. His head will explode."

I snorted. But Mom wasn't wrong. Trina was a daddy's girl, and Dad had always put her on a pedestal. "Just let me know," I said. "And I'll have a chat with said sophomore at school tomorrow."

Mug halfway to her lips, Mom paused. "Cooper."

"I said talk, Mom. Not planning to threaten him yet." I spread my hands. "I'm the reasonable one." Jake could handle all the threatening for me. He would probably even enjoy it.

"Uh huh. Have a good night, baby, and check in with me tomorrow."

"Yes, ma'am!"

It was still raining as I let myself out, so I stuck to the walkways and jogged from cover to cover. Frankie's place was literally right down and around the corner on the other end of the building from my apartment. We'd been close for years.

But now that I'd been staying there so much?

I didn't even want that much distance.

I unlocked the front door, and the sound of Frankie's laughter had me grinning at the sound.

"You are such an *ass*," Frankie declared, and I raised my brows as I closed and locked the door behind me.

"If you say so," Jake answered easily before he shot me a grin. He was kicked back on the sofa, a remote in his hand, and the television paused on a very interesting movie. "Hey, Coop, everything all good?"

Frankie glanced up at me, and her grin lifted the rest of the load off my shoulders. Her flushed face and over bright eyes intrigued me, and I glanced back at the screen.

"Yeah, all good. What are you two watching?"

Dissolving into laughter again, Frankie put a hand over her face.

"Or do I not want to know?"

"Porn," Jake said, without missing a beat. "I'm critiquing it."

"Heh," I laughed. "I'm in." I dropped my bag before I slid over to sit on the sofa on Frankie's other side and nudged her lightly. She shot a look at me, still laughing. A little mortified, but maybe a little turned on. Oh, this could be fun.

"See," Jake said with an evil grin. "Coop's in."

"Oh shut up," Frankie said, groaning. "When you said you wanted to watch experimental videos, *this* was not what I thought you had in mind."

"No?" With a laugh, he hit play, and I flicked a look to the screen.

There was a woman on the bed with two very huge dudes spit roasting her.

"That doesn't even look comfortable."

"It's not supposed to look comfortable," Jake said.

"He's right," I admitted. "They want it to be photogenic, which means those positions are done more for camera angles than pleasure…" Course, the woman let out a scream as the one guy came all over her face.

"And that right there…" Frankie pointed. "Hell no."

It was my turn to laugh, and I slid a look at Jake behind her back. Like what the hell? He shrugged, then nodded to her. She was laughing. And distracted.

Eh, worked for me.

"No facials," Jake said. "Duly noted. But the rest of this is okay?"

Yeah, I didn't miss the way she bit her lip. Hey, like I said, a guy has to have some fantasies.

"Ass," she muttered, and I grinned. That was not a 'no.'

"So," Jake continued, still grinning. "Next we have…"

For the next fifteen minutes, he teased her with different porn videos, and it was hilarious. Particularly when we hit the superhero re-enactments. Some of her embarrassment went away, and she just started laughing her ass off.

When she finally ordered us to pick something new and headed to the kitchen to make popcorn, I glanced over at Jake. "Feel like helping me with the sophomore interested in Sis tomorrow?"

He slanted a look in my direction. "Intimidate or beat the crap out of him?"

"We'll start with the warning."

"Got it." Jake lifted his soda and toasted me with it. "Just tell me when."

"Thanks."

"Anytime."

We were still looking for a movie when Jake's phone buzzed. "It's my mom," he said, rising and hitting answer. He carried it with him as he headed for the bedroom and some privacy.

I kicked back and watched Frankie as she moved around the kitchen with care. She got the popcorn made without us interfering, though I wanted to. She had it down pretty slick, too. When she carried the big bowl out, I rose. "You want me to grab drinks?"

"Yes, please. Do you need real food? Jake and I saved dinner for you."

"I'm good," I told her, then touched her chin gently, and when she lifted her face to me, I dropped a kiss on her lips. "Thanks for saving me food."

"I'm getting awfully used to you guys being here."

"Good," I said with a wink. "I like being here."

Studying her expression, I gave her a minute.

"You want to talk about it?" Despite her earlier laughter, there was something more going on.

"Not yet," she admitted. "Maybe tomorrow?"

"Anytime," I promised her.

She hesitated, then glanced to where Jake had gone, then back to me. "Ian wrote me a song."

Schooling my expression, I nodded. "Cool?"

"It's very cool, but…"

I waited her out.

"But I haven't listened to it yet."

"Do you want to listen to it?" I already knew the answer. She wouldn't have brought it up otherwise.

"I do, and I don't." She made a face. "I thought we settled this, and now…"

"There's no rush," I reminded her. "But Bubba cares about you. So when you're ready, you listen to his song." Then I stroked my finger down her nose.

"Rachel wants to hang out tomorrow."

"Okay. What do you want to do?"

Frankie groaned. "I want to just…be normal. Go to work, get homework done. Hang out with you guys."

"Well, you're doing all of that—except the go to work part. And Marsha said for you to take all the time you need. Your job isn't going anywhere."

I could almost see the "but money" argument flashing in her eyes.

"It's going to be okay," I reminded her. "If you want to go hang with Rachel or have Rachel come over. We'll make it happen."

And one of us would keep an eye on them.

When Frankie leaned into me, I wrapped her up in a hug and held her close. "It really is going to be okay," I said. Jake re-emerged and caught my eye. Then he surprised me. Or maybe not.

He slid right up behind her, and we sandwiched her into the hug between us. It lasted for all of about thirty seconds before she said in a muffled voice, "I can't breathe."

Chuckling, we loosened our grip on her, but that thirty seconds had been pretty perfect.

When we finally grabbed drinks and settled in with the popcorn, she curled right between us. And that was pretty perfect, too.

Chapter Twelve
STOLEN KISSES

JAKE

Frankie shifting against me woke me up. The night had actually been nightmare-free so far, but that didn't stop me from waking at her every little twitch. I curved around her with her back firm against my chest, and one of my legs had tucked right between hers. With care, I lifted my head to make sure she still had her wrist on a pillow—and she did.

Only the pillow was propped up by Coop. They were both breathing steadily, soft, slow sighs that said they were still asleep. Satisfied, I dropped my head back to the pillow and feathered my hand over her hip. I *liked* sleeping with Frankie. The two nights previously crashing back at my place sucked.

This was much better.

She shifted again, and this time, her ass ground against my morning wood and my chances of going back to sleep winked out like a light being turned off. Fuck that felt good and like torture all at once. Every other time, I'd been tempted to tease her awake.

Today, I hesitated.

She was still recovering. The bruises were better. The visible ones on her back were still green and yellow, fading fast. The one on her cheek had taken longer, but it was also just a shadow now. Not the swollen lump of bruise it had been before. The one that made me want to find Mitch and beat the shit out of him all over again.

I shoved thoughts of him right out of my head. He didn't get to be in this bed with her. He didn't get to be anywhere near her ever again. Brushing her hair out of the way, I bared her neck and pressed a kiss there, then another to her ear. She shifted again, and I stroked my hand along her hip.

I loved everything about Frankie—from her sharp mind, to her competitive spirit, to her far too generous heart. The fact that she had legs to die for and sweet curves that fit me like a glove were just a perk. I mouthed another kiss right over her pulse point, even though I knew I should just go back to sleep. The hardest part of this last week hadn't been keeping my hands to myself.

That I could handle.

Between us all, we had years of practice in not getting too handsy with her, even when I ached to roll her over and bury myself in her so deep. Or better, just wake her up with my face buried between her thighs. I'd always liked the idea of going down on a girl, but I loved going down on Frankie. Her reactions were so utterly without artifice.

She wasn't shy about experimenting or telling me when she didn't like something. The porn had been mostly a joke to get her out of her head the night before. She'd started worrying about whether her mother had gotten served and what her reaction would be. Then there was the mountain of homework, even though she'd been ahead and wouldn't need long to get caught up on the rest, and her frustration with her wrist and having to rely on us was getting to her.

More, she needed to talk about what happened, but she didn't want to. She'd talked to Coop, that much I knew. He didn't say a word to us about what she'd said, only that she'd tried to open up, and she was trying to figure out what she wanted to do about her needs.

As much as I wanted to fix everything for her, I couldn't. That part I loathed with every fiber of my being. One thing I'd done in all the years I'd known her was protect her, and the one time she really needed me, I hadn't been there.

Movement had me glancing down as she turned her face toward me. She regarded me with sleepy green eyes, and the trust in them knocked my fury to the side.

"Morning, Baby Girl," I whispered, and the corners of her mouth lifted.

She twisted to curl her left hand up to my hair, and I dropped my head obediently. When her lips parted beneath mine, I sighed and deepened what I intended to only be a soft kiss. Her tongue stroked mine, and a groan vibrated in my throat.

Then the little minx ground her ass back against me. Fuck. Heat and want pounded through my veins. Curling my fingers against her sleep shorts, I fought to keep my libido in check, but she let out a little moan as she tried roll toward me.

Good intentions shredding, I pulled back only enough to help her roll and settled her splinted arm more securely before diving back in to kiss her. Nudging my thigh back between her legs, I groaned when she fisted my hair and arched her hips.

Tracing a path along her jaw, I mouthed little kisses to her skin before easing her back against the pillows. Her breath came out in little ragged pants. With a flick of a look toward Coop, who continued to snore softly, I slid my hands up under her shirt to cover her breasts. I loved how they filled my palms and how her nipples would go all tense and stiff. A little stroke of my thumb, and she'd arch her back.

When she uttered a low sound, I kissed her again, stilling my hands until she quieted. Then nose-to-nose, I flicked another look toward Coop, and she glanced to the side. Her cheeks turned a rosy shade, and I grinned when she met my gaze, her own eyes wide.

She'd forgotten we weren't alone. I gave her breasts a gentle squeeze and raised my brows. Was she up to a little fun?

The skate of her tongue over her lower lip drew me like a moth to the flame, but then she shifted with care and widened her legs until I could settle between them.

Was it any wonder I loved her? Amusement sparked in her eyes along with daring as she scraped her teeth over her lower lip. I caught one nipple and gave it a gentle twist. Her body arched, and I made a shhing sound.

Gaze fixed on hers as I felt more than heard her groan, I dropped my head down to circle one nipple with my tongue. She shifted, almost restless beneath me, and then went still again as I latched onto the nipple. If she didn't want to wake Coop, she had to be quiet and still.

I didn't give a damn if we woke Coop. Little shit had been hinting at it for days beforehand, and I'd read it in his eyes last night. He was as intrigued at the idea of sharing her as I was.

But right now, I was only interested in making her feel good. She'd had enough pain and discomfort the last few weeks. With only the half-light of dawn to illuminate the room and Coop's quiet breaths beside us, we were alone in this little bubble.

She'd slept without a nightmare.

Sucking the pointed tip of her nipple against my teeth, I sighed as she fisted my hair. I slid a hand down to tease under the edge of her shorts. Dampness greeted me, and it was my turn to swallow a moan as my dick almost pulsed at the idea of sinking into her.

Condoms.

That idea floated through my brain. I had them somewhere. Needed to find them, but for now, I satisfied myself with kissing my way down her stomach. I could play with her breasts for days, I hadn't been kidding about how pretty her titties were. I'd been half in love with them since the day I came back and discovered she'd developed them during my absence.

I pushed the blankets back off me so I could tug her shorts down, and she helped by pulling her legs up, which spread them wider, and then I was face to face with her pussy and I sighed. I loved everything about her. Biting down on the juncture between her thigh and her body, I stared up at her. She'd clapped her left hand against her mouth to muffle her own sounds.

I paused to grin, and she half-glared at me and half-dared me with the heat blazing in her eyes. I didn't look away once as I licked her from entrance to clit. Her hips bucked up, and I grinned as I began to nuzzle against her in earnest.

Sweet, musky, and damp, I loved how she tasted. More, I loved how she responded. Her clit seemed to swell under my attention, and I lavished it with more, even as I braced her hip with one hand to keep her still.

My second favorite thing to do while I teased all these responses out of her was to slide in a finger. She clamped down around my index finger as I curved it and eased it in and out. When I added a second finger, I kept swirling circles around her clit.

Her sudden gasp cutting off drew my gaze, and I found Coop kissing her for all he was worth. Satisfaction unfolded in me, and I locked down, increasing the pressure until her cries broke through the stolen kisses and she came in a rush.

I lifted my face to study her flushed chest as it rose and fell rapidly. Her nipples were both peaked, and Coop slid a hand over one, cupping it and teasing the nipple with his thumb as I wiped my cheeks against the blanket.

When Coop finally lifted his head, Frankie looked to me, her eyes glazed over and her lips swollen. For a brief second, worry flashed in her eyes, and I grinned.

"None of that, Baby Girl," I told her as I stroked the inside of her thigh. I needed a minute to get myself under a leash, because I wanted to finish what we'd started. "That was fucking hot."

"Yeah it was," Coop agreed in a similarly ragged tone.

She shuddered from head to toe, and I pressed a kiss to her belly before I stretched over her to the side table. The drawer opened to a roll of condoms I'd stored there. I pulled one out, and Coop moved slightly to lay on his side while still toying with her breast.

"Is this all right?" he asked. While his attention seemed focused on her, Coop continued to twist and tweak her nipples. She arched her back and another full body shudder passed through her. The goosebumps rippling over her skin promised me he was doing a wonderful job of keeping her on edge. I shed my shorts and rolled the condom on.

"I don't mind," I answered when Frankie gave another pleased gasp. "Do you, Baby Girl?"

Licking her lips, she dragged her gaze from Coop to me, and there it was—that daring glint in her eyes. "No," she whispered. "I want both of you."

The words sank into me, riding an edge of triumph, and I ran my hands up and down her thighs, petting her as much as soothing myself. "You're going to get that," I promised. "Maybe not at once, not yet."

She wasn't ready for that yet. Not with her wrist and her still healing bruises. But we could work our way up there.

"Soon," Coop agreed, then slanted a look at me. I nodded at the desire in his eyes. Yeah, I wanted that, too. But right now, I just wanted Frankie, and I was fine with Coop sharing this moment. Fuck, I looked forward to after. "Jake first," he said as he leaned down to kiss Frankie again. The way he went after those kisses, practically devouring her as he pinched her nipple until it flushed deep red, sent an answering pulse to my cock.

Then Coop backed off, and I surged up. Sinking into her was like going home, and even though I wanted to take my time, she wrapped her legs around my hips and dragged me in. When my mouth locked on hers, I thrust all the way home.

Hot, tight, and so damn perfect. I groaned as she sucked against my tongue.

Of all the times I'd ever imagined having her, rocking into her always exceeded my expectations. I planted one hand to keep my weight from crushing her. Not wanting to jar her wrist either, I kept my thrusts sharper, more contained, but she was already spasming around me.

When she pulled back to cry out, I gritted my teeth. The tension in my spine had gone red hot, and I braced my other hand flat to the bed and met her gaze as she arched up to meet me. The rhythm increased, and with every snap of my hips, it was like the edge rushed up to meet me as my balls seemed to drag up tight. When she dug her nails into my shoulder and Coop uttered a quiet "Fuck…" I came.

The hot pulse spilled out of me, and I snapped forward twice more before everything went rigid. Her inner muscles clamped down, fluttering against me as if milking me for every drop. Sweat slicked my skin, and it was hard to catch my breath.

We all lay there for several long moments as I fought to catch my breath, and then with regret, I eased out of her, carefully. She let out a shuddering cry, and then Coop had her mouth claimed again, another kiss as he tugged her to him.

I stumbled back from the bed on rubbery legs. It took me a minute to deal with the condom, and I went to the bathroom to dispose of it. When I came back, Coop had her rolled on her side and he was drilling into her from behind.

Fuck.

That was hot.

I fell back onto the bed, facing her, and then cupped her chin with one hand while I put her splinted wrist against my side to brace it. Kissing her, I wrapped my tongue around hers as she cried out. Coop had his hand between her thighs even as he rocked his hips, and I tasted her orgasm in her kiss a moment before it struck.

I leaned back to watch them, and I loved seeing her come apart, face flushed and sweat beading along her skin, until Coop went rigid and his groan elongated as it filled the quiet room.

They kissed again, and when Coop let go of her lips, she turned to me and I pulled her close for another kiss. The bed dipped and moved as Coop went to deal with his own condom, but I cradled Frankie to me.

Best good morning kiss ever.

It took some real effort to get moving, and I kept an eye on Frankie as I helped her in the shower. Coop had grabbed one first, then he was ready to help her after. She moved a little awkwardly, and I worried we'd been too rough.

"Stop," she shushed me at breakfast while sipping a coffee. "I ache, but I like this one."

Coop chuckled. "Well in that case, what about round three?"

Oh, the body was willing, but the clock worked against.

Her grin lifted some of my concerns. Not pushing her meant also not taking advantage. But the lines of tension in her face were absent, and the shadows that had darkened her eyes since the confrontation with her mother had also eased.

Taking Frankie at her word, I kissed her lightly as we finished getting ready to leave. The cats were fed, and I'd dealt with the litter box while Coop got the trash. I had her backpack and my own. She was riding to school with me, but Coop would bring her home since I had practice after.

In the car, I glanced over to find her smiling at me. "What?"

"Nothing," she said. "Just…that was a lot of fun."

"Yeah it was," I agreed with her. "You're not too sore?" I hadn't been as gentle as I would have liked there, and Coop seemed to have had the same idea.

"Not too much," she promised, then slid her hand over my thigh. "You guys really didn't mind…"

"Hell no, I didn't mind," I assured her. "Trust me. It was hot as hell watching him kiss you while I had my mouth on your pussy. It was hotter still to kiss you while he made you come."

Her face flushed red again, and I grinned.

"You said you had a lot of fun, but is that something you'd be interested in repeating?"

Pressing two fingers to her lips, she said, "I'm definitely leaning in that direction."

"Good to know."

The drive was fun after that, and I liked how relaxed she was. Still, the change that came over her when we got to the school was unmistakable. Her shoulders tightened, her lips compressed. Covering her hand, I pulled it back over to rest against my thigh.

The reduction in PDA at school meant we couldn't offer as much comfort as I'd like, but if she kept this up, I was going to be breaking some rules.

"You know we're not going to let anyone get near you, right?" I asked as we pulled into the lot.

"It's not that," she murmured, though she cast me a wan smile. "But yes, I have noticed the cone of protection you guys are forming, and while I'd normally roll my eyes, I have a hard time doing that when I appreciate it so much."

Good. "Then what's wrong, Baby Girl? Tell me so I can go kick its ass."

She laughed. "You can't fight all my battles for me, Jake."

"Who says I can't? Hmm?"

With a shake of her head, she squeezed my hand. "I do. School just… Everyone knows. It's like when whoever it was decorated my car with all those condoms or Sharon put up those videos, only this is a hundred times worse. They all know what he did."

Wrestling with my temper, I tried to focus on what she was saying. "Yes, they know he's a jackass who drugged you and attacked you. That's not your fault, Frankie."

"I know that," she said, loosening her fingers from my grip to tap the side of her head. "I know that in here. Just like I know I need to distance myself from Maddy."

Only Archie called his parents by their first names. Hearing Frankie do it just made me sad for her. Mom was my biggest champion, and while we didn't always agree, I knew she always had my back.

The fact that Frankie didn't even get that? What a bitch her mother was.

"But my gut?" She continued putting a hand over her stomach. "It's all in knots. Then I'm not sure if I'm angry or sad, and whether I want to scream or throw up."

She sighed.

"I want it to stop so I can just be me."

"You are you," I told her as I parked, then turned to face her without shutting off the car. "You're always you. I get this is messed up. I know you're okay, but I'm constantly checking on you to make sure you're still okay. It's like I have to know… I hated going home the last couple of days, but Coop or Arch always sent me a message after you were asleep to let me know you were sleeping and you were all right."

Wonder filled her expression. "I hate what this has done to all of you. I hate that you're all so worried."

"We'll get through it, Baby Girl. We worry because we care." Fifteen minutes she'd been out of our sight, and look what happened to her. Then again on Monday, she was away from us for one class period, and the bitch showed up to get her.

"If it's ever too much…"

"It won't be," I told her, then brushed some of the hair back from her face. That bruise on her face was still there. It faded each day, but I could still see how bad it was. How still she'd been when we got in there. Barely blinked, her words slurring, then she'd gone so pale.

"If it does," she scolded me, putting a finger against my lips. "Don't hold it in? Tell me?"

Yeah. That was happening. Bubba and I had a session with Diane. Maybe I'd talk about it with her. Not that I was worried about it. "I won't," I said. "But I'm not going anywhere. Trust me?"

Her smile relieved some of the vise locking around my chest. "I do trust you, Jake. I just want to take care of you."

"You do take care of me," I said with a wink. "It just happens to be my turn, so suck it up, princess, and let me be your big bad boyfriend who keeps the world at bay. When it's your turn, I promise to only whine a little when you beat up the people looking at me sideways."

Her laughter was exactly what I'd wanted.

Though her tension abated some, she was still strung tight as we walked inside. I held her hand and to hell with what anyone else thought. When Coop met us at the doors, I let her go so he could sling an arm around her shoulders.

Bubba and Archie were waiting for us. I kept an eye out for Cheryl. So far, she hadn't tried to see Frankie again, but that wouldn't last. Coop nudged me about fifteen minutes before the bell.

"That's him," he said after checking his phone, and I glanced down at the student directory, then across the cafeteria at the target.

"Still just warning?" I checked before draining my coffee.

Coop nodded, but Frankie's speculative glance landed on us. "What are you two up to?"

"Just going to offer some friendly advice," I told her with a grin.

Only Frankie's expression didn't lighten as she glanced from me to Coop, then back. "Uh uh. You have that someone's about to get their ass beat look."

"Not beat," I promised, but it wasn't enough.

With a sigh, Coop gripped my shoulder. "Trina's got a sophomore asking her out."

Archie and Bubba both twisted at the same moment to look where we had been.

"And I'm just going to talk to him," Coop said, his grin easy and his manner relaxed.

"Jake is going because…?" Despite her doubtful expression, the corners of her lips twitched. Frankie damn well knew why I was going.

"I'm going for moral support." Yes, I said with a straight face.

Bubba snorted, and Archie smirked. "You need more moral support?" Archie asked with a glance to Coop.

"Nope, I think Jake is just the right touch. And it's a quick conversation. We'll be right back. Not going to lay a finger on him."

"Hmm-hmm," Frankie said. "I've heard that before." Then... "Just remember, if Sis likes him, you have to be careful."

"So does he," Coop said in an unflinching tone as he locked gazes with Frankie.

She gave it a beat, then nodded. "Well, go get 'im."

"Like I said," Coop spread his hands as he spoke. "It's just a conversation."

She chuckled and shook her head, but shifted in the chair to watch us, and there was something kind of cool about knowing she planned to keep an eye on us. That, and I had to resist the urge to puff out my chest.

"This is going to be fun," I admitted quietly to Coop, and he snorted.

"Not as fun as this morning."

No. Nothing would though. I grinned.

I was still grinning when the table around our target went quiet.

You know, I almost felt sorry for that sophomore when he noticed us approaching.

Almost.

Chapter Thirteen

SAFE WITH ME

IAN

Practice kind of sucked, but the team didn't feel much like a team. Something Coach called all of us on afterward. Mitch may not have been a power player, but he had been popular. There were assholes on the team who resented the fact that he wouldn't be around for the last games of the season. Still more that didn't think it was *fair* that his academic career and potential career were being derailed.

Despite the mutterings, most of them shut up when Jake or I were present. Most. Not all. Maybe they thought they were flying under the radar. I didn't care so much, but if they said one more word about it, I'd be breaking another jaw if Jake didn't get to them first.

Coach, however, offered them no such assurances. "This is the part where you sit with your mouths closed and your ears open," he informed all of us. We were in the locker room, most of us had showered and changed, but no one had been allowed to leave. "For the last few weeks, our heads have not been in this game."

When one of the other kids began to protest, Coach raised his hand and cut him off.

"I didn't ask for your opinion, and I don't want it." Hands on his hips, Coach stared until the mutters stopped.

I leaned back against my locker, and Jake leaned next to me, arms folded. I still couldn't run a pass. If I was lucky, I might get off the bench next week.

Not that I cared much one way or the other. Playing the guitar had been a little tougher, and I'd made that work. That was the thing I cared about more now, rather than the game, as sacrilegious as that might be.

"Are we focused now? Are you hearing me?"

A round of "Yes, Coach," came from all of us.

"Good. What makes a team a team is we work together. What makes a team successful is we support each other."

Jake's whole body went tense, and I bumped his shoulder. The last thing we needed was him unloading on Coach.

"But being a team player is about more than being on a team, it's about being worthy of that support." Coach swung his gaze over all of us. "We've had our ups and our downs. I know you're all saying we lost a good player, maybe we did. Maybe we didn't. While I *can't* comment on it, I am telling you that as a team, you need to pull it together and support the guy standing next to you and the guy standing next to him. The guys who are still here, who are bringing it. Am I clear?"

"Yes, Coach."

He nodded once.

"Get out of here and rest for tomorrow. I expect one hundred and ten percent on that field and to support each other. Got it?"

Another round of "Yes, Coach," and then the team broke up. I twisted to grab my backpack out of the locker along with my duffle. All my training clothes needed to go home for the weekend. Not that I'd gotten them that dirty.

Jake didn't move, not at first, his attention narrowed on a couple of Mitch's besties who scowled and glared back.

Slamming my door closed, I slid the backpack strap over my shoulder and stared at the pair myself. Jackson Taylor and Shawn Abbey weren't my favorite people. Hell, they didn't even rank on the list of assholes above general douche. They were decent players and offered support on the offensive line.

But they were Mitch's boys through and through.

"What are you looking at Rhys?" Shawn demanded when he met my gaze.

"Shut up, Shawn," Coach barked, and Shawn actually jerked at the sound and glanced to where Coach stood in the doorway to his office. He hadn't closed it. "Get your things and go rest up. Save it for the game."

"Sure," Jackson said. "We'll save it for the game." Then he cut a look at us before he slammed his locker door and the pair left.

"Wouldn't take much to catch up to them," Jake said, the threat in his voice anything but idle.

"Don't," I cautioned. "It's what they want." Not that I wouldn't risk a few more broken knuckles to knock them on their ass.

Before Jake could say anything, Coach called us. "Get in my office, boys."

With a sigh, Jake rolled his eyes, but we went. Once inside, he motioned us to sit down and then dropped into his own chair. After pulling his ball cap off, he ran a hand over his balding pate. Coach had been in charge of the football team for more than twenty years. He'd been an assistant coach before that. I'd always liked him—he was a straight shooter, but he loved the game.

That he'd given that speech had to have been hard for him.

"If you want us to drop off the team, Coach, just say the word." Jake's tone bordered on belligerent. "But I'm not helping that asshole's friends accomplish crap."

Well, that was one way to win points and influence people. Not that I disagreed. "Can't say I'm feeling the team spirit there either," I told Coach.

"I know you can't talk about it." That part I understood. There were legalities involved. "But I know what happened. I was there." I'd been involved. "I'm glad he's gone."

"Well, as you said, I can't comment, and no, Jake, I don't want you two off the team. I want you to focus up. You're both in strong positions. You're critical to the team's success. What I want to know is do you want to be here?"

"If I say no," Jake said, "what happens then?"

Wait. I glanced at him. "Really?" This was the first I'd heard he didn't care whether he was on the team or not. We'd been fighting for a position on this team from the spring before high school started. We'd both tried out, practiced, bucked each other up, and earned our spots. We'd fought to keep those spots each year.

"Really," Jake said. "No offense, Coach. I still love the game. But this doesn't feel like a team anymore."

Leaning forward, the older man pinned his look on me. "Bubba?"

"Jake's not wrong," I admitted. Even with all the time we put in, it had been more out of habit than out of real love for the game. At least this year anyway. I thought our best year had been ninth grade. It was all still fresh, Frankie was on the spirit team, and it was another way we spent time together. Now it just sucked time away from where I'd rather be.

"You realize that scouts have seen you both play."

Jake said nothing, but I shook my head. "Not that I've heard."

"That's going to change over the next couple of weeks. They've been watching you, even with the issues and the news stories."

"Not planning to go pro, Coach," Jake admitted. That wasn't a surprise. "I've got my eye on an engineering degree. I'm here because we made a commitment. But I don't have to stay."

Exhaling, Coach settled back in his chair and studied us. I got the impression there was a lot of things he wanted to say and probably couldn't. "Three games left this season, unless we sweep them all and Torrent High loses their next two of three. If they do, we make the division playoffs."

It wasn't going to happen. The team was too scattered. But I heard what Coach asked, even if he wasn't asking directly. I glanced at Jake and read the same understanding there. He nodded to my unasked question.

"Coach, do you want us in the game?" It was my turn to ask.

"Yes," he said. "But only if you're going to give it your all. That means working with Jackson and Shawn, whether you like them or not."

It wasn't just about liking them.

"We'll do our parts," Jake said. "We've always played our best."

But that wasn't a promise to work with them, and I couldn't make it either. Not as long as they held onto that attitude about Mitch. For all we knew, they were in on it, too.

"Play tomorrow night," Coach said slowly. "If you want to walk away after that, I'll make sure you get credit for the full season."

It was better than nothing, I supposed. He wasn't offering to get rid of the other guys, but then Coach didn't have a reason to get rid of them at the moment.

"Sounds like a plan," Jake said. We all shook on it, then Jake and I headed out. Neither of us said anything. The parking lot was nearly empty, which gave me a good view of my bike lying on its side.

Fuck.

Jake saw it a beat after me, because he let out a low whistle. Still silent, we stalked across the empty lot. The side mirrors were smashed. The front tire kickstand had broken right off, and one of the brake grips dangled—it had been cut.

We got it upright, but it didn't matter. I couldn't ride it in this condition. The front and back tires were both flat.

"Fuckers."

"Yeah, we don't know it's them," I said, not that I had any doubts. Who else had this kind of beef with me? Mitch, maybe, but as far as I knew, he hadn't been back on campus since the cops followed him to the hospital. He'd also been arrested. Beyond that, details had been sketchy.

"We don't know, but do you think it was anyone else?" Jake countered.

I shook my head. There had to be a grand's worth of damage done. Fuck.

"Hang tight, I'll go get my car, and we can put the backseat down and load this inside."

"It's not gonna fit."

"We'll make it work. We can at least get it over to the bike shop." We set the bike down again, and then Jake jogged for his car. I pulled out my phone and looked up the number for the bike repair shop. They weren't going to be open much longer.

One phone call assured me a mechanic would be there to check my bike in, but they couldn't give me any promises until they got a good look at it.

Jake was back in no time. "Take pictures of all of it."

"Yeah." I'd need it for insurance.

He also had his phone out and to his ear.

"What are you doing?"

"School resource officer," Jake told me. "We're filing a report on this."

That would take forever.

But I got the pictures of everything, then Jake helped me stand it up again to do more. Coach pulled up while the resource officer was there, and he looked at my bike, then at us. His jaw tightened, but like us, he had no guarantees of who had done it.

We all *knew*, but proving it was something else.

"You okay to get this out of here, boys?" Coach asked.

"Getting it over to the shop now," I told him, and I let the shop know we would be a bit longer while the SRO filled out the paperwork. Coach and the SRO helped us get the bike into Jake's SUV after we spread out some plastic. The last thing we needed was it leaking all over his car, too. The SRO had some rope, and we secured it with the hatch raised.

Now to get it there before it started raining on us again.

"Fuckers," Jake said as we pulled out.

"Yeah," I said blowing out a breath. "I need to text Frankie." I was supposed to be hanging out with them this evening. But without, a ride that might make it challenging.

"Just let her know we're running late," Jake advised. "I can swing by your place and grab stuff if you need it before we head over." At my hesitation, he said, "Coop and I both planned to work tonight, and I'm pretty sure Archie gave you the nod earlier to let you two have some time together."

Guilt sliced at me. "He did, and I appreciate it."

"But?" The warning in Jake's voice just added to the general sour mood in the SUV.

"No but," I said, then scrubbed a hand over my face. "No buts. I don't want to assume she minds if I spend the night."

We all had been. The guys had been sleeping in the bed with her. I didn't mind keeping my distance for that part and intended to until I earned her forgiveness.

"You're not assuming shit," Jake told me as he pulled into the bike shop's parking lot. Considering the number of times we'd run by here while they'd been fixing the bike the first time, it didn't surprise me he remembered where it was. "If you don't want to stay, or she doesn't want you to stay, one of us will get you home. But you aren't going to fix things if you don't have the time with her either."

I turned that over in my head as we got the bike out and I filled out the stuff for the mechanic. Mom and Dad were gonna be thrilled with this, but I'd deal with it. The rain returned as we were getting the bike on a loader. Once back in Jake's SUV, I said, "Yeah, if you don't mind running me to my place—I want to throw on something clean and grab my overnight bag and my guitar."

"There you go," Jake said as he backed out of the spot and headed for the road. "Much better."

It shouldn't humble me that they were all rooting for me, but it did. "How is she? Really?"

"Better," Jake said. "It still comes in waves. She didn't have a nightmare last night—that's something. First time I know she hasn't had one since it happened." He shot me a look. "If you're the only one there tonight, try to stay close enough so if she has one, you can help her."

I nodded. "Not going to let her down."

"Good. Really don't want to have to kick your ass, Bubba."

Shaking my head, I laughed. It shouldn't be funny. It wasn't really funny. At the same time, it was hysterical. Because Jake wasn't kidding. He'd do it, too.

"I'm serious," he warned me, though like me, he wore a grin.

"I know you are," I assured him. "Oddly, that makes me feel better."

"Me, too." He smirked.

We were almost ninety minutes late by the time we'd filed the report, dropped the bike off, and gone by my place. Jake only came up long enough to give her a kiss, then he and Coop were out the door. I thought Archie would be there too, but he'd left earlier because Rachel was supposed to have come over.

"She couldn't make it," Frankie told me after Coop left. "She got called in to work tonight, so I promised that we'd find some time this weekend."

"Okay." I couldn't tell if she was disappointed by the change in plan or not. Still, I studied her as I set my guitar case down. "You mind if I put my bag in your room?"

"Staying over tonight?"

Well, direct question for direct question. "If you don't mind." She sat cross-legged on the sofa, a book open in her lap and her laptop sitting just in front of her where she could pull it to her if she needed.

She'd changed into a pair of boxers and an oversize shirt that kept falling off one shoulder. She'd also pulled her hair up into a ponytail. Well, someone had pulled it up for her.

"I'd like to stay," I continued before she could respond. "I'd like to spend the evening with you. I've missed you the last few days."

The corners of her mouth tilted upward. "You've seen me," she scolded, but the smile took out any sting.

"I want to do more than see you. Do you mind if I stay?" The fact it had been nearly two weeks wasn't lost on me. Over two weeks since she broke up with me. Almost two weeks since Homecoming.

"I don't mind," she murmured, and ducked her head to glance at her book.

Giving her a moment, I grinned. "Thank you. I miss having you come over to swim, too. We might get another week or two out of the pool if we're lucky."

Keeping it light meant I could tease her some, maybe get another smile out of her.

"It's supposed to drop into the sixties next week and stay there."

"Never say never, we've been sweating over Halloween before," I called back.

The room was neat, the bed was disheveled, but the comforter had been pulled up. Not focusing on the who and the how so much as the fact if she was up for that, then that was a good sign, right?

Maybe I should have had a longer talk with Coop about this. He understood the psychology better, and no way was I having that discussion with Dad. Mom had given me some advice. Right now, I'd lean on that.

After setting the bag down, I got changed into sleep pants and debated the shirt then skipped it. Mom told me to be myself. Who I'd always been was comfortable around her.

The awkwardness and stilted interactions were a lot more my fault than hers. "You need anything while I'm back here?"

"No, I'm good. Though if I could talk you into getting me a bottle of water, that would be great."

"You got it." I flexed my right hand and checked the taped fingers. They were still sore, but I could live. Back in the living room, I swung by the sofa and picked up her empty bottle and the empty can. "Did you eat already?"

Frankie put a finger on the line she was reading before she glanced up. I didn't grin at her double-take, just kept moving. I dropped both in the recycle bin before retrieving a couple of bottles of water from the fridge. Jeremy had done a really nice job of stocking it.

"Frankie?" I called when she hadn't answered, and allowed myself a small smile while she couldn't see my face.

"Um…no. We had a couple of sandwiches when we got back after school. Coop helped me work through a lit paper though, so we didn't have time to eat much, and Archie had to run back to his place for some stuff."

"Well, I'm not that great a cook, but I can definitely heat hot dogs and I order a mean pizza."

Seriously, I needed to widen the skillset. Mom had offered to teach me to cook a dozen times, and had I listened? No.

Shit.

"Well, if you can follow instructions, I can walk you through a couple of things." She worked the book off her lap and nudged her laptop aside. Tiddles sat on the back of the sofa, tail lashing. The minute she stood up though, the cat jumped down and settled on her open book. She just rolled her eyes and kept coming.

"I can follow instructions," I promised, opening the water bottle. "Why don't I grab your books and stuff, and you can work at the table and bid me to follow your lead."

She snorted. "Be easier if I can see what you're doing."

Eyebrows raised, I said, "And you don't want to read those short stories."

She made a face. "It's not that I don't want to read them, but I have read them. Going through to pull out citable material is boring as fuck."

I chuckled. "Fine, then tell me what to make." I opened the fridge wider so she could slide up next to me and look. This close, I couldn't miss the smell of her shampoo or the faint hint of the lotion she used. The light from the fridge showed the bare hints of yellow around the bruises on her face. It was almost gone.

Though it would be a long time before I forgot where it had been.

"Hmm," she said, chewing her lower lip as she looked at what was in there. "We can make hot sandwiches. Jeremy got us a lot of roast beef and roasted turkey slices with swiss cheese. So we could even do open faced sandwiches. Or…" She nodded to the freezer. "He got us a bunch of appetizers we could throw in the oven to cook."

"Sure, but what do you want?" I raised my eyebrows.

Lips pursed, she shifted her weight from foot to foot. "Breakfast for dinner?"

"Bacon, eggs?" I guessed.

"Fried potatoes too?"

Well… "With you telling me what to do? What could go wrong?"

Remind me to *never* ask that question again. The eggs were about the only thing that came out right and easy. She promised scrambled eggs, which we could add cheese to after, would not be remotely hard.

But they were also the last thing I made. Cutting up the potatoes was easy, and Frankie gave me very specific instructions on the size of the cuts. The fact that she started punking me about five minutes into that process made it all the sweeter. Anything not cut correctly I had to redo.

Totally fine. I'd do my penance.

I got the oil heating, and then once it was sizzling, in the potatoes went. When she had to keep shifting to get out of my way, I paused to wipe off my hands, and then picked her up and set her on the opposite counter. It was the first time in a while that I'd had my hands on her for more than just a quick hug or to hand her something.

Her swift intake pulled my attention to her lips, both of which gleamed as she licked them.

"Just creating a safer workspace," I assured her, though it took me a minute to convince my hands to slide down to her legs and then off. "Need to do the bacon now."

Maybe that was why I nearly burnt the bacon and set off the smoke alarms because I forgot to turn on the extractor, and the cats lost their minds racing away from the noise.

The potatoes were a little too crispy in the process, too. Also, oil spatter burns suck.

But the smile on Frankie's face and her laughter?

Worth every aching inch.

It was raining again when I opened up the backdoor to get the smoke out. Frankie still had a hand over her mouth, laughing, as I waved the door. "Well," I told her, having to say it louder over the alarms. "Now I know how hard it is."

That just made her laugh harder.

When we finally sat down to eat though, she ate every piece of the bacon. Even the blackened bits, and her smile as she crunched the potatoes helped, but seriously, I just enjoyed the bubble of tension bursting.

She nudged me with her toes. "Okay," she said after she ate the last bite of eggs. "You did good. But I think we aim a little lower next time."

I frowned. "How much lower?"

"Hmm…sausage and waffles?"

I snorted.

"Hey, I'll have you know waffles are easy with a waffle iron."

"Good to know."

She hung out while I cleaned up, and then we retreated back to the living room, and I helped her get settled into place with her book and then went to get my guitar out.

"Do you mind if I play?"

"I never mind if you play," she reminded me. That was true. She never had. She'd always been the one to encourage me. "But…I haven't listened to that song you recorded for me yet."

Well, that was a bit of a knee to the balls, but I nodded. "When you're ready," I said. "I meant it. No pressure."

"It's not about being ready…or maybe it is." She ran her finger over the words on the page, mouth twisting as though she was working through her thoughts.

Guitar in hand, I moved back to sit on the sofa and put a hand on her leg. "Hey, you don't owe me any answers. Or explanations. I gave you the song for you. It doesn't have a time limit or a requirement. Just like me. I'm here. I'm going to be here. This is where I want to be."

She lifted those lashes and studied me. It was like she looked right through me. "Why now?" The question came out so quiet, I almost missed it.

Not playing dumb, I turned so I could face her, and when she didn't reject my hand on her leg, I left it there. "Do you want the whole answer right now? Or is it enough that this is where I want to be?"

Was she ready to have the whole answer?

"I want the whole answer," she said slowly. "I…you hurt me, Ian. When you pulled away, and then when you said I didn't know what I wanted or needed."

"I know I did." Admitting it hurt, too. "It was the one thing I didn't want to do, and I did it. I told you shit you probably didn't want to hear, and I can't tell you if I did it to sabotage them or to sabotage myself." Blowing out a breath, I focused on her. "That was the worst part of it. I hurt you. I hurt them. I didn't… It wasn't your feelings I was questioning, Frankie. It was my own."

She straightened a little. The frown tightening her brows worried me, but I didn't flinch under that laser focus.

"I didn't know if I could handle it. All I've ever wanted was to protect you. Protect you from everyone and everything. Even us. Maybe even especially us." Exhaling, I forced myself to meet her gaze and stay there. "I'm not proud of what I did over the summer, of who I became. I wish… Some days, I really wish I could take it all back." Especially the parts involving Sharon.

"And now?"

"Now that's my problem, and I shouldn't make it yours."

"Wrong."

I blinked. "What?"

"Even if we were just friends, friends talk about problems, don't they?"

I didn't want to *just* be her friend, but I nodded. "Always."

"You've told me I could talk to you about anything."

"Yes."

"So, it would seem fair you should be able to talk to me about anything, too."

"I have," I told her. "You're the only one I ever shared my music with. You're still really the only one I share it with."

"That should change," she told me. "Because you're really good."

I chuckled. "I'm all right."

"No, Ian. You're more than all right…you're amazing."

"You just might be biased."

The corners of her lips twitched. "That doesn't make me wrong."

"No," I agreed slowly. "It doesn't."

We sat there for a beat, and she shifted her legs to stretch them out, and then her feet rested against my thigh.

"Think whatever you practice can help me read through here and find the pieces I need to cite?"

I grimaced. "That's a tall order. Especially if you already think it's boring as fuck."

Her grin lit me up. "Well, I'm prepared to be entertained." The dare in her eyes made me smile.

Challenge accepted.

"All right then," I said, and settled the guitar as she adjusted her feet. When she would have pulled them away, I caught one. "You can leave them there." At the flicker of doubt, I added, "Trust me?"

Though she didn't say anything, she left her feet to press against my leg, and awareness of her sizzled over me as I double-checked the tuning. It took me a few chords to warm up my hand, but when I started to play, Frankie never once looked back at the page.

Maybe I should feel bad about interrupting her homework, but I enjoyed her attention way too much.

And maybe I could tell her with music what I couldn't in just words.

Maybe.

Chapter Fourteen
DANGEROUS CURVE AHEAD

FRANKIE

Something smothered me. Even as I fought against it, the pressure bore down and I couldn't get air into my lungs. They burned, and my eyes teared as I flailed.

"Frankie."

No. I had to get away. I had to…

"Frankie."

Eyes snapping open, I jerked back against the pillows as I stared into the darkness. Then a light shone from Ian's phone, and he had hold of my left hand in his right. There was a red mark on his jaw, and all of a sudden, my wrist hurt like hell.

A groan escaped, and I closed my eyes.

"It's okay," he said gently. "It's really okay. You awake now?"

"Yeah?" I tugged my fingers from his grasp to scrub at my face. Terror churned in my stomach. Unease slid along my spine. Adrenaline pounded in my veins.

"You don't sound too certain," Ian murmured, the bed depressing under his weight as he sat next to me. It was the first night since I'd come home that I slept alone.

I sighed and dropped my hand back to his. When he cradled my hand and then closed his fingers around it, I held on a little tighter. "I'm not." My heart raced, and even though I tried to calm my breathing, it was still coming in fierce pants.

The light from his phone cut out and plunged us back into darkness. "Can I help?"

Archie had texted that something had come up and he might be late getting back over if he made it at all. But he promised to see me first thing in the morning. Jake and Coop hadn't come back either, though they'd texted as well. If I'd asked, they'd have come. But I got it. They were trying to give me and Ian time together.

"Will you lie up here for a little while?" I didn't want to ask. Hell, I didn't want to push, but I didn't want to be alone either.

He shifted without letting go of my hand and put his phone beside the bed, and then he stood. For a second, I thought he would retreat back to his pallet on the floor. Then he lifted the comforter and slid in next to me. For that, he had to let go of my hand.

"How do you want to…?" he started to ask, but I rolled onto my side as he extended his arm, and then I curled up and put my cheek against his chest as he curved his arm around me. I hadn't really been this close to Ian in a while. Not even in the days when he was here day in and day out. The others had let me curl up with them, but he hadn't.

Eyes closed, I burrowed my nose against his shirt as he brushed some of the hair away from my face. His heart beat a steady tattoo. Curled up on my left, I rested my right wrist against his mid-section.

"If that's too heavy…"

"Shh," he said. "Nothing about you is too heavy." Then he pressed a kiss to my forehead. "I should have been right here to chase that dream away before it got to you."

"It's okay," I told him. In the dark, it was just easier. "I don't even know what I'm dreaming about. It's always shadows and running. Sometimes I can't breathe. Most of the time, I'm just afraid."

He sighed.

"It stopped for a couple of nights." So maybe not every night anymore.

"But tonight you were alone." Self-recrimination darkened his tone.

"Not alone." He smelled like Ian. Like sunshine and hot days. Like grass and play. There was always this clean warmth to him. I rubbed my cheek against him. "You're here."

When he pressed his lips to the top of my head, I held my breath for a minute. A few weeks earlier, I'd understood what those little gestures meant. I craved them. Now…

"I'm here," he murmured in agreement. "Think you can go back to sleep?"

I had no idea. "What time is it?"

He shifted, barely, then there was a flash of the light from his phone but I kept my eyes closed. The gentle cadence of his heart soothed some of the jagged edges left by the dream. I could almost see the shadows reaching out, smothering me.

Had Mitch done that? Had he tried to smother me during that time I couldn't remember? My brain kept spinning off little what if and had he questions. Had he chased me down that hallway? The guys told me I was in a little event room not far from where we'd been having the dance. But I couldn't picture it in my head.

I couldn't picture anything. I could barely remember the bathroom. Had there been other girls in there? Where had I run into Mitch? In the bathroom?

"It's a little after three," he murmured, and the light clicked off again.

"Plenty of time to get more sleep."

As tired as I was, sleep was the furthest thing from my mind. Maybe I could just lie here and rest while Ian slept. That would keep the nightmares at bay, right?

I don't know how long we lay there, Ian stroking my hair and my head tucked against him, before he said, "You're not going back to sleep are you?"

"I want to," I lied. Well, not lied really. I would like to go back to sleep if I was sure I wouldn't have another bad dream. Even if my pulse had slowed and my breathing deepened, I couldn't shake the claustrophobic notion of being smothered.

"Want to talk about it?" The offer was there, a gentle olive branch. Would I take it?

Did I want to take it?

"Not too much to talk about," I admitted. "It's all shadows, like I said."

"Shadows and running," he said. "Do you remember anything else about it?"

"I can't breathe." Was it a hand over my mouth? Something else? "Not through my nose or my mouth. I'm fighting, but I can't get it to stop. Then I'm running again."

He flexed his arm around me, and then he cupped my face with his free hand. "No one is smothering you, I promise."

I laughed. "You make that sound like a metaphor."

"Eh." The grimace in his tone echoed loudly. "I'm not going to try and psychoanalyze anything. Doing that before got me into trouble."

"Before?" Okay, I was going to keep digging into this apparently. It was better than digging into my dreams. I hated horror movies, and those nightmares were like living through my own personal one.

Ian went quiet. When I shifted a little closer, he pressed his lips to my forehead again. "You asked me why now."

"I did."

"I said a lot of things."

"You did."

"I really suck at this."

I smiled. "No you don't."

"I do," he admitted. "I suck at it where you're concerned. I want to say all the right things. I want…I want to make it easier for you. Better. I want you to have everything. I want…"

I bit my lower lip and waited him out.

"I want to take back asking my dad for advice and then listening to him. He pointed things out to me, and maybe they were true, maybe they weren't. But I made the mistake of trusting what I was afraid of instead of trusting you."

Lifting my head, I tried to stare at him in the dark, but I couldn't really make out anything other than the outline of his nose. The cats were wandering back onto the bed. Tiddles had settled by my lower back, and Tabby moved her way up onto my pillow, but since I was more lying on Ian than it, I didn't care.

"It isn't just now," he continued, and even though I couldn't see his eyes, I could feel the weight of his gaze. "I was pushing you away because I thought it was the right thing to do, but I never wanted to push you away. When you walked away, you were right to do it. I wanted to undo what I'd done, but I didn't know how."

"Okay," I said, blowing out a breath and settling my cheek against his chest again.

"Okay?"

"Yeah. You suck at this." There was a beat of silence, then his chest began to rumble as he chuckled.

"I do," he said, still chuckling. "I really do."

"I'm not much better though."

"You are far better than me," he whispered. "You didn't shy away from telling me what you wanted."

"What do you want?"

"You."

Simple question.

Simple answer.

"That's what you thought you wanted before," I reminded him.

"Not just thought. It's what I've always wanted. But I gotta earn that right again."

"You have to earn the right to want?" I frowned. That didn't even make sense.

"No, I have to earn the right to pursue you," he said. "I still want you. It isn't just now. I wanted you before Homecoming. I wanted you at Homecoming. I was ready to take any scrap of attention I could get that night, as long as you were having a good time."

"I did have fun," I said slowly, sucking in a deep breath of him. "Until I wasn't."

"I'm glad for the first part." But regretted the second. Well, we all kind of did.

"How is your hand?" I hadn't really asked. I should have asked more.

"It's fine," he said, then stroked my cheek with his thumb. "Barely notice it right now, and I can still play."

"You sounded great last night."

"Thanks for letting me interrupt your homework."

Tiddles began to purr, and my eyes were actually getting heavier, so I closed them and tucked my cheek a little closer to Ian. "Thanks for playing for me."

"My pleasure, Angel." He whispered that last bit.

"Ian…"

"I know, you said I shouldn't call you that anymore."

No, that wasn't what I said exactly. "I was mad."

"I know. I'll stop if it really bothers you." But he didn't want to. That much was clear.

I wanted to trust him. I wanted to believe him. A part of me did.

But another part of me still reeled from having that rug yanked out from under me. "Nothing's changed," I reminded him. "All those things you said—all the stuff that happened. It's all still there, and I'm still dating the other guys."

"I know."

"So maybe…"

"If you want me to stop, just say the word, Frankie."

Stop being my friend? Stop chasing me? Stop calling me Angel? There were a lot of ways to interpret that. But I didn't want to parse it out or pull it apart.

Instead, I said, "Can we pretend?"

"Pretend what?"

"That it's a few weeks ago, and we're still okay."

"We can pretend it's now and we're okay, too." The suggestion made me smile a little. "We can pretend it's now and we're going to be okay, and even if we're not, I'm not going anywhere. I'm here for you."

Tears burned in my eyes. "Okay."

"Then we're pretending it's now or then?" Was that a hint of laughter in his voice?

"Now," I whispered, and he tightened his arms around me. "And we're going to be okay."

"You got it." A sigh escaped alongside the words. Still petting my hair, he began to hum. It was soft at first, but I recognized it. It was one of the songs he recorded for me the night everything went sideways and bad meatloaf were in the house. Songs I'd listened to on repeat until I went to sleep.

Gradually, the adrenaline and the tension drained away as his humming turned into singing. He was on his third song, I thought, when I dropped off. Good to his word, he was still there when I woke up a few hours later.

So was Coop, who leaned in the doorway smiling at us. He mouthed the word 'coffee' and motioned with a thumb behind him.

He could look smug since he'd made coffee. Coop helped me shower and then blow dry my hair while Ian showered. We didn't revisit our middle of the night conversation, but things were a little easier.

It wasn't until we were getting ready to leave that I found out Ian was riding with Coop and me. And I found out what happened to his bike.

"So what happened to his bike?" Rachel asked me after we found a table at the fish place and settled in—me with my beer-battered fish planks and fries while she had her chicken fingers and equally large stack of fries.

"Apparently, someone slashed the tires, broke the kickstand, and dropped it while also breaking the side mirrors on it." They hurt his bike. That pissed me off.

"That sucks," Rachel muttered with a shake of her head. "And sounds expensive to fix."

I nodded. "It's at the bike shop now. Ian's taking it really well, almost philosophical." He took it better than I had. I was incensed on his behalf. While he hadn't said anything about why it happened—they were acting like it was just a random act—I had my suspicions. The swift change of subject when I asked about it suggested I was right.

"Could be karma," Rachel suggested, but at my scowl, she raised both her hands. "Or not."

"Sorry," I muttered, and added some malt vinegar to my fish. The nice thing about this stuff was I could eat most of it with my fingers so the broken wrist didn't get in the way. I used a plastic fork to break up the fish though.

"Hey," Rachel said, nudging my foot with hers. "It's fine. I just like to give them shit. Hell, I'm stunned they let you come out to eat with me by yourself. I mean, I did promise to have you home before dark, but still."

Another difficulty you don't consider with a broken wrist. The fact you have to put your fork down to flip someone off. "They aren't that bad."

"Didn't say they were bad." Pointing one of her chicken fingers at me, she added, "You don't have to be so defensive. You like them. They have been less asshat-ish of late, and they've been looking after you. I'm the critical one, remember?"

I met her gaze across the table and sighed. "I didn't think I was being defensive." Normally, Rachel's attitude about the guys made me laugh. "It's just been…a really long couple of weeks."

"I can imagine. Or maybe I can't. But I'm here, if you want to talk or to mock. I'm very good at mocking."

Despite the hint of bite in her words, all I found was concern in her eyes.

"I haven't really talked to anyone else…the guys have been really protective, which is nice. Maria's not avoiding me exactly. I've seen her a few times, but she always keeps her distance." I snorted. "Even Sharon has kept her distance." I'd run into her a half-dozen times easily, but she changed course.

"Good," Rachel said. "Maria's worried about you, too. I don't talk to the troll queen, but I do talk to Maria. She wants to reach out, but she doesn't know if you want to hear from her." She took a bite of her chicken finger as I reached for my soda. "Kind of like Cheryl." The last bit came out quieter than the rest. "This is me, by the way, not pushing. But Cheryl's a wreck."

I paused mid-bite.

"And I got the impression you don't want to talk to her." She took another bite of her French fries, but the weight of her stare was a tangible thing. "So, tell me what you need, and I'll make sure it happens."

"I don't… I don't really know," I admitted. "Cheryl…makes me uncomfortable."

"She wouldn't hurt a fly," Rachel countered.

"She gave me the drugged water." That fact had been swirling around in my head since I woke up in the hospital. *Cheryl* gave me that water. Not Mitch. Not some random guy. Not some stranger I didn't know. *Cheryl*. "She gave it to me when I was talking to you and Skylar."

Rachel's expression tightened.

"I haven't even asked you about Skylar. Sorry."

"Sky's fine," Rachel assured me. "Seriously. She's great. And…yes, she gave you the water, but Mitch gave it to her." The care with which she made that statement had me studying her this time. There was a marked hesitation there.

"Why would he need to drug his own girlfriend?" The thought made my stomach lurch and just killed what was left of my appetite. The couple of times this had come up with the guys, there'd been a near killing rage in Jake's eyes, and even Coop had vibrated with hostility. They were even more adamant that she stay away from me than I was.

"I don't know," Rachel admitted. "I have no idea why he would or if he has in the past."

Or if he was the one who drugged Maria. "Did Maria talk to you?"

"About what happened to her?" Rachel nodded once. "It came up. She got really trashed after Homecoming and after what went down. Skylar and I made sure she got home. She confessed a lot of stuff."

Chills skated over my skin. "Does she think it was Mitch?"

"She doesn't know. I think that's probably what freaks her out even more. Fuck." She exhaled the last word with the same kind of vehemence rolling through me. "Maria said she tried to warn you—that she thought it might have been your guys for a while, but after the thing with Mitch…"

"It was never my guys." The possessiveness that surged through me had me glaring. *"Never."*

"I know." Reaching across the table, Rachel took my hand. "I'm on your side. Which—even if it makes me throw up in my mouth a little—means I'm on their side, too."

Tears burned in my eyes a little as a laugh escaped. "Don't make yourself sick."

"Oh I'm made of stronger stuff than that," she teased. "I might even say one whole nice thing to them next week."

"Not tonight?" After all, Rachel had picked me up at my apartment to go out to eat. Jake and Ian weren't there because they had to get ready for the game.

Archie had to go back to his place right after school, and I'd told Coop if Archie wasn't back by the time Rachel and I were done, I was going to ask her to take me over there.

Something had been distracting Archie all week. They might be looking after me, but it was up to me to look after them, too.

She made a face. "Do I have to say something nice tonight?"

"Maybe. To one of them?"

"To one of them? Hmm…do I get to pick which one?"

"Nope." I reached for my soda.

"Fine," she said with a roll of her eyes. "I'll say something nice to *one* of them. Your choice."

"Thank you, Rachel."

"You're welcome." She sobered, then nudged my plate. "You need to eat."

"I'm not really hungry."

"See, now I know something is wrong. You always eat."

My appetite had its ups and downs.

"Talk to me?" Rachel said. "Or I can… you know, give you all the gossip. Tell you dirty stories. Ooo. I know, we can mock that truly hideous fucking dress the troll was wearing today. Though I'm pretty sure that Peppermint Patty was really trying to top her."

Had I even seen Sharon today? "I must have missed it."

The very real shock on Rachel's face was near comical as she pulled out her phone and flipped it to her Instagram account, then held it over for me to see.

The dress was yellow, which in and of itself was not a crime. However, it had… "Is that gingham?" I hadn't seen a yellow checked dress except on television in forever.

"Right?" She widened her eyes, almost goggling. "Hold on to your boy shorts." She swiped to the next picture. Patty was dressed in some hideous orange thing.

"Did they lose a bet?"

In all the years I'd gone to school with them, I could honestly say they had fashion sense and taste. Both of them. But…

Suddenly, Rachel smirked.

"Oh my god, they lost a bet."

"Maybe," she answered, all innocence now.

"What did you do?" I demanded.

She nudged my plate. "Eat and I'll tell you."

"Fine," I stabbed a piece of fish and stuffed it in my mouth. It had tasted divine earlier, but my lack of appetite wasn't thrilled with the effort.

"And I bet them on who would be voted off of the Disguised Vocalist this week. They lost."

"Seriously?"

She shrugged. I was behind. "Hey, I can recognize talent, and they were basing it on costume."

"I can't believe they took that bet."

"Sucks to be them. Personally, I enjoyed watching them walk around all day like that. Couldn't happen to a pair of nicer bitches. Besides, I could have done a whole lot worse. But I was all nice and shit."

I snorted. But when she grinned, I laughed and shook my head. "Remind me never to bet you on anything."

"You never have. But then, I wouldn't do something like that to you. Even when you're oblivious, you're not rude."

Yeah. That was something, I supposed. Then she showed me the pictures again, and we both laughed.

I managed to eat about half the food before we circled back to Cheryl. "I don't know what to tell you," Rachel said. "I don't want to think she was involved."

"I don't either."

"But I'll fucking ask her."

"Rachel…"

"No, I like her. I always thought she was too ditzy to do a terrible thing, but…I don't see Mitch drugging her either. They were crazy about each other." Then she grimaced. "I don't want to talk about that jackass, and to think I actually liked the son of a bitch. I guess my taste is questionable."

"I still don't…" I didn't want to finish that thought.

"You still don't what?"

"Don't know why he did it."

"Because he's an asshole."

"But why? He's good-looking, right? He had a girlfriend."

"Assholes don't always need a reason to be an asshole, Frankie. It might be a mistake to look for one, too."

I sighed.

"You done?" She motioned to my food, and I nodded. When I would have cleaned up, she smacked my left hand lightly and stacked everything on her tray. After she disposed of it, we headed out to her car. It was still cloudy and damp, though it hadn't rained, and the temperature was chilly enough to make me glad Jake had dumped his letterman's jacket on me earlier in the day.

Thankfully, Rachel only teased me a little bit about it when she picked me up. Once we were in her car, she asked, "Where to?"

I checked my phone. No message from Coop. Or Archie. So I texted Archie. "One sec?"

"Sure."

Me

You make it to my place yet?

Archie

Sorry, babe. Still at the house. Might be a bit.

Me

Mind if I have Rachel drop me there?

I could just drop in on him. But I didn't want to intrude. His mom might be there, and that was not a position I wanted to put Archie into.

The three dots indicating he was responding seemed to take forever before his message came through.

Archie

You never have to ask. You on your way now?

"Can you drop me at Archie's?"

"Yep," she said, pulling out.

Me

OMW now. Yes.

Archie

I'll be here.

"So," Rachel said as she drove. "I have to say something nice to rich boy?"

I bit back a smile. "Well, we are going to his house."

"Yeah, but I'm verifying that I have to say something nice to him, 'cause it might take me the whole drive to come up with something."

"Then you should probably practice."

She let out a groan. "The things I do for you."

"Thank you," I said quietly.

"You're welcome," she answered in the same tone. "Now…while I think about what I can say to the entitled…" She paused, then made a face like it actually killed her to say, "…misunderstood rich kid, tell me what else you're doing that I can maybe help with?"

"You're already doing a lot."

"Pfft. Give me more work to do, woman. Make me your slave." She gave me a playful leer at the light.

"Save the dirty stuff for Skylar. Besides, you'd like being my slave too much."

"Yes, I would," she admitted. "Trust me, I'd make sure you enjoyed it, too."

The funny thing about it? She was probably right. "You free next Wednesday at lunch?" I'd been sitting on this one all day.

"I can be. Whatcha need?"

"A ride."

"Tell me more…"

She didn't interrupt me once all the way to Archie's. "I can do that," she promised as we pulled in. She took me all the way up to the house, and Archie came out to meet us. "One sec," she said to me. "I have to do my nice thing."

I bit my lip as she rolled my window down, since Archie was on my side of the car.

"Hey, Archie," she called.

"Hey, Rachel," he said, and his sudden wariness at the appearance of Rachel's smile nearly made me laugh aloud.

"I've been meaning to give you a few pointers on the best way to use your tongue so it's really nice for Frankie…"

Oh.

My.

God.

Rachel grinned at me. "See, I can be nice."

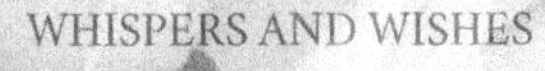

Chapter Fifteen
JUST LIKE HIM

Istole a look at Archie as Rachel waved to us before she pulled down the driveway. His mouth had twisted into a half-grimace, half-smile, even as he suppressed his laughter.

"She means well," I said, trying not to laugh myself. My face was hot, because Rachel hadn't been kidding about her "nice" advice.

"Yeah," he said slowly, then gave me a measuring look. "There something you want to tell me about my tongue?"

If not for the barest hint of a twitch to his lips, I might have died of mortification right then. My shoulders began to shake as the laughter escaped, and I shook my head. "I'm good," I said. "I promise."

"Uh huh." The light in his eyes made me smile wider. The last couple of weeks had been tough, and they'd all focused on me, a lot. "You know, you can tell me if there's something to what she was saying. I'm always willing to test theories."

When he held out his hand, I slid my palm across his and pressed my forehead to his arm as I laughed. "Your tongue is just fine. As I recall, you use it quite well." If it were possible to get heatstroke from embarrassment, I was well on my way.

"Hmm," he murmured, then pressed a kiss to the top of my head. Glancing up, I studied him. While they had been focused on looking after me, I'd tried to pay attention to them, to what was going on, and the last few days, Archie had been distracted.

He had been since Monday, really, and the appearance of our parents at school. Whatever distracted him, he'd been keeping to himself—to protect me, most likely. I hoped he talked to the guys, even if he wasn't confiding in me. But that was why I had Rachel bring me here in the first place. I adored him for wanting to take care of me, but that didn't change the fact that I wanted to take care of him, too.

All of them.

"C'mon," he murmured. "Jeremy is probably fixing something for you right now since I mentioned you were coming this way."

"I just had dinner," I reminded him, and Archie chuckled.

"When has that ever stopped Jeremy? Besides, it might be something with ice cream and cake."

I groaned.

"Or maybe it was brownies." The sidelong look he sent me told me he knew exactly what Jeremy had fixed and he was just teasing me.

"I'll do my best to make sure I don't disappoint him." Once we were inside, he helped me take Jake's jacket off.

"You could never disappoint him," he reminded me. The foyer, with its wide open space and vaulted ceilings leading to the stairs that angled up and then deeper to the larger living and sitting rooms on either side, seemed bigger somehow. "While I wasn't expecting you to come here tonight," he continued. "I'm glad you did."

"Yeah?" Some of my surprise must have shown, not that I hadn't expected to be welcomed, but Archie had said he'd be back at the apartment tonight. In fact, they'd probably all be over after Jake and Ian's game.

"Of course," he said, frowning a bit. "Did something happen?"

"No, I've just been worried about you."

That truly seemed to catch him off guard. He held Jake's jacket by two fingers, even as he caught my left hand in his again. "Worried about me? Babe, I'm fine."

"No," I said quietly, meeting his brown-eyed gaze with a little sigh. "You're not. I saw your face when Mr. Standish and Maddy were at the school on Monday."

"And I saw yours," he reminded me.

"And clearly, we know I'm not all right." He frowned at the comment, but I pressed on, "And you've been…kind of distant. I know I've been preoccupied but—"

"First," he cut me off with a firm look. "You have every right to be preoccupied. There's a lot going on for you, and you come first."

Yeah. That didn't work for me, but I pressed my lips together because he wasn't done.

"Second, I've been working on some things that I wanted to tell you about *after* I lined it up."

"Lined it up?" Line *what* up?

"I think what my grandson is trying to say, and rather indelicately if I might add, Sprout," a new voice announced in a gravelly tone a moment ahead of a tall, steel-gray haired man's approach, "is that he needed to get in touch with me and make sure I could get here. Edward Standish, Sr." He extended his hand. "But you can call me Ted, or Grandpa like Sprout here does."

Sprout.

I glanced from Archie to his grandfather and back. The resemblance was definitely there. Just like the resemblance to "Eddie," but with Ted, at least there was something genial and warm, rather than slick and kind of skeezy. Loosening my grip from Archie's, I took Ted's hand. Fortunately, he didn't seem to mind shaking my left hand. Some people thought it was weird, even if my right arm sported the splint.

"Frankie Curtis, sir. It's very nice to meet you." Stunning really. Archie had called his grandfather? I stared at him as Archie shuffled from one foot to the other and rubbed a hand against the back of his neck.

He looked almost sheepish. "Yeah, Frankie, this is my grandpa. He left me a message yesterday that he would be getting in today."

The last I'd heard, there'd been some falling out with his grandparents, but I wasn't going to ask. "Well, it's really good to meet you," I reiterated. At least Archie's distraction was a good one, right?

"And it's lovely to meet you." He patted my hand once before he let it go. "Sprout was just telling me about you, though he left out some key details. Like how pretty you are." With a wink, the older man clapped Archie on the shoulder.

"Grandpa," Archie groaned. "I told you she was brilliant, funny, and very important to me."

"You did, didn't you?" Ted grinned again, then beckoned to me. "Come on, Frankie. Jeremy was just putting together these hot fudge cake things with brownies. It looks absolutely sinful, and I need to see someone eat it, since my doctors would probably all have a coronaries if I ate that much sugar."

I chuckled.

"Grandpa, if you had a single doctor willing to argue with you, I'd be shocked," Archie countered.

"I didn't say they'd argue, Sprout, I said they'd have coronaries." The older man's humor proved contagious, because even Archie laughed as we headed for the sitting room rather than the dining room. "And I'd say we go eat in the kitchen, but then Jeremy would have an apoplectic fit."

"I do not have apoplectic fits, Mr. Ted," Jeremy said in the primmest tone I'd ever heard out of him. "I do, however, scold quite firmly."

"That's what you kids are calling it these days," Ted said with a smirk so reminiscent of Archie, I had to a hard time not laughing. The older man took a seat in one of the wing-backed chairs while grinning at Jeremy. I got the impression this was not a new argument for them.

"No, sir, it is what you oldsters used to refer to as decorous behavior," Jeremy corrected him, and I smothered another laugh.

Archie caught my hand and drew me over to the loveseat. He tossed the jacket over another chair before sitting down next to me.

Ted snorted, but Jeremy set a cup of coffee down next to him, even as he skipped his gaze to me. "Miss Frankie, it is lovely to see you. I was very glad when Mr. Archie said you were coming over."

"Hi, Jeremy, thank you. Thank you for everything the last couple of weeks, you've been a lifesaver."

"Truly, my pleasure," he insisted. "I have coffee for you, but I could be persuaded to make some hot cocoa. Though the brownies are just out of the oven, and I'll have the hot fudge cake sundaes you so enjoy ready in a moment."

Sometimes, I couldn't get over this man. "The coffee would be great." It wasn't like I had school the next day. Or work yet. "You didn't have to go to all that trouble."

"No trouble at all." He set a cup of coffee down on the low table right in front of me. "I also have the room next to Archie's all set up should you decide to take us up on our invitation to stay." The last he said with a firm look at Archie, who raised both of his hands.

"We've talked about this, Jeremy."

"Yes, Mr. Archie, we have." With that less than subtle reminder, he set Archie's coffee down and then withdrew.

I bit my lip and stole a look at Archie's grandfather, who wore a bit of a bemused expression as he sipped his coffee. "Sprout, would you like me to excuse myself for the evening? Or did you want to continue our conversation?"

Archie shot me a look, then glanced at his grandfather. "After Jeremy brings the sundae, Grandpa, I'd like to continue it, and Frankie can be here for that if she doesn't mind. It involves her, too."

"I didn't mean to interrupt…"

"You didn't," Archie assured me. "Like I said, I wanted to make sure it could happen *before* I told you, but this really does involve you." After a beat, he frowned. "You still good? You comfortable? I should have asked that when you got here…"

"I'm fine, I'm sore and achy, but not hurting." That said, however, I shifted to sit sideways. "But I can call Coop to come and pick me up, or get Jake to swing by after the game. I don't want to interrupt your reunion."

"No," Archie said firmly. "If you need to go somewhere, I'll take you, and you're not interrupting."

He paused on his next words as Jeremy re-entered, and I goggled a little at the tray he carried. I had to shift again so he could place the tray over my lap and present me with the hot fudge cake sundae that had my mouth watering from the smell.

"Jeremy…this looks *awesome*." In addition to the hot brownie square on the bottom and what looked like actual hot fudge poured over a hefty scoop of ice cream, he'd crowned it with whip cream, nuts, and two cherries. There were also two spoons on the tray—thankfully, 'cause no way could I eat all of this on my own.

Well, I could, but I probably shouldn't.

"Enjoy it, Miss Frankie. Mr. Archie may join in when you've had enough."

I wasn't the only one hiding a smile at Jeremy's 'instructions.'

"Can I get you anything else?" Jeremy checked with all of us.

"Thanks Jere," Archie answered. "We're good."

"Feel free to buzz for me if you require anything further." Then he exited as smoothly as he arrived. Even after four years, it was still weird that Jeremy, a butler-cook-house manager and general good guy, seemed always prepared to wait on us.

"Go on," Archie nudged me with an indulgent grin. "Take a bite. I can wait for your chocolate-gasm to dive back in."

My face heated at the tease, particularly when his grandfather chuckled. Still, I settled for just sticking my tongue at Archie rather than retaliating verbally. The first spoonful of hot brownie, cold ice cream, fudge, with a little whip cream and nuts was to die for.

I think my taste buds literally exploded with delight. I was four more bites in before Archie's soft laughter jarred me out of my dessert induced haze.

"Yeah yeah," I mumbled, sure to wipe my mouth with the napkin Jeremy had thoughtfully provided. "Chocolate-gasm achieved. You may proceed."

"You sure?" he asked, still grinning. "I don't mind waiting, and I think Grandpa is just barely holding off sugar shock while you dive in."

Without thinking twice about it, I flipped Archie off, and he cracked up. All at once, my gaze collided with Ted's, and I winced.

"You remind me of Sprout's grandmother," he told me. "She didn't put up with his teasing either."

"Eh, she gave as good as she got." The raw affection in both of their voices made me smile. "Frankie's pretty good about that, too."

Archie and his grandmother had been close. She took him to all those places. Made me wonder what drove his parents and his grandparents apart, or was it losing her that had done it?

Not my place to ask though.

"Anyway," Archie said, after taking another swallow of coffee. He settled a hand on my lower back, just resting it there, and I sighed at the contact, even as I took another bite. "I called because I turn eighteen soon."

"In a little over a week," Ted agreed. "I'm aware. Planned to call you first thing that morning. Then I got your message."

The corner of Archie's mouth quirked up as he began to rub my back in slow, even circles. "It was important. Maybe a little too important to wait."

"Tell me what's going on." Almost at once, the jovial man vanished, and one of sober seriousness faced us, even as he set his coffee cup aside. "You might also tell me where your parents are, while we're at it."

"Muriel's at a spa retreat in Arizona," Archie answered in this flat tone he got when he discussed his parents. I set my spoon down and rested my hand on his thigh in solidarity. He cast me a quick smile before looking at his grandfather. "Edward could be around, or he could be back in Europe. He's not one for informing me of his itinerary."

No surprise flickered in Ted's dark eyes.

"But what's going on is Edward's taken his latest affair a little far."

Ted spared me the briefest of looks before he focused on his grandson again. I had the sneaking suspicion he knew exactly what Archie was about to tell him.

"He's having an affair with Frankie's mother. Allegedly, they've gotten a place together."

"Allegedly?" The mild tone betrayed nothing.

"Allegedly," Archie confirmed. "We haven't seen it. Though they've made some effort to try and get Frankie to move in with them."

"But you've refused?" That question he directed to me, and I nodded.

"I'm really not keen on watching my mother crash and burn with a married man. No offense." He was "Eddie's" father after all.

"None taken." Ted tapped an index finger against the arm of his chair, but it was the only real physical reaction to the news. "Sprout, I'm going to need you to start at the top and walk me through this after we get more coffee. Frankie, are you finished with your sundae?"

I'd already been full, but I had made a dent, so I nodded.

"Sprout, you want to clean that up or slide it over here?"

"And risk the wrath of your doctors?" Archie said with a smirk. "I don't think so." He polished off the last few bites easily enough, though he fed more than one to me, and it was a little embarrassing to be fed in front of his grandfather. But the older man didn't seem to be paying attention to us while Archie seemed to need something else to focus on.

After he'd finished and Jeremy had made a pass through with more coffee and retrieved the bowl, he settled back with me tucked next to him as he recounted the whole sordid mess of our parents, from when he found out to when I did, to what had happened in the last few weeks.

Had it really only been a few weeks? It seemed like it had been ages. Then again, Maddy and Edward had been engaged in their affair for far longer than we'd been aware of it, so…maybe that was part of it. I had no idea. Listening to Archie though, I felt bad for him. The distance between him and his father was so extreme, I doubted it would ever be repaired.

Honestly, I didn't think he wanted to repair it.

Not that I could blame him. As much as I loved my mom? I really didn't like her. After the last few weeks? That dislike had grown. I didn't think Archie even had the love aspect to fall back on.

Throughout Archie's whole explanation, Ted sat quietly, sipping his coffee. When we got to Homecoming, I braced for it, but Archie kept it simple. Detailing that I'd ended up in the hospital after my water had been drugged and I'd been assaulted, and how long it took Archie and Jeremy to figure out where our parents were.

Finally, he summed it up with Edward's threat following their visit to the school on Monday and the uncomfortable discussion in the park. He left out my suit for emancipation, though he did admit he'd paid for my apartment for the next several months to make sure it was done, and nothing Edward could do would touch that money or the place.

It had already seemed like a lot that Archie had done it in the first place, but some of the whys behind it had me biting my lip. He didn't have to pay for several months, but wanted to make sure I was secure. That nothing our parents did would dislodge me if I wanted to stay there.

"That's about it," Archie said. "After I left the park, I sent you the message. Edward can cut me off. I don't care about that. Muriel is just as likely to open the floodgates if he does. The money I don't care about."

"But protecting your friends, you do," Ted summarized, then turned a studying look on me. "Protecting Frankie."

"Exactly."

"Your trust doesn't fully vest for a few years."

"I'm aware of that."

Hands steepled together, Edward sat back in his chair.

"But you will be able to access roughly twenty-five percent of it beginning on your eighteenth birthday."

"Can Edward block it?"

"He could try," Ted said with a mirthless chuckle. "But the terms of the trust are ironclad, Sprout. Neither Edward nor Muriel have control over the funds in the trust. The only control they have…"

Archie tensed next to me.

"…is over whether you can access it at eighteen. They'd have to prove you were too immature to handle the money though, and I don't see any evidence of that. You do well in school. You've applied to colleges, correct?"

"Yes, sir."

"Your attendance continues to be stellar?"

"Well, with a minor lapse recently when I was needed elsewhere, yes, sir. My GPA is good."

"And the reasons you left Andover?"

"Those were always me, not the school," Archie stated. "I didn't want to stay there, and I thought I'd give public school a shot. Neither of them argued."

Curling my fingers around Archie's, I frowned. The more he spoke, the more I hated his parents.

"Sprout, you never explained it to me."

Archie sighed, glancing at me.

"I can go," I offered.

"No, it's just…it's lame." He made a face. Touching his tongue to his teeth, he said, "Promise not to think less of me?"

"I'm sorry, didn't you meet me in the days of glitter in my hair and baking spirit boxes weekly? How could I possibly think less of you?"

"You were adorable," Archie stated, as if it were fact. "Though, I don't miss the glitter."

Me neither. I rolled my eyes, and he chuckled, then focused on his grandfather again.

"I hated the pretentiousness of the school. Everyone was a competitor. The other students were only interested in advancing themselves academically, socially, and financially. I had enough of that when I was with Muriel and Edward. When Nana died…"

"You wanted a real change," Ted said with a much deeper sigh.

"And to go as far from that world as I could get. When Muriel and Edward had that falling out with you and they decided to relocate a portion of Standish here to Texas, this worked." Archie shrugged. "Best decision I ever made. Met the guys and Frankie on my first day, and I've never looked back."

His grandfather smiled. "I'm glad to hear that. She would have been proud of you, too, you know. She always worried about you being away the boarding school. Thought it wasn't right you were enrolled so early."

"I didn't mind it. I got to spend weekends with you two."

"We loved that, too." The thickening atmosphere between them seemed too intimate and too personal, but Archie kept a fast hold on my hand so I couldn't excuse myself to let them have that moment. "We really did, Sprout." Leaning forward, Ted glanced from Archie to me and then back again. "I'll get into it with my lawyers. I'll get them removed from your trust."

He frowned.

"Are you both certain he's asked Frankie's mother to marry him?"

Archie nodded. "They've both indicated that, even if Edward and Muriel are hardly divorced and as far as I know aren't planning to divorce."

"But he's living with…Ms. Curtis?" Ted seemed far more diplomatic in his choice of words than I would be under the circumstances. Of course, this really wasn't comfortable for any of us.

"What are you thinking?" Archie asked.

"Just trying to parse what he's up to, Sprout." Rising, Ted focused on me. "It was very nice to meet you, Frankie. I'll be in town for the next few days. Would you two do an old man a favor and join me for dinner sometime this week?"

"Any day but my birthday, Grandpa. I have plans with Frankie."

Not that we'd discussed, but I was glad he was thinking ahead. I wanted to do something for his birthday, too.

"Makes sense to me. Well, if I can help in anyway, you let me know."

I would have let Archie walk him out alone, but he tugged me along, and now that we'd left the uncomfortable stuff aside, Archie's grandfather turned on the charm. I definitely saw the resemblance.

"You know, I could get us a time at the club this weekend. I'm sure they'll make arrangements for me. You and Frankie could come up, we'll play a round, and Frankie can enjoy a spa if she'd like or join us on the greens."

"Golf?"

Archie groaned.

"I love golf."

"He means real golf, babe. Not mini-golf."

"I know what he meant," I countered, sticking my tongue at him. "I can't really play right now but…could we drive around in one of the fun carts?"

"I like this one, Sprout. Keep her around." Ted grinned, and Archie let out another groan, but it was more in amusement than aggrieved. "Yes, young lady, we will definitely have a cart. If we want to get in a bit of trouble, we could play bumper carts too."

That set both of them off laughing, and the three of us stood in the darkened drive for another fifteen minutes as Ted recounted Archie's learning to drive one of the golf carts for the first time and that they'd ended up having to buy both because Archie insisted on treating it like bumper cars.

It was adorable.

After he left, Archie glanced at me. "Thanks for hanging out with us."

"I like him."

"Me, too," Archie admitted. "You would have loved my grandmother."

I already did.

He sighed.

"Did your father really threaten you?"

"I'm used to it. Grandpa will help. I knew he would. Muriel wouldn't let Edward take away all the funds, but I don't want you in the middle of whatever pissing contest is coming."

Instead of going back inside, we walked along the side of the house and followed the second drive around toward the pool and the gardens.

"You know, you always told us that your parents and your grandparents had a falling out, but you never said over what…and I didn't realize you changed schools because of your grandmother."

"I didn't talk about it as much then. It was still pretty fresh, and I meant what I said in there, I don't regret it." His phone buzzed, and he pulled it out of his pocket. "One sec, babe, just telling the guys we're still here. Jake and Bubba's game is over."

It had gotten a lot later than I realized.

"Huh," Archie said as he tapped away. Crossing my left arm over to hold my right biceps, I watched the way the light of the phone played over his face. He was chewing on his lower lip, and there was just enough scruff on his cheeks to make him look older. "They won. Both seem a little surprised, but they might make playoffs yet. Both lead teams lost tonight, which brings them up closer."

I chuckled. "Oh, they might hate that." At least to hear Jake and Ian talk about it now.

Archie shot me a look. "Right?"

"But it would be kind of awesome if they did get a championship." They'd gotten so close the year before.

He typed a couple more things, then held up his phone. "Smile."

I grinned, but crossed my eyes and then stuck out my tongue at the last second before he snapped the picture. He snorted.

"I'm still sending it."

"I'm okay with it." He finished, then shut off his phone and slid it back into his pocket before holding his hand out to me. "Walk with me for a bit longer? I can tell you those stories if you want."

Clasping his hand, I smiled. "That sounds nice."

It really did.

Chapter Sixteen
FOUR STORIES

Fingers interlocked with mine, Archie headed toward the garden gate. It really had turned into a nice night. The rain had cooled everything down. The breeze was chilly, but not terrible.

"You know Andover," Archie explained, "was a boarding school. Kind of exclusive, though not like some of the European schools where you live there for the whole term, and only go home on breaks. If you had family local, you could leave on the weekends. Edward and Muriel traveled, a lot, but Nana and Grandpa lived pretty close, just one town over, and they were always willing to scoop me up after my last Friday class, and I'd stay with them until late Sunday evening."

The affection in his voice made me smile. After meeting his grandfather, I got it. He seemed a genuinely nice guy.

"They're wealthy, don't get me wrong. The house…their house was huge. Bigger than this one." He nodded to the place overshadowing the garden as we wandered through the greenery. "But it was warm and always full of life. I told you that Nana took me places all over the world, right?"

It was hard not to smile at the depth of warmth radiating off of him. "Yep.

You had all your adventures."

"Exactly," he said with a low sigh. "The house was always full of items from their adventures. Nana collected all kinds of crap. But every room was stuffed to the gills with memories and stories. Every weekend, she'd tell me a new one. When I was little, she promised we'd add our own stories to the house, and we did."

Squeezing his hand, I rested my head against his shoulder as we walked, and he freed his fingers to slide his arm around me.

"The best part of it was when we would trade stories with Grandpa. He had stories, too. It was just our thing. When she got sick and couldn't travel as much, we still had the stories to tell, and when she died…the house was so empty. All the stories seemed to go with her."

My heart twisted for him.

"I had friends at Andover," he continued, sliding a playful if self-deprecating look in my direction. "Not quite the poor little rich boy you might be imagining. But I didn't have friends like you or the guys. Not really. We were more friends of opportunity. If I was there, I hung out with them, when I wasn't, never really thought about them or vice versa."

"That sounds pretty shitty."

"Eh." He shrugged. "It wasn't horrible. Everyone had their own lives. So, when Nana died and Grandpa didn't want to keep the house…I got it. He offered to hold onto it for me, but…"

"It wasn't the place." I mean, I kind of got that. "You missed her, and without her… I'm sorry, Arch."

"Thanks, babe," he murmured, pressing a kiss to my temple as we paused next to one of the taller shrubs. With care, I wrapped my arms around him and just hugged him. "I miss her. It's weird, I can still smile and laugh about her, and then like tonight…it hits me all over again that I can't just call her up and tell her about you. She would have loved you."

The thickness in his voice tugged at me, and I tightened my arms, even when it pulled uncomfortably on my wrist. Archie pressed his cheek against my hair, even as he tangled his fingers up in it.

"The worst part of it all though," he said, a distinct catch in his voice. Combing his fingers through my hair and keeping me close, he cleared his throat. "The worst part…was Edward sued Grandpa over Nana's will and estate."

I opened my mouth, but no words came out.

"I keep mentioning my trust, I told you that comes from them, right?"

"You've said that. Once, I think. That your grandfather set up the trust for you when you were born, and they added to it over the years, invested in it, but your parents can't touch it."

"Correct." His exhale seemed to shudder through him, and I pressed my nose to his throat. Just wanting to be closer to him. "They never seemed to care, until Nana's estate added to the trust. She didn't leave anything to Edward or Muriel. Apparently…apparently, Nana thought that the trust they'd given Edward when he was twenty-one was sufficient. The rest would go to me, and I have a feeling that he saw the slight as something that would then play out with Grandpa."

"So they sued him?" What the hell?

"I don't know," Archie admitted. "At the time, I didn't get it, and then they informed me I wouldn't be seeing him again. They were making a total break. While I have talked to Grandpa a few times since then, usually on my birthday, he's kept his distance until I told him I needed his help."

"All this right before you started at school?"

"Well, that summer," he said. "I know the differences between them aren't my fault and have nothing to do with me. Grandpa cut them off as much as they cut him off. Losing contact with me was retaliation for him cutting them off."

Ugh.

"That's such a mess."

Leaning away from me, Archie glanced down. "That's kind of my whole family. Still think you corner the market on having the bad parent?"

I couldn't help my smile. "Well, we've kind of always had that in common, haven't we?"

"Yeah," he said, then brushed hair away from my face. His fingers lingered over the remnants of that bruise on my face. "I never realized how much until the last few weeks. Just always knew you were the girl who gave me a place to be that first day. You became my anchor. Probably not sexy to admit that."

"I kind of like it."

"Yeah?" He raised his brows.

"Well…you guys have all been my anchors, I'm just glad I got to do that for you before everything went kind of crazy and I turned into a walking disaster."

Eyes narrowed, Archie cupped my cheek. "You've always been that for us. You're like the glue that makes this all work. I know we made some shitty calls…but you are not a walking disaster. You're amazing. Beautiful. Strong. Fierce. A little kooky." His lips twitched. "But you're my kind of kooky."

When he dipped his head and brushed his lips against mine, I leaned right into the contact. Nothing in his kiss demanded, it just gave. Gentle. Caring. It made my eyes burn a little at how slow and easy he was. It ended far too soon for my liking, but this wasn't about me.

Archie was hurting, too.

"So you called your grandfather?"

"Sent a message," Archie said. "I wasn't sure if he was in the States or not. He works more now than when Nana was alive, says it keeps him busy." He licked his lips. "Either way, I needed to make sure you were protected so if Muriel and Edward do decide to cut me off, I can still take care of you."

Nose wrinkled, I fisted his shirt. "Well, my apartment rent is paid up for the next few months, and you're already staying over there a lot."

He chuckled. "Telling me that you'll take me in if I find myself homeless?"

"In a heartbeat."

"Would you support me? 'Cause I'm not sure about this getting a job crap."

I laughed. "It's not crap, and you'd be fine."

Arm still around me, he started us walking again. "You got a job when you were fifteen."

"I was almost sixteen, Marsha just *trained* me while I was fifteen on a really part-time basis."

"Then you started working your ass off at sixteen. Frankie, I've never had a job."

True.

"Then get one."

He snorted. "Just like that?"

"Coop is delivering food, so is Jake. Coop worked at a store before that. Jake used to mow lawns. He and Ian both—all the lawns they mowed." Three years running, those guys had mowed more lawns than I cared to count, and they'd made good money doing it.

"So I think it's a little late in the year to start mowing lawns and not sure I'd be any good at delivering food," he admitted with a wry smile. "Maybe I'll come get a job at Mason's and work with you."

I laughed. "Well, at the rate I'm going, I'm not going to have a job."

"Nah, Marsha loves you."

She did. But it was hard to do anything with my wrist all locked up in the splint, and they might yet put it in a cast.

"You know it scares the hell out of me if I can't go back to work, I'm going to have to figure out a way to do it even with this…"

"Woah," Archie said, leading me toward one of the benches nestled in the garden. It was identical to the one I'd sat on with Rachel the night of the party.

It seemed like a million years ago.

"First, no matter what happens, you're going to be okay." Twisting on the bench to face me, he pulled his knee up and it pressed against my thigh, even as he took hold of my left hand. "When do you go back to the doctor about the wrist?"

"Monday morning. Coop was going to take me."

"Let me do it," he said. "I'll take you, that way I can also make sure the bill is paid."

"Archie…"

"Yeah, I know, I don't have to pay for everything. You don't want me for my money. You have *never* wanted me for my money or been anything more than exasperated with me when I spend it. As long as I have it, let me use it to do this. You're worrying about everything…"

"If they put this in a cast, it could be another four weeks, maybe longer, and then there's the PT after." It all cost money. So much money, and it would keep adding up.

"Frankie," he said, squeezing my hand, and his tone accompanied by the hard look in his eyes demanded I listen. "You got a scholarship."

"Yes, but…"

"You got a hell of a scholarship."

I had. I'd been over the moon about it.

"And didn't you just get offered that internship that could lead to more grants?"

I had but…

"You have a lot already in savings."

"But life is bills, Archie…"

"Okay. How much?"

I glared at him, and he blinked back at me, seemingly undisturbed by my irritation. "You can't just pay for everything."

"Sure I can, as long as I have it and you need it, what the hell else am I going to do with it? Frankie, I just told you I've never had a job. You're right, I need to get one. I need to understand what it is to work for a living. But I also have money. Okay fine, my *family* has money."

"I'm not my mother."

"No," he said fiercely, sliding a hand up to cup my nape. "You're nothing like her. Look, I'm not making excuses for them or anything. This—you and me? We're not them. Who they are and what they are to each other, it has *nothing* to do with *us*."

I swallowed.

"Dammit."

He blew out a breath. "What? C'mon, babe, I'm trying to fix this, work with me here."

"I came here to be here for you, not so you have to fix it for me." Ugh. The whole reason I'd come to the house tonight was because I was worried about him, and we were right back to discussing my problems.

"Well, I happen to like fixing your problems," he told me tartly. "So deal with it, buttercup."

I scowled at the mere mention of that nickname, and he grinned. "You don't get to enjoy me being annoyed."

"Why not?" He raised his brows. "Get pissed off at me, Frankie. Snap at me. Thump me. I can take it."

I let out a little scream, and he actually laughed at me.

Asshole.

"I love that look on your face," he told me, stroking his thumb along my neck. "I love it when you push back and put me in my place. You have *never* been a pushover."

I snorted. "Really?"

"Really," he confirmed. "You set all the rules. All the boundaries. The only thing I've ever done was try to play inside them."

"Bull. Shit."

I spit each syllable out with emphasis, and he laughed.

That was it. I pulled my hand out of his and thumped him. His grin widened—if it was even possible to be wider than he was already grinning—as he cupped my face and kissed me.

Not a sweet, gentle kiss, but a hard, fierce kiss. It was all tongue, teeth, and heat. It was impossible not to kiss him back or to fist his shirt. My wrist protested when I tried to reach for him with my right hand and then had to set it down, but he chased my tongue with such a singular focus, I almost forgot I'd been irritated with him.

Almost.

In between biting nips, I panted, "This doesn't mean I'm not mad."

"I know," he said before closing the gap and sealing his lips to mine. Heat scorched through my system. Archie tasted like chocolate and coffee. With a groan, I moved to stand, and he pulled back and straightened.

"Hey…"

"Hey," I answered with a breath before straddling his lap, placing one knee on either side of his thighs on the bench. It put my head a little above his. "You don't get to win disagreements with kisses."

"Okay," he said, tracing my lips with his gaze before lifting his eyes to study me. "Can I win them with my tongue? I got some advice earlier…"

Laughter burst through me, and I tilted my head back. "You're impossible."

"No, Frankie, I'm infinitely possible. But I love to make you smile and to laugh…"

"…and to piss me off," I mocked him.

"Sometimes," he admitted, squeezing my hips gently. "I hate it when you're sad or lost or lonely. When you push back, when you're fighting, you get so demanding. It's hot."

"What am I going to do with you?"

"Keep me?" Archie suggested.

I huffed out a breath and squinted at him like I needed to think about it. "I suppose."

"You *suppose*?" Outrage blossomed in his voice, but even in the near dark of the garden with its solar lamps scattered around, the gleam in his eyes was clear as day.

"Yeah, I mean, it would be kind of cruel to kick you when you were down."

Eyes narrowed and lips twitching, he asked, "How am I down?"

"Well, you're a man on a mission, worried about spending all your money before it's taken away for what, four or five whole days before your birthday?"

A snort escaped him. "Practically pathetic."

"Right. And I couldn't do it on your birthday."

"No, that would be cruel," he agreed.

"So…I suppose I'll keep you." But I couldn't resist tweaking him a little. "For now."

His mouth slammed against mine as he slid a hand up to fist my hair, and I didn't resist for a second. This was exactly the response I'd been looking for.

"You know what, babe?"

"Hmm?"

"You're…"

The gentle clearing of a throat quieted him, and he leaned slightly sideways to glance behind me.

"Yes, Jeremy?"

My face heated, but I didn't turn around.

"My apologies, Mr. Archie, Miss Frankie. I wanted to inquire as to the evening's plans. Will Miss Frankie be staying over, or will you be taking her home and staying there?"

I bit my lip as Archie glanced at me and grinned. "Want to spend the night? Or want to go back to your place and spend the night there?"

The guys were expecting us back at my place…

"Whatever you want," he reminded me, but…

"Friday nights are your nights."

A quiet kind of joy lit up his face. "You feel safer when everyone is there."

That wasn't entirely true, except…

"We're going back to Frankie's tonight, Jere."

"Very well, Mr. Archie, Miss Frankie." Disappointment hugged those words. "I do expect at least one sleepover this week, perhaps the night before Mr. Archie's birthday so you can have breakfast here, Miss Frankie."

"Jeremy, my man, you have my back, always," Archie said without once looking away from me.

"Absolutely. Now, if you are taking her home, it is late, and she likely hasn't taken any pain meds this evening."

I had to bite my lip to keep from laughing. When I went to stand, Archie helped me up and I glanced to where Jeremy stood. Sure, my face was on fire, but he met my gaze with a gentle smile. "Thank you, Jeremy."

"My pleasure, Miss Frankie. Shall I come by this weekend to collect the laundry?"

"Tell him yes," Archie said, sotto voce. "It will make him happy since he can't make you breakfast in the morning."

I elbowed Archie. "You really don't have to. Archie promised to help, and I'll take pictures."

A delighted look creased Jeremy's face. "Well in that case…"

"I did, huh?" Archie asked.

"Hmm-hmm." I canted my head to look up at him. "You want to spoil me. I want to make sure you have all the skills you need to handle life on your own."

"So a little tit for tat, huh?"

"I don't have any tats." I dared him to say it with Jeremy standing right there.

Something the older man clearly understood as he cleared his throat again.

"Mean," Archie said with a little snap of his teeth before he kissed my nose. "Yes," he continued wrapping his arm around me and looking to Jeremy. "I will be doing the laundry this weekend, so you may need to rescue the wreck I make of it."

We were all still laughing as we made our way out of the garden. Archie left me with Jeremy for a moment while he ran upstairs to grab his bag.

"Jeremy…if I ask you a question about his grandfather, do you think you can answer it?"

"I'm not promising anything, Miss Frankie," he told me. In the light cast by the porch, it was easy to see some of the gray in Jeremy's hair. He didn't have much. A little around his temples gave his darker hair a little more regal appearance. His expression, always kind, sobered as he studied me. "But I shall do my best. You're worried about Mr. Archie."

"He loves his grandfather." Not a question. "I know he wouldn't have reached out to him if he wasn't worried himself. Do you think he can count on him?"

The last thing I wanted was to see Archie disappointed by another member of his family. It sucked on so many levels.

"I believe Mr. Ted will do his absolute best by his grandson," Jeremy told me. "The family is…complicated. The affection, however, is genuine. On both sides."

"So, I shouldn't worry about him?"

Jeremy gave me a considering look, hands folded behind his back. In all the time I'd known him, I don't think I'd ever seen Jeremy stand in anything that wasn't almost attention. Even with all his formality, he was a thousand percent warmer than Archie's parents.

"I can't caution you to not worry. I think someone should worry about Mr. Archie. He would cut off his arm for all of you. He would go to war with his parents for you. His grandfather is different."

Different? Before I could ask what he meant though, Archie appeared through the front door with a duffle bag and his backpack. "I'll talk to you tomorrow, Jeremy."

"Very good, Mr. Archie. You two get some rest and look after Miss Frankie." Though he didn't say anything more, the look he gave me spoke volumes.

"I'll look after Archie," I promised him. "He's gonna be a pro at the laundry thing in no time. I taught Ian to make food. How hard could it be?"

Considering Ian did burn some food, maybe I'd make sure Archie had no whites to wash.

That might be safer.

Jeremy almost smiled.

Score a point for me.

In the car, I sent a text to the guys that we were on our way back, and they lit the phones up with requests.

Jake

Want us to order food? Or can you guys pick some stuff up?

Coop

You're out of milk. Sorry. I'll grab some tomorrow. Pizza?

Ian

Brought over some of my mom's brownies. Wanna grab coffee and do a movie marathon tonight? We're all free tomorrow morning.

We hadn't even made it to the end of the drive. Archie leaned over to read the messages and snorted. "Still time to go back to my room, sleep here, have semi-wild sex, and get spoiled by Jeremy in the morning."

"Tempting—wait, semi-wild?"

"Well…" Archie hedged, even if he was smiling. "I get that you've been a little more active but…"

A little more active. I was definitely active with Coop and Jake. I stole a look at him, eyes narrowed. Had they told him?

"I don't want to push for anything."

They hadn't.

"You wouldn't be pushing, Archie." Sobering, I put the phone down and gripped his arm. "I mean it. I know I've been a mess. But I'm not afraid of you guys. I thought you were all…afraid of me."

Coop had proved that wrong. So had Jake.

"We don't talk about it," Archie said quietly. "You don't bring it up, and I feel like an ass if I try to ask you."

"I don't remember much." At all.

"I know. And I know it bothers you."

I nodded.

"I asked Rachel to take me to a counseling appointment next week," I blurted it out, and he frowned.

"You made an appointment?"

Was he mad about it? "Coop and I went through the names and numbers Denitra gave me. I called a couple of them…the ones that looked like they might be a good fit." I didn't look at him. "One has an opening on Wednesday at lunch time."

"And you asked Rachel to take you."

"You guys haven't really been letting me take my car and…" I held up my right arm.

"Babe, I get that, but I have no problem taking you anywhere you want to go."

I made a face and then looked over at him. "I know you'll think it's stupid, but…you guys have already done a lot, and going to talk to someone is…Mom— Maddy always said Curtises don't do therapy. It's already feeling weird that I'm going to go at all."

Weirder still because it was right before his birthday.

"Yeah well, I don't think much of Maddy's opinion. I think the world of yours. I'd rather be the one taking you, but I'm glad you told me. If you want Rachel to take you then…I'll help with the guys."

"I don't want to tell them." I made a face. "I mean, Coop kind of knows that I'm looking, and we talked about that…"

"And Jake knows you need to talk to someone," he reminded me. "I'd bet you a dollar that Bubba does, too."

"A dollar?" I laughed a little. We were still idling in his car at the end of the drive, and Archie made no move to pull out.

"I'm trying to practice frugality. How's it working so far?"

I snickered, which had probably been his intention.

"Frankie, this will sound weird, but…we all have four stories. That's what Nana used to say. There's the story we share the world, our public face. It seems like a lot, but really, it's only a little. Then there's the story we share with acquaintances and people we know. Then there's the story we open ourselves up to with the people we care about. But there's always a story that's just ours. The one we don't know how to share. Sometimes, we get to glimpse that in the ones we are really close to, but the only person who knows that whole story is you."

I swallowed. "That sounds lonely."

"Yes and no. You know your story. You know what you need. Babe," Archie continued, reaching over and sliding his hand into my hair and tugging gently so I'd meet his gaze, "no one is going to think any less of you for going. Fuck, I'm relieved you want to."

What? "Really?"

"I don't know how to make those dreams go away. I don't know how to fix what that asshole did so you don't hurt anymore. I am clearly not the poster child for healthy parent-child relations. So yeah, I'm relieved you're going to talk to someone who might be able to do all those things."

I swallowed. "You know you're pretty awesome."

"I know," he agreed. "I'm just glad you finally came around and figured it out."

With a roll of my eyes, I shook my head. "You are such an ass."

"Yep," he agreed, running his thumb over my cheek gently. "Sometimes. But you need me to be an ass sometimes. I'm pretty sure that's what you like about me, too."

I made a face. "I will neither confirm or deny that."

"Good, make me work for it." He winked, then he sobered. "I'm serious. Go, talk to them. If they aren't a good fit, we try someone else. I want you to take what you need."

"What about what you need? Or the guys?"

"Eh, I have what I need right now."

My skepticism must have showed, because he grinned.

"Oh, trust me, babe. I have you. I got my best friends. I have my grandfather back. Birthday in a few days. It's looking pretty golden here, even if I have to learn how to do laundry because my girlfriend is a tyrant."

I shoved his arm away from me, and he smirked. "So tell those losers to order pizza if they're hungry, and yes, we'll grab coffee if you want some. Then we'll go do whatever…but I'm sleeping in the bed tonight. I want that much if I'm not going to have you to myself."

"Well," I said, reaching for my phone, "you do have a birthday coming up."

We locked eyes for a moment. "Only if you're ready," he told me.

"I'm ready. I would have been ready earlier tonight, but…"

"But we needed to talk. This is good, too. At least I know you don't just want me for my banging body or my money."

"Nope," I agreed.

"Wait." He frowned. "I do have a banging body."

"Hmm." I was trying to type one-handed.

His little grunt made me grin.

"Yes, Archie, I like your body just fine, but that's not what I want you for. Though it is a perk."

"Better." He paused a beat. "It's the car, isn't it?"

I grinned. "Guilty."

He threw his head back and laughed. "Yep, you have good taste."

Chapter Seventeen
BE CAREFUL WHAT YOU WISH FOR

The weekend went better than I could have expected or planned for. First, not only did we end up having a movie marathon, but the guys turned up the mocking as we picked the films apart. Luckily, they were all movies I'd seen before, but it didn't matter—it was still funny.

As requested, Archie curled up next to me in the bed, but to my surprise and everyone else's, Ian grabbed the second spot on my other side.

"If you don't mind," he'd murmured. While he had ended up crawling into bed with me the other night, it was only after nightmares had freaked me out.

Jake and Coop made faces, but rolled with it. Though, like Ian, they didn't crash on the sofa and grabbed spots in the room.

"Bigger bed," Archie muttered as we settled in. It should have been awkward maybe to be tucked between them. I was used to Archie, Coop, and Jake, but not so much Ian. Still, when I tucked my feet against his legs, I hesitated. He let out a hiss at the chill, and when I would have pulled them away, he locked his calves around one.

The giggles hit a minute later.

"Dude," Archie complained with a grin in his voice. "The icy feet you gotta deal with."

"I'm dealing just fine."

"If you can't handle it, we can always swap," Jake offered.

Ian snorted and then managed to trap my other foot, and the giggles had me biting my lip.

"Or we can just keep making her laugh," Coop drawled. "Because that's an effective way to get her to go to sleep."

I snorted mid-giggle and then hiccuped.

That successfully cracked all of them up.

Needless to say it was another hour before we shut up and stopped laughing long enough for me to go to sleep. What little awkwardness had been there when Ian first claimed the spot was gone. I went to sleep with my head on Archie's shoulder and my feet tucked against Ian's legs, while he had a hand on my hip and Archie held my left hand.

The cats had picked their places with Tiddles nestled in the divot between Archie and I. Tabby and Tory abandoned us for Jake and Coop respectively. It was a little bit like a game of Twister, but it was comfortable and sweet.

Despite a couple of nightmares, Saturday proved to be laid back. We slept in. Well, I slept in. Coop got up and fed the cats. Jake got up and ran to the store and picked up donuts and coffee. Ian got up next, then he, Jake, and Archie all went for a run.

I was aware of none of this until after the fact because I slept until nearly eleven. Coop teased me a little for sleeping through his best moves.

"Clearly, they weren't your best then," I snarked around a yawn that just set Coop off laughing.

As promised to Jeremy, I got pictures of Archie doing laundry. He didn't do too badly. Course, he had Coop and Jake advising him with Ian showing moral support. In all honesty, I didn't think I'd ever laughed so much just doing chores.

Then again, I'd never had my panties and bras folded or rated by four guys before either. The argument over whose of their boxers I had, however, that they were in the midst of when Mrs. Tagaliono—an elderly neighbor who lived in one of the apartments between Coop and I—entered with her own small basket of laundry just about killed me.

Dead.

Seriously.

I was pretty sure I was redder than the boxers Jake had been twirling around his finger—Coop's by the way, that had somehow been added to my drawers along with another pair from Archie, and two from Jake. I gave them fair warning if my old ones from Coop vanished, there would be hell to pay.

The whole time though, Ian watched with a speculative glint in his eyes, and I found myself wondering if he'd end up giving me a pair of his. Then I gave myself a mental shake.

I shouldn't be wondering those things. The subtle and not-so-subtle shifts in his behavior left me wondering where this was going.

Again.

The minute those questions cropped up, I just shut them off. I didn't want to borrow trouble. Ian was there. We were talking. It was enough.

For now.

It had to be.

Trina showed up at dinnertime, pissed. She knocked on the door like she was ready to yell "police" or something. Jake opened the front door and just backed up a step as she charged in.

"You *threatened* him?" She practically vibrated with outrage. Her shoulder-length sandy-blonde hair, so much like Coop's, flew as she spun from him to look at me. I was perched on the arm of the sofa with my feet tucked under Archie's thigh.

He paused the show on robot builds they'd had on.

"Frankie? Did he tell you what they did?" Agitation climbed along with her tone.

"Trina," Coop said. "Stop shouting."

Whirling on her brother, she glared. "You *threatened* him." Yeah, she wasn't going to stop shouting anytime soon. "I told you he asked me out and I wanted your help, and you threatened him."

"Point of order," Jake said, folding his arms. "Coop didn't threaten him."

Rolling her eyes, Trina put her hands on her hips. "Having you do it, Jake, is just playing semantics. If any of you guys threaten someone, they know they're getting all of you. I'm not an *idiot*." Then she looked at me again. "Frankie. Talk to them. Fix this?"

"Um…" I had parts of this conversation. Jake and Coop threatened someone. That I got. It had to do with dating Trina. That I also got. "Who asked you out?"

"Does it really matter?"

You know, before Homecoming, I'd probably have still said yes. But that was because Trina was Coop's baby sister. Now?

"Yes, it matters. Because some guys are just assholes."

Trina glared at me for a long moment, then the heat in her eyes faded as she snapped her mouth shut. Archie wrapped a hand around my calf as Trina all but deflated.

"I thought you'd be on my side."

"I am on your side." I was. "So is Coop. So is Jake." I swallowed. I hadn't been out with some unknown guy when bad things happened to me. I'd been with people I trusted. "So, who is he?"

"Noah is a great guy, he lives across the street from Mandy, and I've hung out with him."

I wrinkled my nose. "Doesn't he smoke?"

"Thank you," Coop said, tapping his nose and earning his sister's ire all over again.

"That doesn't make him a bad person." Trina damn near growled the words. For a moment, it struck me she wasn't a kid anymore. She was, but she was almost the same age I was when Archie came into our lives. Four years.

It didn't seem like much, until it was.

Still, she was Coop's baby sister, and as much as she could aggravate him, he loved her to pieces.

"Smoking doesn't mean he's awful," Trina insisted, looking to me for support.

"No," I agreed. We all had vices. The guys liked to drink. Archie often supplied alcohol because he could get it from Jeremy. Definitely not legal. They had other habits over the summer that we weren't going to dredge up right now. "But that's literally the only thing I can think of when I think of him. So, he asked you out…"

I needed a little more data. Not much, because the scenario practically wrote itself. Trina got asked out by a boy, told Coop because she needed his help with something, and all Coop heard was some older kid was sniffing around his sister. Jake also had sisters.

They had threatened the guys who'd apparently been interested in me and warned them off. It was no great leap to think they would do the same if not more for Trina.

"He's a nice guy. He's a lot of fun." Trina shifted from one foot to the other and shot looks to where Ian and Archie were both doing their best impressions of watching without staring. They did not have sisters, so it was always kind of funny to watch them around Jake's three and Coop's one.

Guys? No sweat.

Younger girls? Yeah, they weren't so smooth then.

Well, honestly, Archie seemed twitchier than Ian, but after everything I'd been learning about his family? I totally got that. Would siblings have made his life easier? Or harder?

He could withstand his parents, but it had definitely affected him. The last few weeks had given me a front row to how much he would do and how far he would go to protect me. If he'd had to look after siblings against his parents?

I almost shuddered at the thought.

"Look, Trina," I said, sliding off the sofa and ignoring Archie's grumblings as I pulled away. "C'mon, let's talk. Just you and me."

"Yeah…wait, what?" Coop demanded. "Why just you and her?"

"Because you have dangly bits," I informed him with a flick of my finger to the tip of his nose. "And this is girl stuff."

Jake snickered, but Trina's dour face brightened. "Where?"

"My room," I told her. "And the boys will stay out here."

"No problem," Ian said.

"Yeah, dangly bits stay out here." Trina marched ahead of me, and Coop groaned.

"Did you have to use that term?"

I shrugged. "I happen to like your dangly bits." Luck and the fact he was on my splinted side saved me from retaliation. I cut a look to where Trina had gone, then eyed him. "Did you really threaten that boy?"

"Jake did," Coop said, sticking with the story.

"Yep," Jake volunteered. "I have three sisters, I told him Trina was almost a sister to me, too. We didn't like boys who do stupid things with our sisters. So he should consider his options before asking her out."

I rolled my eyes to stare at the ceiling.

"Did you tell him he couldn't ask her out?"

"Nope." Arms folded, Coop wasn't even a little bit sorry. "But he's not using my sister to score points."

Period.

The firmness to his jaw and the flash of guilt in his eyes were all the confirmation I needed. "Okay." I pressed a kiss to his cheek. "You guys figure out food? I'll talk to her."

"Thanks," he murmured, then just before I hit my bedroom door, he called, "But don't promise we'll double-date with them 'cause I'll just be planning how to break his legs."

Trina stared at me from where she sat on the foot of my bed, and I was fairly certain we wore the exact same expression.

Boys.

"I hate my brother."

"No you don't."

"Well, sometimes I don't like him very much."

"It's okay. I'm pretty sure there are days he feels the same way about you."

She crossed her eyes and made a face.

Bumping the door closed, I slid against the pillows to sit at the head of the bed. "Okay, tell me all about him."

Surprise stamped her features, and she gawked at me. "What?"

"You heard me, tell me all about him."

Confusion filled her eyes, and she frowned. "What do you want to know?"

"Well, what do you like about him? What does he do? How does he talk to you? What are you hoping for if you go out with him…those kinds of things."

They were the kind of things I used to talk to the guys about back when they were first dating. Some of the girls, too. Though arguably, those were the same girls pumping me for info on how to date my guys.

Not that I ever shared that much.

"Um…wow. I thought you were going to try and give me the sex talk or tell me all the reasons this is a bad idea."

"Do you need the sex talk?"

"*No!*"

I didn't laugh, but it was a close thing.

"Okay. Do you know all the reasons it's a bad idea?"

"He's older than me, we go to different schools, he might have expectations because high school boys like it when you put out. But I've only been kissed a couple of times, not sure about the other stuff. I know it can be hard to tell them no, or at least, that's what Laurie said. She cashed in her V-card at camp over the summer.”

“Wait, she didn’t want to, but she did?” That bothered the hell out of me.

“She said she got kind of scared, but he got her through it and it wasn’t so bad. It wasn’t so great either. That’s not really a ringing endorsement, you know.”

“No,” I said, slowly. “It’s not.”

Trina deflated in front of me. “I just…he likes me, and I like him. I like hanging out with him. He asked. Coop was supposed to talk to Mom, but Mom said she’d think about it, but he called me an hour ago and said that after Coop threatened him that maybe it wasn’t a good idea.”

“Okay, well the guy gets points for actually calling and not blowing you off, but… I’m taking away at least one of them for using your brother as excuse.”

Her whole expression screwed up in a frown. “Why? Coop and Jake can be scary when they chase guys off. You forget, I’ve seen them do it when it came to you.”

“Because, you’re a package deal.”

Trina blinked. “What?”

“You have a big brother,” I reminded her. “His job, at least the way he sees it, is to protect you. Big brothers threaten guys who want to date their sisters. It’s a guy thing. If that guy can’t handle it…” I spread my hands.

“So, you think if some guy had stood up to them and asked you out anyway, you might be dating him instead of Coop?”

“We’ll never know.” Considering my first date was with someone who hadn’t been “in the know” it was very likely. “I know…what it is to want someone to like you for you. To have them want you and want to do things for you. I can blame the guys for a lot of things in warning people off and making me this… isolated and untouchable person. Trust me. I do. We’ve had our moments. But at the same time? No one else was willing to stand up to that heat, which means I wasn’t worth it to them.”

I’d never really voiced it aloud that way before, but it was true. I went from being furious to yelling at them, to finally admitting what I wanted, and the one-eighty we all took had been heady and intoxicating.

But the truth was, I adored those four, even if I'd never really admitted it to myself before.

"You want to be wanted, and that's cool. But want to be wanted for the right reasons. Sex isn't status. It should be…fun and intoxicating and make you feel more connected. It should really feel good. It doesn't matter if his dick is in you or not or you've been making out for hours, no still means no."

Trina paled. "Frankie…"

"It's okay. That part is okay. I know what 'no' means, and that guy didn't get that far. I was thinking about your other friend."

"Yeah." She sighed. "Fine, you have a point though, if a guy is gonna bail just because Coop looks at him crosswise…"

"Exactly."

Nose wrinkled, she blew a raspberry. "Okay, so it's not totally Coop and Jake's faults."

"Oh sure it is," I countered with a grin. "Just, they weren't totally wrong, either."

"I am never telling my brother that." She gave a firm nod, and I laughed.

"Your secret is safe with me." It was an easy promise.

"You know I used to wish you were my big sister," Trina admitted.

"You might have said that a few times."

Red stained the other girl's cheeks, even as she laughed. "Still wish it sometimes."

"Consider me adopted," I told her. "You hungry?"

"Yes, but I'm not eating with the Dangly Bits crew."

It was my turn to laugh.

"I'm gonna call one of the girls, then probably go binge something on Netflix."

Ten minutes later, she was out the door and I flopped back on the sofa.

"Well?" Coop asked, and I raised my brows. "How did it go?"

"It went fine," I told him. "What are we eating?"

"That's it? Just fine?" He squinted at me. "C'mon, Frankie, tell me, you know you want to."

"What I want is food…and a chance to see which of you is going to win the races tonight…"

Yep, dangle the video games and they went for the bait. Well, not all of it. Coop gave me a worried frown, and I smiled before mouthing 'she's fine' and to 'trust me.'

Despite his grunt, he let it go after that, and I got to tuck there between them as they argued, raced, and drove each other crazy.

Eventually, we even got food.

Sunday started out much like Saturday, except I didn't oversleep, thanks to the smoke alarm going off.

Ian tried bacon again.

The laughter and grumbling from the kitchen added a flash of joy to the day.

Fortunately, I had a lot of homework to do and so did the guys. So after we managed to salvage some of the not blackened to charcoal bacon, Jake and Coop took over the cooking while Ian and Archie went for coffee. My arm ached like crazy, but I did my best to ignore it. The pain meds helped, sure, but it made studying a pain in the ass.

I really hoped the doc didn't stick my arm in a cast. The splint was bad enough. A cast would suck.

We also went to get Ian's bike from the shop. From the repairs, it looked to be in good shape. I still couldn't believe someone had vandalized it. My car. Then his bike. Only they'd done some damage to his bike.

Serious damage.

"Yeah, I could have lived without that bill," Ian admitted as he tucked his wallet into his back pocket. I leaned against Jake's SUV. "You know," he said.

"I'd offer to give you the next first inaugural ride…"

"No," Jake said crisply.

"I wasn't going to," Ian snapped at him. "Not while her arm is still in the splint."

Not for the first time, I wished the splint was history. "Well, maybe when I'm better," I suggested, and Ian jerked his attention back to me.

"Really?"

"Maybe."

"I'm going to hold you to that maybe."

"Yeah, because it says so much for my level of commitment."

He snorted. "True. But I'd still like to take you for a ride. Just say the word."

My heart did a little fist bump with my ribs, and I swallowed. We never had really gotten to go on our date.

What he asked right now wasn't pretending. Even if it was a simple offer to go for a ride on the bike, it seemed heavier somehow, far more meaningful.

The silence stretched out uncomfortably, and Jake shifted his stance. "C'mon, you got the bike, let's head back. You coming back to Frankie's or heading home?"

The weight of Ian's stare pressed in on me. Meeting his gaze, I read the question in them.

Did I want him to come back?

"I have a doctor's appointment in the morning. I might be in a much worse mood tomorrow, so tonight would be good."

A flash of a smile softened his expression, and he winked. "Then let's go."

If I thought I was off the hook 'cause Ian was on his bike and Jake in the SUV, I was wrong.

"You okay over there, Baby Girl?"

"I don't know," I admitted, not bothering to pretend I didn't know what he was talking about. "I don't know what I want right now."

"That's okay," he said. "That means you haven't closed the door entirely."

"But I did."

"No," Jake argued. "You broke up with Bubba and told him if he didn't want to date or couldn't trust you to know your own mind, then maybe you just needed to be friends. That wasn't closing a door, Frankie. That was giving him a solid kick in the ass."

"How does he know he really wants to do this when he didn't before?"

"I don't know," Jake admitted as we sat waiting for the light to change. "How do any of us know? Sometimes…sometimes we have to have reality dump cold water on us. Sometimes we have to see the girl we want is about to go out with some total stranger and realize the thing we've always wanted suddenly became attainable again."

"Sometimes, we have to find out our best friends are the best cock blockers there are?" I glanced at him, and he grinned.

"Damn straight." He brushed his thumb over my chin. "Whatever you want with Bubba. I mean that. I know you've got a lot on your plate, but he's here. He's been here. I don't think he's going anywhere."

Again.

I didn't think he was going anywhere before, and I leaned my head back against the seat. "I want to believe that."

"Then make him work for it," he whispered. "I'll help. I'll model how good boyfriends behave."

Laughter shivered through me. "You are a good boyfriend."

"Damn straight."

The quiet settled there, and I chewed the inside of my lip. "He was just asking me to take a bike ride. It doesn't have to mean more than that."

"Nope," Jake agreed. "It doesn't. I mean, it does mean more than that, but it doesn't have to."

I rolled my eyes. "You're not helping."

"Sorry, I gotta call bullshit when I hear it. You want it to mean something, but you're gun-shy about believing it does until you can see it in clear black and white letters. That's okay, he earned that bit of mistrust on your part."

And that was what it came down to. I wanted to trust him.

But I wasn't sure how.

"You know what, adulting sucks."

Jake laughed, but the shock of masculine warmth cut off abruptly as we neared the parking spots near my apartment. Following Jake's gaze, I found out why.

My mother stood on the sidewalk, arms folded, posture rigid, and definitely radiating hostility, even if sunglasses hid her eyes. Despite the jeans, she wore an expensive blouse and jacket, both in brighter colors. Her hair had been pulled up into a knot, and a pair of teardrop earrings glistened in the mid-afternoon sun.

The papers she had fisted in her hand drew my attention, and I sighed. This wouldn't be pretty.

"Fuck," Jake muttered. "We can just go."

"Nope, I live here." And I reached over with my left hand to open the door. He was out and walking around to meet me before I'd even touched my feet to the pavement. Ian pulled in scant moments behind us.

One heeled foot tapping, Maddy waited for me only as long as it took me to step up on the curb. "What the hell is this?" She waved the papers at me in demand.

"You should have your attorney talk to my attorney."

My voice didn't quaver. Go me.

Jake put his hand against my lower back. "Ms. Curtis," he said.

"Shut up, Jake," Maddy snapped, and I raised my brows.

"You don't talk to him that way," I informed her. "You have a problem, take it up with me. Oh wait, you don't do that unless you want something."

"What I want right now is an explanation for this ridiculous and, may I mention, *frivolous* suit."

"If you have a question about that, I already told you. Talk to my attorney."

I pivoted to walk past her, and she slammed a hand out and gripped my right bicep. It was just above the splint, and it fucking hurt. Jake gripped her wrist a split second later.

"Let her go," he ordered.

"She's my daughter, I'll do as I damn well please. Would you like to face another assault charge?"

Oh hell no, she wasn't going to use that against Jake. "Would you?" I demanded in the same breath as Jake said, "Knock yourself out."

"Let her go, Ms. Curtis," Ian said in an almost kind tone. "No one has done any harm—yet."

Maddy glared past me, and in her sunglasses, I caught Ian's reflection and his upraised phone.

"But to be clear, we will document every moment of this interaction. You have been asked to go and to take your questions to an attorney. Jake has asked you to let Frankie go. You're hurting her, and she's already injured."

Lips compressed, Maddy transferred her attention back to me and let go of my arm. The abrupt cessation of pressure was a relief, but I refused to let it show. Jake dropped her wrist like the contact disgusted him.

"I would like a moment with my daughter."

"You're already having one," I reminded her. "Right here. The child you so often forget you have."

"Alone, Francesca. Do not be an idiot on purpose."

Yeah. Another reason I hated that name. It sounded way snootier than I would ever be.

"Not happening," Jake informed her as he pulled me back a step and edged slightly in front of me. "You aren't cautious or caring enough with her. I have zero intention of letting you take that temper out on her, lady."

There was the faintest tremble to Maddy's hand, and the color in her cheeks went hot. I bet if she pulled off those sunglasses, her eyes would be blazing. "I will not air our personal business in front of others."

"Whatever, see you later then." I took a couple of steps, with Jake keeping himself between me and Maddy. "Or not. I know it's a crapshoot with you."

"Frankie."

I stopped.

"You can't ignore me forever."

"Sure I can," I said, and this time, I didn't bother to try and soften the derision in my voice. "Just following the example you set, Maddy."

I was almost to the stairs when she let out a little scream. "I could have given you up for adoption."

The words stung.

They always did.

"Or an abortion. I could have done that. Then where would you be?"

"Bitch," Jake muttered, but I turned around and stared back at my mother. She was the one making a scene. I had to guess at least one of the neighbors heard it. But still…

"Where would I be? Better off in the first case, I would imagine, and in the second? Well, I wouldn't have to deal with you then either."

"Go away, Maddy," Archie said as he descended the steps. "Don't make us get a restraining order."

She glared. "This isn't over."

But that was it. She turned on her expensive heel and walked back to her… Holy shit, that was not her car. It was far more expensive than the car she'd owned.

My heart raced and sweat prickled along my skin as she slid behind the wheel of the Mercedes and stared at me for several long seconds, then Jake, before the engine purred to life, and she pulled away.

That car so did not belong in this parking lot. Not even with the nice SUV and the pricy Ferrari currently parked there.

Ian lowered his phone and then moved toward us as Jake slid an arm around me.

I needed to call Mr. Wittaker. Whatever happened, I couldn't let Maddy take it out on the guys, and the way she'd looked at Jake worried me.

Maybe Mad Maddy wasn't the joke she'd always made it out to be.

Maybe it was a warning.

Chapter Eighteen
HIGH ANXIETY

The doctor elected to put me in a cast. Archie and Coop had both taken me to the doctor's appointment while Ian rode with Jake to school. I'd really wanted different news, but he was concerned about the fracture itself.

On the upside, the swelling had reduced, and he'd made the fiberglass cast red—Archie picked the color—and it was kind of pretty. On the downside, it could be six weeks in this cast.

Six. Weeks.

What the hell was I going to do for work in a cast?

The doctor assured me fiberglass was easier to care for. I'd still have to go back every other week to get it x-rayed and to check on the swelling. We had another long list to call him about if any of them happened.

All the way through the process, Coop and Archie kept an upbeat patter and I pasted on a smile. They were all killing themselves to make this easier for me. The least I could do was roll with it.

We made it in by just after lunchtime. I didn't want to miss anymore days than I had to, even if the guys didn't care about the attendance records. I didn't even make it to study hall before I got pulled into the principal's office.

Maddy waited for me there.

The smile on her face made my blood run cold. I dug my phone out as Mr. Dillard ushered me into his office. Thankfully, I'd texted Mr. Wittaker the day before, so his message was right near the top. I told him my mother was at the school and I'd been pulled into the principal's office with her.

Message sent, I stopped at the door and refused to take another step. "I apologize, Mr. Dillard, if you want to have this conversation with Ms. Curtis in the room, but I'll be waiting for my lawyer."

The principal hesitated. One thing about our principal—he was a good person. He knew everyone's names. He greeted us in the hallways and had treated us like old friends from our first day here. The man showed up to all the football games, debate tournaments, academic decathlons, cross-country meets, and band tourneys—if there was a contest or someone from the school competed somewhere, he did his absolute best to be there.

Unequivocally, he was on our sides.

He was also a huge proponent of family.

Huge.

Like massive.

Religious, too. Not in your face and drive you crazy religious. Not remotely hypocritical. The man lived his beliefs and truly embraced talking out problems and using love to heal everything. He so wasn't going to get us.

No. Not even a little.

"I understand why you might feel that way, Frankie," he told me kindly. "Your mother came in this morning to get my help, and she's asked me to sit in on this discussion for *your* comfort. She's very concerned about you."

Bull. Shit.

I didn't bother to look at her. "That's very kind of you, Mr. Dillard. I'm still not having a conversation with her without my attorney." Who would ever think I'd need to utter these words where my mother was concerned?

Instead of being remotely put off, he gave me another patient look. "Well, how about this? She has some things she'd like to say to you. We can sit here, and she can talk and you can listen. You don't have to say a word."

"I'd rather not."

"I understand, but I think this is important, and I'll be here with you. I can even call the student advocate to come down and join us."

No. Diane had already gotten an eyeful of my crappy situation. My phone buzzed. A glance down showed a message from Mr. Wittaker.

He was ten minutes away.

"Mr. Dillard." My mother's voice turned all kinds of breathy, and I swore I threw up in my mouth. "Frankie's always been a bit difficult. It's better to just start talking than to wait for her to agree." She smiled, all sugar and light. "Honestly," she continued, and glanced at me with a smile that set off every warning bell I possessed.

Look, I got the good mother today. The one who would probably like to bake cookies and shit with me. The one who used to take me for hot cocoa every day before kindergarten. The one who used to encourage me to climb onto the back of the sofa each evening and brush out her hair for her.

Little things that probably didn't amount to much, but those scraps had been gobbled up by younger me.

Not responding took everything I had. Maybe I should have just texted the guys. It was one thing to have them swoop in when my mother showed up with Archie's father to drag me out of here—wait.

Where was "Eddie"?

This was twice in as many days that I'd seen her sans the new boyfriend-fiancé-dirty little secret. Well, not so little or secret anymore, but definitely dirty.

Had he dumped her? Archie said it was coming. Sooner or later. His grandfather was in town. Had they ended up having a fight?

I wasn't sure whether to be relieved, wary, or flat out terrified.

Mr. Dillard pulled at his lower lip as he considered me, then my mother, then back to me. "Would you like to close the door, Frankie? I would prefer to give you ladies some privacy."

"If you're staying, Mr. D, then we're hardly going to be in private." Not that I needed or wanted privacy. My arm ached like hell, and my gut churned. If I could drag this out a little longer, Mr. Wittaker would get here.

"Frankie, darling," my mother said. Apparently, I wasn't the only one watching the time. "I think we really have just shared a classic misunderstanding. I know that you aren't comfortable with my engagement, and perhaps I did things a bit out of order."

Was she high?

I didn't look at her no matter how much I wanted to figure out the answer to that question.

"Yes, Eddie and I have been almost inseparable. I've almost forgotten what it is to be so enamored." She let out a breathy little sigh. "Mr. Dillard, you remember what that first flush is like? It's been so long, and I let myself get swept away in it. The simple truth is—we're in love."

It was official. I just puked.

My mother rose from her chair and took a couple of steps toward me. "But you have always been my first priority."

Okay, that did it. I looked at her. The cloying nature of her sentiment cluttered the air like the sticky humidity after a late day storm in the middle of summer. I could barely breathe through the thickness of crap she put out.

"Those boys, however," she said. "I'm just worried about what they've put into your head. Drinking the way they do. Partying…the trains of girls they've run through."

My jaw locked.

"Archie and his father…they are having their issues, sweetheart. I don't want you getting caught up between them."

Don't say it. Don't rise to the bait.

"And that Jake," she said with a tsk. "I've never wanted to be judgmental, but he's been in how many fights now?"

"Ms. Curtis," Mr. Dillard interrupted. "I think we're getting off subject."

"Actually," she said, pivoting like a shark slicing through the water. "This is part of the problem. They're filling Frankie's head with a lot of noise when she should be focused on finishing school and keeping her head, rather than making irreparable choices and engaging in God knows what with those boys." Another glance to me, and as thick as she was laying it on, the act still hit me as a calculated gesture. "Baby, I know what I saw them up to this summer, and it's nothing that I'd ever want you around."

Wow.

She really went there.

A sound of the main office door opening had me glancing down the hall. Mr. Wittaker paused at the front desk, then motioned toward me before he headed right for me.

"Miss Curtis." He managed to sound just a tad out of breath and utterly collected. Must be a legal trick. "Sorry for the brief delay, this was an unexpected summons."

"You're right on time." Now, I stepped back a foot to let the lawyer enter the principal's office before I followed him. "Mr. Wittaker, this is Mr. Dillard, my principal, and the woman standing there is Madeline Curtis. The defendant in my suit."

The verbal slap landed, and Maddy's civilized veneer thinned as she glared at me. "Your mother," she corrected me.

I bit my tongue to curb the response. Mr. Wittaker gave me an approving nod after shaking Mr. Dillard's hand. Smoothly, he glanced from one to the other, including them both in the conversation. "Mr. Dillard, I'm actually glad you could be at this meeting, it will save me a little time."

He set a case down on a chair and opened it before he removed two sets of papers. He passed the first one to Mr. Dillard and the second to my mother.

"I would recommend you have your attorney review that, Ms. Curtis," Mr. Wittaker informed her. "As Frankie's attorney, I represent her interests. This is an emergency injunction granting Frankie temporary emancipation until the court hears her case. As such, Ms. Curtis' rights and privileges are hereby revoked. She will have no more access to Frankie's records, accounts, or the right to check her out of the school. Frankie will self-manage in the meanwhile with moderate support from my office."

Mr. Dillard frowned as he reviewed the document, then glanced at my mother. Disapproval flashed in his eyes, but he focused on my attorney, then me. "I see. Thank you for bringing this to my attention. Frankie, I'm sorry for inhibiting your day. If you would like to return to class, just get a note from…"

"Wait a damn minute," my mother said abruptly as she snapped her gaze up. "You can't just emancipate her and remove my rights. I'm her mother."

"I applied for the injunction," Mr. Wittaker said smoothly. "The judge granted it. All the pertinent details are in that document. Consider yourself legally on notice, Ms. Curtis. You are to have no further contact with Frankie, beyond having your attorney speak to me, and I will transmit the messages to her."

I wanted to smile. But I didn't.

Freedom from Maddy was what I'd wanted, but it wasn't a good thing. The hurt in my mother's eyes cut at me. It didn't matter if it was a play or just one more calculated maneuver. I didn't think she faked it.

Guilt nibbled at me, and I locked my jaw.

"Frankie, it's been you and me from the beginning. You can't want this…" She tried to get close to me, but Mr. Wittaker shifted his stance.

Until that moment, I hadn't realized how big of a man he was, but he blocked my view of her easily enough.

"You don't get to just take my child away!" Something in my mother's voice cracked. "No one gets to take her away. She's *mine*."

"Frankie," Mr. Dillard said, hustling around his desk. "Go to class, hon." Oh, he did not have to tell me twice.

"Yes, go to class. I'll call you later," Mr. Wittaker told me. I didn't even make it halfway across the office before my mother's voice turned strident, harsh, and threatening.

Yeah. I was gone.

Jake was on his feet as soon as I arrived in the library. There wasn't even five minutes left to study hall. "Where the hell have you been?"

The hissed question reminded me about my phone on silent. I dragged it out. Messages from the guys filled the screen—all of them worried.

"One sec," I told him. After I sent a message telling them I was fine and would fill them in after school, I told Jake my mom had been in the office and what happened with my attorney.

His expression darkened significantly, but the relief spilling through his eyes when I said Mr. Wittaker came through with the temporary injunction pulled at me. I glanced around us and found no one nearby or watching, and then just wrapped myself around Jake. His arms folded me close, and I closed my eyes.

"Baby Girl," he said in a hushed voice. "You're shaking."

I had to get a grip.

And all too soon, I had to let Jake go. "I'll be okay." I pasted on a smile.

Fake 'til I make it, right?

Yeah. That didn't really fly with the guys.

Jake filled them in before I could, and after school resulted in a tense meeting at my apartment. Archie left after to talk to his grandfather. Ian had to go home for the evening, but promised he'd stay over on Tuesday. He even asked if I'd be willing to just go out with him for an hour Tuesday—just the two of us.

"On a date?" Yes, I probably sounded as skeptical as I felt. As much as I wanted to figure this out between us, I wasn't sure I was up for it. Not really.

The sick feeling in my stomach just wouldn't go away.

"Nope," Ian said, surprising and disappointing me all at the same time. "I need your help. Promise I'll tell you all about it." Then he glanced to where Coop and Jake were making no pretense of not listening. "It's a secret."

I rolled my eyes. "That's not code for it might be a date if it goes well?"

He grinned. "It can be a date if that will get you to say yes."

"Yes to an hour doing whatever your surprise is."

"So that's a date then," he said the last bit with a teasing grin, and it helped. Dammit. It was hard to stay irked with him, even in my current uneven mood. Still, would dating him be a good idea?

If he hadn't freaked out…

If he hadn't told me all those things about the guys and their points…

If he hadn't walked away, saying he just wanted to be friends…

If… If… If…

"Maybe," I told him, and he nodded before brushing a kiss against my lips so fast I barely had time to register the contact before he was already heading for the door.

"I can work with maybe. I'll call you before bed, Frankie. Call me if you need me." Then he was gone.

I touched a finger to my lips.

"That was good, right?" Coop mused.

"I don't know," Jake answered. "On a scale of one to ten, I'm thinking a five because vague as fuck, but two points extra cause he did actually get her to say yes."

"And a kiss, he scored a kiss."

"That wasn't winning a kiss. He gave her a kiss," Jake argued. "That's different. Pretty shitty kiss, too."

Sliding a look at them, I said, "You're not funny."

Coop grinned. "We're hilarious."

"And you adore us," Jake added on. "So what are we doing tonight?"

"You, I hope," Coop continued. They both grinned widely, knocking elbows once like they'd coordinated it.

"Asses. Both of you. And no—you're not *doing* me…at least, not right now." Because…well to be honest, the other day had been all kinds of hot and intense. I grimaced and glanced down at my cast. It was a little lighter than the splint, but that wasn't saying much. I swore my bones ached.

"You hurting?"

"Yeah, but I can't take anything yet. I need to try over the counter stuff first, 'cause I still have homework and I need you guys to take me to the mall."

They both paused, then asked in a dead similar tone, equal parts dread and caution, "Why?"

"Archie's birthday. I need to go buy him a present." I'd totally blown it on Coop's. "And you still need one, too."

"I got my present," Coop said with a sly smile. "I got a day with you. And the night after. Best present. Ever."

"I'll remember that the next time you start bitching you want your game system upgraded," Jake muttered.

"Oh like you wouldn't give up a game system for a day with Frankie. Please."

I grinned. It was a ridiculous conversation, but it helped.

"Mall?" I asked. "Please? Before this hurts so much I don't want to do anything."

"Sure thing, Baby Girl. We'll even swing by that Indian place there and let you get all the naan bread you can eat." Jake's offer had my stomach snarling.

Yeah. I was easy.

Now, what the hell did I get Archie for his birthday?

Hopefully, Tuesday would go better than Monday, save for the rocky start. There had been no sex with guys, as nice as that might have been. After a damn near fruitless shopping trip and getting homework done, I hurt too much and I was too tired. But curling up with them while I talked first to Ian, then to Archie before we went to sleep had been nice.

When I had a hell of a time relaxing, Jake had gone to work on massaging my feet while Coop stroked his fingertips against my scalp. I was out in less than five minutes.

Nightmares had woken me a dozen times. It was probably the worst night's sleep I'd had since my first couple of days after Homecoming.

The guys hovered, even when they weren't trying to. I was a mess. And Ian still wanted to go do a surprise that night. As hard as I tried not to be cranky, I was losing that battle.

Mr. Wittaker hadn't called on Monday like he said, but he did call on Tuesday and left me a message. He had all the pertinent details, like what the injunction covered, and he sent a copy to my email to keep on hand, another would be couriered over before the end of the day.

By the time school wrapped for the day, I half-wished I'd told Ian no, but I wouldn't back out at the last minute. Jake drove us back to my apartment while Ian followed on his bike.

Before I could ask how we were going anywhere, Ian opened the passenger door of Jake's SUV. Coop had planned to run some deliveries right after school. Yes, I was a little sour that they were finding ways to work and I still had to call Marsha about my arm. It wasn't their fault.

"Mind if I drive your car?" Ian offered. "Or if you're up for it, you can drive."

Some of my bad mood dissipated.

"Um…" Jake started.

"It's an automatic. Frankie's a good driver," Ian said. "And she hasn't driven her car in weeks." Then he looked back at me. "That said, if you're tired or you hurt, I can totally do it. I just… Not the bike yet."

I liked his bike.

I'd liked it a lot from the first time I got to ride it.

But now that he'd brought up my car…hell yes, I wanted to drive it. "Maybe I drive there, and if I'm too tired, you can drive us back?"

Ian's cheeks curved with his smile. "Sounds like a plan to me."

Jake still scowled, but I pressed a kiss to his jaw. "I'll be careful," I promised him.

"You better be," he said tersely, but he wasn't looking at me so much as at Ian.

Yeah, yeah. Jake was the one who said I should give him a chance if I wanted to. Same should apply to the car, right?

Once in the driver's seat, I let out a breath that felt like I'd been holding for weeks. I really hadn't driven my car all that much, not since it got covered in condoms. To work and back, sure. A couple of errands even, but after Homecoming? Not even that much.

It was a little awkward to buckle my seatbelt or start the car with my right arm in a cast. "Can you…?" I asked Ian after he settled into the passenger seat and belted in.

"Yes, I can," he said easily enough, reaching past me to pull the seatbelt down and then locking it in. Then he slid the keys in and started it. "Want me to change gears, too?"

I made a face. It would be easier if he did it. I didn't think just how much I needed my right arm. Fuck, I hated Mitch.

Agitation buzzed under my skin.

"Please," I ground out between my teeth.

"Hey," Ian said softly. "I'm not trying to be pushy."

"You're not," I said, blowing out a breath. "It's just…"

"You want to be able to do it yourself."

"Yeah," I admitted. He put the car in reverse, and I backed out. I wasn't rusty, but it still took adjustment 'cause I kept reaching to use my right hand and I had to remember to keep it up. It was better to keep it above my heart.

Aware of Jake watching us until I headed for the street, I tried to get a grip. "I'm sorry that I'm being cranky."

"I can take it," Ian offered.

When I shot him a look, he shrugged.

"Angel, I can take just about anything where you're concerned, except you shutting me out. Granted, I'm the one who put myself on the outside, but

I'm at the gate. The minute you let me in, I'm never going to waste my chance again."

It was sweet.

It helped.

"I don't…"

"You don't have to," he hurried on. "I mean it. You don't. When you're ready, you're ready. Until then, let me have it with both barrels. If you need to vent, especially if you need to vent, or if you just want to scream it out. I can take it."

"I'm not mad at you."

"Eh," he said, making a so-so motion. "You're at least a little still mad at me."

Okay. Maybe I was.

"I don't want to be mad at you."

"That means everything," he promised.

A real smile tugged at my lips this time. "You're kind of crazy."

"About you? Absolutely. Now, do you want to know where we're going?"

"That would help," I told him.

He grinned, "Bonner Street Music, off of Main." Which to anyone else probably wouldn't make sense, except where Main Street wasn't downtown, it was called Bonner.

I turned out before I asked, "Why there?"

"It's a surprise," he reminded me, and I rolled my eyes.

"Right." Then I made a face as a dozen different ideas tumbled through my head. I'd gone to Bonner Street Music with Ian a few times in the last couple of years. It was a music school, mostly for younger kids. Ian had apparently studied piano there when we were all younger. But most of the time, when we went it was to get sheet music or to repair one of his guitars. They had a great music shop there.

It was where I'd gotten him the sheet music for his birthday.

When we got there, I found a place to park in the little lot behind the building. The drive had been a little more nerve-racking than I wanted to admit. One hand controlling the wheel made me extra cautious. Still, when we got there, it was totally worth it.

I loved that the guys would take me anywhere and they *wanted* to do it. But I didn't realize just how much I'd missed my freedom driving on my own.

"Feeling okay?" he asked after I parked.

"Um, a little nervy, but…yeah. I'm okay." Better, actually. It had helped with some of my shitty mood. "I'm ready for my surprise now."

Ian grinned. "Then come on."

Inside, he made a beeline for the main desk and got a key, then signed in to the logbook. "Thanks, Marlene."

"Have fun, sugar," said the older woman behind the desk with her bright maroon, clearly from a bottle hair, with a genuine smile. Ian held out his hand, and I clasped it, the gesture a little easier than all the other contact combined.

He led the way through what was a series of semi-darkened hallways, past practice rooms—soundproofed because they had all kinds of students from drums to guitars to pianos to a dude actually playing a tuba. Ian didn't slow long enough for me to do more than glimpse in to each door.

When we got to the one in the corner, he unlocked it and let us into a practice suite and recording studio.

"You're going to record something." I didn't even have to manufacture the excitement.

Ian's eyes gleamed, and his smile grew.

"Actually, Angel," he told me. "You are."

"What?"

"Trust me?"

Oh, I wanted to say yes but… "Ian, I can't sing."

"Trust me? Please? Just for the next hour. I promise, I won't let you down." He studied me with those intense blue eyes.

I bit my lip.

Did I trust him? Even this little bit?

"Promise me this isn't going to be like the karaoke incident?"

He grinned. "I swear, Angel. You won't be embarrassed. If I have my way, you're going to be thrilled."

Exhaling, I took the leap. "Okay."

Light seemed to fill his whole expression as he grinned. It was a real one, the first one I'd seen on his face in a while. It warmed his eyes and reminded me why I'd wanted to kiss him that day in the pool.

Five minutes and after he'd explained his plan later, I burst out laughing. "Are you shitting me?"

"Nope," he promised. "What do you think?"

"I *love* it."

I really did.

Schadenfreude

WEDNESDAY

Bubba

AM canceled today. Where's lunch?

Jake

What?

Bubba

She just texted me. Didn't you get one?

Archie

Jake

Nope—wait. Got it.

Coop

Parking lot. Now.

Archie

OMW.

Bubba

What happened?

Jake

Fuck me. You're about to get it.

Archie

I'm going to kill that cunt.

Bubba

Shit.

Coop

Less talking. More walking.

Jake

Where's Frankie?

Archie

With Rachel. Her 1st appt is today.

Jake

Shit.

Coop

Just get out here. Txting Rachel.

Archie

Fuck.

Bubba

What now?

Jake

Where is that bitch?

Archie

It's lunch. Check the cafeteria, I'll check her car.

Bubba

Guys.

Coop

Don't. We make a decision together.
Nothing impulsive. Parking lot.

Jake

…

Archie

Fine.

Bubba

Almost there.

Coop

J?

Jake

I'm seriously done with her.

Archie

Me 2.

Jake

BRT

Chapter Nineteen
THERAPY SCARES ME

The interior of the office had pale gray carpet and a half circle formed by three sets of leather loveseats covered in colorful pillows. There was a hum in the corner from a small fountain along with another little fan in the other corner. The white noise was kind of pleasant.

Across from me, Erin Thom sat legs crossed and her demeanor relaxed. Probably good one of us was. Even after making the appointment, I'd done my best to not think about it. I'd been distracting myself for two days. All the way here though, I'd barely heard a word Rachel said. No matter how hard I tried to pump myself up, my stomach was in knots by the time Rachel pulled into the parking lot of the tidy little office building.

Red brick construction, kind of L shaped, with a handful of trees serving as landscaping, the building was utterly unremarkable. There was absolutely no moisture in my mouth by the time Rachel pulled into a parking slip.

"I'll wait out here," she said. "Unless you want me to come in with you."

Clammy palms, racing heart, upset stomach, and a dry mouth. Yes, I wanted Rachel to come with me. "No," I told her with a lot more certainty than I was feeling. "It's kind of hard enough to do this at the moment."

"It's always hard the first time," she cautioned. "Don't expect miracles, Frankie. Just go in there and talk about as little or as much as you want."

Curtises don't do therapy. "You make it sound easy."

"It's like putting one foot in front of the other when you're walking on stone bruises across hot pavement. It hurts, and it's awkward. You're tempted to run, but that's gonna hurt in an entirely different way, and if you trip, it's worse."

I made a face and then looked at her. "That's a horrible analogy."

"And painful," Rachel told me with a wry smile. "But you're thinking about that and not the appointment. So take advantage and go on in. You got this."

I blew out a breath. "Thanks, Rach."

"I'll be *right* here."

That promise buoyed me. It helped me keep my chin above water all the way inside to the quiet little waiting room. There was a light on over the door where I was supposed to have my appointment and a note that read, *Press the button when the light is on and take a seat.* My fingers had trembled more than I cared to admit. But I pressed the damn button and then took a seat.

I took my phone out and checked my messages. The guys knew I was out for lunch. They knew where I was going. No one had given me even an ounce of teasing over it. If anything, the only question I'd been asked was did I really want Rachel to take me? When I said yes, they backed off on it.

As weird as that response seemed in some ways, I'd been damn grateful for it. All the joy from the night before seemed like a distant memory. Ian and I had fun at the studio.

So much so, I'd agreed to go with him again the following Tuesday. He'd been booking studio time for the last couple of weeks, putting in serious time. Recording the…

"Frankie Curtis?"

I nearly jumped out of my skin at the greeting. I'd been so focused on trying to think of anything else, I hadn't noticed her door opening or the woman standing there.

"I'm Erin Thom," she said, smiling. She was about my height with long dark hair, faint Asian features, and I swore she couldn't be that much older than me.

This was supposed to be my therapist? What was she? Twenty-one? Twenty-two?

No, she had to be older, right?

After shaking my hand, she ushered me into her pleasant little office with its all of one room. While she had a notepad next to her, the pen lay capped and on top of it while she focused on me.

"I've never done this before," I admitted.

"That's what you said on the phone," Erin told me, her tone patient and easy. "That's perfectly fine. Why don't you tell me a little about yourself?"

"I'm…I'm seventeen. I'm a senior in high school."

That was probably not what she meant, right?

"I'm—um…" I curled my fingers into my palms again. "I don't really know how to do this. My friend Coop, he's easy to talk to about things, and he wants to do what you're doing, but this is weird."

"I understand. What I hear you saying is you're not comfortable discussing personal things with someone you've just met."

"No, I'm not," I agreed readily, and looked at my hands. "It's more than that though. I was raised to believe we handled our own problems and that…" Fuck, consider the source, I told myself. "Maddy always said Curtises don't do therapy."

I winced.

"That sounds kind of insulting. Sorry." Licking my lips, I flexed my fingers. "A few weeks ago, I was holding that line firm, even when the school advocate was offering to talk, and yeah, I probably needed to talk to someone, but not her. She's…too close. She's right there at the school. Knows the people."

"Understandable, you want privacy because you're not comfortable discussing any of these topics in the first place, much less with someone who might have a more personal tie."

I nodded. "A little bit like that, yeah. I don't…" I shifted and pulled my legs up to sit cross legged before I gave into the urge and got up to pace. The longer I sat here in this serene, peaceful room with Erin's kind eyes on me, the more restless I became. "This is so messy, and I don't know how to explain this to myself, much less to anyone else."

"I hear you," she told me, and not once did she flinch from meeting my gaze, even when I kept pulling mine away. "Would it be easier for you if I ask questions?"

"Maybe." The truth was I didn't want to talk about any of it.

"Okay, let's start with something simple then. Tell me what you hope to get from coming to see me."

"Peace of mind?" That was more of a question than an answer. "Something…a lot of somethings have been going on, but…I was drugged at Homecoming, and I don't remember parts of that evening, like…how I got this." I motioned to the cast on my right arm. "I know my friends…they saved me. They stopped the guy, and I know who, and considering the battery of tests I had to do afterward when I woke up at the hospital…well, I know what he wanted to do."

A slick of ice seemed to race over my skin.

"He didn't. I mean, that's one upside. At least that's what they could tell from the tests they did. There was a really nice woman—Denitra. She was my SAFE advocate."

Erin nodded.

"I had some bruises, the broken wrist…some bruised ribs. And the guys took me home afterward, and they've all stayed with me. I haven't been alone, and that's a good thing. But I have nightmares most nights that wake me up, and it's hard on them. I know they remember—I can see it in their eyes. But I don't, and there's this hole where something bad happened, and even though it could have been worse, it's…like I want to fill in all the blanks with the worst thoughts and ideas." I tried to laugh, but it came off hollow even to my own ears. "I should mention I'm absolutely terrible about horror movies. Can't sleep for days after watching one."

"It sounds like you have a vivid imagination."

"Sometimes." I licked my lips again, desperately wishing I'd brought something in with me.

"Would you like some water?" Erin motioned to a small mini fridge. "I've got some bottled water."

My stomach did a flip-flop. "That was where the drug was. In a bottle of water."

"Okay. Doesn't change my question, unless bottles bother you. In which case, we can grab some empty plastic cups and step into my private bathroom there and you can fill it with water from the sink."

"That probably comes across paranoid, doesn't it?"

"Not at all. It comes across as healthy caution and wariness after your trust has already been abused. I'm assuming the person who gave you the water bottle is someone you trusted."

I nodded once.

"Then I can understand why you would be wary of taking a bottle of water from a friend, much less a stranger."

She didn't make it a big deal or sound remotely critical. Just took it in stride. We both grabbed plastic cups, and she opened her tidy little restroom. I filled my cup from the sink, and the tap water was probably the most welcome thing I'd drunk in a while.

When we were back in our seats, she studied me again. "You told me about some of what happened to you and that you're looking for peace of mind. What do you need to find that?"

"Those hours back," I admitted. "To know for certain what happened, because it can't be worse than I what I keep imagining. To not worry the guys anymore. They're spending so much time looking after me and trying to shield me from stuff. I'm *not* a fragile person, but I feel so…"

I didn't have the words for what I felt. It didn't fit into a tidy little box. If anything, it spilled out like chaos and scattered all over in a disorganized mess.

"I don't know what I feel. I just don't feel like me."

"Do you mind if I ask where your parents are in this? Can you talk to them?"

"I don't have a dad, or at least, not one that I know. He's never been a fact of my life. My mother…um…I'm suing in court to be emancipated, because she's currently having an affair with the very married father of one of my closest friends and…they're living together. She moved out of the apartment a couple of days before Homecoming."

Yep. Erin blinked.

"I have a temporary injunction granting me emancipation status while the court reviews my case. My lawyer has good feelings about it, because my mother moved out and has had limited time for me over the last couple of years." Longer, but probably better to stay on target.

"I'm sorry to hear that. It has to be tough."

"I'm kind of used to it. She's never been… The words 'emotionally available' would never apply to her." I chewed at my lower lip.

"You said your friends have been staying with you."

"The guys," I told her. "They've been my best friends for years…Coop goes all the way back to kindergarten. He's been in my life pretty much for as long as I can remember. Jake's been there for a long time, too. Ian came later, and Archie last. But…we've been tight." I made a face. "I'm dating them."

"So you have a boyfriend."

"I kind of have three," I admitted. "I had four, sort of, but Ian and I broke up. Well, I broke up with him because he was…he was doing this push and pull, and I didn't know where he was coming from and he wouldn't talk to me, and

I never knew where I stood with Maddy so I thought it would be easier if I just stopped the dating part before our friendship tanked. I don't want to lose any of them as friends, and there are some lines that once you cross them, you can't come back."

I squinted one eye closed as I met her speculative gaze. Okay, to be fair, it might not be speculative, but she definitely seemed to be focused on me. Which, I supposed, was her job.

"Not sure how you categorize train wrecks, but I just might be one."

"Hmm, I think that might be an extreme view to take of yourself. What I hear is a lot of things have been happening, not all of which are under your control. In fact, as with most things in life, the only thing we can truly control is ourselves."

"Not really sure what to do with that advice."

"It's not advice, it's an observation. We're not to the advice portion of our program. We're unpacking things right now. Laying it all out so we can look at it."

I picked up the water and took a really long drink of it. "What else do you want to know?"

"Let's talk about your mother. Tell me about your relationship with her."

We could be here all night. "How much time do we have left?"

"Enough," Erin assured me. "Don't worry about the clock, just focus on me."

So, I told her about the relationship between Maddy and me. I explained why I'd decided to call her by her name. I had to keep jumping back and forth, partially because a part of me wanted to defend her, and the rest of me want to put my foot down on the accelerator of the bus and drive it right over Maddy.

When a little ding sounded, I paused and Erin glanced over at the clock.

"Our hour is up?" Somewhere in there, the hammering of my heart had chilled out and the sick feeling in the pit of my stomach quieted.

"Not quite, I always leave five minutes so we can discuss what we want to do next, particularly because this was our first session. What I would like to do is schedule future sessions with you—I think we have a great deal more to unpack."

More sessions. "I barely made it to this one."

"Was it as terrible as you were expecting?"

"No," I admitted. "But…is this really going to help? I can try to talk to the guys more."

"You can absolutely talk to them. Having people you trust, a strong support network who will listen, that's vital. At the same time, therapy isn't a cure-all, it's a treatment plan. It's a way to help you focus on the issues, and tackle them. I'm here to help you find the answers that work best *for* you."

I swallowed. "So you can't just say like, take these two pills a day for the next few days and it will clear it all up?"

"No," Erin told me kindly. "It doesn't work like that. How comfortable would you be coming in three times a week?"

Three times a week?

"Um…maybe two?" The guys were seeing Diane two or three times a week. "I'm not driving yet. I mean, I did drive yesterday. But it's still challenging." But the guys said they'd bring me, too.

"Well, let's start with two. You came today, I would normally suggest Friday at lunch, but I already have an appointment then." And it was Archie's date night, and his birthday was this weekend with us racing toward Halloween.

"How about next Wednesday? Then we can do that Friday at lunch? Is this a good time for you? We can do it later in the day if you want."

"No, this is fine." I was really going to see a therapist.

"All right, I have you down, and it will email you a confirmation."

I nodded and rose along with her.

"Frankie, do you journal?"

"I'm supposed to be keeping one for class, but I'm pretty behind on it." I held up my right wrist. "The guys are doing a lot of my handwriting, and we kind of skipped over the journaling thing."

"I can understand that, but you can still type with your left hand, yes?"

I could, so I nodded.

"Good, I want you to work on a couple of things for me between now and Wednesday. Also, if you have any questions, email me. You can call and leave a message, but it's not always easy to get me on the phone. I check email between every session."

After she explained my homework, she told me she was looking forward to working with me, and then it was done. I was out of the door and leaving the office building through the glass doors. Rachel was parked right where I'd left her, and she was busily typing away on her phone when I opened the passenger door and let out a waft of burgers, fries, and spotted the drinks in the cup holders.

"Hey," she said with a grin. "I got a vicious case of the munchies after I bitch-slapped some asses on Snapchat. I doubled the order so you could eat, too."

Before I went into the appointment, the thought of food made me want to puke, but my stomach was growling like hell as I unwrapped the cheeseburger. "Thank you."

"Got to take care of my girl," she told me, then clicked her phone off and glanced over at me. "So…do you want me to ask how it went, or just give you your space on that and we talk about the rest of the world?"

I took a bite of the burger and damn near groaned. While it wasn't super hot or anything, it was really tasty. My stomach growled happily as I swallowed that first mouthful. "It went okay. I'm…I'm not sure what to do with it all. But I think I'd rather talk about other things for now, if that's all right. She does want to see me again next week."

"Tell me when, I'll make sure you get here."

"Rach, I'm really glad you're my friend."

"Right back atcha." There was a moment of silence, then she said, "Now, moving on to other things—Sharon is a cunt and she must be destroyed."

"What?"

"She decided to post more of her fun little videos."

I groaned. I needed to add Sharon to the list of people I hated. But I just didn't have the energy for her right now. "Of the guys?"

"No, of you and Mitch. She cut together this lovely piece of trash to suggest you led Mitch on, but phrased it like, well what was he supposed to think since everyone else is tapping you."

Every ounce of my appetite fled.

Rachel grimaced. "I wasn't going to tell you. I went back and forth on it, then I thought if it was me, I'd want to know. Needless to say, I've reported it, and I've got my girls on it reporting the hell out of it. I also might have emailed it to the cops."

Setting the burger back in my lap, I stared out the window. "My phone is on silent at the moment." I'd put it in do not disturb for the appointment. I squirmed to reach for my back pocket when Rachel cut her head in a sharp negative.

"Don't. Believe me when I say *you* do not need to see that trash. It's lies. Anyone who was at Homecoming would see the lies."

"Not everybody went to Homecoming, Rach."

"No, but the people who matter did, and bitch showed her hand this time."

"So she posted it as her?"

"No, it came from an anonymous account. I don't know it. She, however, added it to the school mailing list, and it went out to all the accounts. That shit right there is enough to get her busted."

I swallowed. Phone out, I stared at the screen.

Jake

Call me before you do anything else.

Coop

We'll meet you in the parking lot when Rachel gets back with you.

Archie

Unless you decide to blow off the rest of the day, and if you do, just text us and we'll meet you at the apartment.

Ian

Whatever you need. Just say the word.

Whatever that video showed, it must have been truly awful. They weren't mentioning it all, and there was an intense vibe of protectiveness in each of those texts.

"Why does she hate me so much? I'm not trying to be dense. But, when did I become the enemy? She and Ian weren't even dating when he asked me out. Not that we're dating right now, but what did I ever do to her?"

"You're you," Rachel said with a shrug, stopping at a red light. "You're the girl they all want. Everyone knew it, Frankie. All of us. The only one oblivious to it was you. Every single one of those girls always knew they were on borrowed time. Jake, you couldn't nail down with a power tool. Coop drifted, half the time I was never sure he was even aware he was dating when he broke up with girls. Archie? Yeah, he knew. But he was never serious. It was always a passing fancy for him, and Bubba? Who the hell knows with that guy? Sharon was probably the girl he dated the longest, and even then, it wasn't him chasing her. He never chased any of the girls. They always came to him."

"Believe it or not, that part I know." I'd had a front row seat for it all.

The light changed, and she accelerated. "Yeah, but that's my point. You were always too close to it. But you were the one they couldn't supplant. Because whether you noticed the guys' interest or not, every single one of those girls was in full on competition with you."

"We were friends before that."

"Oh, honey, I love you, but no. You might have been friends with some of them, but definitely not all. Actually, I take that back, you were probably friends. They weren't. Not all of them. You were their ticket in. Making friends with Frankie might get you an intro, and then there's always the confidence that happens when the guys actually ask them out. But it doesn't take long to notice—if you wanted or needed something, they'd drop those other girls without a second thought."

"That's asinine."

Rachel shrugged. "I don't make the rules. I'm just telling you what I see. Right now, Sharon doesn't hate you anywhere near as much as she hates herself for not being you. Maria's gotten over it. I think Maria wouldn't mind being your friend again, she just doesn't know how."

"And Patty?"'

"Eh, fuck Patty. Fuck Sharon, too. Fuck that little junior chick who got stupid with you."

A laugh slipped out, and I shook my head. "I just want the crap to stop. I've tried ignoring it and being understanding."

"And you know that's not going to work, right?"

"Yeah." I did. "I slapped her down a while back."

"Good. You need to do it again. I'll help." She sounded almost eager.

"Oh that terrifies me. What you would do for revenge?"

"Revenge is such an ugly word," Rachel informed me as we pulled into the parking lot. Sure enough, all four of my guys were right there waiting just feet away from Rachel's assigned parking spot. "I call it just desserts. After all, she's asking for it. Making sure we deliver it would seem to be the polite thing to do."

I shook my head, but I was focused on the four of them.

My guys.

I'd included Ian in that. But he seemed to want to be included. I really was messed up.

"Also, I think I'm going to be a little sick with the sugar waiting for you." As soon as the car stopped, Jake opened my door and Rachel looked at them. "I already told her what the bitch did, and she still needs to eat. So blow off fifth period, eat the food, and let's talk about what we're going to do."

"You're in?" was all Jake asked her as he popped my seatbelt for me and then searched my face. "You're okay?"

I glanced from him to the guys, then to Rachel, before I swung my gaze back to Jake. "Yeah," I said. "I'm okay. And I think Rachel's definitely in. She's diabolical."

"You might be a prick," Rachel informed Jake. "But I'm a whole damn cactus."

Coop snickered. "Yeah, Rachel gets my vote."

"What the hell," Archie murmured as Jake gathered up my food for me before I slid out of the car. Coop snagged my backpack from Rachel. "At least we know she can actually hit her."

"Yes," Rachel said, in a tone smug as fuck. "I can definitely hit her."

I searched Ian's face. This was his ex we were discussing. But all I found in his eyes was concern for me.

The text he'd sent earlier echoed in the back of my mind. *Whatever you need. Just say the word.*

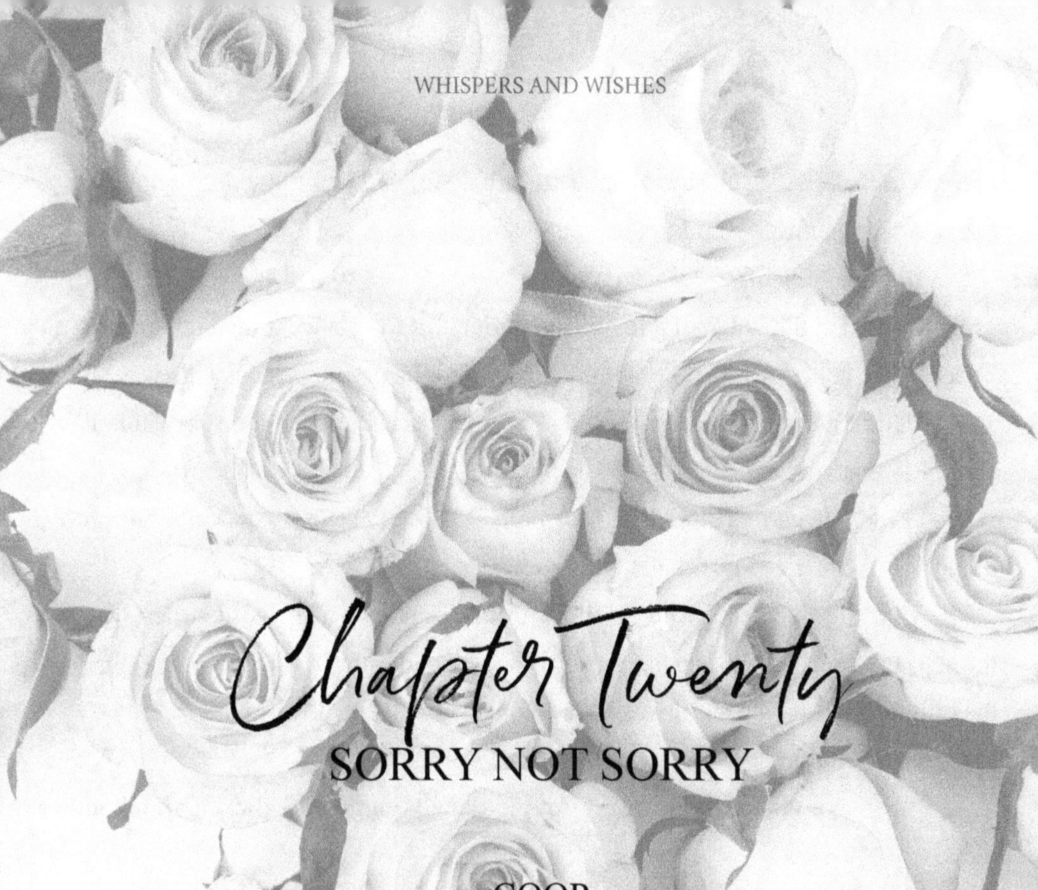

Chapter Twenty

SORRY NOT SORRY

COOP

We found a spot away from the main doors and set up for Frankie to eat while we talked plans. The air practically radiated with anger rolling in waves off of Jake and Archie. They were so pissed, they couldn't see straight. Another reason I didn't want anyone making an independent decision. Jake had enough problems because of his temper, he didn't need any new ones.

Rachel wasn't so much pissed as vindictive as fuck. Remind me to never get on her bad side. I was beginning to think we'd gotten off light that she'd only told Frankie about us warning guys off her. That could have gone a lot worse.

Bubba, though… Bubba wore a toxic combo of guilt and rage. Guilt because he'd dated her, and rage? Well, the same reason the rest of us were pissed off.

The earlier actions had been bad enough. Posting the pictures. Tagging

Frankie to make sure she saw them. The verbal taunts. Even the video about our behavior and painting Frankie in a negative light.

But this bullshit?

I stared at the video playing on my phone. I'd long since muted it. Not that I needed the sound track to go with the text captions on the screen. This was an attack. This was using what happened *to* Frankie against her, and no way in hell could I let it stand.

"Fine, we can't strip her car for parts," Jake conceded. "It would be fun though."

That didn't even garner a smile from Frankie as she worked her way through the fries. There was no gusto to how she ate. In fact, I was pretty sure the only reason she ate at all was because we were all checking on her.

Fuck Sharon.

"We have video of our own," Archie pointed out, and I flicked a look at him.

"Dude," I said with a slight shake of my head.

"Let me guess, video from the summer?" Frankie asked.

"Yes," Archie admitted.

"How does that make us any better than she is?"

"Right now, I don't care about being better," Jake admitted. "The attacks have to stop. The only language that bitch understands is just as mean as what she's been spewing."

Frankie's shoulders sagged, and I scowled. My girl was not a quitter. She just preferred direct fights. Probably because of all the passive aggressive crap with her mother. "Frankie," I told her. "We can't do nothing. I know you have never been a fan of bullying. I get it. This isn't that."

"No," Bubba said slowly. "It's not. It's retaliation, and right now, she really deserves retaliation."

Rachel leaned her head back and stared upward. Her sunglasses hid her eyes from me, but she drummed her fingers like she was thinking. "You have to three-prong the bitch."

"Excuse me?" Archie asked.

"Hit her from three different sides. We're not just going after her for this video, but for all of them. Right now, it's the only power she has left. She keeps doing it because people are listening to her. So we have to humiliate her the same way she's trying to humiliate Frankie. Chip away at what support she has left and leave her looking petty as fuck, if not dumber than a box of rocks. The kind of chick no one wants anything to do with…not even jocks who don't care where they get their rocks off. No offense."

Jake grunted, but Bubba just looked pained.

I felt for the guy. Except… "Look, Laura fucked with Frankie. She tried to mess with her head, and she was cruel. Own the fact that we made shitty choices and move on. We all made mistakes. Those mistakes aren't allowed to lash out at her. They want us? Bring it on. But not her."

"Oh, it's a good thing you're pretty," Rachel told me with a pat on my arm, and I narrowed my eyes at her. "Dude, why do you think Sharon is going after her so hard?" She pointed a finger at Bubba as if I couldn't guess. "Because she wants to punish him. She hates Frankie because she wants to be her and can't—oh."

A slow smile crossed her face, and almost as one, Archie and Jake eased back an inch.

"I'm not alone in saying that smile is evil, am I?" Archie asked.

"No," Frankie answered, shocking all of us. "Rachel is really good at being bad."

"I'm a cactus, touch me and get stabbed." Turning speculative eyes on Bubba, Rachel said, "How willing are you to get your hands dirty on this one?"

"What do you need me to do?"

I raised my brows, and I wasn't alone. Bubba didn't hesitate. At the same time, a smile pulled at the corners of my lips. The guy had been trying to make it clear he was all in.

With a glance at Frankie, he added, "Name it. I'll do it."

Perched where I was at the end of the table, I didn't miss the small smile on her lips or the way her gaze snared on Bubba's for a beat longer than necessary.

Well, well…it was about damn time.

I just had to hope he didn't screw it up.

"Tell us the plan first," I reminded everyone. "We all have to agree, or we don't do it."

"Pfft," Rachel said, sticking out her tongue. "Democracy sucks. You should be a matriarchy, that way what Frankie wants, goes."

Jake snorted, and Archie grinned.

I didn't mind that so much, except…

"I prefer democracy," Frankie said, and even Bubba laughed at that.

"You keep spoiling my fun," Rachel told her in a mock whisper.

"Sorry."

"No you're not."

"No," Frankie said with a real smile. "I'm not. So what's your evil plan?"

At least the next bite she took had a little more effort in it and a little more interest.

That was something.

Course, by the time Rachel was done, I wasn't sure whether we shouldn't be more terrified than amazed.

Evil plan was right.

JAKE

Bubba had upped his game some from side-eye to eye bang, and I was all for it. Later. Right now, we needed to focus on dealing with the Sharon situation. This shit had gone on way too long. I was beyond over it. If she'd been a dude, I'd have already kicked her ass sideways.

As it was, I was half-tempted, but my mother would have my ass in a sling if I raised a hand to a girl. She'd be right, too. Still, it was really fucking annoying. I'd encourage Frankie to punch the bitch, but she had her arm already in a cast.

"It'll take a little coordination," Rachel said. "But we can do it. But you all have to agree." Almost as one, we all looked at Frankie.

There were days when she was too damn nice. But it was that compassion that we all valued, too. The openness of her heart and ability to embrace dating all of us, and honestly, I never felt like I was getting the short end of the stick. I knew what I mean to her.

More, I knew what she meant to me.

"You'd have your hands pretty much clean," I told her. What Rachel described would only involve Frankie indirectly. Say what you wanted about Rachel, and trust me, I could say and had said a lot, she got our girl.

"That doesn't really seem fair," she pointed out. I didn't groan, though I did scowl at her. "Not the plan," Frankie corrected, meeting my gaze, and the challenge in those gorgeous green eyes dared me to disagree with her. "Keeping me out of it is sweet. But she's targeting me. Whether to get even with you guys or to punish me or both. I should be involved, too."

"You're a part of the decision," Coop offered. "You don't have to play a part in anything else. Sharon wasn't your problem until we made her one."

"Until I made her one," Bubba corrected him.

"No," Frankie argued, twisting until she locked gazes with Bubba again. "She made herself a problem."

I wasn't alone in sighing. Frankie would give us a lot of slack, and she'd forgiven a lot of our shit. But I was with Bubba on this one. We made Sharon Frankie's problem. It really was on us to fix it.

On Bubba.

He was manning up to handle it, so we'd have his back.

"Are y'all done?" Rachel asked, bridging the silence. "Because the sweetness is going to give me a cavity at this rate."

Frankie laughed and bumped her shoulder to Rachel's. "You're just jealous."

"Hmm," Rachel said thoughtfully. "Maybe. Just a smidge. But I know I'm your favorite girl, and I bet they have arguments over who your favorite is. So I win."

Arms folded, I rolled my eyes, but Frankie cracked up so I'd take the needling. Not that I'd ever ask her to pick favorites.

Ever.

"Back to the plan," Archie said, leaning forward. "We have about five minutes before the bell rings, then we need to hit sixth period."

Rachel nodded. "I'll prime the pump, since I don't have sixth or seventh periods. A few well placed text messages, and the rumors will be generating. She'll have heard about it by seventh."

"She still stalks your path," Archie said with a nod as he transferred his attention to Bubba.

"Yep," he said with a sigh. "Unfortunately."

"Would it be better if she could do it in front of me, or do I need to be out of sight?"

Personally, I wanted Frankie nowhere near it. Neither did Archie from his expression, but Coop said, "She might not go for it if she sees you. Bubba's been giving her a hard pass."

"Actually," Bubba said, twisting to look at her. "It might play better if you do 'catch' us and then slap the shit out of me."

"Oh, I vote for that," Rachel said, arm shooting into the air, and this time, I had a hard time biting back a laugh. The girl was nuts and into our girl. Still… she was funny.

Frankie, however, frowned, but Bubba wasn't done. "Think about it. We've looked rocky from the outside, and we have been. This just takes it up a notch, and you get to play a role." His gaze fixed on her, and I almost whistled.

Nice. Well, at least someone had found their damn game, finally.

"You really want me to hit you?"

"No, but I kind of deserve it, don't I?" When she didn't deny his teasing, he nodded. "You bust me, slap the shit out of me, and walk off. We won't have a lot of time in that window, and that will amp the pressure."

"I'll be with Frankie," I said. "I'm usually walking her out to the lot to hand off to Coop or Archie."

Frankie wrinkled her nose and then stuck her tongue out at me. "You make me sound like a football."

"Nah, you're way more valuable." I winked, but Coop had straightened.

"That works. I'll make sure I'm close to intercept—if we're going with football metaphors—then Frankie can cry on my shoulder, and I'll offer her big comfort."

"Yeah, that's what you'll offer her." Archie slapped his shoulder. "So you have a tight window to drop that bomb in there, and Rachel has the reaction primed, and we just wait to see what she does?"

"Best we can do," Bubba said. "And I'll do it every damn day until I have what we need."

None of us liked that plan.

"Ugh. Kill me and can the dramatics, guys." Rachel gagged and stood, gathering up the trash. At least Frankie had eaten most of her food. I caught Archie studying the food too, and then lifted my chin when he glanced at me. We needed to get her favorites tonight. The decline in her appetite had been noticeable over the last couple of days, particularly after her mother's last drop in visit on the heels of being stuck in a cast.

I leaned over and caught Frankie's left hand as she stood, then pulled her to me and dropped a kiss on her lips. Yeah, no PDAs at school, but fuck it at the moment. She sighed and leaned in to me for a few seconds, and I murmured, "It's going to work, Baby Girl. Trust us?"

"Yes." I never realized just how much power that one word could have, particularly when it came to asking her to believe in us.

No way in hell would I let her down.

Ever.

"I'm walking her to class," I decided, and Archie snorted but he nodded anyway. Rachel just rolled her eyes. "Hey, Rach."

"Hmm?"

"You got a little something there on the corner of your mouth." Coop cracked up before I'd even finished speaking.

"Yeah, drool," Archie added on. "Definitely noticeable."

She flipped us all off, but I grabbed Frankie's backpack with my free hand and tucked her under my other arm.

"Rach," Frankie said as we started walking away. "Thank you."

"My pleasure," she called. "'Cause this shit is gonna be lit. Excuse me, I need to go fan the flames."

The bell rang, and I cut toward the doors that were always unlocked during the day and let us bypass hitting the office.

"You good for sixth period?" I asked.

"Yep," she said. "How hard should I slap Ian?"

"Really hard. It'll be therapeutic for both of you. Just make sure you use your left hand."

That got me a pinch, a shove, and a grin.

Worth it.

RACHEL

I waited a second as Jake ushered Frankie away. Coop and Archie didn't waste any time in following, and then it was just me and Bubba. "Not going to class?"

"I wanted to talk to you," he said.

"Well, I guessed that, shit for brains. What did you want to talk to me about?"

"How are you planning on winding her up specifically?"

I shrugged. "That's really for me to know and you to just to take advantage of."

Pretty boy scowled, and I smiled. Objectively, the guy was good-looking. Not my type, but he had some hidden emotional depths, when he wasn't being a blithering idiot who tripped over his own tongue and crapped on the best thing that ever happened to him.

Not that I was bitter.

Nope.

I'd nursed my crush for as far as it went, and I got a new friend out of it, so win win for me.

"Yeah, but I need to know because I don't want it to blow back on Frankie."

Yeah. "Tell you what, you let me do my part, and you just make sure you do yours. Tripping over your tongue is a specialty, and I really would hate to see it fall into that bitch's mouth and burn any bridges you might be in the process of rebuilding. Catch my drift?"

He scowled at me, and I had to admit, *that* was a good look on him. "You're protecting Frankie, so I'll let that slide. Don't ever say shit like that to me again. Wanting her has never been the problem, and I would rather cut off my tongue than touch Sharon with it again."

"Good boy, there might be hope for you yet. Now shoo. I have work to do, and I stir shit better when someone isn't watching me." Utterly untrue, but he needed to go away. "Besides, Frankie slapping you is a stellar idea. It might actually help her forgive you."

He let out a little sigh and shifted his backpack strap. "Not sure I'll ever deserve it."

Ugh. Okay. "Look," I said, relenting. "You screwed up. But it's not irreparable."

He frowned. "Are you giving me advice?"

"Shut up and take it, but do not comment on it, or I'm walking away. Got it?"

Hands raised, he said, "Got it."

"Good. You hurt her. You hurt her a lot, because you didn't know what you wanted and you projected that on her. Like you thought she didn't know or wouldn't. You decided you knew how she felt better than she did. Stupid mistake. Huge. Never ever tell someone how they really feel. It's patronizing and dickish. That said, you seem to have woken up face down in the cow pasture and tasted the manure. Good job. Now clean that shit off and just go for it. She's not throwing you out the door, and you've been stepping up since that fucktard put hands on her. I can't say whether you did before or not, but that's neither here nor there. Stop hesitating. Grab that girl and kiss her like you mean it. Sometimes, actions speak a fuckton louder than words."

I took two steps away and then whirled back as the bell rang again. Dude was so getting a tardy. Not my problem. "But to be clear, you hurt her again, and what we do to Sharon is going to look like a picnic next to what I'll do to you."

He opened his mouth, then snapped it shut again.

Good boy.

Maybe he could learn.

"See you in a couple of hours for Operation Bitch Slap." Such a stupid name and funny at the same time. "Toodles."

I was halfway to my car before I glanced over my shoulder. Bubba was gone. I could only hope he took my advice.

Back in my car, I had my phone out and my feet up as I scrolled through my contacts.

Who was in Sharon's sixth period class?

ARCHIE

Both classes dragged like hell, probably because I was itching to get back out there. From the moment that video dropped, all I could think about was crushing those bitches like a bug. While we hadn't really discussed it, I had zero doubt that Patty wasn't involved in that shit. She'd had a hate-on for Frankie because she was under some delusion that Frankie was the reason Patty and I weren't getting back together.

She wasn't the only girl gunning for her. I used to think this girl-on-girl shit was funny before it involved Frankie. I didn't mind when they fought over us. Hell, it entertained me. The lengths some girls went to get our attention.

But this?

Nothing funny about this at all. The verbal attacks had been one thing. This bordered on criminal. Seriously, painting Frankie as someone who invited being drugged and assaulted? That crossed so many lines, she was in another county.

As far as I was concerned, crushing her like an insect would be too good for her. I would go along with the plan for now, but I wanted contingencies in place.

It might take a little finagling, but my grandfather was in town, and if anyone knew how to pull strings and make shit happen? He'd be the guy to ask.

I might have already sent him a text to do just that, but I had to be careful, too. Frankie didn't want to hurt Sharon—that compassionate heart of hers was too much. I wanted to hurt the bitch, but Frankie didn't. So I just needed to make the problem go away.

Jake hit me with a text during classes, verifying I'd be in place before it went down. Coop was always the first one to the lot, but I wouldn't miss it for the world.

We needed all the camera angles.

He texted a few more times, going over the plan in the group chat. Bubba and Coop indulged him, and I just paid attention in case something came up that I needed to know.

My phone buzzed *again* about five minutes before the end of the day. Jake was on edge, but I'd expected it to be Bubba. Instead it was a number I didn't recognize.

Unknown

This is Maddy Curtis. I would like to speak to you privately.

I snorted. Was this bitch for real?

Me

Give me one good reason why I shouldn't just block your ass right now.

Unknown

Because you seem to care about my daughter.

Seemed to care. What a cunt.

Me

You'll have to do better than that. You wouldn't know caring if it bit you in the ass.

Unknown

The three dots hung there for a long while, and the bell rang. Too late, I muted the message and then slid it off the screen as I abandoned the class. I wanted a front row seat to the action.

I didn't quite run, but I still managed to hit the shortcut down the band hall and then right outside where I could circle back toward the doors Bubba usually exited. Switching the focus on the camera, I turned it on to record before sliding it into the pocket of my shirt. As long as I angled toward them, it would catch everything.

Rachel sat cross legged on the grass, not far from the same doors, with her phone in her hand while she looked for all the world like she was texting.

If I didn't know what she was up to, I would have bought it.

Coop strolled through the door first. He lifted his chin toward me as he headed in my direction, and I nodded. Why would we ignore each other? It wasn't like we didn't usually hang out or anything.

Not ten seconds later, Sharon exited with Bubba, and he had his head angled toward her like he was listening. There was no physical contact. Just Sharon talking a mile a minute while Bubba pretended to be interested.

"Showtime," I murmured as Jake pushed the door open to let Frankie out. The sun hit her blonde hair and gave it a glow. She already had her sunglasses out and tucked them on. Half-turned toward Jake, she made a show of noticing Bubba.

I held my breath as she locked on to where he and Sharon stood. Sharon noticed her first—well, seemingly. I highly doubted it, but Bubba's body language was hard to read, considering how stiffly he stood there already.

Frankie's lips compressed, and the anger flashing over her face was so close to the day she'd ripped into us about her mother's affair with Edward that I winced.

Blowing out a breath, I fought the surge of hot cold and my stomach bottoming out. I never wanted her that upset again.

Jake caught her arm as if trying to half-heartedly hold her back, but she shrugged him off as she marched toward them. Sharon had a hand on Bubba's arm and stepped into him.

Fuck, I wished I could hear what she was saying exactly, but then Frankie was there.

He jerked around to face Frankie, and the crack of her hand colliding with his cheek echoed across the quad.

No missing that.

I swore Sharon grinned before she snarled at Frankie and took a step toward her. Oh fuck no, but I'd only taken one step before Jake was there, inserting himself between them.

Okay, not the plan. But we rolled with it. Particularly when Jake said something to Sharon, and her face mottled with rage.

Fucking bitch.

Okay, walk away, Frankie. Time to walk away.

She was, but she didn't look happy about it, even if Jake brought her straight toward us.

Red hand print blazing on Bubba's cheek, he tracked Frankie's progress with a look so close to devastation, I almost thought it was real.

IAN

The sting on my face barely registered as I tracked Frankie stalking away from me. The hurt and anger in her expression had seemed damn real. It made me raw and ache inside.

"Are you all right?" Sharon asked, reaching up to touch my still smarting cheek. It took everything I had not to wrench away. As it was, I still flinched a little, and she slowed her action. "Does it hurt?"

Had she not been paying attention? "I'll live," I gritted out. "You were saying something. You know, before."

Because the sooner we got this over and done with, the better. "I've just been worried about you," she said, then stepped in closer to me. I shifted back until we were out of the flow of people exiting the building. More than a few curious gazes flew in our direction.

Maria, for one, and that junior Coop had been dating, and Cheryl. I didn't catch where she went, but I trusted Coop and Archie to keep Frankie safe.

"Look, Sharon," I tried to pitch my voice a little lower, as if I liked having her this close. "I have to get to practice."

"I know, it's that day. I could wait for you. We could go hang out after."

I'd rather dip my dick in bleach. "Probably not a good idea," I admitted with a sigh. "Things are just…messy at the moment."

"How can I help?"

I shook my head. "You can't." If she'd just fuck off and leave Frankie alone, that would be great, but she wasn't going there on her own, so now we'd make her go there.

"Bubba," she continued, clasping my arm, and as much as I wanted to shake her off, I had to play my part. "You know there's nothing I wouldn't do for you. I'm pretty sure I proved that this summer. Remember?"

"Yeah." The thought made me sick. "I was pretty much an ass to a lot of people this summer. Not sure that's something you should be proud of."

"Why not? I made you feel good. I mean, I know you played with some others, but you came back to me."

Wow, did she really think so little of herself? I fucked around on her, and that was okay? To be strictly fair, I didn't specifically cheat when I was with her, but I wasn't *with* her that long.

"You know I'll do anything for you."

"Look, Sharon, being around me isn't a good idea. Look at the crap Frankie's taking. People won't leave her alone, and we're not even dating anymore."

Her eyes glittered with unsuppressed joy. I clenched my fist on the strap of my backpack to keep from responding when she dug her nails into my arm.

"The last thing I'd want is for someone to do to you what they've been doing to her."

"Oh, baby, you don't have to worry about that." She laughed. "Frankie needed to be taken down a few pegs. Stuck up little bitch thinks she can walk off with everyone's guys, and we wouldn't do anything about it?" A very unfriendly sound escaped her in a snort. "Let's just say I'm providing her with a crash course in real life. All that repressed bad girl coming out in her is turning her into a slut. You know the whole team is talking about it, and then her setting up Mitch that way…"

Was she really that delusional?

"…I mean, sure, he probably just wanted to tap that because he wanted to tap everyone you guys did. But it doesn't matter, right? I'm on your side, and you don't have to worry about me."

"No?" I raised my brows. "You already fuck Mitch, Sharon?"

"Maybe." She gave a little shrug. "I figure a little tit for a little tat is fair. You strayed. I tested out your teammates. I figured I'd get your other boys, but I wouldn't do that to the girls. I have some sense of loyalty."

I just shook my head. "That's what you call loyalty?"

"What?" Sharon frowned.

"Hey," Jake said, cutting in. "We gotta go, Bubba."

"Fuck off, Jake. We're having a moment," Sharon informed him.

"Wasn't talking to you, skank. I'd tell you to suck my dick, but I wouldn't want it to fall off."

"I wouldn't touch your dick anyway…you know I'm all about Bubba."

Yeah. I couldn't do this anymore. I wanted her hands off me. But the look of pure malice on Jake's face kept me still.

"Really? I'm pretty sure that was you begging me the last night before school started. You were horny and Bubba wouldn't fuck you, but I looked free, so you all but tried to crawl onto my cock, and I had to dump your ass in the pool to get you off of me."

Sharon's eyes blazed, and her face went red. "That's not true."

"Well, we can always check the video," Jake taunted her. "You like video. You and the girls were all over us, and you didn't seem to care who you got as long as you got one of us, so spin your bullshit for Bubba, and if he wants to buy in, I'll be sure to get him an appointment for that STD panel."

"Fuck you," she snarled at him, then looked at me. "Are you going to let him talk to me like that?"

I shrugged. "Is he lying?"

She froze. "What?"

"Is. He. Lying?" I enunciated every word clearly.

"Well, we might have had a moment, but we were drunk."

Translation. Jake wasn't lying.

I didn't care, other than that I hadn't seen through this crap in the first place. Rachel was right. I fucked up royally.

"And all your little attacks on Frankie? Those lies?"

"No—they're just—well—they're true. From a certain point of view."

Jake snorted. "Cunt."

"Fuck off," she growled at him, and he smiled. It was not a friendly smile. "Make me."

She let out a little scream. "Bubba?"

We had an audience now, not just the folks who'd planned on watching it—like Archie, Coop, Rachel, and fuck me, Frankie was right there. But there were other kids, too. Sharon was really making a spectacle of herself.

"What? You're a big girl. You just told me you can handle it."

She flushed a deep crimson. "Of course, I can. Should I meet you after practice, since you have to go?"

"Why?"

"Why what?"

"Why should you meet me after practice?"

"So we can talk about getting back together again. I'll make it real nice for you."

"No."

"What?"

"I said no," I repeated for her. "You must have a hearing issue. People tell you no, and you don't hear it. People tell you they aren't interested and it doesn't fit your narrative, so you twist it. You make up lies and then call it creatively telling the truth from a certain point of view. You're the worst kind of person. The worst kind of girl. Backstabbing. Manipulative. Shallow. Even worse than all of that—you're pathetic."

Yeah. Not the plan. Didn't care anymore.

Her eyes widened.

"I dumped you months ago. Get over it." With that, I turned and stalked away from her with Jake right next to me. He actually laughed when we were halfway to the stadium.

"Damn, Bubba. I didn't know you had it in you."

Yeah. I didn't know it either. "She's the second worst mistake I ever made."

"Yeah?"

I nodded. "Letting Frankie think I didn't care was the worst."

"Dude, you can still fix it."

I intended to.

Rachel had the right idea. I pulled my phone out and switched it off from recording, then tapped the file to send it to Archie. "Think we got it?"

"I know we did." Jake slapped my back. "She isn't going to know what hit her. Besides, she made such a scene, everyone was checking it out and filming it."

I snorted. "I thought that was Frankie's slap getting their interest."

"Oh, that definitely earned some play. How's the face?"

"Hurts."

"Good," he said with a grin.

"Ass."

"Definitely. But you deserved it."

Yeah. I really had. "Fuck, I hope this works."

On all counts.

Chapter Twenty-One
SLEEPING ARRANGEMENTS

ARCHIE

Soon as Bubba and Jake stalked off from Sharon, I looped my arm through Frankie's. "Time to go."

"I should have slapped *her*." The hostility edging Frankie's voice was pretty damn sexy. More telling was the possessiveness in her voice.

"You can slap her later," Coop promised, and I shot a look at him. The very last thing Frankie needed was to be getting in a fight. She still had a damn broken wrist. "C'mon, we need to grab food."

She made a scoffing noise.

"And we need to work on the rest of this," I said, hoping the verbal nudge would get her moving. It worked. We split up at the cars, Coop heading for his while Frankie climbed into the Ferrari with me. Thankfully, she was inside the car and didn't see Sharon glaring after her. But I did.

I made sure the bitch knew I saw her. She better remember where she was and who I was before she started something up with me. After one last filthy glare, she cut away and headed across the parking lot. Coop swung past my spot, the lot had emptied pretty rapidly, and he rolled down his window.

"What are you doing?"

"Just keeping an eye on her."

"Yeah yeah," he said. "Let's go."

I snorted. Coop had always been the cooler of the heads among us, and he'd always been the most relaxed. Today, he'd also been the most in charge, and the fact that he got Jake to calm the fuck down and listen was a minor miracle. "Sure thing."

Inside, I glanced at Frankie, who stared through the windshield toward the stadium. "Hey," I told her, reaching over to clasp her left hand. "Bubba's fine. He knew what he needed to do, and he did it."

"I know," she admitted. "But how much of a hypocrite am I that watching that, even knowing what I knew, pissed me off because I didn't want her touching him? Particularly when *he* didn't want her touching him."

Lifting her hand, I press my lips to her knuckles. "I ever tell you that your left is almost as powerful as that right you can throw?"

The distraction worked, she glared at me. Hey, I'd take what I could get. "You're not funny."

"You wound me."

The corners of her mouth gave the barest of twitches. "You're impossible to wound. You have a magnificent ego."

"I do, don't I?" I winked at her. At least some of her scowl had diminished. Starting the car, I backed out and spotted Coop waiting for us. He'd given me time to settle her. Five bucks said he was aware of how uneasy that whole scenario would have left Frankie.

Part of that was why we hadn't wanted her involved in the first place.

She sighed.

"Talk to me?"

"About what?"

"Anything," I said. "Do you want to tell me how the appointment went? How are classes going? Do you want to see if you can record the classes, or are you getting the notes and stuff from the teachers? Halloween would be good. Anything you want to talk about, babe."

"How is this going to work exactly? Rachel made a recording, you did, Jake did, and I know Bubba was recording it, too, right?"

Okay. So we would talk about how it would work. I diverted toward Starbuck's. Conversation like this required coffee or liquor. With the pain meds she had, no liquor needed to be involved. Behind us, Coop followed right into the drive-thru line. I waved at him and he shot me the bird.

Aww, poor Coop. Stuck without Frankie in his car. I should shed a tear.

"You're smirking."

"I am. But I'm picking on Coop in my head, and it's really funny."

She snorted.

"As for how it will work, let me order the coffee and I'll walk you through it again." I thumb nailed it down to the bullet points. "Step one—Rachel already happened. Step two—with Bubba we just witnessed."

"And participated in," Frankie pointed out. "I hope I didn't hurt him."

I did not laugh. I deserved a medal for not laughing. "Bubba can take a hit. Besides, if you'd really wanted to hurt him, all you had to do was have Jake pop him."

"Jake has already hit him. A lot."

True. "So, see, if you'd really wanted to hurt him, you wouldn't have been the one hitting him. At least not bare-handed. I've seen your golf swing. You can do serious damage."

She laughed.

It was like winning the pennant race. "Okay, point taken. So step three is splicing all the recordings together?"

"Yup," I said. "I'll work on that once we're back. I may need to head over to my place, but I'll try it on the laptop first."

"Are you sleeping over there?"

"Why?" I teased. "Going to come with me?"

"Yes."

Oh.

Well, hell yes.

"Frankie…"

"Don't say if you're ready," she mused. "Someone told me my left is pretty mean, and it's almost over the slap I gave Ian."

"Noted." I slid a sideways look at her. "Babe, if you coming over means you're just sleeping in my bed with me, that's fine. If we're doing anything else in that bed, that's fine, too. I'm not telling you no."

"But you're worried about me."

"I am. Kind of comes with the title." I pulled into a parking spot and eyed her. "Not going to ask me what title?"

"You're my boyfriend," she murmured, then lifted her eyes to meet my gaze. "I worry about you, too."

"Comes with the title," I said.

"Exactly."

Coop opened her door. "And what are we doing in here?"

She smiled at me. "Discussing titles."

"I'm partial to Master of the Universe." The easy smile on Coop's face and the softer tone relaxed some of the tension right out of her. "What do you think, Queen of the Cats? Or Feline Woman?"

"Feline Woman?"

Yeah, I was with Frankie on that one. That sounded terrible. "Dude, no. Catwoman."

That might have been a mistake, because as we slid out of the car, I found myself imagining her in a slinky black bodysuit. Leather.

Oh. Yeah.

My gaze collided with Coop's as he licked his lips. Okay, I was down with sharing that fantasy. "We still need to pick out some Halloween costumes."

She hesitated, glancing from me to Coop and then back. "I am not dressing up as Catwoman, you dirty, dirty boys."

"Aww," Coop groaned. "But you would be in all that leather and have a whip."

She rolled her eyes. "No."

"Not even if one of us dresses up as Batman?" I offered, and she strode away from me, laughing.

"Not even."

"We'll work on that," Coop said, and we both grinned.

While I downloaded the files that Bubba, Rachel, and Coop sent over, and Frankie took care of the cats with Coop before putting some things together.

"You going over to Archie's tonight?" he asked. I was in the living room, but they weren't exactly being quiet about the conversation.

"Maybe," she told him, and I smiled. "If he has to go over there to work on this project, I'm going with him." There was a beat. "You don't mind, do you?"

"Well, I kind of like sleeping here with you, but we can give Archie a night if he has to go back to the big lonely mansion without you. He's had a few nights away, seems only fair."

I smirked and called, "Your benevolence knows no bounds."

"I know, right?" he answered, then his voice dropped to a more normal tone. "And no, I don't mind, Frankie. You guys can stay here if you want, we can all make ourselves scarce and let you have an evening to yourself. Or at least part of it, and I can always come sneak back in after you're all warm and naked and sleepy."

"Subtle, man. Real subtle."

"Not even trying to be subtle. I like sleeping with her."

Who didn't? Whatever Frankie answered, I didn't catch, but I managed to get all the clips downloaded and laid out in the video program one after the other.

It would take some time to play them all.

"I also don't mind sharing her," Coop pointed out as he wandered back into the living room. I glanced past him but didn't see Frankie.

"Jake called," he said. "So she's talking to him. I think he needed to know she was okay after all of that."

I nodded. Made sense to me.

"How's she look to you?"

"I think that was harder on her than she cares to admit."

Yeah, I got that, too.

"Well, this better work, 'cause if Sharon comes after her again, I don't know what I'm going to do exactly, but it won't be pretty." I'd already decided I could reach out to my grandfather. Ted Standish knew exactly how to deal with people who did him dirty. Maybe I could get Sharon's parents transferred to the ass-end of New Mexico or something.

That would be a feat.

No Sharon, no problem, right?

"If this doesn't work and Sharon goes after her again, we might need bail money for Jake and Bubba." Coop tugged at his lower lip, and I eyed him.

"Bubba's not going to snap." Jake? Yes. Three weeks of anger management did not a solution make.

"I don't know about that. Did you look at his face when he was talking to her?"

It hadn't been that bad. Had it? "Not really, I was focused more on making sure we had a good angle to catch her face." That and keeping an eye on Frankie. She'd done an admirable job of a poker face. Too admirable. Maybe a result of having to cover for her mother all these years.

Shit. Her mother.

I pulled my phone out and looked at it. Sure enough, there were several messages from Maddy waiting for me.

"We'll keep an eye on Bubba," I said. "Hopefully, some of this is catharsis for him."

"Put the past to rest?" Coop mused.

"Something like that." While I hadn't had this conversation with any of them, I was pretty sure the real problem was Bubba built Sharon up to be someone else in his mind. Another blonde we all had a thing for. Unfortunately, she had never been Frankie. Never could be her. I'd steered away from most blondes, to be honest. None of them were Frankie.

Jake and Coop? Eh, if they'd dated any, it hadn't lasted more than once or twice. Made sense, 'cause they weren't Frankie. Not Bubba. Sharon had paid him all the attention in the ways Frankie hadn't, and the sap had soaked it up but it hadn't been enough, and I doubted he'd seen it himself.

But he'd been getting an eyeful of the real her now.

Unknown

I don't expect you to understand.

Unknown

I also don't expect you to take my side.

Unknown

However, it's in Frankie's best interests that we smooth this over. You know how your father is.

Oh, I knew exactly how Edward was.

Unknown

Can we meet?

I stared at that last line and shook my head.

"Problem?" Coop asked.

"Maybe." I closed the messages without answering. I needed to think about that and talk to Frankie before I took a single step. Personally, I wanted nothing to do with that crazy bat and her idiot choices. She was putting Edward before Frankie, and only an idiot would do that.

"Need help?"

"Not yet."

And I wanted to talk to Frankie about it before I brought it up to the guys. Right now, we had enough crap on Frankie's plate. Wittaker deserved a damn raise for the efforts he was putting out there to block her mother. The emergency order had been a great first step.

Frankie emerged from the hallway with her phone in hand.

"Hey, babe," I greeted her with a smile. The endearment had stuck. I loved her name, but I liked that she was my babe, too.

"Hey," she said, crossing over to collapse on the sofa right between me and Coop. "How's it going?"

"Got them all," I said, motioning to the screen. "Everything good with Jake?"

"Yeah, he was worried about me." She chewed at her lower lip, and Coop nudged her until she moved and then sat with her back against his chest and he could wrap his arms around her. I envied him the position, but I could still see her at least, and that was something. "Can you do the thing here?"

"Gonna try," I told her, and I had to admit, when a flicker of disappointment crossed her face, it boosted my ego. "But we can still go back to my place if you want that time."

"Or I can take off," Coop offered easily. "I can also text the boys and tell them to take a powder for the night." He rubbed his chin against her hair.

She frowned. "I hate asking you to do that."

I met Coop's gaze and caught the concern in his eyes. Yeah. I heard the waver in her voice, too.

"You're not asking," Coop said firmly. "I'm offering. We all need our alone time. You two haven't had much, and neither of you have complained."

"Oh my hand has complained," I interjected. "But he's not used to the quality time with me anymore."

Frankie gaped at me, mouth forming a cute little 'o'.

"What?" I asked, raising my eyebrows. "Babe, I told you before. Wanting you has never been a problem. I'm pretty sure Coop's been looking after you, and I'd bet Jake, too." The sudden flush to her cheeks confirmed it. While I might be envious of the time, I wasn't jealous. Go figure. "Good. 'Cause you can't hang out with Rosie Thumb and her four sisters while in that cast. Arguably, you could do it left-handed I suppose…"

Her sudden peal of laughter pierced through the gloomy little cloud hanging around her. Achievement unlocked. Go me.

"I'd like an evening with you, but I should call Ian before we go to bed. I want to make sure he's okay."

Sounded like a plan to me. I looked at Coop. "Get out."

Frankie gaped again, and Coop snorted with laughter.

"Archie!"

"What?" I played innocent. "You said you couldn't ask him. So we didn't ask. I just told him to beat it."

"It's cool," Coop said, eyes laughing. "Besides, I can probably squeeze in a shift and check on Sis before I go."

Ugh. Sisters. That whole thing the other day had been uncomfortable as fuck. When I met his sister, she'd been in braces and elementary school. Now she was talking about dating someone at the same school as us? Never had I been so happy to be an only child.

Well maybe when I thought of Edward and Muriel as parents. Anyway.

I went back to looking at the tracks as Frankie walked Coop out, and I didn't even gawk at them as Coop pinned her to the wall and kissed the hell out of her. At least he wasn't noisy like Jake. Damn, no way to miss what Jake was doing to her, even if I wasn't looking.

Not that it wasn't hot, but I still needed to splice the video, and the fact that Frankie wanted to just hang with me tonight already had me semi-hard. Video. Feed her. Help with homework. Then play.

When the door closed, I glanced up to find her watching me. The flush to her cheeks, brighter eyes, and wet lips began to chip away at all my good intentions. There wasn't anything wrong with dessert before dinner, right?

"Archie, am I hypocrite?"

"No, we covered this already."

"But…I didn't want Sharon touching Ian. I mean, it physically repulsed me that she'd put her hands on him, and I'm with you and Coop and Jake, and I just asked Coop to leave so we could be alone. That's hypocritical."

"No," I told her slowly. "It's not. One, we all know about each other and we're all in agreement that we're sharing." Granted, the implied *until Frankie chose* had been there. But I didn't mind the guys. Not even Bubba, granted he'd been an idiot, but he was still one of us. Just without all the benefits.

For the moment.

Frankie settled back on the sofa next to me, and I snaked an arm around her to pull her close. "Listen, you were mad at Sharon touching him because you care about him. That hasn't gone away. Caring is a good thing. It means there's still hope for you two, and I for one will be glad as fuck when it gets sorted out *if* it makes you both happy. You also didn't like her touching him because you knew he didn't want it."

The light bulb clicked in me.

Fuck. I was an idiot. She'd *just* been assaulted. Of course she'd react to someone forcing their touch on someone else. No matter the circumstance.

"Frankie, I'm sorry, babe. I wasn't even thinking."

"It's okay," she whispered. "I wasn't either, not until toward the end when I got a good look at his eyes. He hated every moment of it, and he did that for me."

"Yeah, he did. The difference between what happened to you and what Bubba did? Bubba chose to do that because it was important to him to take care of this for you." Respect, man. I needed to tell him that. "It wouldn't have been my first choice to do, but if I'd had to endure it so we could get what we needed to slap her down? Yeah, I'd probably have done it, too. I get it."

"But I hate that he had to do that."

"I know you do, because you care." I pressed my lips to her forehead. "Tell him."

She looked up at me, and my heart squeezed. "You make it sound easy."

"Nope, it's not." I rubbed my cheek against her hair. "None of this has been easy. But it's okay to care about him. It's more than okay. If you're not ready to tell him, then you wait. Remember what I said to you a few weeks ago when I wanted to take you up to my room and kiss every inch of you?"

One of the best nights of my life, hands down. The only thing I wanted to change was the shit that went down the next day. For a few hours, we'd had damn near perfect. Then I almost screwed it all up.

We came back from that, though.

She forgave us. Forgave me.

"Tell you no, and you'd stop?"

"Hmm. That's part of it."

"And nothing would happen that I didn't want to happen." Trust glimmered in her eyes, chasing the shadows away. "Nothing did happen that I didn't want."

"Exactly. Same principle applies here. You want Bubba? Go for it. If you're not ready for that, then nothing happens until you're ready for it to happen."

"I want to trust him, Archie."

"I know you do, babe." I trusted him, *now*. But my point of view and Frankie's were different. He'd screwed up, and he'd been paying for that. So had she. "No pressure."

She tucked her head against my shoulder. "Do you mind if I watch you work rather than do my homework?"

"Nope," I said. "Long as you don't beat yourself up for not doing it."

Her groan made me smile. I knew my Frankie. "Fine." But rather than move away, she tilted her head up, and I took the invitation and kissed her.

I loved kissing her. What little hesitation she might possess would slip away, and she'd kiss me back with equal fervor. Sometimes our teeth clacked, sometimes we warred over whose tongue was in whose mouth, and sometimes I forgot that we both needed to breathe.

Frankie was the drug whose addiction I never wanted to recover from. When she shifted, I put a foot against the coffee table and shoved it farther away, then helped her straddle my lap. The cast bumped against my arm, and I braced her biceps and leaned back to lift her arm to rest on my shoulder better. At her grimace, I smiled.

"Was the kiss that bad?" The ache straining my cock promised me I was all in.

"No." Nose wrinkled, she gave me a glare that came off more sultry than pissed. I loved how her lips would get that swollen look after I kissed her a few dozen times. Just made me want to bite that lower lip and kiss her hard. "I just… I hate that stupid cast. It gets in the way."

She hated why she had to wear it more.

"As long as it's not hurting you at the moment, we can work around it." I hadn't been pushing. Between the nightmares, the trauma, and the pain she'd been in, encouraging sex had just seemed like a bad idea. I wanted it to be right for her, and I could be patient.

"Not hurting me at all. Just unwieldy," she complained as she smoothed her left hand over my shirt.

"What can I do to help?"

She glanced up at me from beneath those lashes, and all the blood in my body drained south. Frankie was a stunner. There was no getting around it. With a roll of her hips, she ground against me, and I hissed out a breath.

"Help me get up?"

Fuck. Not my favorite four words, but I dropped my hands to her hips and lifted her. She'd never seemed fragile to me before. I swore she'd lost weight the last few weeks. Once I had her on her feet, I started to stand, but she pressed a hand to my chest.

"Not you."

I raised my brows and sat back. When she knelt, I said, "Frankie…"

"Shh." She pressed a finger to her lips. "I might need help in a minute, but I have this."

Then she reached for the snap on my shorts, and I groaned. It took her a moment to loosen them, and it took everything I had to keep my hands away from helping her. She moved forward on her knees, nudging my thighs apart, and I let them spread.

The gentle rip of sound as she lowered my zipper sent tingles skating across my skin, and my balls grew tighter. The want was real. Frankie darted another glance up to me, and I licked my lips. "You're beautiful." The words slipped right out.

She laughed as she tugged on my shorts. "Going to need your help again."

"Yeah?" I glanced down to where her hand rested against my hip. "What can I do for you, babe?"

"Take these off?"

I hooked my thumbs into the sides and pushed them down. I braced my feet to lift my hips so I could them off without her having to move. As soon as they were over my thighs, she took over and tugged, leaning to let me slide them off my legs before she was in front of me again.

"Better?"

"Hmm," she murmured, and stroked one finger over my erection through the boxer briefs. The fabric was thin enough I felt every inch of that contact, and not thin enough because it denied me the feel of her skin. "Almost. Think you could take these off, too?"

Was that even a question?

I dragged the briefs down and over. She leaned away and helped me get them off, and then smiled when my very eager cock bounced against my stomach as I settled back. The cold air did nothing to chill out the need at having her this close to me. The first time she'd touched me, I damn near came in her hand. If she did it now, I might just blow, but damn what a way to go.

"You know, this is usually me going down on you," I said as she rested her right arm against one thigh and spread her left hand against my skin. It was hot and cool in equal measure, and pre-cum leaked. I *wanted* her so bad, it was a physical effort not to drag her up and just kiss her before I got rid of her clothes, too.

Speaking of which, to save time, I stripped off my shirt and tossed it behind her. Her pupils dilated, and I grinned.

"You've never let me do this."

"Babe, it's not a matter of let," I told her. "Seriously, when we're naked, I just want to sink inside of you. I love fucking into you until you're screaming."

She shuddered.

"I love that, too," she said, and then slid her hand against my balls, and it was my turn to suck in a breath. "I love it when you kiss me and tease me and drive me crazy. But I like this, too." Then she leaned in and licked across my tip, and I closed my eyes and fisted my control. I wasn't going to blow my wad like a pre-teen in the middle of the best wet dream of his life.

I'd had dreams of her like this.

When she swirled her tongue over the tip, I bucked a little. It was too much and not enough. A tease. A promise.

"I've wanted to try this on you since that first night." Yep, that declaration sent a bolt of lust right through my system. The hot heat of her mouth wrapped around me as she fisted the base of my cock and swallowed almost half of it. Her tongue teased along the underside, and I let out another groan.

"That feels so fucking good," I told her, and dug my fingers into the sofa cushion, even as I reached with my free hand to tangle in her hair. Not responding other than to bob her head, she set up a rhythm that sucked every thought I had down to my balls.

The brush of her breath as she exhaled through her nose on the downstroke teased against my abs. She sucked me deeper, and I had to fight to keep from thrusting up to fuck her mouth. The pace was just the right side of agony to keep my balls tingling, and not quite enough to push me all the way over.

A little bit of drool escaped her mouth, and I tracked it for a moment.

Even that was hot.

Fucking drool was hot when it was her mouth on me, and I groaned as my cock hit the back of her throat. She made a gagging noise and eased back. I fisted her hair, ready to pull her off. "Babe," I grunted. "You don't have to."

The look she hit me with said 'shut up, I want to.' Then she eased to the tip, and finally, I popped out of her mouth and we both let out a shaky breath. "I want to," she verbalized the words. "But if you don't…"

"Oh, I do," I promised in a hurry. "I want you to touch me. I *love* your hands on me, and your mouth is fantastic."

"Is it enough pressure?"

"You could do more," I said. "I won't break. But whatever you're comfortable with."

She studied me for a beat, then glanced down at my cock. I followed her gaze. The fact that she'd had her swollen lips wrapped around me was totally doing it for me, and my dick twitched.

"You want to control the speed?" That offer almost had my eyes rolling back. She opened her mouth a little wider. "Do to my mouth what you like to do to the rest of me?"

"Frankie…"

"I want this," she told me. "I want you, and I want to feel you."

I don't know who thought consent wasn't sexy, but fuck me. "Yes, I want to. Ease back a little." She moved back on her knees, and I grabbed a cushion, then helped her kneel on that while I stood. It would be easier for me to thrust at that angle. "Hand on my thigh." She slid her left hand up, and I reached around to tug the coffee table. "Right arm there."

She gave me a grin. "Lot of set up for this."

"Yes, but then we're doing it my way, right?"

"True." Her lips quirked, but it was laughter and heat in her eyes, and the combination made me harder.

"This is how it goes. Relax your jaw, suck and lick as much as you want, but I'll push. If I go too deep or you can't breathe, you slap my thigh once, and I'll ease off. Deal?"

My balls were tingling at the thought of it. I was still half-tempted to just strip down her shorts and eat her out until she screamed, then fuck her. I pocketed the first half of that for later. If she was doing this for me, she was going to come as many times as I could make her.

"Deal," she whispered, then pressed a kiss to my tip, and I groaned. When she opened her mouth and sucked against the tip, my thoughts splintered. She threatened to shred my control, but I had to hold onto it. I was not going to hurt her.

Gathering a handful of hair, I murmured. "We're going slow at first. Just relax, this is how I'll control the rhythm. I'll try not to pull."

"You can pull my hair." The vibration of the words against my dick sent lust streaking through me like a wildfire. "I like it when you pull my hair."

I had, usually when I fucked her from behind, and now that image painted itself across my eyelids as I worked my way past her lips and tugged her head forward to let her take me as deep as she could. At the first hint of gag and spark of dampness at her eyes, I eased back.

Twice more, then I had it.

"Ready, babe? I don't know how long I'll last." I wanted to come so bad, at this point, it wasn't funny.

She nodded a little, then smiled around my cock. Someday, I wanted a picture of that. I wasn't likely to forget the image, but I still wanted one. She sucked me deeper, and I rocked my hips forward, guiding her head. Slow at first, shallow pumps, and every stroke of her tongue was exquisite torture. Then faster, fighting to keep it careful, I pushed a little deeper, a little further each time, always easing off when the choke of her gagging escaped.

Tears trickled down her face, and I almost hesitated, but she dug her fingernails in and moaned. A real moan, she was getting off on this, and that did it to me. I let go, and she took every thrust until my balls dragged up tight.

"Babe, I'm going to come…let me…" She dug her nails in again and fought to stay with me. Then bliss ripped up my spine and spilled out of me in a heated wave as she swallowed around my cock and I shuddered.

Best fucking feeling in the world. My legs were weak when she pulled off of me, and I sat abruptly. When she pressed her head to my thigh, I stroked her hair.

"You're beautiful," she whispered, and I cracked my eyes open to find her watching me.

"Nah," I said, still trying to catch my breath. Sweat trickled down my chest, but all I needed was another moment, and then it was so her turn. "You're the beautiful one in this relationship."

"You're beautiful when you let go and trust me," she corrected. "And I had the best view in the house."

Chuckling, I dragged her back up carefully and kissed her. Sweeping my tongue into her mouth, I half-tasted myself still on her tongue, and if that wasn't the sexiest fucking thing, I didn't know what was. "I beg to differ, babe." Then I scooped her up, and she let out a shriek of laughter as I stood.

Oh yeah, my legs were still wobbling a little.

"The best view is the one I'm about to have," I informed her as I carried her toward her bedroom.

"What about our homework?" Playful tease licked each word.

"It'll still be there."

Five minutes later, I had her naked and sprawled in front of me. Like I said, best view in the house.

Chapter Twenty-Two
LOVE BITES

JAKE

"**H**ey, Baby Girl, you ready?" I called as I let myself in. Football practice had run late. Coach ripped into all of us. Fine by me. I was about ready to put Barry Jenkins out with a permanent injury. I had zero doubt who was behind sabotaging Bubba's bike. He might not be the only guy behind it, but he was definitely in on it.

"Yeah," she answered, coming out of the hall to her room. The tank top and sweats look was really working for her. "It's colder, isn't it?"

The temperature outside had dropped into the fifties, and the sun was already on its way down. The cold front sweeping in promised a chilly Halloween. "Yep. Need help with a sweatshirt?"

We both looked at her cast.

"I bet I can cut one of mine for you." It was a suggestion, but she made a face. "And I can braid your hair," I offered. "If you want."

She laughed. "I managed to brush it today."

"I know, I still like doing your hair." I caught her fingers and tugged her back to the bedroom. "How was your 'me' time?" After school, Coop had taken her home, and she'd said she wanted a couple of hours just to herself. Coop texted that he wasn't gonna run deliveries so he could be close by, and I headed over as soon as practice ended.

"I liked it," she said. "I even went and checked my own mail."

In her bedroom, she perched on the end while I went through the clean clothes stacked on my duffle. It looked like Jeremy had swung by. The man popped by two or three times a week, and always did something around the apartment. It was tidier each time. Even Frankie had noticed, and she always got this little exasperated look on her face.

It would be amusing, except the fact that she had limited mobility was making her crazy, so I did my best to refrain from teasing her. I found one of my football shirts, it just had the team logo on it. I think we all got these back in junior year. Didn't matter. I only wore it to work out or run on really cold mornings.

"Scissors?"

She pointed to her desk. "You don't have to cut up your clothes for me."

"Come on, Baby Girl, do you know how sexy it is when you wear my stuff?" She rolled her eyes, but there was a pleased little smile on her face. "Besides, we're going to get our Halloween costumes tonight."

"Yeah, about that…"

I pulled the scissors out and then cut the cuff off so we didn't have to squeeze it over the cast. "You decide to be Catwoman after all?" Archie painted an excellent picture of Frankie in leather. I could definitely get behind this idea.

"No," she muttered, and thumped me when I reached her. "You guys all have sex on the brain."

"You in leather?" I snorted. "No, that's us all having *you* on the brain."

That snagged me another smile, but it faded too quickly. I pulled the sweatshirt over her head. The thing dwarfed her, but it worked to cover her arms, and I tugged it down. "What's going on, Baby Girl?"

"Haven't decided on costumes yet."

"Uh huh, that doesn't make you moody." I helped pull her hair out from under the collar before I stood to grab her hairbrush and some ties. "Talk to me."

"I got mail."

Apprehension crawled up my spine. "Yeah?"

She ducked her gaze when I faced her before she rose and walked over to her desk. Opening the top drawer, she pulled out two envelopes.

"Early decisions."

It hadn't even been four full weeks. That would have to be the fastest on record for getting any decisions. The envelopes were small.

"That doesn't mean anything," I told her as I walked over. "You heard the same overview as I did, a lot of stuff is online, so they don't send these giant packets anymore."

"I know, but I'm kind of terrified to open them. Which is stupid. These are the things I've been dying to hear about, and I'm scared to open them."

"Is it Harvard?" I'd bet money neither was. Not yet. No way she'd hold off on opening that.

She shook her head and moved to sit in her chair when I pulled it out for her.

"Okay, so who is it?"

When she held them up, I read the return addresses—NYU was on the first one, and Fordham on the second. Those were both in New York.

"Kind of Harvard adjacent," she joked, but it fell flat for her, and I didn't push it. Instead, I just started brushing her hair so I could braid it. She let out a shuddery breath. "What if I didn't get in? They weren't my first picks."

"What if you did?" I countered. "You're pretty awesome, you know." They still weren't her first pick. "New York could be cool."

"Have you seen what apartments are like there? They're so tiny."

I grinned. "We'll make sure we have space for a big enough bed, and we can all pile onto it."

Her snort made me grin wider. With a few careful twists, I began gathering her hair back into a loose French braid, more to get it out of her way because we would be trying on costumes.

"Crowded."

"Snow."

"Where would you run?"

"They have parks," I drawled. "A really big one that takes up several acres as I recall. They have a zoo, too."

"What if you guys get in, and I don't?"

"What if you open the letters and stop making yourself nuts?" I tied off the braid and moved around so I could face her again. Leaning back against her desk, I folded my arms to keep from tugging the letters out of her hands and opening them myself. "C'mon, Baby Girl. Open them. You don't have to believe in you if you don't want to, but I have all the faith in you."

Wherever we all decided to go, I would make sure there was no distance between me and Frankie. Between all of us and Frankie. I wanted this to work. That meant making the choices that were right for all of us.

"You won't know until you open it," I reminded her softly.

"You're right." With a roll of her eyes, she tore open the first one and tugged the three pages out. The first line read *Congratulations!* and I bit back my reaction while she scanned it. Pride was a fist in my chest. She shot me an incredulous look, and I let my smirk out.

"You just need to remember I'm right more often."

After sticking her tongue out at me, she passed the first one to me while she opened the second. I hadn't been by my place, but I'd swing by later and check my mail. Her little excited gasp had me grinning again. Fordham was in my hand, but she had NYU.

"They're offering me an out of state waiver."

"A what now?"

She glanced up. "It's a grant for out of state students, it means my tuition will be a lot lower than the out of state rates, and there's a second scholarship offer for Exceptional Futures."

"Well, well, my sexy little brainiac," I murmured as I set the Fordham letter down and tugged her up and into my arms. She hugged me fiercely, and I squeezed her. "Look at you and your badass self with those two acceptances."

Scholarship already in the bag. More offers. The injunction giving her temporary emancipation, and now two yes letters. Her laughter came off giddy as I picked her up.

"This calls for a celebration."

She groaned. "We don't know if the guys got theirs—oh my god, Jake, what if you got yours?"

"I'll find out later."

From wild disbelief to giddiness to a stern glare, she poked me. "Let's go, Mister. We need to stop at your place."

"Yes, ma'am." I was not going to argue. I did, however, snag my letterman's jacket and drape it over her shoulders before we headed out. The guys were meeting us at the Spooky-Spot, the Halloween pop up shop that opened every autumn. They usually had the best costumes and the most variety.

The drive to my place took us ten minutes out of the way, but I let the guys know we'd be a few minutes late. I'd let Frankie give them the good news herself. For the first time in days, she practically vibrated in the seat next to me. It was probably the most upbeat I'd seen her in the last few days, and for that I could kiss whoever those recruiters were who got the acceptance letters fired off so quick.

"What are you doing here?" Louisa demanded when Frankie and I came in.

"I live here, brat," I reminded her, and she flicked her fingers at me dismissively. Ugh, she'd been spending too much time with her friends. Suddenly, big brothers weren't cool anymore. Becca and Blake had done the same things at her age.

"Couldn't tell by me," she retorted, then grinned at Frankie. "You live with Frankie now."

"Louisa," Mom's voice cut through from the other room, and Louisa made a face as I snorted a laugh. "Watch your mouth, young lady. And don't you have chores to do?"

With a roll of her eyes, Louisa said, "Yes, Mom. Your long-lost son is home."

I caught her pony tail as she tried to dart around me and tugged it gently. Then I managed a few good tickles under her ribs that had her squeal-screaming, and Frankie laughed. Mom walked out from her make-shift office and bedroom. "Hi, Frankie, dear. Please ignore my hellions. Are you two hungry?"

"Starving, but we're meeting the guys," I told her as I let Louisa go. She streaked away but flipped me off when she was safely out of Mom's sight, and I just grinned. At least I could still make her laugh. Blake was finally coming out of the big brothers suck phase just in time for Louisa to slide in. Fun stuff.

"Ahh," Mom crossed over and offered Frankie a gentle hug. She gave her that Mom-inspection look, then said, "Well, I'm glad to see you. Is my boy behaving himself?"

"Absolutely not," Frankie promised, and Mom laughed.

"Good."

"I just came to check the mail. Frankie got some news, and she insisted we find out if I did." I smirked again when Frankie widened her eyes at me impatiently. Oh no, she needed to strut this news, and I wasn't going to let her bury it. Her mother sucked, mine did not.

Mine would do what real moms did when their kids got awesome news.

"Oh?" Mom took up the gauntlet like a pro and looked at Frankie. "Tell me."

"I can't believe you," Frankie hissed at me, but I just gave her a smile as I went over to where the girls had sorted the mail. I actually did have a few envelopes. Four to be precise.

Fuck.

One of them was Harvard. I glanced over my shoulder. "Just tell her. You know you want to."

"Your son is annoying," Frankie informed my mother, and Mom chuckled.

"True story," she said with a grin. "Now stop delaying and tell me the news. I could use some good stuff in my life right now."

Was something wrong? I frowned but slit the envelope from Harvard open and read the contents swiftly, then tucked it deeper down and hid it. Until Frankie got hers, I would act like I hadn't received mine. NYU was in my stack too, and the *Congratulations!*

Hell yes. One university locked down for two of us, now we needed to get the others in. I didn't see one for MIT, but it was probably too early. There was no out of state waiver on my letter, but that was fine. Dad's military benefits were going to help with my tuition. Yay.

"Frankie, that's fantastic! Congratulations!" My mom did exactly what I expected her to do, she hugged Frankie carefully but with every ounce of her enthusiasm. "I'm so proud of you."

I wandered over and dangled two acceptance letters of my own. "Can I get in on some of this action?"

Mom's gaze fixed on me. "You got in?" She and Frankie chorused it as one.

"Well don't look too surprised, I'm pretty damn awesome."

Where she'd been reticent about celebrating her own, Frankie let out a scream for me, and the joy on her face had me laughing before I got a crushing hug from both her and Mom. The noise pulled the girls out of their rooms, and there was an impromptu bout of yelling and hugging. It actually took effort for me to extract Frankie from there and get her back in the car.

I promised Mom she could take us out for a celebration dinner soon, but maybe we'd wait until we all decided on the school. The air was electric all the way to the shop, and Frankie damn near bounced out of the SUV when we got there.

"It's about damn time," Archie groused. "Did you two get lost?" He wasn't remotely ticked, if anything, he gave Frankie's glowing face and happy smile a speculative look. I knew what he was thinking, and yeah, that would have been fun, too.

Frankie had her arms around Coop when she looked at me and raised her brows. I spread my arms and bowed my head, motioning for her to take it all from the top.

"We got in," Frankie said. "Jake and I both got into NYU and Fordham. The first acceptance letters were in."

"Hell yes," Coop said, squeezing her to him before he let her go to Archie, who also scooped her into a hug. Coop slapped me on the shoulder as did Bubba. When Frankie turned from Archie toward Bubba, I crossed mental fingers as he grinned at her.

"I'm so happy for you," Bubba told her. Frankie's hesitation landed for less than a second before she stepped to him and wrapped her good arm around him. All but sagging in to her, Bubba held her close and pressed his face against her hair. The hug didn't last long, but it was a hug and that was a good step forward as far as I was concerned.

Even better, she didn't move away from Bubba but stayed there next to him. The night was just improving.

"Let's shop," Coop said. "We have people to be."

Inside, we meandered together, but Bubba stuck close to Frankie and I paralleled, just keeping an eye on the people who were there. The place was pretty packed, but Halloween was a couple of days away. The party was on the weekend, so we needed to pick out what we wanted.

"Sexy maid?" Coop suggested.

"No," I answered along with Archie. Sexy was fine, but we weren't making her parade anywhere wearing anything she didn't want.

"Well, we have the options of sexy nurse, sexy firefighter, sexy doctor, sexy—"

"Coop, man, different section." I thumped him, but Frankie laughed.

"I'll totally wear it if you four will."

"And on that note," Coop said. "Next section."

She flashed a smile at me, and I grinned.

We waded through monsters from vampires to werewolves, to Frankenstein and his bride. That had some potential, but Archie pointed out we'd look like some goth metal band if we went as the Frankensteins. Point. Frankie liked the elf ears and the *Lord of the Rings* costumes, but the cast would prevent her from really using a bow.

Bubba pulled out dwarf costumes and got Frankie snickering when he offered her a full beard. Dwarf women were bearded after all, and as funny as that sounded, I'd prefer her lips weren't hidden behind nasty faux hair.

We made it to superheroes, but Frankie kept walking when Archie pulled out the Catwoman costume and followed her with a teasing if pleading smile. Serial killers and slasher film costumes were right out. I wouldn't mind one of those, it'd be fine, but I also wanted to be able to kiss her some time that evening.

Decisions. Decisions.

Fairy tales and nursery rhyme costumes were in the next section, and Frankie stared at some of those thoughtfully. "The problem," she admitted as we huddled. "Is you guys wanna theme, and there's not a lot of options that means all five of us can coordinate."

"I don't care if we're all wearing the same thing," Bubba offered.

"Neither do I." I gave her braid a little tug, and she slapped my hand. "The trick is to just find one we all like."

"What about Sexy Red Riding Hood?" Coop suggested with a wicked grin, and all of us groaned. "C'mon, then we're all the big bad wolf. All the better to eat you, my dear." The leer at the end had her groaning even louder, and she pinched him. Absolutely irreverent, he at least circled us back to where we'd started. "If you gave us some guidance here, Frankie, it would definitely help with the decision-making process."

"She could go as the Invisible Woman," a familiar feminine voice offered. "You know, all wrapped up in bandages because she's so good at not letting you see her if she doesn't want to be seen."

Archie let out a quiet "Fuck" as I pivoted to eye Cheryl. Of all the people to run into tonight, just fucking no. Frankie was having a good night. "Go away," I told her. "No one invited you to join us."

She frowned at me. "It's a public place, and I want to talk to Frankie." Glancing past me, she focused on Frankie, who let out a sigh.

"I don't really have anything to say to you, Cheryl," she admitted. "We're trying to find a costume so…"

"But I'm so good at shopping," the ditz pushed forward, but Coop blocked her from getting too close, and Bubba and Archie both had Frankie's back. There would be no going around them to close that distance. Frankie didn't want to talk to her, and as long as that was the case, the ditz could keep her distance. "I helped you find the perfect dress for Homecoming, remember?"

What vague sense of goodwill I tried to muster erased. "Go away, Cheryl, before I pick your ass up and dump you outside with the rest of the trash."

She gaped at me, but she didn't get a word in before Coop said, "There's air-headed, and then there's just flat cruel. You are digging a grave here, Cheryl. Now fuck off."

"You know, I don't have to listen to any of you. Frankie and I are *friends*." She looked past us to Frankie. "Right? We're friends."

"Did you know what Mitch was going to do when you gave me that bottle of water?"

All the air evacuated, and I clenched my fists. Cheryl needed to be very careful with her answers here. She shifted her footing, but Frankie pushed up next to me, and I wanted to drag her back and put her behind me, but this was also her fight.

"If we're friends," Frankie said slowly, "then you'll tell me if you knew what he planned to do when you gave me that bottle of water."

It wasn't a difficult question.

Cheryl's face crumbled.

Son. Of. A. Bitch.

"He never hurt anyone before…"

"Before?" Archie shot that word out like a bullet. "How many people did you hurt, Cheryl? How many of your friends?"

"It's no big deal, he showed me." The pleading on her face begged us to believe her, but she just made me sick. "Really, he did… He said it was…it would make things easier. You guys were getting all the girls, and he wanted to be able to keep up but he wasn't a manslut."

"No, he's just a rapist," Bubba said dryly. "Big step up."

"You drugged your friends," Frankie said. "You drugged them and set them up. He has sex with them and they can't remember, and that's okay with you?"

"He never hurt anyone," Cheryl attempted again and took a step toward Frankie, but stopped at the look on Frankie's face. "He didn't Frankie, I swear. He never hurt anyone before what happened with you, and if you hadn't fought him, maybe he wouldn't have gotten mad."

"Are you for fucking real right now?" Archie demanded.

Tears slid down her face. Were we supposed to feel sorry for her? I wanted to pop her upside her head, but I doubted there was anything rattling around in there. "He got mad over the summer when he thought I'd slept with you guys."

"Why the fuck would he think that?" I had to know.

Cheryl bit her lip and flashed those damp eyes at me. Sorry, not buying the bullshit or the histrionics. She swallowed and took a step back. I didn't have to look to know I wasn't the only one glaring at her.

"Maybe I should just go," she said, turning away.

"Why did he think that?" Frankie asked. "What did you tell him?"

"I wanted to make him jealous because he was hitting on someone else," she admitted. "I wanted to prove I didn't need him."

"So you told him you slept with the guys?"

"Just Archie and Jake. I had pictures of everyone. I showed him them on my phone. He assumed it was all of you because he was really mad. He didn't talk to me for two weeks. I thought I blew it and then…"

"And then what?" Jake asked. "Then he said, drug some girls so I can screw them, and everything will be all right? What is *wrong* with you?"

She pushed toward Frankie, big fat tears rolling down her face. "I just wanted him to be happy. I know he's not the greatest guy but…he was going to leave me, and it was my fault for lying. None of the others were hurt. You know…"

"When you fought over the summer," Frankie asked slowly. "Why did you fight?"

Cheryl shook her head. "It doesn't matter."

"The hell it doesn't," Coop stated bluntly. "What did you fight about?"

"You wouldn't do it." Frankie answered, not Cheryl. "The fight over the summer was when he first asked you to do it, and you wouldn't."

"I'd done it for him at a party, but I didn't know anyone there…it was my punishment."

Oh fuck me. I grimaced. I knew what she was about to say before the words came out.

"He made me watch. Said if he had to live with knowing I had sex with all of you, then…I had to see him have sex with someone else. It would be okay 'cause she wouldn't remember…it was just for me."

"Then he wanted you to do it to your friends." It wasn't a question.

"Frankie, I promise I didn't know he meant that for you. I didn't know until that night after we'd all been dancing. But…he really hates them and wanted what they have. I figured it would be quick and you wouldn't know, and it would be all right…"

I had no words. She was delusional.

The tears fell hot and heavy on her face, and she stepped toward Frankie like she would hug her, but Frankie withdrew. The disgust on her face waging war with sympathy. Yeah, I didn't have any sympathy. Mitch was scum of the fucking earth, but Cheryl wasn't much better.

She'd willingly served her friends up.

Willingly served Frankie up.

"It's all over now… I mean, Mitch has a broken jaw and he's been arrested. My parents won't let me talk to him… I'm so sorry."

"Me, too," Frankie said and turned away. "I can't do this."

"You don't have to," Bubba said, and I nodded to him then blocked Cheryl. Archie had his phone out, hopefully calling the police. As far as I was concerned, Cheryl was as guilty as Mitch. When they showed up, that meant another round of statements, and it was late by the time we got out of there. Cheryl's parents had shown up, and they left with her and the cops.

We didn't end up picking out costumes after that. We went back to Frankie's, and she took pain meds, and we got her to sleep. I didn't think I'd be sleeping anytime soon though, because one thing kept playing over and over in my head.

Yeah, Cheryl lied. She told Mitch she'd had sex with us. Stupid lie, but whatever. Mitch had gone after Frankie because of us. Because of all this.

Sick asshole.

The next day, we'd deal with Sharon and celebrate Archie's birthday and the college acceptance letters, but where we should've been feeling good, there was only a darkened pall.

I wasn't alone sitting in the living room. Bubba and Archie were there, too. Coop had stayed in with Frankie.

"Think they'll arrest her?" Bubba asked, and I shrugged.

"I hope so. Fuck, Frankie needs a break."

"She liked Cheryl," Archie said. "I have no idea why, but she liked her."

And Cheryl served her up to Mitch.

"Are we done with high school yet?" Bubba stretched his legs out and tipped his head back.

"Nope," Archie said. "Soon."

Couldn't be soon enough.

"She's going to be okay," I said. This was a setback. But at least we had a question answered, so maybe it wouldn't haunt her anymore.

"Yes, she is," Archie agreed with me. "Because we're going to make sure of it."

"Damn straight," Bubba added. At least that little bit of good also came out of the day.

"Still need to get costumes," I mused.

Archie snorted. "I have an idea, and I'm pretty sure it will make her laugh her ass off."

After he explained, I had to agree.

She'd laugh at us.

But I didn't mind. We drew straws, Coop got stuck with whatever was left since he was asleep. Lucky bastard on two fronts, but Bubba just chuckled.

"I can totally be the dog. Maybe it will get me out of the dog house."

Maybe.

Chapter Twenty-Three
EVERY STEP

FRANKIE

Archie's birthday got off to a fun start when the guys pounced him for a birthday pillow fight first thing. I clung to the laughter. It was a much better feeling than the despair I'd gone to bed with the night before. As if conjured by the thought, Cheryl's tear-streaked face popped to mind. I discounted her. In some ways, I let myself believe that just because she was an 'air-head,' she couldn't possibly hurt me. Hurt us.

Wow. Had I been wrong.

"Hey," Archie said, dropping onto the bed next to me, face flushed and eyes gleaming. "Birthday boy still get his way?"

I smiled. "Absolutely."

"Then you don't worry today," he said, touching his finger to my chin before he tilted my head and gave me a proper kiss.

The slant of his mouth over mind left no room for escape or breathing. I drank in the taste and touch of him, even as Jake whistled and Coop chuckled. Archie didn't let up until some of the tension cording my shoulders eased and heat flash-fired through me.

When he lifted his head, he smiled. "Better," he whispered.

"Happy birthday," I told him, and the curve of his lips deepened.

"It is now." Then he brushed my nose as he stood. "Need help with your shower?"

"Not telling you no," I admitted, and let him tug me up. "Birthday boy gets his way."

I locked gazes with Ian for a moment and braced for the hint of rejection. He'd not been thrilled with all the kissing before. Instead of objection, I found sweetness and a smile. Taking that little kernel of hope, I bumped his hip on my way past. I really hadn't gotten to talk to him about the Sharon thing the last couple of days. We'd literally not had the time.

But I promised I would make a point of it this weekend. After Archie's birthday. Archie got his first birthday present in the shower. Or maybe I should say he gave me a present, too. Either way, I was a lot looser and more relaxed after the shower than I'd been when we went in. The fact that he'd pinned me against the wall and made me come until I'd actually screamed had me flushing red the minute I came face to face with Coop's knowing eyes.

"I hate you right now, Arch," Coop told him without an ounce of real heat. "I'm gonna be fighting a boner all day now."

"Fighting one? I already lost the battle," Jake said. "That was hot." He snaked me close for a hug.

"It definitely sounded good," Ian commented, and I glanced at him. "But I think we should be giving Archie hell, not Frankie."

"Not giving her hell," Coop argued, but when I snorted, he grinned. "Okay, maybe a little bit of hell, but I'm dying to ask what he did right there at the end that had you screaming."

"Consider it a challenge," Archie teased while he grabbed a Pop-Tart and dropped it in the toaster.

"Oh, the make Frankie scream challenge?" Jake perked right up, and I swear, all four sets of eyes locked on me like laser beams.

"Challenge accepted," Coop said, clapping his hand down on Jake's shoulder. His gray-green eyes twinkled with absolute mischief when he continued, "But I'm pretty sure Jake and I are already ahead on that, aren't we?"

"Really?" Archie raised his brows. "Already keeping score? C'mon, babe, gotta tell me where I fall. Birthday boy gets his way, remember?"

"Nope," I said, shaking my head. "That's a trap. Not falling into that trap."

"You said my ass rated a seven, and you still won't tell me a seven on what scale," Coop argued. "If we're going to have a make you scream contest, we need rules and to know where we stand."

"Screaming orgasms?" Jake offered. "Number of?"

"Overall or per event?" Archie asked. "Because I go for three or four at least every time."

I ducked my head to eat my cereal and found Ian watching me with a sympathetic smile. "For what it's worth, I know what my score is," he murmured. "But if we play this game, I definitely want in."

Frozen, I stared at him as milk dripped off the spoonful of cereal halfway to my mouth. Had he just said…?

"Oh man, Bubba's starting in the handicapped position," Jake mused. "We should account for that in the scoring system."

"Boys." I was so proud my voice didn't crack. "Do you ever want to get laid again?"

"Okay, new topic," Archie said. "We'll discuss this later."

I dropped my spoon back into the bowl and snagged a placemat off the table to whack Archie with, even as he laughed. He wrapped his arms around me from the back and started nuzzling my chin and then my neck until I laughed.

"Forgive us? We love to compete," he whispered against my ear. "You know we do. You're not a prize, though admittedly, I do feel like I won the lottery."

"Dude you have more money than the lottery," Coop supplied, and Archie glared at him. Raising his hands, Coop still grinned, utterly unrepentant. "Just saying. Archie's right, we're not counting you as the prize."

"We're counting your pleasure as the prize." Jake leered playfully, and I groaned.

"You're all terrible."

"Hey," Ian argued. "I'm not, Angel. Not yet anyway." The playfulness in his eyes beckoned to me. I hadn't lied when I told Jake I wanted to trust him. I really, really did. "But I think they have the right idea. Wanna help me cheat?"

"Cheat?" All three guys echoed.

"Sure," Ian said with a grin. "I'll be on Frankie's team. It'll be us against the three of you. The one who gives her the most orgasms wins."

Yep, I was pretty sure I was going up in flames, and I must have lost some braincells in the conflagration, because I was seriously tempted to take him on the offer right then and there. Not appropriate, yeah, I know.

"Well, this should be interesting," Archie mused, kissing my cheek. "Now everyone stop picking on her. My birthday, I'm the only one who gets to do this."

That elicited more laughter, but at least we got breakfast finished.

"We need to get moving or we're going to miss the fireworks," Jake said.

"Definitely don't want to miss those." Archie's grin grew. "I personally want front row seats."

Even after everything I learned from Cheryl the night before, I couldn't bring myself to feel bad for Sharon. Honestly, I had—for a little while anyway—felt bad about how things had worked out for her. But that feeling had effectively died in the bathroom that day when she went on and on about how she'd only wanted to get rid of me. She'd waited until I was out of the picture to make a move on Ian.

I still needed to talk to him, but it was Archie's birthday and I liked to spoil the guys. I'd find time for him though, I had to. At school, we were all at our table in the cafeteria when the video sent. It buzzed everyone's phones, and I was sipping coffee when the first wave of laughter hit.

Rachel dropped into the chair on my other side and held out a bag of M&Ms. "Too early for popcorn," she admitted, and I grinned.

With Archie's arm around me, we queued up the video on my phone. Ian and Jake had their own phones out, but Coop had his gaze planted across the room. Stretching out my foot, I bumped Ian's, and he glanced at me.

'You okay?' I mouthed the words more than spoke them. His whole expression softened, and he nudged my foot back as he nodded.

The video opened with a close-up of Sharon coming out of the bathroom. Dude, I did not want to know where that shot came from. But the voice over was all her.

"You know what's the worst part? I would have done anything he asked but he's only got eyes for her. He could have me anywhere, anytime, but nope. No dice. What the hell does she have that I don't?"

The word *self-respect* flashed across the screen. Followed by *#justsaying*.

I bit my lower lip as Rachel cackled. I'd been there while Archie made the video, splicing all the different pieces together, but I hadn't really watched it so much as him.

The next bit was splices from her earlier videos about me before it hit some shaky cam footage of me stalking toward Sharon in the hallway. She had her phone pointed at me and I got right in her face. Oh crap. That was the day I'd decided I'd had enough of her doing that shit to Ian.

"I'm ready for my close-up," I told her, and then lifted my middle finger. "Just in case you wanted a real message for your next little puff piece."

A scattering of giggles went up around us, and Sharon lowered her phone the rest of the way. "You really think you're funny."

"Oh, honey, I'm not the one obsessed by me and every step I take."

A little woo went up around us, and red flushed Sharon's cheeks. "You know, sooner or later, they're going to figure out you aren't worth it."

"Maybe," I agreed. "If that day comes, I guess I'll look to you for all your experience with it and what I really shouldn't do after."

The camera froze on Sharon's face as I walked away. Her mouth open, her eyes hot, and her face scarlet. *#BURNED* flashed over her face.

A narrator's voice that I swore had to be Jeremy asked crisply, "Do you know what she's doing wrong? Because clearly, she hasn't figured it out."

Then the videos from that day outside the school filtered in. Every single word she spat at Ian and those Ian gave her back.

Girl, he is just not that into you. Let. It. Go.

I put my good hand over my mouth as Rachel snorted. "This is gold."

Finally, the last clip was a close-up of Sharon as Ian and Jake walked away.

#PATHETIC

The next voice over was definitely not Jeremy, and I flicked a look to Coop.

"So what did we learn? Only time will tell. But let's be honest here. Sometimes you need to call people on their behavior. No one is perfect. Let's count all the ways…"

Images flashed by rapid-fire and in nearly every single one, Sharon was doing something—laughing at people, throwing things, scowling, and her voice echoed over that last clip of her vicious expression. *"I don't care what I have to do. But I'm going to make her miserable. It's all I have left."*

Had she *really* said that? I cut a look to Rachel, who shrugged. "I did my part," she murmured. "Girl needs to remember that when she is sticking knives in people, they are going to pull them out and might stab her back."

Across the cafeteria, Sharon stood up from a table, shell-shocked eyes and red-faced. She glared at us, and I did my best to look innocent. But I didn't start this war. I would happily, however, participate in ending it. The rise in conversation hushed abruptly as she took one step in our direction. Ian never turned around, and Jake wore a faint smirk, like he was just waiting for her to do it. I glanced away from Sharon to meet Ian's gaze.

He gave me a small smile and bumped my foot again. A flash of movement had me looking across the room again in time to see Sharon marching out of the cafeteria—alone. None of her 'friends' went with her.

"Too bad, so sad, mean girl," Rachel said as she mimed and explosion with her hands and added a sound effect. "You play with fire, you're going to get burned."

I snorted. "I almost feel guilty."

Five voices in unison said, "Don't," with such vehemence that I raised my good and wounded arms at the same time.

"I said *almost*."

"Good," Jake told me firmly, but it was Ian who leaned forward and stretched his hand out to me. When I laid my hand in his, he locked his gaze on me.

"It wasn't pretty, and it wasn't fun. It was necessary," he told me. "She only understands social power. So, we had to take that away from her. She also knows we're not going to pull our punches a second time. If she leaves you alone from this point forward? Worth it."

I squeezed his fingers and sighed. "Agreed. I want her to leave you alone, too."

"Not a problem." His eyes warmed. "She's not even a blip on my radar."

"Did you sink her battleship?" The question prompted a round of groans, and Rachel stood up with a laugh.

"Okay, nerdette and her merry band of dicks, I'm off. Be good. That was fun. The next time you want to take someone down a peg or four, lemme know. I'm all in." She took a step, then pivoted and looked at Archie. "Happy birthday."

"Thank you," he replied, and they both did this incline of their heads followed by the cheesiest of grins.

"Nice, right?" Rachel asked me, and I laughed.

Yes, it was nice.

The rest of the day went better than I could have expected really. Even with so much to think about and obsess over, I focused on Archie. I had a few hours before I got to give him his present, and the closer we got to then, the more I focused on that.

Math was probably the most relaxed class it had been in weeks. Ian slid into the desk next to me, and it was like he was right back to where he belonged. That awkward strain between us had eased, or at least lessened. Unfortunately, Jake and Ian weren't at lunch—they had their anger management meeting with Diane that both claimed was going well. I didn't ask for details though, and they didn't offer. That seemed pretty fair, considering they weren't asking me about my session with Erin.

In fact, pretty much the only question asked so far had come from Coop. Did I like her?

When I said I'd said yes, he'd just hugged me and said good. That was that.

We ate lunch at the sushi place because Archie's birthday and that was what he wanted. The guys had a game that evening, but Archie and I were going to have dinner with his grandfather. I offered to let him have the time with him on his own, but he said no. He wanted me there with him. Plus, Ted liked me.

Birthday boy gets what he wants.

So after school, I bribed Rachel into helping me fix my hair, since we were going out to some nice place for dinner and Jake was at football. No, I did not tell Rachel or anyone else that Jake would have been my first choice to do my hair. I figured that was fair. Besides, he and Coop were getting really good at scalp massages. I might never go back to doing my own hair again.

I debated what to wear on and off all day. The thought of dress shopping kind of nauseated me. Too soon. I didn't think Archie would care if I wore one I'd worn before, so I went with the little black dress. It was classic and sleeveless which meant I didn't have to worry about the cast. Rachel helped me get dressed, then eyed me critically when I stood in front of her. She'd done something with my curls to tame them, piled them up, and now they spilled down one side of my head. It was a little complicated and looked a whole lot pretty.

"What?"

"You need jewelry."

I glanced down. "I don't have that much, and a bunch of my stuff is still with the cops." My charm bracelet for example. I needed to call them and find out when I could get that back. Surely they didn't need it the whole time, right?

"Hmm. What do we have in here?" She pulled a jewelry box out and flipped it open. My stomach dropped. It was a gold necklace with charms on it. Real charms.

Like the ones on my bracelet.

There was a present on the necklace, a birthday cake, roses, four heads—which was the only way to describe them—and each one had a name inscribed, one for each of my guys. There were also three cats scattered on it. And keys.

Four keys.

One for each head.

"Rachel, what did you do?"

She gave me a saucy grin. "I wish I could say I did it, but I'm totally just the messenger. Feel free to kiss the messenger. I don't mind."

"You're terrible."

"I know." She winked. "Read the note."

There was a note folded and tucked into the top of the jewelry box. I opened it while Rachel got the necklace out of the box.

Frankie,

It's my birthday, which means it's the birthday boy's choice. These are all charms meant for your bracelet, but at the rate we're going, we're going to fill it up so I started a necklace, too. I'm pretty sure you can figure out the meanings to all of them, but in case you need a hint, I'll be there soon. Wear it for me?

Archie

I bit my lip.

"Don't cry," Rachel ordered as she unhooked the necklace and helped put it on me. "That mascara is good, but let's not push it. Besides, rich boy did really good with these. Look, I'm even on here." She tapped the roses and I grinned.

"Yes you are." I hugged her. It was an impulsive act, and Rachel returned it easily. "Thank you."

"My pleasure." She loosened her grip and stepped back. "So, about that kiss…"

"Ahem," Archie said, clearing his throat. "We talked about this, Manning. No making moves on my—*our* girl."

Archie looked fantastic. He was dressed in a suit that was black with a charcoal gray shirt underneath it. The dark colors were doing wonders for him, giving him that air of sophistication and mystery.

"No promises, Standish," Rachel retaliated. "But since it is your birthday, I'll give you a free pass tonight."

He snorted. "Thank you." But his gaze was on me, not her. "You ready, babe?"

"Thank you for my necklace."

"You are very, very welcome." He had a jacket for me—not Jake's letterman this time, but more a wrap which was easier than a real coat. "Coop's ordering pizza, Rachel, if you two want to bond and play video games."

Coop's outraged yelp from the front room made me laugh, and Rachel just rolled her eyes. "Sorry, he's going to have to survive without me. I have a date of my own."

"Oo, Skylar?" I was oddly hopeful. I liked her.

"Could be," Rachel said, all coy as she gathered her stuff together. "Call me tomorrow, and I'll confirm."

"Are you bringing her to the Halloween party?"

"Eh," Rachel said with a shrug. "Undecided. I might swing that one stag.

We'll see."

"Find us if you go with or without her?"

"Promise." She brushed a kiss to my cheek. "You two have fun tonight."

Coop made us take pictures before we left. He also gave me a lovely pinned to the wall kiss with great care not to wrinkle my dress. He did, however, succeed in removing nearly all of my lipstick. A fact that made him particularly cocky when I had to duck back to the bathroom to fix it.

Thankfully, it also gave me an excuse to grab the small purse for my phone and keys. "Don't wait up for us," Archie called as we left. "I might not bring her back until tomorrow."

"Have a good birthday, man," Coop said. The guys had gone in together and gotten Archie a new sound system for his Ferrari. It was an upgrade on what he already had, and it would get installed this weekend. Archie and Jake would do the work themselves.

Of all of them, Archie had always been the toughest one to get presents for. He had everything. So the gifts I got him always had to mean something. I'd found a couple of concert shirts for him from his favorite classic bands, but those were more like what I would give him at random than as presents. I'd actually saved one to "give" him later after I'd worn it, naked, in his bed. I figured he'd appreciate that.

Once we were in the car though, I put a hand on his arm. "Before we go, can I give you your presents here?"

"Right here?" he said, eyeing me. "'Cause the seats aren't the best for it, but I'm totally game to try."

I rolled my eyes. "Not that and not here, perv." The insult slipped out easily.

He grinned. "Damn. Though after the other night, you're really going to need to work it to match that as a present. I still get hard thinking about it."

Okay, now I was hot. "Archie. Let me give you your present."

"Fine." He gave a mock sigh before he mimed zipping his lips. Then looked at me expectantly.

"Thank you." I pulled out my phone. "Do you mind if I pair this with your car?"

He reached forward and hit a couple of buttons while I pulled up Bluetooth. It was paired in nothing flat, then I opened the music app and took care not to show him the screen as I queued up the song.

"Have I mentioned how hot I find it that you're giving this moment a soundtrack?" The cocky grin on his face just made me laugh.

"Hush."

Leaning back in his seat, he tilted his head so he could watch me. The first strains of piano and guitar came across. Ian had played both when we were at the studio, mixing one with the other. It was a little on the ballady side and not quite what Archie liked to listen to, but I was already half-in-love with it and over the moon that I'd gotten to help do it.

"The first step was the hardest one. You walked in and I invited you to sit and talk. I smiled at you and you joined in. You were a stranger then you were a friend."

I bit my lip at the sound of my own voice. Ian had worked with me on every line recording it until I hit every single note. Archie's eyes widened.

"The second step was harder still. You wanted me and I was blind. Whispers and wishes, so many misses. Dancing. Playing. Laughing. Crying. You were the one who wanted to take my dreams flying."

He reached over to catch my hand as the music played. It was awful.

It was cute.

Did I sound as terrible to him as I did to me?

I mean, it wasn't as awful as that karaoke night, but the beats were there.

"The third step and we fell off. My whispers became shouts and my wishes so many doubts. You were there every step of the way and when I tumbled you had to have your say."

Archie raised his hand to my cheek and stroked it.

"But here we are, crash and burn, rise and fall, song and singer, friends and lovers…" The last word trailed off. *"If I have my way, this is where we'll stay but I want your whispers and your wishes every day."*

The music rose again and then trailed off.

"Happy birthday, Archie. I always want your wishes to come true. So whisper them or shout them, but this song? It's just for you."

Then it ended, and I sank my teeth into my lower lip, alternately horrified and delighted at the raw expression on his face. He kissed me. No room for thought or hesitation, just a kiss that stole every ounce of my breath.

"God, I love you," he admitted, and my heart did a fist bump with my ribs. But before I could say anything else, he was kissing me again.

We were late to dinner.

Chapter Twenty-Four
WHEN YOU NEED SOMEONE TO LEAN ON

We were late, but Ted—or Grandpa, as he kept insisting I call him—had been more amused than annoyed by our tardiness. As soon as we were seated, a waitress brought over drinks. Wine for the whole table, and I cut a look at Archie. We drank at his place…

"Don't worry," Ted assured us both. "They aren't serving you, and Mary would have wanted me to toast your birthday, young man, and she would have wanted you to toast along with us."

"A sip won't hurt," Archie told me. I hadn't taken any pain meds today, so I nodded. Once Ted had poured the wine, he set the glasses in front of each of us. The restaurant we were in was expensive, exclusive, and we didn't sit out in the main dining room, but had this private room to ourselves surrounded by tropical plants and artwork.

The place didn't even have a name. You couldn't walk in off the street. It was just the kind of reservation-only exclusivity for people with more money than I would know what to do with.

Archie and his grandfather fit right in, but they were both including me, which helped to ward off the sensation that I didn't belong.

Lifting his wine glass, Ted said, "I'm proud of you, Archie. You made it to eighteen, but you remember what you said at eight?"

With a groan, Archie said, "Grandpa, are you really bringing that up?"

The older man laughed. "Damn straight, my boy. Mary laughed for a week after you proclaimed at your eighth birthday that you were of the right age to be Pharaoh, and by eighteen…"

"I'd be a real god." Shoulders slumping, Archie actually looked moderately embarrassed. Even the tips of his ears had gone red. I'd never seen him so self-conscious. He was almost always the picture of confidence.

It was adorable.

"Exactly," Ted continued, extending his glass. "Welcome to your godhood, Sprout. May it be everything you dreamed of."

We clinked our glasses together, and I was grinning so hard my cheeks hurt. "A god, huh?"

"Don't." Archie shot me a pleading look. "Please."

"Oh, I won't share it. But if I'm dating a god, I think I have the right to at least tweak you a little."

Chuckling, he rubbed his hand against my thigh below the table. "*You* can do whatever you want."

"Your secret is safe with me," I promised, and he chuckled.

Grandpa Ted nodded. "A keeper that one. All right. Have a drink. Let's order, and then we're discussing your birthday present, Sprout."

"Grandpa, I'm good. Really."

"Nonsense," the older man continued. "Your trust has been there for you since you were born. That's fact. Presents are supposed to be fun. And I have one for you…" Amusement glimmered in the man's eyes. "You're going to let me give it to you, Sprout."

Archie raised his hands in surrender. "Yes, sir."

I liked this side of Archie—the openness and warmth he shared with his grandfather. This was the side so few got to see. I did. He'd been like this with me from the beginning.

If I'd known him better, it might have clued me in to his real feelings long before I got there. Looking back, it was a lot clearer to me now.

We took our time picking out our meals. The waitress appeared as if summoned by magic when we'd decided. She also brought sodas for me and Archie. The wine was nice, but two swallows had already left me with a warm buzzy feeling, so probably better to dial back on that.

After she left, Archie's grandfather focused on him. "All right, I've done some research. Your father might be engaged, but he's not divorcing Muriel. At least not yet. He hasn't filed papers anywhere. I also checked with the attorneys to go over a copy of the prenuptial they signed. He may not have to worry about that much longer. Either of them."

"How so?"

"After twenty years or their youngest child reached his or her majority, several of the clauses would fall away."

"And I just turned eighteen." He scoffed and shook his head.

I covered his hand on my thigh with my own. "I'm sorry."

"You know," he said, cutting a look at me. "I don't really care beyond the crap they're pulling with you. Let them get divorced. It might make them happier."

Leaning forward, Ted considered Archie. "I have friends on the board still, it wouldn't be that hard to oust him. You're a bit young to take his place though."

What were they…?

"I'm good, Grandpa. No offense, not really into running Standish."

Ted shrugged. "I could take over for a few years for you. Serves him right after he shoved me out the door."

Were they…?

"Grandpa, really, I appreciate it. And I know you built that company. But I don't want it. I want… I want to make my own mistakes. Build my own future.

I want to build things, period."

"Sprout, I respect that, but you also asked me to deal with your father. Now it sounds like you want me to back off." Ted glanced at me, but the reality of Archie running the family company had never really sunk in before. I mean, sure, I knew they had one. But I didn't picture him in suits—no matter how good he looked in them—wheeling and dealing, and doing whatever it was his father did.

Honestly, I had no idea what "Eddie" did, except date my mother and apparently, have affairs. So maybe it was a good thing I couldn't picture Archie in that role.

"You're already moving forward with your emancipation, young lady?"

I nodded.

"Then that's one thing we can take care of. As for your father, neutering his power reduces his ability to threaten any of you." Ted paused as our first course arrived.

This was not the conversation I pictured having on Archie's birthday. Through most of the appetizers and the entrees, they debated it back and forth. I fought a silent battle with myself. A part of me wanted Ted to just stop and let Archie enjoy his day, but each time the conversation lulled, Archie would bring up another point and they'd be off to it again.

So maybe Archie did want to have the conversation.

When dessert arrived, Archie cut a look to me. "We're boring the hell out of you, aren't we?"

"Not boring me so much as worrying me."

He raised his eyebrows, and for a moment, we were back in the car again and he said those three words that had rattled around me as he kissed me and buoyed me through most of this meal.

"How so, babe?"

"It's your birthday, and Eddie makes you miserable. I'd rather you were having fun." Try as I might, I couldn't help a bit of a reproachful look at Ted.

"You two are together again, surely there's something else fun you can talk about."

The two men shared a look, then they both chuckled. Lifting his wine glass, Ted said, "I told you she was a keeper. She lasted about as long as Mary did when my father and I had this debate."

"Excuse me?"

Archie covered my hand. "Grandpa likes to test people." There was a glimmer of apology in his eyes. "If you haven't noticed, my family is filled with hard heads and stubbornness."

"No?" I deadpanned. "Really?"

Chortling, Ted dabbed at his mouth with his napkin before setting it aside. "Blame me, pretty girl, not Sprout. I did this to Muriel and she failed it abysmally, but Junior wouldn't listen to me. Thank God for that now, though then I was pretty cross." He lifted his chin. "Don't get me wrong, Muriel was a good woman, and she gave us Archie here. But she and Junior were ill-suited from the beginning. You're good for Archie. You look out for him, but you're also trying to support him. I see him doing the same thing for you."

I wasn't quite sure what to say to that. "He's one of my best friends," I finally said. "I'd pretty much do anything for him."

"Ditto, babe," Archie replied, dropping a kiss to my bare shoulder before he pressed a kiss to my ear and whispered, "Just another reason I love you."

Shivers chased up my spine. It was one thing when he said it in the heat of the moment over the song in the car. This was different.

"It's a good thing. Hold on to that. But enough with the business talk. I heard there are congratulations in order for you."

Archie grinned. "I told him about your acceptance letters…and mine."

"Yours?" I gaped. "You didn't tell me about yours."

He ducked his head a little as he twisted his glass on the table. "Mine aren't anywhere near as amazing as yours. Really, they aren't."

Before I could argue, the waitress returned with a cake topped by lit candles along with a host of the other servers. They sang a beautiful a cappella version of a birthday song as they set the cake in front of him. Archie blew out the candles as they applauded and squeezed my hand. When he turned to me and slanted his mouth across mine, I sank into the feverish kiss, half-forgetting we even had an audience.

Soft chuckles popped the bubble around us, and Archie lifted his head with a smile. Heat rushed to my face, but I didn't really care so much. It wasn't long until we had slices of tiramisu cake in front of each of us.

"Don't tell Jeremy," I admitted two bites in. "But this is amazing."

"Your secret is safe with me," Archie told me with a wink.

"Okay, now spill. Tell me where you got in." My stomach knotted. I was over the moon that Jake had gotten accepted to the same schools I had so far. We still had more to hear from. Coop hadn't gotten his letters, and neither had Ian. But that didn't mean they weren't coming. Maybe they got them today, and we just hadn't heard yet.

"It's really not a big deal, babe," Archie said, cutting into his cake.

"How can you say it's not a big deal?"

"Because he's a legacy," Ted said bluntly. "And he has money. Most schools are going to leap at a chance to take him, thinking it will get them endowment money from the family."

"Which it probably will," Archie admitted. "You getting in is way more interesting to me."

I rolled my eyes. "You're important to me."

"Sprout just means you getting in is a reflection of your hard work and merit, Frankie-girl. He's very proud of you."

"Well, I'm proud of him, too." Pointing my fork at Archie, I said, "So tell me. I want to know."

"NYU," he admitted. "Fordham. MIT. Harvard." He ticked them off one after another, and when he got to the last two, pride surged through me. I dropped the fork to turn and hug him. He wrapped his arms around me.

"That's so cool!"

I didn't know about Harvard for me yet. "But you got them all."

"Yeah," he admitted. "I did. It's the STEM programs."

"I'm so proud of you," I told him. "Don't dismiss it. That's awesome. We're just one step closer to all being up there."

I had mental fingers crossed for Coop and Ian, too.

That called for another glass of wine, which both Archie and I turned down, but we did toast. By the time we wrapped the meal with his grandfather, Ted had regaled me with the most delightful stories of Archie as a kid, and he'd taken it all like a champ.

We walked out to the cars together, and the two shared a hug, then Ted surprised me by giving me a kiss on the cheek and clasping my shoulder gently. "Sprout's going to make sure you have my number. You call me if you need anything. Don't worry about your mother or Junior. We'll get you clear of any fallout. And I still expect you two out at the golf course."

"Promise, Grandpa." Archie slid his arm around me. His driver arrived with his car first, and he gave us a little salute before he slid into the back.

Once we were in the car, he said, "Sorry about the test thing."

"It's fine," I promised him. "Now that I get it, it's almost funny. Annoying, but funny."

"He just worries, but he really likes you."

"I'm glad. I really like him, too. It's hard to believe that…"

"He's my father's dad? Yeah. But I figure he's mellowed as he's gotten older. He's tough as nails and it's still there, under the surface. Maybe he was a different guy. I don't know."

"He reminds me of you," I admitted.

"Thank you, I'll take the compliment."

"And, Archie, I am proud of you for getting in to all the schools. I know you think it's just because of your last name, but you are worth so much more than that. You work hard, and you are so smart. You and Jake make robots and shit."

"Maybe."

"No maybe about it. You're a smart cookie. Just another reason I like you so much."

"Yeah?"

"Yeah."

"What are the other reasons?"

Laughing, I shook my head. "I plead the fifth."

"It's going to incriminate you?"

"No, but it might stroke your ego."

With a snort, he countered, "You can stroke anything on me you want."

The drive didn't take us as long as it had to get to the restaurant. "We're not going home?"

"Nope," he said. "I got us a room for tonight, if that's okay with you. I wanted an evening away from all of it—the house, the worries, school, or the nascent fear Edward would show up at my place or your mom will come to yours."

He wasn't wrong.

"And I want to be greedy. I want you to myself." He pulled straight through to the valet before glancing at me. "If that's okay with you."

"I'm not complaining." I wasn't. "Do we need to call the guys?"

"Nope. They know."

Of course they did.

"Coop and I packed you a bag for you yesterday, so you'd have a change of clothes, but I don't plan on you needing clothes much until we leave."

A shiver skated right through me, pumping the little bubbles of elation higher. Once out of the car, the colder air brushed my face, but it felt good since I was overheating.

Inside, we didn't even have to wait that long to get checked in or the key. Excitement and nerves vied for dominance in my stomach as we took the elevator up. We weren't talking, but every time our gazes clashed, we both grinned.

All the way to the top.

He got a penthouse room.

It was easy to forget Archie was rich until he did things like this and I had to pinch myself. His money wasn't what I wanted. Once inside, he set our bag down, and I glanced around the sitting area with its fireplace and rich furniture and sumptuous carpet. It looked more like someone's fancy apartment than a hotel room. There were French doors leading out to a balcony and another set that opened into a darkened bedroom with a huge king-sized bed in the middle.

"How's your arm?" he asked as he set the room key, his wallet, and phone down on the coffee table before he stripped off his jacket. His dark hair hung over his forehead, a hint of a wave that softened his face. The clean cut of his jaw would be smooth, he'd probably shaved before he'd picked me up, and his dark brown eyes held so many promises and warmth, it heated me as he walked to the entertainment system.

"It aches," I admitted. "But I'm almost used to it. So not bad."

"I hate that you've gotten used to it," he said as he flipped on the sound system, then reached over and dimmed the lights. "But I'm glad it's not bad. Would you dance with me?"

We hadn't danced since Homecoming. While he didn't say a word about it, it was written all over his face. This was what I'd been struggling with verbalizing. What happened to me didn't just happen to me. It happened to them, too. I couldn't remember, and that gap in my memory sucked. But they remembered all too well, and it colored how they interacted and handled me.

Sometimes they were so careful, it made me want to scream, and at others…at others, it squeezed my heart so tight, I didn't think I'd ever be able to get over it.

Sliding off my shoes, I met him halfway, and he braced my cast against his shoulder as I slid my left hand against his nape. The slow song barely registered, just the fact that I was dancing with Archie, slowly swaying to the music.

I don't know how long we danced, but the songs kept playing and we kept moving. We just let it all fall away. Eventually, we shed the clothes, and he was right, I didn't need them until the next morning.

With my arm in a cast, some of our options were limited, but he made the most of all of them. Sprawled next to him, my arm propped on a pillow while he lay on his side drawing patterns over my skin with his finger, I studied him.

"What's wrong?"

"Nothing," he said. "Everything is great."

"Then why do you look worried?"

"'Cause I don't want to get too comfortable. It's usually when things are at their best that everything goes horribly wrong."

"Hey," I murmured, cupping his cheek. "Even if it does go wrong, we'll deal with it. All of us."

A smile lifted one side of his mouth. "You're the best, you know that?"

"Someone keeps telling me that," I whispered, and he buried his face against my throat, wrapping an arm around me. When he slid his leg over mine, it was like having an Archie blanket. "Someone I love, too."

He went very still.

I licked my lips as my heart hammered. It had been hard to say that. At his continued silence, apprehension fisted in my chest. "I don't…"

"Shh," he said, jerking his head up. "It's okay. I just needed a moment to process that without getting up and making a fool out of myself by rushing buck-ass naked out to the balcony and shouting that you love me."

I cracked up at the image. "You wouldn't…"

I didn't even get to finish the thought. He rolled off the bed and charged out to the living room and then to the doors.

"Archie…"

They opened before I made it to the bedroom door, and he walked out there and put his hands to the side of his mouth. "Frankie Curtis loves me!"

When he turned around, he wore a delighted grin, and I gaped at him.

Even the cold air rushing in couldn't cool the heat raging through me. I wasn't just turned on—though admittedly, him standing out there on that chilly balcony wearing nothing definitely did it for me. He marched back in and closed the doors, then swept me up.

"You're crazy," I informed him.

"About you? Absolutely." Then he kissed me. Even the roots of my hair seemed like they were on fire. Still kissing me, he carried me back to the bed. "I love you," he whispered in between kisses, and I shuddered. "You're always there for me…"

"Archie, that's not entirely true."

"That was then," he said, dismissing my concern about the summer. "If the guys had actually gotten to you and told you about the tonsillectomy, would you have come?" Everything in his expression demanded an answer. "Even mad as hell at us for what we did, would you have come?"

"Yes." No hesitation. "I wish I had known, that I hadn't ignored the calls…"

"You had a reason. See, this is how I know, you've always been there for me. I want to always be there for you."

"You are. You have been."

"Good." Then, "Does this mean you picked me?"

My stomach bottomed out, and I hesitated. That wasn't what I'd meant. Suddenly, I was trembling. "Archie…"

"Eh," he said with a wry smile. "A guy can dream, but no—that wasn't what you meant."

I shook my head slowly. "Not in a, I'm not going to date the other guys kind of way."

Oh man.

"I do love you though." It got a little easier each time I said it. "I loved you before."

"Yeah?"

"Yeah." I loved all of them. I had for a long time, but admitting it aloud was different. Admitting it to them was something else altogether. "I didn't—I don't say that to anyone a lot. Maddy's not demonstrative, if you haven't noticed."

"I get that," he said, settling against me again until we were curled together. "And I'm glad you can tell me."

"But I don't want to choose between you guys." It took everything I had to say that. "I know you all think I'm going to—especially Ian." I swallowed and met Archie's gaze. "But I don't want to. I like...love all of you."

"Good," he whispered, then nuzzled a kiss against the corner of my mouth. Really?

"I want you to choose me," he said. "If you're going to choose, I want it to be me. No lie. I'll fight with everything I have to prove to you I'm the right pick. But if you don't choose—then I get to keep my best friends and you, and I don't have to fight them."

Relief swarmed me.

"You know I have no idea how this works."

"One day at a time," Archie said. "I think we've been doing pretty awesome the last few weeks. We're almost living together."

We were. "I've gotten really used to having you guys there."

"So, not kicking us to the curb yet?" he teased.

"No..."

"Does that mean we can finally clear out the master and fix it up so we have more space and get you a bigger bed?"

I groaned. "Archie..."

"Look, I like how snuggly we get in your bed. But more space never hurt anyone, and I think getting rid of the rest of her things would be good for you. I don't want you holding on to some idea she's going to come back and suddenly everything will work out."

Was I doing that? "I don't even know how we would start over, or even if we could. Especially now..."

"Because she knows you're suing for your emancipation."

"And the whole thing with your dad and their living together."

"Their lives," Archie said slowly. "Not ours. We don't need our lives to be about bad meatloaf."

A giggle floated up through me. "We deviated on your birthday again."

"Babe, you told me you loved me. Best. Birthday. Ever. I win. Hands down."

We talked for another hour about everything and nothing. Eventually, the tired caught up with us, and I was listening to the drum of his heart when I went to sleep. I woke up to Archie nudging my legs apart and eating me out with a gusto that utterly destroyed sleep and left me a trembling, shaking mess before he moved up to slide into me.

An hour later, we'd showered and ate room service breakfast before we got ready to check out. It was almost lunch time and a lot later than I expected, but Archie hummed all the way back to my place. The guys were waiting for us. We'd texted to say we were on the way. The moment Archie got out of the car, he got hit with super soakers from three different directions. While it wasn't as chilly as it had been the day before, it couldn't have been warm.

"Oh, you assholes," Archie said before handing me his keys. Someone had set a super soaker down for him, and he grabbed it. "Be right back, babe."

Then they were racing around the parking lot, ducking in and around cars, hitting each other with water.

It was hilarious, and something inside of me unlocked as I watched the shenanigans. I really wished I could be out there doing it with them, but at the same time…I adored my front row seat.

And the fact that I was base. Anytime one of them got too close to me, they were suddenly safe.

Jake stole a morning kiss that way. So did Coop.

But Ian startled me when he slid an arm around my waist, turned me around, and half-lifted me like a shield before his mouth closed over mine.

Already breathless, I think something in my brain short-circuited at the glide of his tongue against mine. I'd missed him. Missed kissing him. Missed feeling the hard heat of his muscles bunching as he moved. The kiss lasted three seconds and seemed to last forever, then suddenly, he set me on my feet and grinned.

"Good morning, Angel." Then he winked before he raced back into the fray. I was still touching my tingling lips when I caught Coop's knowing look.

Wow.

Leaning back against the Ferrari, I tracked them all as my guys darted in and out.

My guys.

Seriously.

Wow.

Chapter Twenty-Five
YOU HAD ME AT GOODBYE

The Halloween party was in full swing when we got there. It was rare enough that I attended parties, much less parties thrown by other kids. Clearly, I'd gone to Archie's or Ian's places when they'd had parties—more often at Archie's than Ian's, but the principle was the same.

This was Corey Kaplan's party though—another senior. Our arrival had snared some notice, we'd all come over in Jake's SUV. The costumes the guys had picked out cracked me up and worked, too. They'd even made it so I could put my cast arm in a sling to ease the weight and added this faux basket.

I was Dorothy.

Jake took the Cowardly Lion, which made him laugh, and he kept growling at me. Coop was the Tin Man, but swore he wasn't remotely rusty, though they had drenched him in this silver body paint. Archie had tackled the Scarecrow, and he had the loose arms and goofy hop-walk down. But Ian?

He'd gone for Toto, and I laughed so hard when he yipped at me that even the guys cracked up. Once we got to Corey's though, Ian planted himself at my side.

"Toto and Dorothy go everywhere together," he reminded me. "Even the bathroom."

That got three firm nods from the guys. I couldn't really argue with it. As it was, I wasn't even sure I wanted to come to the party. But I think this was kind of our do-over. Homecoming had been spoiled, but not all of it. I still loved all the dancing we'd done and the silly pictures, but I couldn't think about them without the gap in my memory swimming to the surface or waking in the hospital.

Tonight was about all of us, or so Jake and Archie insisted, while Coop said we'd stay as long as I was comfortable. Corey's parents had a place almost as nice as Archie's.

Almost.

Halloween was chilly, so the heavy costumes were actually comfortable, which was good 'cause the skirt I had on also had layers. At least the ruby slippers had chunky heels.

Inside, drinks of all variety including alcoholic were flowing. Kids were dancing in the living room where all the furniture had been shoved back against the walls and draped with covers, probably to protect them.

There were witches and sorceresses, superheroes and cops, a few firemen and enough naughty witches, nurses, and more to turn all the guy's heads. There was even a naughty Dorothy.

Rachel found us five minutes after we arrived.

"Nice costume," Jake told her as he eyed her Hogwarts School uniform. "You are…?"

"Hermione of course." She gave a toss of her hair. "The only intelligent one."

I grinned. "I like it."

"Looking good."

"I know, right?" So modest, too. I glanced around, looking for Skylar, and Rachel gave an exaggerated sigh, then nodded toward the bar where the sodas were flowing and, without a doubt, alcohol. Another girl in a Hogwarts uniform waved at us. The platinum blonde wig threw me though. "Luna Lovegood. I love long time."

Coop groaned at the tease, but I just laughed. "Good."

"You want to dance?" Rachel asked me, then glanced at the guys. "'Cause I'm not sure there's a Yellow Brick Road for you to skip on."

"Go torture Ron and Harry," Archie suggested. "You're supposed to be a *good* witch."

"Ha." But the laughter that followed was real, and I was grinning all over again. At least they were getting along. Skylar joined us with drinks at the same time Ian nodded to the make shift dance floor and "Who Let the Dogs Out" started playing.

"We have to," he said, then grasped my hand and tugged me with him. Yes, we absolutely did. Ian danced with gusto, singing along with the lyrics, and it wasn't long before the guys joined us.

The rooms were getting more crowded, but they kept a barrier up around me. Rachel and Skylar got in, no one else.

On one cool down break, I spotted Maria. It was the first time I'd really seen her since everything happened. Our gazes locked, and I gave her a small smile. She offered the same back. I'd been the lucky one, I knew that. We might never be close again, but we had been friends once upon a time, and I really didn't wish her ill. Then people moved between us, and I lost sight of her.

Mathieu came by with his date and introduced us. There was a lot of grumbling from the Cowardly Lion until I stepped on his foot, and the Tin Man elbowed him. Whether he was aware of the grumbling or not, Mathieu only stuck around for a couple of minutes before he wandered.

Patty appeared, hanging off the arm of one of the football players, but I didn't remember his name. Ian wrapped an arm around my middle and pulled me back against him because there were more and more people filling in.

"Want to go outside?" he asked against my ear.

I kind of did. There were so many people here. So many costumes. I knew some of them, but not all. Coop and Jake had gone to get us drinks. When Ian jerked his chin toward the door and said in a little louder voice, "We're taking this outside," Archie nodded.

"You got her?"

"Yeah."

"Good, I'll let the guys know."

Like I wasn't right there. Then again, Ian hadn't moved from my side all night. My one and only trip to pee, he'd gone into the bathroom first, then parked it inside with me, back turned while he leaned against the door.

It had been very sweet.

Hand in hand, he guided me out while Archie headed for the bar. I looked around for Rachel, but Ian found her first. She and Skylar were lip-locked in the corner. And the ferocity of those kisses suggested they should find a room sooner rather than later.

The tempo from the bass throbbed through me, and the sudden cessation as we made it outside was a relief. The colder air was more than welcome against my flushed cheeks. I hadn't even realized I'd gotten a little sticky and clammy, though that made sense from all the dancing.

Some of the party had spilled outside, but we walked around toward the drive. Despite the open-air, Ian held onto my hand.

"You know," he said. "I'm glad we're finally getting a minute."

"Yeah," I agreed. We really hadn't, not since he helped me record the song for Archie. "I wanted to tell you thank you. Archie really loved the song."

"I'm glad," he told me as he paused near the covered porch and leaned against the railing. Looping his arms around me, he tugged me to him. We were in the shadows with only a couple of dim outdoor lights offering any illumination. The cloudy skies overhead added to the general darkness. "I'm also really glad I'm here."

"You kissed me today." I ripped the Band-Aid right off. While we hadn't avoided the topic per se, we hadn't really addressed it either, and the guys hadn't commented.

"I did," he murmured, then reached up to brush some of the hair away from my damp forehead. "I plan on kissing you again."

"You do, huh?"

"I do." The smile in his voice tugged at me. "I want to kiss you and make up for every single time I didn't when I wanted to."

My stomach see-sawed a little. "Ian…"

"Angel? I'm in. No more hesitation. You take all the time you need to forgive me. I know I need to earn it. But from the moment you said goodbye to me, it hit me what an enormous jackass I'd been. You were right, you deserved so much better. You deserved someone who knows what they want and isn't afraid to go for it. I might be slow…but you're where I want to be and who I want to be with. Think you can give me another chance?"

The sick, fluttery feeling was back in full force. "What if you change your mind again?"

"Not gonna happen," he promised.

"Ian, you don't know that."

He cupped my chin when I would have looked down and kept my gaze up. "I know what it's been like since you broke up with me. I know you've fought to stay my friend, even when it was hurting you. I know a lot of crap happened between then and now. But there's good things too. I know what I lost, Frankie. I know what I want back, too. I'm not changing my mind. I'm not assuming you will or you won't. I'm just asking to be here with you, to have a chance to prove to you that you weren't wrong about me that day in the pool."

The first time we kissed.

"I screwed up," he whispered, pressing his forehead to mine. "I'm sorry I hurt you."

"I know," I answered him. "I am too. I'm sorry it was so hard for you that I'm…"

"Honest?" Challenge inhabited the word. "You haven't lied to me. I see how you feel about them. I just want a chance for you to be able to feel that for me, too."

Swallowing, I laughed a little. "You're kind of an idiot."

"I think we established that."

"I'm kind of an idiot, too."

"What's the point of having friends if you can't bitch, moan, and be idiots together?" He had a point.

"If you get scared again, talk to me first?"

"Promise. If I can't find the words, I'll fight to find them. I won't just make sweeping decisions."

"You know I want to trust you?"

"Yeah?" Surprise filtered through his voice.

"Yes," I told him. "I don't know if I do…all the way yet. But I want to. But I'm scared, too."

"What are you scared of?"

"Everything some days. Of being selfish. Of making the wrong choices. Of not getting into college. Of getting into college. Of getting my emancipation. Of not getting it." Then I focused on him. "Of caring about you guys and losing you."

"You won't lose," he promised. "I'd tell you I'd follow you anywhere, but that's a little stalkery."

I laughed.

"A little, true."

"How about this? Will you go out with me, Frankie? Real dates. You and me. Let me buy you flowers and take you out to eat. Let me take you for rides on the bike as soon as that arm is healed. Come listen to me work on my music, work on it with me? You inspire me, Angel. Everything I've written in the last few weeks, it's all been you."

I swallowed around the lump in my throat. "We're going to need rules."

"Agreed."

"And you guys don't get to be the only ones who make them."

"Totally down for that."

"You owe me a night of dancing."

"Agreed."

"Karaoke." That was a concession. I hated the karaoke, but he was so good at it.

"Name the time and the place, I'm there."

"You're easy."

"For you?" Ian cocked his head. "Haven't you figured it out yet, Angel? I'd do anything for you."

Oh, I wanted to believe him so bad. I'd hated the distance between us. The gulf. Even holding on with my fingers and toes to our friendship, a piece of me had been missing.

"I—"

"Well, well, well," a raspy voice gritted out, and ice slithered down my spine. Ian jerked up straight and glared.

"What the fuck are you doing here?"

I turned, but Ian was already shoving me behind him.

Mitch stood there—a creepy Frankenstein—and he had a few friends with him.

"Believe it or not, Bubba…" Mitch gritted out. "We were looking for the pair of you. Trick or treat…"

I didn't even get a chance to scream before something was yanked over my head.

* * *

Frankie and the boys return in *Hangovers and Holidays*.

To keep up with Heather and all her series join her reader's group:

https://www.facebook.com/groups/HeathersPack/

About Heather Long

USA Today bestselling author, Heather Long, likes long walks in the park, science fiction, superheroes, Marines, and men who aren't douche bags. Her books are filled with heroes and heroines tangled in romance as hot as Texas summertime. From paranormal historical westerns to contemporary military romance, Heather might switch genres, but one thing is true in all of her stories—her characters drive the books. When she's not wrangling her menagerie of animals, she devotes her time to family and friends she considers family. She believes if you like your heroes so real you could lick the grit off their chest, and your heroines so likable, you're sure you've been friends with women just like them, you'll enjoy her worlds as much as she does.

Follow Heather & Sign up for her newsletter:
www.heatherlong.net

Also by Heather Long

UNTOUCHABLE

Rules and Roses

Changes and Chocolates

Keys and Kisses

Whispers and Wishes

Hangovers and Holidays

Brazen and Breathless

Trials and Tiaras

Graduation and Gifts

Defiance and Dedication

82ND STREET VANDALS

Savage Vandal

Vicious Rebel

Ruthless Traitor

Dirty Devil

ALWAYS A MARINE SERIES

Once Her Man, Always Her Man

Retreat Hell! She Just Got Here

Tell It to the Marine

Proud to Serve Her

Her Marine

No Regrets, No Surrender

The Marine Cowboy

The Two and the Proud

A Marine and a Gentleman

Combat Barbie

Whiskey Tango Foxtrot

What Part of Marine Don't You Understand?

A Marine Affair

Marine Ever After

Marine in the Wind

Marine with Benefits

A Marine of Plenty

A Candle for a Marine

Marine under the Mistletoe

Have Yourself a Marine Christmas

Lest Old Marines Be Forgot

Her Marine Bodyguard

Smoke & Marines

BRAVO TEAM WOLF

When Danger Bites

Bitten Under Fire

BOOMERS

The Judas Contact

Deadly Genesis

Unstoppable

Chance Monroe

Earth Witches Aren't Easy

Plan Witch from Out of Town

Bad Witch Rising

Her Elite Assets

Featuring:

Pure Copper

Target: Tungsten

Asset: Arsenic

Fevered Hearts

Marshal of Hel Dorado

Brave are the Lonely

Micah & Mrs. Miller

A Fistful of Dreams

Raising Kane

Wanted: Fevered or Alive

Wild and Fevered

The Quick & The Fevered

A Man Called Wyatt

Going Royal

Some Like It Royal

Some Like It Scandalous

Some Like It Deadly

Some Like it Secret

Some Like it Easy

Her Marine Prince

Blocked

HEART OF THE NEBULA
Queenmaker

Deal Breaker

Throne Taker

LONE STAR LEATHERNECKS
Semper Fi Cowboy

As You Were, Cowboy

MADISON, THE WITCH HUNTER
Every Witch Way But Floosey's

MAGIC & MAYHEM
The Witch Singer

Bridget's Witch's Diary

The Witched Away Bride

Mongrels

Mongrels, Mischief & Mayhem

SHACKLED SOULS
Succubus Chained

Succubus Unchained

Succubus Blessed

SPACE COWBOY
Space Cowboy Survival Guide

WOLVES OF WILLOW BEND
Wolf at Law

Wolf Bite

Caged Wolf

Wolf Claim

Wolf Next Door

Rogue Wolf

Bayou Wolf

Untamed Wolf

Wolf with Benefits

River Wolf

Single Wicked Wolf

Desert Wolf

Snow Wolf

Wolf on Board

Holly Jolly Wolf

Shadow Wolf

His Moonstruck Wolf

Thunder Wolf

Ghost Wolf

Outlaw Wolves

Wolf Unleashed